SOUNDS OF
DIAMONDS

Printed in the United Kingdom

Cover design and layout by www.spiffingcovers.com

SOUNDS OF

DIAMONDS

NICHOLA K JOHNSON

‘Where is she?’ Mark asked, standing at the door of Abigail’s flat with his foot halfway in the doorway just in case she shut the door on him.

Abigail, with her hand on her hip, stood in the doorway with an uneasy and slightly irritated look on her face.

‘I told you she’s not here, she’s out with her aunt for the day.’

‘Are you gonna invite me in, I’ll wait?’

‘No, there’s no point,’ she replied, ‘they’ll be ages. Only left about half an hour ago, in fact you just missed them. Plus I’m busy today anyway, I’ve got to go to the laundrette, do some shopping, it’s just not a good time.’

Something wasn’t right, she was full of excuses as always. This was the eighth time Mark had visited with no luck.

‘I really need to see her, Abi. It’s been months. Savannah still won’t return my calls. I’ve got no idea of what’s going on. Every time I come by she’s not here. It doesn’t make sense.’

‘Yeah, well, I can’t tell you more than I just have,’ she replied.

‘Can you just get Savannah to call me? This is ridiculous.’

‘I’m really sorry Mark, can’t help you,’ she responded.

This time she looked quite sincere as she lit a cigarette and exhaled. He looked deep into her eyes as he tried to figure out if she was telling the truth or not. She looked away. She’s hiding something, he thought to himself, he could see it in her eyes.

‘I’ll see you soon, Abi,’ he said as he turned and walked away leaving her on the doorstep.

He knew she was hiding something, but couldn't figure out what it was and couldn't get anything out of her. In truth, he had only seen me a few times. I was just over one year old. He didn't get the opportunity to visit too often, he was young, just turned 18, he'd just started a new job in IT. He was a well-known DJ and the head selector of a huge music sound so his weekends were taken up playing out at parties and clubs, plus he was in the process of buying a new flat with his current partner. Things were quite busy for him, but he promised himself he wasn't going to give up. As he walked away, he decided he was going to get to the bottom of whatever it was going on, no matter what it took. And he wouldn't stop until he found the truth.

* * *

Abigail stood at the door in the exact same position – bold as ever, cigarette in her hand, other hand on her hip – as he returned the next day.

'Abi, I've had enough of this, trust me I'm not leaving until I see her.'

He was firm, almost quite threatening.

'You either tell me where she is, where Savannah is, or I stay here until she's back. I don't care where you might have to go or how long it takes, I promise you, don't fuck around with me Abi. She's my daughter and you lot have been keeping her from me for too long now.'

Abigail looked at Mark, quite shocked at his response. She certainly wasn't one to find herself lost for words and although she felt his tone was slightly aggressive, she could see how serious he was.

'You'd better come in, then, hadn't you?' she said as she turned and walked into the kitchen.

Mark followed and they both sat down at the table. Abigail reached for a cigarette and lit up.

'So,' Mark asked, 'where is she this time?'

'She's not here.'

'Yeah, you already said that.'

'No, she really isn't here.' She took a drag of her cigarette and exhaled. 'I don't really know how to say this, but she hasn't been here for a while, neither has Savannah.'

Mark calmly sat back in the chair to get more comfortable.

'Savannah's in Amsterdam, has been for about five months. She was in a really bad place, Mark. Depressed, not coping with life, drinking, some days she wouldn't even get out of bed. And Nikki, that kid, was such a burden to her. Do you know most of the time I had to take care of that little girl myself? I didn't sign up for that. I was done with kids a long time ago and that child, god she has a way about her. She's uncontrollable.'

'What the hell are you talking about?' Mark asked. He leaned over and took one of her cigarettes. 'Where is my daughter?'

'I'm sorry to have to tell you this, Mark, but she's gone for good. Savannah met this guy and he made her happy again. Honestly, if you saw her you'd understand. He's wealthy and offered her the world – big house, money, everything she ever wanted – but he had one rule, no kids.'

Mark couldn't believe what he was hearing. The palms of his hands began to sweat, but he remained calm, not wanting to interrupt or give any reason for her to hold any information back. He sat quietly while he listened. He knew Savannah was emotionally unstable – I believe his words were 'fucked up' – but Mark was smart, he could outsmart this whole family, a bunch of emotionally challenged women who could never stick at anything worth doing in life were his exact thoughts. He wasn't interested in Savannah's new life or love interest, he just needed to know where his daughter was.

'So, where is Nikki?' he asked again, looking straight at her so he could read her behaviour.

She got up to put the kettle on.

'I'm gonna ask you one more time, what the hell has this woman done with my girl, Abigail?' He raised his voice.

'I tried to do it!' she cried, as she broke down in tears.

Abigail breaking down was a first for the record. She was generally the head of the family and called herself the big white chief; she was a strong, stern, big-boned woman with short blonde hair and the deepest blue eyes you've ever seen, a very straight-to-the-point type of woman you didn't want to mess with. Deep down she liked Mark, she knew he was a decent guy despite him walking out on Savannah.

'I tried, I really did, but I told you this wasn't what I asked for, I mean a baby. Nope, I couldn't, please believe I tried Mark. Savannah couldn't cope so when this guy came around, I told her to go, told her to be happy. She's my daughter, I wanted the best for her, I couldn't bear to see her throwing her life away at such a young age. We were going to take care of Nikki, but when it got tough, I wrote to her and begged her to come home, but I got no response. I wrote and wrote until one day I got a postcard from her saying she wasn't coming home. Ever. Wasn't interested in her old life anymore, told me to do what I wanted with Nikki. In the end we agreed, we all agreed.'

'Agreed what?' he asked as he puffed on his cigarette.

'To put her in care. She'll be better off in the end. It's going really well for her, she's been with a lovely family for a while now and they're soon to adopt her. They'll offer her a much better life than we can even imagine Mark. I mean, you wouldn't be able to take care of her would you? You're just a kid yourself, you're both kids, darling. It's for the best, I promise. If you love that little girl you'd leave her where she is, leave her where she has a chance in life.'

* * *

The walls are grey, and the floor is blue and really shiny, silver-framed single beds in a row with blue and grey striped bedding. One big room with rows of metal-framed beds with blue blankets. This is my earliest memory. A few boxes of old toys at the end of the room, my favourite, a raggedy doll with a green skirt and orange face. It was tatty and a little bit dirty, but I loved her. I named her Jemima and literally took her everywhere. Along the front of the room were three really large windows. I often tiptoed to see if I could see outside, but we were so high up that all I could ever see was the sky. I was two and a half and had been in this place for over a year. There were lots of other children who also lived in this room; we often played together, but most of the time we fought over toys or just fought for the sake of it. Some of the children were older and helped take care of the smaller ones like me. Most of the time they weren't very nice, and bullied us. There was never anything we could do to defend ourselves.

We had our daily routine which was exactly the same every single day – get up, make your bed, Weetabix with hot milk for breakfast (which I hated), bath time, back to the grey and blue room to dress and play for a few hours, an hour in the outside playground, back to the room to wash our hands and faces to get ready for lunch, TV/reading in the afternoon, dinner and back to bed.

Night after night I cuddled Jemima while I tried to sleep. There were no curtains at those big windows, so the light of the moon always shone through making it really difficult. Most nights I just lay there staring at the moon, holding Jemima wondering why I was there; it was really lonely. And at night, when I did sleep, I often suffered from really bad nightmares. One particular night I woke up from in a cold sweat from a crazy nightmare that felt so real. I woke up screaming, hysterically crying, looking for Jemima, but she wasn't there. I cried out loud in that silver-framed bed, alone, looking around for someone to help, comfort me, tell me everything was OK. But nobody came. I curled up under the covers and cried until the moonlight turned into sunrise.

The next morning, very sleepy and puffy-eyed, I looked across the room and noticed one of the older girls a few beds away had my dolly. I cried to the matrons, but they didn't care one bit. 'Find another doll,' she said. I was so upset. That girl had my doll and I was determined to get her back. She was much bigger than me and laughed as I jumped up trying to grab her while she held the doll high up to the ceiling. As usual with the bigger kids, I couldn't win, so I gave up and got back into my bed. I glanced over and watched while the girl was about to cut my doll's hair. I couldn't help myself. I jumped out of my bed, ran up to her and literally laid into her; I was punching, kicking and screaming at her to give me my doll back. She shoved me to the floor and laughed. 'Go away little girl, it's my doll now.' I got up, crawled towards her and bit her so hard on her leg it pierced her skin. The girl screamed and fell to her knees; there was blood everywhere. Everyone rushed over to see what was going on while the girl screamed and shouted out names at me. This time the matrons came, but to her rescue, and dragged me away kicking and screaming. They took me to some other room where this time there were only two beds. They shoved me in without a word said.

A young boy sat by the side of his bed playing with a train set. It was obviously my punishment for biting the girl, but actually this room was better. It wasn't so cold and the windows were smaller. I quite liked the boy, and after I calmed down and stopped crying he let me play with his train set. So we sat together and played for the rest of the afternoon. We didn't play outside or have reading time, we were hidden away in that room all day.

That evening, after dinner while we were in bed, I asked him why we were in this room alone. He was slightly older than me, probably about five or six. He told me we were there because we were bad and had to stay on our own.

'We can't play with the other children because they think we can be a danger. We can't do anything to the other kids while we're in here and we have to be good,' he continued. 'So when a family comes they'll like us and then we can have a mum and dad.'

My eyes lit up at the thought.

'My mum and dad will come?' I asked

'No,' he said, 'a new mum and dad.'

I was so confused. Why did I need a new mum and dad? Where were my real mum and dad? I didn't understand, but went to sleep a lot easier than I ever had in the blue and grey room. I liked the thought of a mum and dad regardless of who they were; it would be much better than this place. From then on I dreamed of it often and wondered when they were coming and how I would get them to like me.

* * *

My day had finally arrived. One of the matrons came to wake me earlier than usual.

'It's a special day for you today, Nikki, you're going to meet a new family.'

'Really?' I replied with excitement. My mum and dad had finally come to get me! I was so excited I couldn't wait.

We went down for breakfast, I had my bath and even had a new dress to wear. The matron brushed my hair into two bunches and tied them with pink ribbons. I looked in the mirror and swung from side to side so my dress would swirl, and felt so pretty. Matron took hold of my hand and away we went. We walked down the corridor together which felt like we were walking for miles, until we eventually entered a room where a really tall man and woman were stood. They both turned to look at me, their faces beaming with huge smiles. I stood still looking back at them, my excitement quickly drifting away.

'Here she is, this is Nikki,' the matron said.

They both said, 'Hello Nikki' in sync with each other.

I stood in silence holding matron's hand tightly.

'Oh yes,' said the man, 'she definitely is beautiful.'

This isn't what I imagined at all. They looked like really nice people, but they were definitely not my mum and dad – even though I didn't know who they really were, it definitely wasn't these guys. These people were white. At this point I became really nervous. I was set to go home with these people but didn't feel comfortable at all. Was this really the family I was supposed to be good for? If so, it was all wrong. I was internally panicking but powerless to do anything, my legs shaking with nerves.

'You've made a mistake,' I cried. 'Don't send me away with those people, please. I want my real mum and dad, I don't like these people.'

I held onto matron crying and begging.

'She just needs time,' matron suggested to the couple. 'Don't worry, this reaction is pretty normal with children of this age, it's a natural defence mechanism, doesn't last. Happens all the time.' And just like that, that was it. There was nothing I could do. I was definitely going.

* * *

Claire and Dave were indeed very nice people. After what felt like a drive that lasted forever we arrived at their home, a massive white house with a huge driveway, a big front garden with a pond and a swing. There was a lady sat on the garden wall watching over two boys playing football. I had cried myself into a deep sleep halfway into the journey, so it was all a bit of a blur when I eventually woke up. I looked up at the house as we walked towards the steps – it was like a palace with a grand entrance, a large central staircase surrounded by big stained-glass windows in the hallway, chandeliers hung from the ceilings, it was amazing.

Claire took off my coat while Dave left us together. She took my hand and walked towards what would be my room, a big bright yellow bedroom with two sets of bunk beds. Claire was overexcited about it all, extra nice with a constant smile on her face. I think she felt being super sweet would put me at ease.

'This is where you will sleep, Nikki. Shall we put your clothes over here? I brought you lots of toys, I hope you like them. Are you hungry? You must be, it's been a long morning hasn't it? I'll prepare lunch and ask Monique to get the boys ready.'

Overwhelmed by her enthusiasm I asked, 'Who's Monique?'

'Monique is the babysitter darling, she looks after Peter and Paul sometimes. I can't wait for you to meet them, I guess you can call them your new brothers, you'll absolutely love them.'

'The two boys playing in the garden?' I asked.

'Yes darling.'

I didn't want brothers, I just wanted my real mum and dad. Tears came to my eyes, it all felt too much to deal with. I suddenly felt heavy, tired and wanted to sleep again. It was bad enough knowing I'd have to get to know Claire and Dave, but now there were two other boys. I was quite shy and just no way near ready.

'I'll be back shortly,' Claire said. 'You can play over here for a while with these.'

Under the bunk bed was a box full of new toys and books. I dug through the box in the hope there would be a dolly that looked similar to Jemima, but there wasn't. I sat on the floor feeling nervous, with my legs crossed, waiting for whatever was next. Moments later Claire entered with that big smile on her face again.

'Are you ready Nikki? We're all ready for lunch now.'

As I looked up at her, terrified of meeting these guys, she noticed I'd been crying. She came over, wiped my face with a tissue and kissed me on the cheek.

'It's OK little princess, no need to cry, everything with be fine. There's nothing to be frightened of, I promise. The boys are dying to meet you and you'll love them.' She held out her hand. 'Come on darling, let's go and have lunch. Let's go and meet the boys, you'll feel so much better after, I promise.'

* * *

I sat quietly at the table with Peter, Paul and Dave, still exhausted from the long journey and hours of crying, while Claire pottered between the kitchen and the dining room table with plates, bowls and cutlery. Dave was sat back reading a newspaper. He looked over the paper at me, smiled and went right back to the paper while the boys were deep into some sort of finger game. I sat quietly waiting for Claire to do something to introduce me. Although she seemed so overexcited and was constantly shuffling herself around, I decided I liked her. I liked Dave too, but there's no way I was ever going to speak to him unless he spoke to me. He was way too tall and scary; I felt that I'd annoy him if I spoke and I wouldn't even know what to say, so I remained quiet.

Eventually the table was prepared. Claire came over and sat by my side. The boys were still bickering over who had more points in the finger game, while Claire tried to get their attention with no luck.

'Boys! Quiet!'

'Listen to your mother!' Dave shouted, with such a deep voice it scared the life out of me.

He folded his paper and drew his attention to the table. This is exactly why I wanted to keep out of his way. I never ever wanted him to speak to me with that tone. The boys shut up right away and Claire asked us to all hold hands to say grace.

'Peter, Paul, you remember our conversation last week about Nikki, don't you?'

They both stared at me with their big brown eyes.

'Well this is Nikki, your new little sister, and I want you both to be good boys and look after her, share your toys with her and always make her feel welcome. She is part of our family now, so say hello to Nikki please.'

'She's not my sister!' shouted out Paul. 'I've already got a brother and your tummy didn't grow so she can't be a sister. Brothers and sisters come out of your tummy, don't they mummy?'

Claire smiled at Paul with that big smile she gave me earlier. Paul was five years old and Peter eleven.

'There are lots of other ways to expand a family, Paul. And mummy and daddy just chose a different option, OK? We are all very lucky we have this chance to expand our family and offer more love to each other.'

'I don't love her,' he whined.

'Right, that's enough Paul,' shouted Dave. 'You're being incredibly rude. We all talked about this last week, remember?'

'But mum!' this was now Peter who had something to say. 'How can she be our sister and she's black?'

Claire was stuck for answers. She looked over at Dave for help, but he just nodded to allow her to answer.

'We'll talk about this later,' Claire snapped. 'Can we just all be nice to Nikki, please, like I've asked, and let's eat.'

* * *

Months went by and these guys really did become my family. The grey room, the shiny floors and all its drama were a distant memory. I was happy here. I hung out with Claire all day playing games, making cakes, visiting friends or just generally hanging out together watching TV or Disney movies. Claire and I chatted and laughed together every day; she adored me, and I adored her, she was tall, very slim and extremely pretty with mid-length brown hair and hazel eyes. She wore the most beautiful dresses with neat heels, even at home. She would dress me up in similar dresses to hers when we were out, so we were almost matching. My little princess, she'd call me, and I thought I would be with her forever. She taught me new things, which was always so exciting, and did absolutely everything she possibly could to make me happy or make me laugh. In the afternoons, she'd prepare dinner while I sat at the kitchen table colouring or playing with dolls. After lunch, Monique would come home with the boys. They arrived with their dirty shoes, grubby faces and their leather satchels full of books and pictures they brought out to show us while yapping away about what they did at school. I would then follow them out to the garden while we played together on the swings, or I would run around chasing them while they played football. Although they were still so confused as to why I was black and asked constant questions about my skin and hair, I grew to love the boys and deep down they loved me too.

Dave was usually at work all day and night. Whenever he was around it was only ever for a short time and when he did come home we would all run into his arms. He'd hug the boys and ruffle their hair, he'd pick me up, swing me around and shower me with kisses while I giggled away. Claire watched on with an uncomfortable smile on her face, not like the smile she gave to me or the boys. He'd briefly kiss her on the cheek, brush past her and sit at the table waiting for dinner. We all ate together as a family, then Claire would bathe Paul and I after an hour or so and put us to bed.

One evening I jumped out of bed in the middle of the night to go to the toilet and quietly tiptoed to the bathroom. I slowly opened the door hoping not to make too much noise and found Claire sat on the floor in floods of tears. She looked up, startled to see me, quickly wiped her eyes and straightened her hair. I stood looking at her wondering what was wrong. It was strange to see her cry, it seemed like she was always happy. She held out her hand and sat me on her lap.

'Why are you crying, mummy?' I asked.

She stroked my face and hair.

'It's OK, Nikki,' she said. 'It's nothing. Mummy just misses daddy that's all. Daddy's just gone back to work and I miss him, just like when we miss the boys while they're at school,' she smiled.

'Oh,' I said, 'but why does daddy always go to work in the night as well?'

'All daddies have to go to work, darling, so they can provide for their families. And I want you to know that daddy loves us, OK? He loves us all so much so he works very hard for us.'

'Even me?' I asked.

'Of course, Nikki, even you,' she hugged me and kissed me on my forehead. 'You're just as much a part of this family as anyone else is,' she replied and gave me a big hug. 'I love you so so so much,' she said, as she smiled at me and cupped my face. 'There's nothing to worry about OK? Now come on missy, it's late, let's get you back to bed.'

* * *

Over the next few weeks things drastically began to change. I still hung out with Claire during the days, but it wasn't as fun as it used to be. She was different. She wasn't as radiant or as bubbly as she usually was, her pretty face looked drawn and tired, she wasn't wearing make-up or pretty dresses anymore, she didn't talk or play with me as much as she used to and was always in a rush to do things. We had to collect the boys from school ourselves instead of Monique, so we didn't have much time to prepare dinner together like we used to either. I often asked Claire where Monique was, and she'd sharply snap back 'I don't know'. 'But where is she, mummy?' I asked again and again. 'She just had to go away so we need to forget about her for now.' It wasn't like Claire at all to be so jumpy, and so out of character to snap at me the way she did. I wondered why Monique left us as she was also a part of our family. As far as I knew, Claire and Monique were great friends, so I was surprised she didn't even know where she was.

I played with the boys in the evenings, but we were bathed and sent to bed much earlier than usual. Often the boys and I would stay awake chatting after Claire turned off the lights and closed the bedroom door. Sometimes we'd hear her crying downstairs, which was always sad for us but we never knew what to do. One night we were all tucked in bed chatting as usual.

'Why does mummy cry at night?' Paul asked Peter.

Peter sighed, but didn't respond. He was older and always knew a lot more than we did and sometimes ignored us.

'Peeeter!' whined Paul.

'Shut up and go to sleep,' Peter snapped.

'But why?' Paul began to cry, mainly to get Peter's attention.

'I've told you before, mum wishes dad didn't have to work so much, that's all, so just stop crying and go to sleep.'

Paul climbed out of bed crying and sniffling and went to the door. He wanted to find Claire to ask her himself. I quickly jumped out of bed and ran after him. Peter also jumped down from his top bunk to try and get us back, but we were way too quick so he had no choice but to follow. We scarpered down the hallway, Paul and I holding hands until we got to the top of the staircase and stopped still. We could hear screaming and shouting coming from downstairs, and we all huddled together at the top of the stairs.

'What is it Peter, what's happening?' asked Paul.

'I'm scared.'

'Shhh,' Peter said. 'I can't hear.'

We all sat on the step clinging on to each other and listened.

'How could you do this to me? How could you do this to us? I've given you everything and her, her, how dare you! You're disgusting! I fucking hate you!'

The voices were loud and so clear we heard everything. We were so scared of the shouting Paul began to cry again and so did I. Poor Peter tried his best to comfort us both until we stopped crying, just like

Dave would have done. He looked up to Dave so much that he pretty much copied everything Dave did. We sat on his lap on the top step and continued to listen.

'I didn't want this, did I? I had no choice, you were never happy. I gave you a home, two beautiful boys, but that wasn't enough was it? I was never enough. I even agreed to get Nikki for you, to make you happy, but no, you don't recognise that do you? You wanted her to distract you from me.'

'How dare you!' screamed Claire. 'This has nothing to do with Nikki. This is about you and what you've done to us, we both agreed.'

'No, you went on and on and I gave in, gave you your perfect little girl and that was all you wanted,' Dave replied.

'But why Monique?' screamed Claire. 'Why her? Tell me, she was my friend! She looked after our kids, how could you betray us like this?'

'I can't talk to you when you're like this,' Dave shouted. 'You know why Claire, this marriage was over way before all this happened. Another child wasn't going to fix us and on top of that, you went and got a black kid. Do you know the grief I get at work for having a black kid? I should have never agreed to it. I'm leaving. We'll talk when you've calmed down.'

'You're the one who's screwed this up,' screamed Claire. 'It's got nothing to do with Nikki, whatever colour she is. It was you, fucking that bitch.'

Dave rushed to the front door to leave.

'When you've calmed down we can talk, but I'm not listening to this now,' he replied and opened the door.

Claire was hysterical. She ran over to him and grabbed his arm.

'Don't you walk out on me, I swear David don't you dare do this!' she screamed.

Dave shoved her off so hard she hit the door.

'Mummy!' Paul screamed out.

Both Claire and Dave stopped in surprise and looked up to see us all sat at the top of the stairs. Paul and I were crying again, while Peter held us.

'Oh my gosh, my babies!' Claire cried. 'Now look what you've done!' she scorned at Dave. 'Get out, go!'

But Dave didn't leave. He ran up the stairs towards us, while Claire followed behind him trying to get to us first.

'What's going on, dad?' asked Peter, he was so calm.

'Nothing, Peter,' Dave replied. 'Your mum and I are just having a disagreement.'

Claire was crying as she held Paul and I in her arms.

'Did Monique do something bad?' asked Peter.

Dave was silent.

'No no,' said Claire. 'Monique had to move away, that's all. Come on, you all need to go back to bed, it's late.'

'Is daddy leaving because of me?' I cried.

'No Nikki, daddy's not leaving us darling,' she looked sternly over at Dave as he rubbed his head with his hands. 'Daddy's not leaving us,' she repeated.

They put us all back to bed, kissed us and shut the bedroom door. Paul fell asleep pretty much straight away, but I was still unsettled.

'Nikki,' whispered Peter, 'are you OK?'

'Yeah, how can I get daddy to like me more, so he doesn't leave us?' I whispered back.

Peter jumped down from the top bunk, got into my bed and cuddled me.

'Daddy won't leave us, Nikki, I promise. He's a good man, he's always taken care of us and always will.'

'But he might leave now because he said he didn't want me. Is it because I'm different?'

'No, Nikki, don't be silly. Dad loves us all and he tells me all the time how much he loves you too. He loves all of us, and even if you are different, it's what makes you special. Now go to sleep, it'll all be better in the morning.'

* * *

'What? She's where?' asked Maria.

'I know,' Mark sighed as he poured himself a brandy. 'I don't know what to do, or even what I can do. I knew that family was fucked up, I knew something wasn't right. Why did I leave it so long?'

Maria rubbed Mark's shoulders while he sipped his drink.

'I'm her father! How can they even think of doing this behind my back, this is bullshit!'

'I don't understand,' Maria said. 'It just doesn't make any sense to me.'

'OK, so you know all those times I went to see her and for some reason or another she was never home?'

'Uh huh.'

'Well it turns out it wasn't just wrong timing, they've been lying to me all this time. They fucking knew where she was. They've given her away, they put her in a children's home and now she's with a foster family. They gave her away and there's nothing I can do about it. Savannah fucked off abroad and they didn't want to deal with her. She's about to be adopted by the family she's with.'

A tear rolled down his face.

'My baby girl gone to a family I don't even know, she doesn't belong there. I can't even believe they thought they could do this without me finding out.'

Maria listened in shock while Mark held his head.

'If only I went sooner,' he said. 'If only I went more often, something could have been done.'

'Well you know what we've got to do,' Maria demanded. 'We've got to go get her.'

Maria was a sophisticated and an extremely smart woman who was so devastatingly in love with Mark she would have done anything he wanted.

'You're right,' he replied. 'I can't let this happen. I need to get her.'

* * *

Claire screamed and fell to the floor.

'This isn't true! Please tell me this isn't true! She's mine, she's ours, they can't do this.'

In floods of tears, she was crouched on the floor with a letter in hand, distraught.

'They can't do this, she's mine.'

She looked up at Dave in desperation for help while he stood looking down at her.

'Don't let them do this, Dave, please don't let them.' She hysterically cried out like a baby, hopeless. 'She's ours.'

For once he actually felt sorry for her. He knew how much she loved me and believed she would have me forever. He kneeled down beside her and held her while she rocked in his arms, her cries lingering through the whole house.

'Please don't let them take her,' she repeatedly cried.

She became weaker and weaker until eventually Dave left her alone on the floor and walked away.

* * *

It was clear after a few months that things had changed quite a lot. Dave had officially left to start a life with Monique, and came for visits. Remembering the fight on the stairs, we were all quite reserved when he came over, even though he brought us toys and sweets. It was better when he wasn't around, when it was just Claire and us, we were happier because she was happy; when Dave came over Claire was different, she was on edge, didn't laugh as much, and didn't smile, she sent us all outside to play while she sat forever in front of the mirror trying to conceal her drawn face with make-up. She was vulnerable to Dave and completely lost without him. We heard their conversations at night, although they always thought they were being discreet.

'This is all your fault,' she screamed. 'If you didn't betray us we wouldn't be in this position right now, they'd have no right to do this if we were still a tight family. You did this, you abandoned us and now I have absolutely no leg to stand on.'

Dave sighed, 'You knew the risks, Claire, we both knew the risks. We knew there was a chance this could happen, we talked about it and you said you'd handle it. We are where we are, let's just deal with it. She'll probably be better off with her own flesh and blood anyway, her own people.'

Claire sobbed. She walked over to him and looked deep into his eyes. She pointed in his face.

'I hope you're happy with yourself. You better pray that girl's parents will love her as much as we do, and give her a better life than we could because she deserves nothing but the best. And while we're on the subject, I can't believe I married such a racist pig. I want a divorce.'

* * *

'Oh my god, she's here again,' Mark shouted out to Maria. 'Hide this shit, quick.'

Mark was lounging on the sofa, chilled out with a can of beer and a spliff burning in the ashtray. Stevie Wonder played in the background on the turntable while Maria sat at her computer working. He hated these moments. They both jumped up and rushed around like lunatics as they speedily disposed of any unruly evidence around the house, and opened the door to Mrs Smith. Mrs Smith was from social services and had been sporadically visiting the home in an attempt to get to know them on a personal level. She needed to report if she felt it was a sufficient household and environment to bring up a child. Mark and Maria had been in battle with the courts for almost two years in order to gain parental custody. These visits were always unexpected, at random and had been going on for two years. It was tiring for them both. Mrs Smith could arrive at any time of the day or night unexpected to spot check the family home. Mark, only 20 years old, was doing so well on the DJ scene he was rarely home in the evenings, but somehow it always seemed to work in their favour.

'Please take a seat,' Maria offered. 'Coffee?'

'No thanks,' she replied. 'You'll be pleased to hear this will be a shorter visit than usual.'

She took a seat and opened up her briefcase.

'Mark, Maria,' she smiled. 'I understand this has been a challenging journey for you both. I've thoroughly enjoyed working with you and getting to know you both over the years. I know we've had some ups and downs over the time, but I believe I got a real insight into you both and how you run your lives.'

She shuffled through the paperwork in her briefcase and presented Mark with a formal letter.

'I'm so proud of you both, all of your hard work has definitely paid off. It's good news for you.'

Mark sat, eyes wide in anticipation.

'Following the evidence provided, along with my satisfactory visit reports, the courts are happy and agree that the best place for Nikki is to legally reside with her biological father and have granted full parental custody to Mr Mark Johnson.'

Mark couldn't breathe.

'Really?' he managed to say after catching his breath. His eyes reddened. He had been fighting this battle for so long and although it was hard to deal with the unexpected visits, the constant interrogation and questioning, he couldn't actually believe he'd come this far. All the hard times and struggle had worked out. It was an extremely tough and long road, and at times it was so hard he wanted to give up, but he persevered. He held his hands to his face and completely broke down, his emotions completely overwhelming him. He was so happy he'd won. Maria sat beside him, rubbed his shoulders and kissed him.

'Well done baby, we did it. She's coming home.'

* * *

I slowly climbed onto the back seat of the car. It really was a sad moment I was so unprepared for – I was leaving. I had a small understanding of why, as Claire tried to explain it to me many times, but couldn't help but think Dave wouldn't have left if it wasn't for me. I'd finally got my wishes to know who my real family were, but I loved Claire and the boys so much I didn't want to go. It was all my fault, I thought to myself. Had I ruined everything for Dave and Claire? Was the colour of my skin the real reason why I had to leave? The questions went round and round in my mind, although Claire promised it had nothing to do with me. She gave me the biggest and tightest hug ever – I was almost crushed to death. She held me tight, planting wet and teary kisses all over my face, telling me she loved me and would always have a special place in her heart for me. I clung to her, not wanting to let go. I knew the moment we let go would be the moment I would have to leave.

'Please can't I stay?' I asked her. 'I'll be good, I promise.'

She unwrapped my arms.

'No darling, you can't. You need to be a good girl now and go with your mother and father, OK? They'll take good care of you and you'll have an amazing life, the life you've always deserved.'

She wiped the tears away from my face, kissed me, turned her back and ran back into the house sobbing, while I walked away hand in hand with Mark and Maria. The boys stood at the door waving. I don't think they really understood I was leaving for good, but I waved back anyway. Sadly there was no sign of Dave. As the car pulled off I looked back out of the window as the house became smaller and smaller. I looked to the front of the car, at Mark behind the wheel and Maria sat next to him, and looked back again. The house was now completely out of sight. I had no choice but to try and embrace my new surroundings. I sat quietly and looked down at the shiny new shoes Claire had brought me and wondered if I would be as happy with my real family as I was with her. I also wondered if I'd ever see any of them ever again.

* * *

I remained silent the whole journey, whilst Mark drove in silence also. Every now and then Maria turned around to ask if I was OK.

'Are you hungry? Do you need to go to the toilet?'

I didn't answer. I already decided I didn't like her. I don't know why, I just didn't get the best vibe from her. Not like Claire, I knew straight away Claire loved me from the first day we met. I wanted Claire so badly and now I had to get to know Maria instead, like replacing one mother for another just like that. I was sat in the back of this gold Capri on my way to god knows where, yet all I could think about was Claire. I wouldn't be sitting in the kitchen with her and the boys for dinner tonight. I wouldn't be able to play in the garden in the afternoons. I wouldn't have Claire's hugs and kisses.

We finally arrived at the house. It was nowhere near the size of Claire's house. It was an average mid-terraced ground floor flat with a garden. Maria took my hand and walked me in. I still hadn't spoken a word at this point. I sat on the sofa while Mark and Maria whispered together in the kitchen.

'I'll leave you with her for a while,' I managed to hear her say. 'You need some time alone to bond with her, just talk to her, it will be OK.'

I looked up at Mark blankly as he sat me on his lap. He stroked my hair and face.

'So pretty,' he said with a smile.

He seemed really nice, he was my real dad so I automatically felt at ease with him. I studied his face, and tried I tried to imagine what the future would be like from day to day in this new environment. I smiled back at him.

'Are you really my real dad?' I asked.

He kissed me on both cheeks, my forehead and my nose. 'Yeah, I am.'

* * *

A whole year had gone by relatively quickly. Things were very different to how they were with Claire and the boys, but I expected that and knew it wouldn't have been the same or even close. Although I learned that Mark was my real dad, something didn't seem right. I never felt that Maria was my real mum. I called her mum, but it never felt natural to me. I didn't even like her; I used to look in her eyes to see if I could see what my dad or Claire had in their eyes when they looked at me, but there was nothing, she seemed cold and never embraced me like they did. She was pregnant and soon to give birth to a baby boy. Maria was completely different to Claire, she hardly looked at me, never smiled and most of the time she dragged me around on her daily travels like I was a burden. She did the bare minimum with me – bathed me, clothed me, did my hair, fed me – but it felt like it was just what she did because she had to, it was never with love or affection. She did however change her tune and seemed to pay more attention in dad's presence, which was so annoying because he thought she was an angel. He actually praised her so much for doing so well with me and told her he loved her even more for accepting me. But I knew deep down it was all a front; she didn't accept me, she tolerated me, and although I didn't know much, I knew in my heart she wasn't my mum. But there was nothing I could do to prove it.

* * *

Dad and I drove together on the way to the hospital. He had let me sit on the front seat for the first time ever, which was so exciting. I shyly giggled at his jokes and all the fascinating things he pointed out to me as we drove along in the night – where he used to live, where he went to school, where he had great parties. Soul music played in the background and I sang along to the songs I recognised. I happily stared out of the window as we drove along, and as we passed the common, I could see loads of moving lights way in the distance.

'Dad, what are those lights?' I asked. 'They look like fairies.'

'Nah, they're not fairies,' he replied. 'They're Smurfs.'

'Smurfs,' I repeated as I giggled. I loved the Smurfs and looked again.

'Yes darling, they're Smurfs.'

'Wow,' I said excitedly as I tried to wave to see if they could see me. The truth was they were just lights from other cars in the distance, but for as long as I could remember they were Smurfs in my mind, which always made our trips much more fun and exciting.

I was looking forward to meeting my new baby brother. I missed Peter and Paul so much and was really excited to have someone new to play with again. I looked around at all the faces in the hospital room, family members of Maria, some of them knew of me, some didn't. I stood close beside dad holding his hand, almost hiding behind his legs. I could see some of them whispering and talking about me and wondered what the issue was. I watched them chatting, looking over, nodding and smiling. I became extremely shy and paranoid and literally stuck by dad's side as they hugged, kissed and congratulated him on the baby. As well as the baby, one by one they all put their two pence piece in on me. 'Oh she's so pretty.' 'She's so cute.' 'Lovely.' 'Hasn't she's got a lot of hair.' One woman just looked at me and walked away. It was weird, most of these women were Maria's family, yet some of them didn't make me feel very welcome. I kept my head down and stuck by dad. I could sense that no one really cared too much for me, they were here for Maria and the baby.

Dad walked over to the bed where Maria was, kissed her and went to the cot to get the baby. I pretty much stuck to his leg as I followed. He was so cute, but as soon as dad picked him up everyone crowded over to get a glimpse and I couldn't get a look in. I became invisible and completely shut out. Claire was always so happy to show me off and include me in whatever she did, yet here I was, stood hiding behind dad's legs as if I didn't exist. I couldn't help but wonder if this really was my real family. Why did it feel so false? And why was I made to feel like such an outsider?

* * *

Rashid was so cute. I loved him so much and played with him as much as I could. He didn't do anything but sleep, cry and get his nappy changed, but it was like having a real-life doll to play with. I was at nursery during the days and was always so excited to get back so I could play with Rashid, who'd be wrapped up in a white blanket sleeping most of the time. He was so cute, even touching his little hands while he slept kept me entertained for ages. One afternoon I came home, as usual desperate to play with him (it literally was the highlight of my day).

'Don't wake him,' Maria scorned. 'I just got him to sleep.'

I was pretending to feed him with my Tiny Tears dolly bottle. I ignored her and continued pressing the little bottle into his mouth. He woke up, which was the result I secretly wanted.

'Hello Rashid!' I happily said. 'Wake up so you can have your milk.'

Rashid screamed at the top of his lungs.

'Don't cry Rashid,' I said, trying to shove the toy bottle in his mouth which made him scream even louder.

'Didn't I tell you not to wake him?' Maria shouted. 'What the hell are you doing?'

'Nothing,' I replied innocently and tried to push the bottle further in his mouth.

She ran over to the basket and hit me so hard across my head I fell to the floor. The pain was excruciating. I lay on the floor holding my head, in so much pain I couldn't stop the tears. Thinking she would realise she'd made a massive mistake and apologise, I looked up at her, still crying and in shock, waiting for her to say she was sorry. But she didn't.

'What's the matter with you?' she screamed. 'I told you not to wake him, didn't I? You stupid girl.'

* * *

Completely wrong in thinking that was a one-off due to stress, it actually became a regular occurrence. She hit me for spilling my drink, not finishing my meals, not tidying up my toys, if my clothes were dirty, anything. She hit me for any reason she could think of. Sometimes it felt like she even made up excuses to hit me. I started to wet the bed at night, probably due to the constant anxiety, and she beat me for that too. It got to the point that no matter what I did, she found wrong in it. It sadly became the way of life that I became so used to. I actually learnt to disguise the pain. She would strike me, I would flinch and just carry on. I couldn't give her the satisfaction of knowing she was hurting me. I hated her so much, she was literally evil and I tried so hard to pretend she wasn't getting to me. It got to a point where I never really understood what was right or wrong anymore and didn't quite know how to behave because I got hit for pretty much anything I did. Living day to day on edge and confused wondering what I was going to do next to piss her off, I figured the best thing would be to just stay quiet all the time and do as little as possible, so she wouldn't get angry. This meant I completely stopped speaking, to her or to anyone in case I said the wrong thing. I tried my best to do absolutely nothing to annoy her. I never answered her when she asked me anything, I'd just nod yes or no. I ate anything she put on my plate or gave me even if I didn't like it. I played alone really quietly with my toys. I daren't touch Rashid in case he cried, so I stopped playing with him altogether. If we were out, I wouldn't even tell her if I needed the toilet because we'd already been there and that was always a huge problem too. So sometimes if we were out I would pee in my knickers so I didn't bother her. It'd happened so many times before that I'd get hit on the street for wanting to go to the toilet and that was the biggest embarrassment ever. If I'd peed my pants, she didn't even notice. I'd sneak to my bedroom when we got home and quickly change my knickers and put the messed-up ones in the wash. This way, in my mind, I thought I was winning. I looked at it as if it was a game, that I could outsmart her, it was the only way I could distract myself from the pain and how I really felt on a daily basis. I lived on constant eggshells each day, to survive without being noticed for anything that would start her off, I learned how to suppress myself and became very good at living in her life unnoticed.

It wasn't always so bad. It was great when dad was home, but unfortunately that wasn't very often. I had birthday parties and got lots of toys when family came around just like any other kid, I was always dressed well, and we always got loads of toys at Christmas. To the outsider, we were absolutely fine, but it was all a united front to show that perfect family life in front of other people.

* * *

One afternoon we went out to visit one of Maria's friends. They both sat in the kitchen chatting while the friend gave Rashid and I some orange juice and a few biscuits. We happily played together while we munched our biscuits and when we finished, I asked the lady if we could have some more. Maria looked at me with those stern eyes,

'Yes of course you can,' the friend replied as she went to the cupboard to get the biscuit jar.

I looked at Maria confused. I hadn't done anything wrong, but from the way she looked at me I could tell I shouldn't have asked for more biscuits.

'You just wait till we get home,' she whispered in my ears.

I suddenly felt that sense of dread. I knew exactly what was coming. My stomach turned in fear. She was going to start there and then. I'd only asked for more biscuits, surely that wasn't the worst thing in the world. I sat quietly at the table and slowly ate the biscuits, wishing I hadn't said a word, hoping it would be OK. Everything seemed fine for the rest of the evening and we got home, but I hadn't forgotten about her comments at the house. It would be too good to be true if nothing was going to come of it. I was secretly terrified but tried to act normal, hoping she had either forgotten or would let it slide for once. I still kept myself to myself though and kept really quiet just in case. Anything else, just one thing, could upset her and trigger her off.

We got home, and I figured all was OK. She hadn't said anything, but the anxiety still ran through me. Completely on edge, I sat quietly on the sofa to watch TV while she put Rashid down in the bedroom to sleep. She came back into the living room and closed the curtains. It was a bit early to close the curtains as it was still sunny outside, but nevertheless I continued watching TV as she came over to me and sat by my side.

'Go to the bedroom and get your belt,' she said. Her tone was calm, and she was smiling as she spoke which made it feel like everything was fine, but deep down I knew it wasn't.

'What belt?' I nervously asked. 'Why do I need my belt?'

'Just go, and get your belt,' she repeated.

I quickly jumped off the sofa, not wanting a blow to my head, and slowly walked down the corridor towards my room to get the belt. I returned, slowly handed her the belt, interested to see what she was going to do next. She looped the belt, grabbed me by my arm, dragged me towards her, pulled up my dress and struck me over and over on my bare legs with it.

'You do not ask people for food. Do you want people to think I don't feed you? Children should be seen and not heard.' She shouted each word with a blow to my legs.

I screamed, pleading her to stop, but she just carried on. It felt like my legs were on fire. Through my tears, I got a glimpse of her face. She looked so satisfied with what she was doing. I couldn't understand why she was doing this, why she hated me so much. I cried and cried for ages that evening, not only because of the pain but because of how distressed I was. It felt like there was no way out of this life, the constant fear, the anxiety, the embarrassment. This was actually my life and it was exhausting. I was so tired of trying to avoid her or trying to do the right thing, it was clear that this was a no-win situation, and I quickly realised it wasn't about how I behaved, or what I'd done or not done, it was about me and nothing else. Once I'd realised this was the case, I saw no end to this living nightmare. I longed for my dad so badly, but with what was going on I figured he didn't care. If he cared this wouldn't even be possible. I actually believed he must have known what was going on and what she was like. I thought perhaps he agreed with it and perhaps it was normal. I never once thought she could be deceiving him too.

* * *

A couple of years in, I became so accustomed to this life I learned that no matter what, it was never going to change, this was normal life. But inside I was angry. I hated everyone, hated the world including dad, this was the life I'd left Claire for, and it was a living hell. I was now six and Rashid was three. Dad as usual was never home to witness anything or understand how things really were. I still had thoughts in my mind that he must have had some idea and never really trusted him anymore. As well as his full-time day job he played out in the sound three, even four evenings a week. The sound was called Diamonds, and the name was everywhere. Everyone who was into the music he played, followed that sound every week, and he was at the very forefront of it all. He'd become a bit of a legend, almost like a celebrity, and was becoming more and more popular, and obviously busier. Everyone knew Mark Johnson from Diamonds. Men respected him, other DJs wanted to learn from him and women absolutely loved him. In his outside world he was having the time of his life, but at home this was going on. In my eyes if he loved me so much he'd be home more, he'd pay more attention to what was happening at home. I wondered why he didn't realise how quiet I was, or how much my personality and behaviour had changed. He obviously didn't care enough to notice anything, I figured, therefore, I had no faith in him either. How he could allow these things to happen to me right under his nose was beyond me. I wished I could tell him what was going on to see his reaction and to see if he knew anything, but then I'd think he'd tell her and everything would get worse while he was out, so I decided the best thing to do was keep quiet.

I was in school at this time and absolutely hated it. I spent most of my time alone. I had no friends because I was always so nervous or worried about how to act. I didn't know how to be myself, I thought whatever I said or did would either be the wrong thing or unworthy, so I spoke to no one, didn't smile, laugh or answer questions in class. I sat at the back not wanting to be seen. I never knew how to make friends, I wasn't confident enough to think anyone would have any interest in me. In my mind I had learnt it was always better to not say anything at all, that way I could avoid anything bad happening. At playtimes I sat alone reading books while the other children ran around playing in the playground. I became a great target for bullies as I never knew how to stand up for myself. Kids called me names, pushed and shoved me around. I had long curly afro hair which was usually tied in two side bunches, so they'd run around me calling me Mickey Mouse, pulling my bunches. I had a gap in my teeth so they'd shout out all sorts – buck teeth, rabbit teeth, vampire – and run away. I got so used to it I didn't even respond, I just let them say or do whatever they wanted. I spent most of my time reading with the teachers who always said I was very intelligent and beautiful. Being around the teachers was the only time I felt safe, but I certainly didn't feel beautiful.

* * *

On Monday mornings, Maria sent me to school with my weekly dinner money in a brown envelope. She never gave me any extra money for sweets or the tuck shop. I'd once built up the courage to ask but I was completely ignored. Every day at first break all the kids ran to the tuck shop to buy sweets and chocolate. Every day I sat on my own in the corner and watched the other kids with their treats. I pretended I didn't care but I did. I wanted to be like them, I wanted to have friends and buy sweets just like they did. I was tired of being the odd one out, the one that always had to go without. One particular Monday morning as usual, Maria handed me the dinner money. I looked down at the envelope in my hand and at that moment I knew exactly what I was going to do and didn't care about the consequences. I was going to use this money to buy sweets, even if it was just for one day. I wanted to feel normal for a minute and today I was going to, and if the other kids saw me as normal, maybe they would begin to accept me.

The bell rang for playtime, I was so excited with my philosophy and hoped it was going to work. I took the five pound note out of the brown envelope and went along awkwardly ahead of the other kids to the tuck shop, and put it down on the desk. I ordered nearly everything available and stuffed my face. I then began to give away some of my sweets to a couple of kids behind me in the queue. Within moments, a bunch of kids surrounded me wanting sweets as I gave them out. I put my hand in my pocket and pulled out the remaining change and handed it all out while they happily thanked me. For a minute I felt like these kids actually appreciated me while they crowded around taking the money. I thought I'd done it, I'd finally made friends, and from now on things would be better, at least at school. It felt like spending that money was the best decision I'd made and I was prepared to take whatever punishment I was going to get for it. At least that's what I thought.

By lunchtime everything went right back to normal and I was alone again, being mocked and laughed at. I didn't understand, I thought I'd worked it out, I had brought nearly everyone in my class sweets only a couple of hours ago, but they still didn't want me around. Go away rabbit teeth, they pushed me and ran away laughing. I felt so stupid and didn't understand how they could be so horrible after this morning, and now I'd have to face the consequences with no result. It felt it would be a sacrifice worth taking, but everyone still hated me. I thought about the children's home when they said I was bad and a danger; I thought about Dave and Claire. Dave didn't want me because of the colour of my skin and I wasn't good enough. I thought about Maria, she must have really hated me to do what she did and thought it was all my fault, that I must be ugly, or bad, or different. It was the truth in my head, and the reason this was happening to me.

At the end of the school day, of course my teacher asked if I had my dinner money. I don't know why, but the easiest way to answer the question was to lie.

'No, my mum didn't give it to me.'

'That's not like her,' the teacher replied. 'She must have forgot. Oh well, that's easily done,' she said. 'I'll give her a call.'

My heart completely dropped. The thought of her finding out made me feel sick. I don't know what I expected to happen, but I knew the punishment was going to be insane. I started to cry immediately at the thought, but the teacher didn't understand why. She tried to comfort me and asked what was wrong, but I was too scared to tell her the truth so I lied again and said I had a tummy ache.

* * *

I dreaded going home that afternoon. The school was only five minutes away and I usually walked straight home, but today I walked and walked for hours, around and around street after street, completely terrified, wondering if I could stay away forever. I walked around for almost three hours until I became hungry and needed the toilet. Maria came to the door with Rashid running behind her. She picked him up and went back into the front room; she didn't say anything to me or anything about the money or why I was home so late. I walked into the front room and one of her friends was there which was a huge relief. Bags full of clothes and boxes of shoes were scattered on the floor, they'd been shopping for the afternoon in the West End and both seemed to be in a good mood. I said hi to the friend and quietly sat on the sofa hoping everything will be forgotten. Maria and her friend opened the bags and pulled out dresses to admire.

'Oh that's so nice,' said the friend while Maria pulled out a long black dress.

Maria smiled, 'Yes, it is isn't it? I'm going to wear it on Saturday for Mark's birthday with these shoes.'

She opened the box of shoes and pulled out a pair of white pointed stilettos.

'Perfect,' said the friend. 'So how are things with you and Mark? Are you getting to spend more time with him?'

'I don't know,' Maria replied. 'Let's talk about it later.'

She put her head in my direction as if to say, not in front of Nikki.

'OK, yeah, we'll talk about it later, I'll call you.'

She got up to leave and ruffled my hair.

'She has such beautiful hair, doesn't she?'

Maria looked at me and smiled. 'Yes, she does.'

I looked at her so confused. Half of the time she was either battering me black and blue or completely ignoring me, yet she acted like everything was perfect in front of her friend. That was the first time I'd seen her smile at me in ages. I hated her so much, but figured I'd take advantage of her good mood in the hope she wouldn't be that bothered about the money.

As her friend left I sat on the floor playing with my Barbie. Rashid was also on the floor playing with a puzzle. Maria slowly entered the room and went to close the curtains.

'Why did it take you so long to come home from school?' she asked.

'I went to my friend's house,' I replied.

'What friend?'

'Just a friend.'

I could see the expression on her face changing and knew that look so well. It was such a dramatic change; a minute ago, she was excited about her new dress and shoes.

'So, what happened to the dinner money?'

I didn't answer.

'What happened?' Her voice calm but slightly raised with that same smirk on her face.

'I spent it in the tuck shop.'

I didn't want to tell her the real truth or why I spent the money. I was so embarrassed at what really happened or even why I did it.

'What do you mean, you spent it at the tuck shop?'

'I spent it at the tuck shop to buy sweets and I brought my friends some too.'

I wanted her to believe I had friends; I didn't want her to know her actions were affecting me so badly that I never knew how to behave, that actually I had no friends and was always alone, that the kids chanted at me and pushed me around because I was so weak.

'I'm really sorry,' I quietly replied, my head hanging down, my heart pounding with fear, praying something would happen to distract her.

She looked at me with her face full of thunder – you would have thought I'd done something a lot worse – and in no time at all she scarpered across the floor, grabbed one of the white stilettos from the shoe box and struck me in the face with the heel of the shoe three times. It all happened so fast. My face on fire, I screamed out so loud that it frightened Rashid and made him scream too. It was chaos. How she could change her mood so quickly was shocking. I sat holding my face, screaming out loud it hurt so much.

'Shut up,' she screamed at me while she tried to comfort Rashid. 'You're scaring Rashid. Shut up and go to your room.'

Just as I was about to go to my room I heard the key in the door – dad was home. It was the distraction I was so desperate for, but a little too late. I wanted to see him so he could see me crying, I wanted him to ask what was happening. I wanted him to see this because he never actually saw it, I always thought he knew but he never saw it. Maria quickly put the shoe back in the box and rushed over to me.

'Shut up and get to your room now,' she whispered in my ear. 'I don't want to hear another word from you.'

Terrified of what would happen if I didn't, I held my breath, stopped crying and quickly went to my room without seeing dad or having dinner, and cried myself to sleep.

* * *

About a week later, on a sunny Saturday afternoon, Rashid and I were playing together in the garden. I was skipping with the new skipping rope dad had bought me, and Rashid was running around with a toy car. We were having so much fun together, but randomly and very typical of British weather the sky went completely grey and it poured with rain. Rashid and I, laughing and screaming, ran to the front of the garden and quickly shuffled inside the house to continue playing.

'What shall we do now?' Rashid asked. 'I know, we'll play shops,' he said.

'Yes,' I replied.

Maria was in the kitchen preparing dinner. Rashid ran to grab the pretend till that he loved so much, and we began to play.

'Fifty pence, please,' Rashid said, after he scanned the pretend items.

We were playing with one and two pence pieces for the money, but for some reason I decided I wanted a 50 pence piece and knew there were coins in Rashid's money box. The money box was a ceramic NatWest pig dressed as a policeman. I wanted one of those so badly but of course only Rashid got one. I ran to the bedroom to go get it, brought it back to the front room, knelt on the floor and frantically shook it upside down to try and get the money out. I quickly realised the money came out from the bottom and you had to open the hatch so I tried and tried with my fingers but couldn't do it. I looked around the room thinking of Plan B and saw a pair of tweezers on the side table which would work. I grabbed the tweezers and attacked the money box so hard that it smashed into pieces. I quickly looked at Rashid.

'Shhhhhh,' I whispered to him.

We both sat there in silence for a moment, knowing we'd be in serious trouble.

'Say it was you,' I said. 'Please, just say it was you. She doesn't hit you, you can say you dropped it.'

It was the truth, she never ever hit Rashid.

'What the hell was that?' we both heard Maria shout out from the kitchen.

Rashid and I sat still on the floor with the shattered money box in front of us, looking as guilty as ever. I prayed Rashid would stick to the plan.

'What happened?' she asked as she entered the room standing over us.

Please Rashid, please, I prayed in my head with my fingers crossed behind my back.

'Nikki did it mummy,' Rashid said really quickly.

I looked at him in shock. I couldn't believe he could do that to me. He knew what was happening, he saw it every time, it would have been so easy for him to just say it was an accident. She scorned at me and left the room. My stomach turned, I knew something awful was about to happen and the dread was awful. I literally prayed I could disappear. She arrived back with my new skipping rope. She didn't even say anything, she just grabbed my arm, pulled down my jeans and started lashing my bare legs. This was the worst yet. I remember that skipping rope so clearly, it was fluorescent yellow with orange handles. As she lashed me over and over I screamed and screamed in agony, begging her to stop, until it got to a point where it didn't even hurt anymore, and suddenly I felt a strange warm sensation. As I looked down at my legs I saw blood, blood dripping down my thigh, the plastic rope was actually piercing my skin as she struck me with it and I don't even think she noticed or even cared.

I began to hysterically panic and screamed out at her, 'It's bleeding, stop, look at me, please.'

I was shouting as loud as I possibly could to get her to stop but she continued.

'Look at me!' I screamed. 'It's bleeding!' I cried.

She continued slashing, it was like she was another person, like an out-of-body experience or something because she didn't hear me, her face so full of anger I couldn't recognise her. I didn't know why she was so angry with me all the time, breaking the money box didn't warrant this. I was so tired, I began to move in slow motion to the rhythm of the lashes, my eyes filled with tears. I tried to think of something to block out the pain, but I couldn't think.

When she finally stopped, she pulled my jeans up, dragged me into the bedroom and shoved me on to the bed.

'Go to sleep and don't let me hear your voice,' she said as she turned away and shut the door.

I cried and cried into the pillow on my bed. I had absolutely no control of what was happening to me. I needed to get away from this somehow, but had no idea of how, my legs were stinging so badly but I couldn't move. Once I'd managed to stop myself from crying, I peeled myself off the bed and pulled down my jeans to take a look. My legs were red raw but the worst was my thigh – four bleeding slashes right across my thigh, the wounds so deep I could see flesh. I didn't know what to do. I couldn't tell her, I was too scared of her reaction. I had completely run out of energy and had a splitting headache. I wanted to sleep but the mess from my legs was so bad I had to clean myself up. I went over to the drawer, pulled out a t-shirt and wiped away the blood which stung so badly. I hid the t-shirt at the back of the wardrobe and tried to go to sleep on my left side, but it hurt so much I couldn't sleep. I snuck to the bathroom and found some plasters to put on my legs, but there weren't enough to cover all the wounds, so I did the best I could and put baby wipes over the rest. I was emotionally and physically drained, my mind went round and round in circles trying to think of how I could get away from her. I looked at my leg which was still bleeding through the baby wipes so I snuck again to get some more, wiped the wounds as best as I could and fell into a deep sleep. The next day I washed my wounds in the bath and covered them with baby wipes and Sellotape since I'd used all the plasters. Whether she knew I was bleeding or not was always a mystery to me. I was old enough to bathe and clothe myself, so she wouldn't have seen the wounds, but how she didn't notice at the time was beyond me. She had gotten away with it, yet again.

* * *

'Why on earth did you cut her hair?' dad asked one morning.

'Oh I just don't have the time to be sorting out her hair every day, it's a bit of a nightmare and I'm too busy with getting Rashid ready in the mornings to deal with it. It's no big deal though, it'll grow back.'

'I see,' dad replied and nodded his head. 'Yeah I guess it's easier.'

I looked at him with a look to say she was lying but he didn't notice, he believed her. It wasn't the biggest deal in his world to have to worry about, but that wasn't the truth. I had long thick curly hair which fell right down my back and yes it was very hard to manage a lot of the time, but most people said it was my beauty, people always commented on how beautiful my hair was. She had cut it the day before, but I believed she did it on purpose. I sat between her legs with tears running down my face as she did it.

'This hair of yours is way too much to deal with, it'll be so much better short,' she said.

She took the scissors and began hacking off my hair. The curls dropped to the floor as she cut away and every time I cried out or begged her not to do it. She whacked me in the side of my face with the hairbrush and told me to shut up. She cut nearly all my hair off, leaving me with nothing but a tiny afro. I literally looked like a boy. When she finished, I stood at the mirror staring at what I saw, ugly, puffy-eyed from all the crying and no hair.

'That's better,' she said and left the room.

I watched her leave and turned back to the mirror. I cried as I looked at myself in that mirror trying to find an answer, trying to find a solution, but when reality hit and I realised there was no solution, it became more apparent and so sad that this was it. The thought devastated me so much I sat on the floor and cried for what felt like forever.

* * *

It was the school holidays. Rashid was in nursery and I went to a childminder in the daytimes which I also hated. The kids at the childminders were actually worse than the kids at school. At least at school the teachers were around and had the ability to stop anything really bad from happening. At the childminders there was just one woman looking after all of us and she never seemed too fussed about what we were doing. She did the bare minimum. Other than lunchtimes, she pretty much left us all to it in the playroom all day. The playroom was a large room with loads of toys, books and games lying around. Just like life at school, I usually sat in a corner alone reading books while the other kids played together. I was the only black kid there so that was another reason they never wanted to play with me. They shouted out racist comments and called me names.

'Go away black monkey, you can't play with us.'

'Urgh don't touch her, you might get black too,' one of them said.

I hated it there and the days always felt so long. When Maria picked me up in the evenings, I begged for her not to take me there again. I told her the kids were mean to me and called me monkey, but nothing changed, she ignored me like she always did. It got to the point again where there was no point in speaking about it.

'Shut up and stop moaning,' she said. 'Do you know how much money I pay for you to go to that place?'

This particular morning with my hair cut so short I knew it was going to cause a drama; the kids would mock me even more. I literally knew I was on my way to torture. As usual I picked out a book from the box and went to the corner to sit and read.

'Look at the monkey's hair!' one of them pointed at me and shouted.

They all laughed and chanted monkey sounds at me. They ran around hitting and pushing me laughing as I sat there with silent tears running down my face, counting numbers in my head until they would stop. They eventually stopped when the childminder popped her head in the door to tell us she was going to the shop downstairs and would be back in five minutes.

'Quick,' one of the kids shouted, 'let's rub poo on the monkey girl.'

'Isn't that what she's made of?' another giggled.

It was like I was paralysed, I couldn't move, I couldn't do anything, I had no effort or energy in me to even attempt to get away. I sat there with dry tears on my face, tired from all the crying. I'd already cried so much this morning when my hair was being cut. I watched the kids giggling and running around, plotting, excited about their plan. They came back with a yellow potty full of poo. It was so calculated, one of the kids ran for the potty while another pooed in it. They rolled around in fits of laughter while I sat frozen, more tears running down my face as one of them threw a piece of poo at me. It was so funny to them, but for me, I literally wanted to die there and then. They became more and more excited and egged each other on, getting carried away with excitement.

'Make her eat it,' one of them shouted.

'Yeah,' shouted another as they laughed hysterically, 'she probably eats poo for dinner anyway, that's why black people are black, 'cause they eat poo.'

They all laughed so much, but I didn't know what to do or how to get away. These kids were not messing about, I knew they were going to follow it through. I looked to my left at the window. Can I jump out of that window? I thought. They can't make me do this, they can't. My mind was racing with thoughts of how to make this stop, yet I was powerless to do anything. Surely they wouldn't really go that far? I was praying, please don't let this happen.

They circled around me, jumping, laughing and egging each other on.

'Go on, do it, make her eat it,' one of the kids said to one of the boys.

The boy looked at me, looked back at the kid, looked at the potty. He was just as scared and didn't really want to do it.

'Just do it,' the kid said. 'Don't be chicken.'

'I can't,' he said.

The kid punched him in the stomach.

'Do it,' he said, 'or I'll beat you up every day.'

The boy reluctantly picked out a piece of poo from the potty and slowly walked up to my face. I could hear the sounds of laughter and chanting drift away until I heard nothing, my mind totally shut down in disbelief, it was unreal. I knew exactly what was happening, but I couldn't hear it anymore. The boy bent down and shoved the poo right across my mouth and ran away. The sound became clear again.

'Hahahahahaha,' they threw themselves on the floor crying with laughter.

With utter shame and embarrassment, I ran to the bathroom to spit out what was remaining in my mouth and washed my face. I stayed in the bathroom for as long as I could, ashamed to leave. I sat on the toilet seat and stared at the floor. I had no tears left to cry so I sat there wondering why the world was so evil. I wished there was a way to become invisible, I just didn't want anyone to look at me or acknowledge me ever again.

The childminder eventually came to find me in the bathroom and told me to come out to play. I was so humiliated I couldn't go back out there, but I couldn't bring myself to tell her what had just happened, so I quietly walked back into the room, sat right in the corner with my legs crossed, my head face down, reading the same page of the book over and over and didn't move until pick up time.

'Please don't make me go there again,' I begged Maria while we were in the car on the way home. 'The boys made me eat poo.'

'What?' she asked as she turned around to look at me.

'They made me eat poo.'

'Oh my god, shut up and stop lying,' she replied. 'Don't be so ridiculous, I'm sick of your lies.'

* * *

It had been five years since I arrived at this hell hole. I was now eight and Rashid was five. Nothing much had changed, it was just how things were. On so many occasions I wanted to tell dad everything, but was just too scared of the outcome. I wouldn't even know how to tell him or if he'd even believe me. I wasn't confident enough to bring the conversation up, every time it was almost possible to tell him I'd freak out. I thought he'd never believe me over her anyway and I still had that doubt in my head that he knew all about it. Maria was still Maria, she was just who she was and there was no changing that. I was still completely on edge in her presence and terrified of what she was capable of. The major incidents had slowed down, but I still got a slap over the head, in my face, or behind my legs every now and then for whatever reason, but it wasn't as dramatic as previously, or perhaps I'd just got used to it.

Rashid and I had become really close. He was no longer a baby, he'd grown into a cute little boy and became my little best friend. We now shared the bedroom which was cool; it felt much better having Rashid in the room with me. He looked up to me and even though he was younger, he became quite protective. He'd seen all the bad things happen over the years and tried his best to comfort me by giving me his toys to play with or saving his sweets for me. I still hadn't figured out why she would only hit me and never him. I had seen him do so many things worse than I ever did and he always got away with it.

One night whilst in bed, I stared up at the ceiling thinking about everything. I crawled out of bed and went over to the other side of the room where Rashid's bed was.

'Why do you think she hits me and not you?' I asked.

'Who, mummy?'

'Yeah.' I rarely called her mum or mummy, I called her 'she' or 'her'.

'I don't know,' Rashid replied.

'I know why,' I said. 'Because she's not my real mum.'

'Yes she is.'

'No Rashid, she isn't,' I sighed. 'I don't know who is but I know it's not her, I just know.'

'That's stupid,' Rashid said. 'Course she's our mum.'

'No it's not stupid, it's true, she's not my mum,' I snapped back disappointed he didn't believe me.

'So, if she's not your mum then why do you live here?' he said confused.

'I don't know,' I replied.

Slightly frustrated I got back into my bed and continued to stare up at the ceiling. The feeling became stronger than ever. I don't know what came over me but something was telling me she really wasn't my real mum. I could feel it, there was someone else out there somewhere, someone who was my real mum and the idea excited me so much. I hoped whoever she was, she was looking for me too, and would take me away from this house, this life and her. It gave me something to look forward to and gave me hope that somehow, one day I would find out the truth which would be my chance for things to change.

* * *

'I'll see you soon,' Maria said as she hung up the phone.

Her best friend Sheila was on her way over for the afternoon. Rashid and I liked it when she came over, she brought us sweets and sometimes she'd even bring new toys for us. We'd sit in the corner of our room together playing, totally left to our own devices while they chatted and drank wine. About an hour later she arrived with a bottle of wine and they sat around the table for a chat while Rashid and I played in our room.

'So what really is going on?' asked Sheila as she sipped her wine.

Maria sighed a long sigh. 'Oh Sheila things have been really bad,' she said. 'Mark is never home, never, you know how big Diamonds is now, and it's just getting bigger and bigger. I'm constantly hearing rumours about him with other women, I just can't deal with this. How can he expect me to be sat at home alone every day and night, taking care of his child while he's out there doing whatever he wants with other women? It's disgusting, I feel like he's taking me for granted.'

Sheila was surprised at what she heard, she always thought they were the perfect couple and everything was fine.

'But you love the kids, don't you?' she asked.

'Rashid's the love of my life, I love him more and more every day,' she replied.

'You love Nikki like your own too, don't you?'

'It's not as easy as that,' sighed Maria. 'Honestly, it's really hard taking in another woman's kid as your own, as much as you try to, you'll never love them like your own.'

'I'm sure you can,' Sheila replied. 'Loads of parents do.'

'I know, but the way things have been going I don't even know if I want to. Savannah's back.'

'What?' Sheila shrieked. 'She can't be.'

'Yep she's back, she's been calling here saying she's come back for Nikki, even though Mark won the custody battle.'

'Oh my god, what are you going to do?'

'I don't know. Mark's even seen her, apparently, to discuss the situation, but guess what, he didn't come home that night.'

'Are you serious?' sighed Sheila.

'Can you believe I actually found out she came back a couple of years ago and apparently he's been seeing her behind my back all this time.'

'No way,' Sheila said. 'He wouldn't do that to you.'

'Well she told me herself when she called. How do you think she has this number?'

'Oh, she'll say anything to piss you off Maria. Honestly, you can't believe her, she's crazy right, isn't that why she left in the first place?'

Maria shrugged her shoulders.

'What a mess, she's probably lying just to hurt you. Surely Mark wouldn't go there, especially after everything you went through to get her out of care. She can't just come back and take Nikki after all this time.'

'Perhaps that would be the best thing,' Maria said under her breath.

'No Maria, you don't mean that, you're just angry.'

'Angry?' Maria replied. 'Yes, I'm angry, of course I'm angry, I have to look at that child's face every single day. And do you know what I see when I look at her? I see him and I see her. Honestly, it's torture, I hate it. If they really are "seeing" each other or having an affair then why am I the dumb idiot at home dealing with "their" child. She can bloody well come and take her back for all I care, I don't know,' she sighed. 'It's all messed up. My friend Chris reckons I should just give her back and get on with my life.'

'Chris, who's Chris?' Sheila looked at Maria wide-eyed.

'Oh he's just a friend from work, he's good to me. He's been really great actually and he understands what I'm going through.'

'Oh Maria what are you getting yourself into?' Sheila sighed.

'I didn't ask for all this,' Maria laughed. 'Mark's never home, all I do is cater for these kids while sat at home hearing all these rumours about him with other women.'

'So you jumped into another man's bed?'

'No, it's not like that,' sighed Maria. 'We're just friends. He knows the situation, he's not gonna cross the line.' She sighed again and took another sip of her wine. 'Oh Sheila, what am I going to do, it's all so messed up?'

* * *

I jumped right out of my sleep suddenly awoken by chaos, shouting, screaming and banging coming from the front room. I ran over to Rashid's bed to wake him up.

'Rashid!' I shook the bed. 'Wake up!'

Rashid sat up rubbing his eyes. 'What's wrong?'

'Can you hear that?'

'What is it?'

'I don't know.'

We sat together on his bed quietly listening, and realised it was dad and Maria arguing. We listened while they screamed at each other at the top of their voices. Rashid and I sat cuddling on the bed while we tried to hear what they were arguing about, but it was so intense we couldn't work it out.

'I hope daddy doesn't hit mummy,' Rashid said.

I secretly kind of wished he did, that way they'd become enemies and I could tell him what she did to me and he'd hate her like I did. The shouting became louder and louder and then we heard a huge crash. It sounded so loud, like a window had been smashed or something.

'Let's go and see,' I whispered to Rashid.

'No,' he said. 'I'm scared.'

'Come on,' I said and grabbed his hand.

We crept down the corridor and hid in the kitchen. It was the only place we could hide without being seen. We quietly peeped through the kitchen door into the living room which was an utter mess. The table and lamp were on the floor, there was mess everywhere, dad and Maria were at each other's throats, Maria was hysterical.

'It's you, you're not a man, you turned me to this, what was I supposed to do when you leave me every night with her, your child?'

'What has this got to do with Nikki?' he shouted. 'This isn't about her, it's about what you've been doing behind my back with him.'

'Yes, it is about Nikki,' she shouted back. 'It's everything to do with her. I was the one who helped you get her back, I'm the one who takes care of her while you fuck around with her mother and other women.'

She raised her hand to hit him, but he grabbed her arms to stop her and pushed her away into the wall. She then ran over to him and slapped him across his face. I grabbed Rashid's arm and we both ran back to the bedroom. I was too scared to see any more and so scared we'd get caught. We both sat in Rashid's bed hunched together wide awake listening to it all through to the early hours of the morning until we both fell asleep.

The next morning Rashid woke up quite a bit later than me. I had been up for ages unable to get out of bed, wondering what happened last night and what the mood would be like today. I couldn't help but feel guilty, it seemed the problem was me and it was clearly confirmed that she hated me just as I always knew. It also confirmed 100 per cent that she wasn't my real mum, so deep down I was kind of relieved. I was right all this time. I looked over to Rashid's bed to see him sat up looking at me.

'Are you OK?' I asked.

He started to cry. 'Why did mummy hit daddy?' he asked.

'I don't know.'

'What's gonna happen?'

'I don't know.'

'Shall I go and see?' he asked.

'I don't know,' I replied.

The truth was, I didn't know. I didn't know what to expect, I didn't want to even see Maria. She pretty much confirmed she hated me and she'd hit dad. However, I was secretly happy that he had finally seen her evil side, maybe it could be a good time to tell him about what she was doing to me.

'Come on then, let's go and see,' I said.

We held hands and went together to the living room. Dad was in there sitting on the sofa drinking a brandy. He called us both over to sit with him as we entered.

'Where's mum?' Rashid asked.

'She's upstairs,' he replied.

'What's wrong dad?' I asked.

He sat me on one knee and Rashid on the other.

'Nikki and I are going to go away for a while,' he said while he cuddled us both.

'Where?' I asked.

'Just away for a while.'

'Can I come?' asked Rashid.

'No, not for now Rashid, you need to stay here with your mum.'

'Why can't I come?' Rashid started to cry.

'It's OK,' dad said as he cuddled him. 'It won't be for long. I need you to be a brave boy and look after mummy OK? Can you do that for me?'

Rashid nodded. 'When are you going?' he asked.

'Today.'

'Today?' I asked in surprise. 'Where too?'

'I'll tell you later Nikki, don't worry OK?'

He looked so sad, I'd never seen him like this. I looked up at his face and saw he was almost crying. I felt so sad I began to cry too. I had no idea what was going on but whatever it was, it was really sad.

'Go and have a bath,' he said as he put me down on the floor. 'Have a bath, get dressed and we'll get ready to go.'

I got ready as quick as I could just as he asked and went into the living room. Maria was there, this time with Rashid in her arms. Dad was sat on the sofa with three suitcases by the side.

'You ready?' he asked.

Still unaware of why or what had happened, I nodded.

'Let's go,' he took my hand.

Maria didn't say a word and neither did I. Rashid was painfully crying out our names, holding his arms out for us, but we were going. Maria stood there and watched while dad and I began to leave. I looked back at her, she had that uncomfortable, sarcastic smile on her face. I looked right into her eyes, and if my eyes could have spoken, she'd know exactly what I was saying. She looked back at me, but her eyes were ice cold. I turned away, walked out the door behind dad and got into the car. Not a word said by either of us. Dad went back inside to get the suitcases while I sat on the front seat of the car staring back at the house. From the outside looking back it was just a simple house that looked exactly the same as any other house on the street, but for me, that house was misery. Everything that happened in that house made it hell and I was happy to see the back of it. I could still hear Rashid's cries which tore me apart. I felt this huge sense of sadness all round, but deep down I knew the nightmare was over. I knew one day it would have to end, but never knew when that would be. And here I was, on this morning, on this particular day, looking back at that house, knowing today was the day. I had a feeling of relief I couldn't describe, I was so weak for so long but today I felt strong, I'd got through it. Dad finally put the last case in the boot, got into the car and off we went. We drove for some time in silence, not knowing where we were going and what was going to happen next. I wished it was night-time, so I could see the Smurfs and daydream about them running around for a distraction, but it was broad daylight. We stopped at a traffic light and dad turned to me.

'You know, sometimes daughters need to be with their dads and sons need to be with their mums.'

I smiled at him and nodded, I really didn't understand completely what that meant for us, but somehow I felt everything was going to be OK. I had dad, and Rashid would be OK with Maria. I wound the window down to feel the breeze as we drove by and decided not to ask any questions, and just waited to see what was next when we got to the destination.

* * *

We arrived at Grandma's house a little while after. We'd visited Grandma's house a few times before, but not too often. I didn't have the closest relationship with her, but it was nice to see her all the same. We both sat at the table in the dining area while Grandma brought in a beer for dad and a packet of crisps for me.

'Hi Nikki,' she said, 'aren't you going to say hello?'

'Hello,' I replied looking down at the tablecloth.

I was tired and a little bit nervous in her company, so I figured it would be best to keep quiet as I had previously learnt when it came to people I wasn't familiar with. I listened across the table as dad spoke to her.

'It won't be for long,' he said. 'Just until I sort myself out.'

'What about school?' Grandma asked.

'I'm not sure yet, we'll have to sort that out when I get my new place,' he replied.

'Well of course she can stay, Mark, but not forever. You need to make sure you sort yourself out. You have responsibilities now, you need to grow up and deal with this properly, you can't just rely on me.'

'I'm going to,' he replied, quite annoyed at her response.

It wasn't rocket science to figure out they were talking about me. I actually thought we were just visiting.

'I just need some time, that's all. She's a good kid, just a bit quiet, she won't give you any trouble.'

'It's fine,' replied Grandma. 'Where's her stuff?'

'I've got some in the car and I'll bring the rest later.'

I was so looking so forward to it being just dad and me, getting closer to him again. I was going to tell him what 'she' had done, but now I have to stay here. I was so disappointed I could feel my eyes welling up.

'Come on Nikki, we're going to the shop,' dad said.

I got up and followed him out with my head down to the floor in a huge effort to hide my welled-up eyes. We went to the shop, got some sweets and sat in the car for a while.

'I'm gonna need you to stay with Grandma for a while,' he said.

I nodded, I couldn't hold back the tears any longer at hearing the words.

'It won't be for long, I just need some time to sort out my own place and then I'll come back for you, OK?'

I nodded as I wiped my tears.

'And I'll come to see you as much as I can.'

* * *

Living with Gran wasn't the best but wasn't bad either. It was the school holidays, so I spent most of the days at the house watching TV, or in my room listening to music or reading. Sometimes I'd wander alone to the park and just walk around. My aunt Cara also lived there with her little boy Dylan. She usually got up really early to get Dylan ready for day care before going to work, and when she arrived home, she pretty much stayed in her room with the baby, so I didn't see much of them.

On Saturdays Grandma took me to the markets in the mornings to help her with the shopping, then we'd go back and do chores together. The days were so boring, but it was easy to swallow because dad always came over on a Saturday evening giving me something to look forward to. Usually we went for a little drive for a catch up and have a chat via McDonald's.

'When can I come and live with you?' I continually asked.

'Soon darling,' he'd reply.

Weeks went by and everything was the same. I became willingly used to my own company and spent most of my time alone in my room, and although most times it felt quite lonely or boring, I preferred it that way. I listened to Prince, Michael Jackson and Whitney Houston tapes on my Walkman over and over to pass the time and lived in a constant daydream. I spent my time dreaming about how life would be when I was an adult, dreaming about love, the future, my real mother, everything, but mainly dreaming of the moment dad would sort himself out so we could live together.

Every day I woke up thinking it could be the day, but when each day passed with nothing happening, I began to stop thinking about it. Time was going so fast the holidays were almost over and Grandma and I began visiting school open days. It was obvious dad hadn't worked anything out yet and the thought of staying with Grandma forever and going to one of those schools freaked me out a little bit. One evening Grandma and I arrived home after being out shopping for school stuff to see dad there with a friend. I ran to sit on his lap as I usually did to talk about the week.

'Hi dad!'

It was literally the highlight of my week, I looked over at his friend while we chatted, quite stunned at how pretty she was and how nice she was dressed.

'Nikki, this is my friend Savannah,' dad said.

Me being me, a little bit shy, said a quiet hello. I could feel her staring at me which made me feel even worse.

'Right, come on you,' dad said. 'Go get your coat, we're going to McDonald's. Savannah's coming with us too.'

'OK,' I said as I jumped off his lap to go and get my coat.

'She's really shy,' I heard him say to her as we got in the car.

'Yes I can see that,' I heard her reply. 'Why is she so shy?'

'Don't know, she just is,' he replied.

* * *

The three of us went to McDonald's, and in that time I began to realise Savannah was actually quite nice. She had a lovely, almost permanently fixed smile on her face, she was extremely chatty and asked loads and loads of questions. What's your favourite colour? What food do you like? What's your favourite song? Do you like school? Do you like reading? What books do you like? It was actually the first time anyone had paid so much interest in my likes and dislikes. I learned quite a lot of things about myself I was totally unaware of. I mainly answered with one-word answers, thinking she would stop, but each answer I gave prompted another question. I'd usually find this sort of set-up extremely uncomfortable, but she was kind of nice and I quite I liked her. I guessed she was dad's new girlfriend and would probably visit us more often when we got our new place, so I slowly opened up a bit more.

'What did you think of Savannah?' dad asked.

We'd just dropped her home and were on our way back to Gran's.

'She's nice,' I said as I climbed over the chair to sit in the front. 'Is she your girlfriend?' I giggled as I asked.

'No, she's just a friend,' he replied. 'She'll probably be around for a while and actually, I've asked her to do me a big favour,' he said. 'I've got to go away for work for a few weeks, so I've asked her to spend some time with you at the weekends and take you out. You know, to McDonald's or wherever you want to go.'

I liked her, but not that much. I didn't even know this woman which made me panic slightly. Anything could happen I thought. He hadn't even known her for that long, yet he was prepared to allow her to get so close. I wasn't ready to let this happen personally due to my past experiences; she might have been all nice and sweet in front of dad but god knows what she could do while he wasn't there.

'No, it's OK dad,' I replied. 'I just won't go to McDonald's until you come back. I'll stay at Grandma's.'

'Don't you want her to take you?' he asked.

'No,' I shook my head. 'No, it's fine. I'll wait for you.'

He could tell it was making me uncomfortable.

'OK,' he said. 'It's cool, but I might ask her to just come and see you at the house then, just to check you're OK. Would you be happy with that?'

'Yeah fine,' I said.

I wasn't overly happy with that either, but it was a relief knowing I wouldn't have to be alone with her.

* * *

The next week I was sat in my room one afternoon with my headphones on when Grandma came knocking on the door.

'Remember your dad's friend?' she asked.

'Yeah.'

'She's downstairs, she's come to see you.'

'Oh, OK,' I replied and followed Grandma downstairs to go and say hello.

'Hi,' I said as I went into the dining room.

'Hello darling,' she replied.

I admired her as she stood up. She was stunningly pretty with beautiful long black wavy hair that fell way past her shoulders. She wore a long black leather mac with high-heeled knee-high boots. She was a lot different to Maria, definitely a lot prettier, better dressed and at least this woman smiled. It didn't surprise me that dad liked her.

'How have you been?' she asked as I sat down at the table.

'Fine,' I replied.

She put her hands through my hair. 'Have you always had short hair?'

'No.'

'What happened?'

'I had longer hair before, but my mum cut it.'

'Your mum?'

'Yeah.'

'Why?' she asked.

I shrugged my shoulders.

'Well you're still very beautiful, whether you've got long or short hair,' she said.

I didn't quite believe her, but I replied anyway to be polite.

'Thanks.'

'What were you doing before I got here?' she asked.

'Listening to music.'

'That's nice, what were you listening to?'

'Michael Jackson.'

'Oh really? I love Michael Jackson!' she said. 'We have a lot in common.'

I smiled. Grandma brought in a tray with cups of tea and biscuits and sat at the table. I could tell she wasn't too pleased about something but that was generally her personality, so I thought nothing of it.

'So, where've you been all this time?' she asked Savannah.

All what time I thought to myself.

'I've not come here to argue, I've come to see Nikki,' she replied quite sternly. 'We all just need to be 100 per cent focused on Nikki, isn't that correct?'

Grandma got up, grunted a word or two under her breath and left the room. I knew Grandma could be a bit tricky sometimes, but she certainly didn't like Savannah for some reason. But Grandma being Grandma was indeed very choosy of who she liked and disliked.

'Do you like staying here?' Savannah asked.

'It's alright. I'm waiting for dad to get his own place. Do you know if he's got it yet?' I asked.

'No I don't think so,' she replied. 'I think it's taking him a bit longer than he thought.'

'Are you dad's girlfriend?'

'No,' she said with a giggle. 'We're old friends.'

After another 15 minutes of small talk Grandma entered the room.

'I think it's time for you to leave now. Nikki needs to tidy her room.'

Savannah got up and reached for her coat.

'Well it was lovely to see you again Nikki,' she said. 'I'll come and see you soon, OK?'

I nodded as I watched her walk towards the door. Grandma followed her out. I could hear them talking at the door but couldn't quite make out what they were saying so I crept a bit closer to listen.

'You can't stop me,' I heard Savannah say whilst Grandma slammed the door shut.

* * *

After a few days, Savannah came back to visit again. We chatted for a minute or so before she asked if I wanted to go to the park. My initial instinct was to say no, but it was a lovely sunny day and I'd been cooped up in the house for ages, so I happily jumped at the chance. I looked back at Grandma for approval. She was stood in the hallway with the washing basket in her arms.

'Two hours,' she said. 'And I mean two hours. I need her back by 6pm.'

As we walked down the street, Savannah took my hand.

'She's a right tough one your Grandma is, isn't she?'

I giggled as I pulled my hand away. We walked around the park together while she chatted away about herself and her family.

'You're very quiet, aren't you?'

I shrugged my shoulders and looked down to the floor. I wanted to ask her questions but was unsure if I was allowed. I wanted to know exactly who she was and why dad was making her visit me.

'Shall we get some ice cream?'

'Yes please,' I replied.

We walked along towards the ice cream van and again she took my hand and this time I didn't pull away. We sat on a bench while we ate our ice creams.

'Are you usually this quiet?' she asked.

'I don't know,' I replied.

I didn't know what she expected from me and was beginning to feel a little bit uncomfortable with the questioning.

'Do you know when dad's coming back?' I asked to change the subject.

'I think he'll be back next week. Why, do you miss him?'

'Yes.'

'Do you miss your mum too?'

'Not really,' I said shyly.

'That's strange,' she said. 'So you don't miss your mother?'

I shook my head. 'No.'

'What about Rashid, do you miss him?'

'Yeah, I miss Rashid a lot,' I replied. 'Do you know Rashid?' I asked.

'No darling, I've never met Rashid, but I've heard all about him.'

'Have you got any children?' I asked.

It took her a while to answer. 'We'll talk about that another time,' she said. 'Come on, I'd better get you back, it's getting late.'

We arrived back at Grandma's and for the first time in ages I felt quite happy. I'd had a really nice afternoon and was growing to like Savannah. She was fun, pretty, chatty and she made me feel comfortable. As she left she gave me a big hug and a kiss on the cheek. Grandma was standing at the door with a stern look on her face.

'See you soon!' she said as she blew kisses at me while she walked away.

I waved back at her until she disappeared round the corner. I ran up to my room and laid on my bed feeling excited. I put my headphones on and let my thoughts wander while I stared out the window. Dad was coming home next week, he'll get his new place and I'll live with him, Savannah and her children. I had figured it all out in my head, this was going to be so much fun, all I had to do was wait for dad to get back and it would all work itself out.

* * *

Over the next week I counted the days until dad was back, looking forward to our new life. But after a week, I hadn't heard from dad at all. He used to call a couple of times a week to see how I was which hadn't happened, and Savannah hadn't come for a while either. The next day, Grandma sat me down at the dining table.

'Come and sit here,' she said as she pulled out a chair. 'I need to talk to you about something.'

I sat down in anticipation wondering what this was all about.

'So, you know we have a place for you at the school around the corner?'

I'd totally forgotten about school and I thought I'd be living somewhere different.

'Well, we only have a week to make a decision.'

'What decision?' I asked.

She took a deep breath and began to explain. 'Well, if you start at this school you'll need to stay here with us for a lot longer. Your dad's not going to get a place for now because his work isn't settled, he hasn't had a chance to sort anything out and probably won't be able to for a while.'

My heart dropped with disappointment while I quietly listened.

'Or, if you want to, you can stay with Savannah for a while and she can find you a school where she lives.'

I sat silent for a minute. 'I can stay with Savannah?' I asked.

'If you want to,' Grandma replied.

'Does dad know about this?'

'Yes, of course he does,' she replied.

It was a no-brainer in my eyes. I could go and stay with her until dad comes back and when he does, we'll all be together. It made sense and seemed like a really good idea.

'I'll go with Savannah,' I said quietly. I didn't want to upset or offend Grandma, but I was secretly beaming with excitement.

'Well, your dad's coming back next week so he'll take you and sort everything out.'

I felt so relieved and looked forward to it; it was finally all coming together the way I'd had it all worked out in my mind.

* * *

A couple of days later, I was lying on my bed reading *The Lion, the Witch and the Wardrobe* when I heard a knock on the door. As I opened the door I saw dad standing in the doorway with a new Barbie doll in his hand.

'Dad!' I screamed with excitement, jumping up on him.

'Aww my little baby,' he said as he kissed my face. 'Have you been OK?'

'Yes,' I replied. 'Grandma said I can live with you and Savannah. She came to see me and she took me to the park, she brought me ice cream and we had a really nice day, and she's really pretty,' I giggled.

He laughed as he put me down. We sat on my bed while he stroked my hair.

'So, you like her then?' he asked.

'Yeah, she's really nice. Is she your girlfriend?'

'You'll love it with her,' he said. 'She's looking forward to having you.'

I was so excited I didn't even realise he hadn't actually answered the question.

'When are we going?' I asked.

'Today.'

'Really?' I yelled. 'Today?'

'Yes darling, we've got to go soon, she's expecting us. Get your things ready and we'll get going.'

He went downstairs to talk to Grandma and Cara while I quickly jumped off my bed, pulled out the suitcase from underneath and began packing. As I folded each item my heart filled with relief, I was so excited – me, dad and Savannah living together would be so cool. I wouldn't even need to tell anyone about Maria or what she did, it didn't even matter anymore. I'd never have to see her again and we'd all be happy, I'd finally be able to just put it all behind me and move on.

* * *

I said thank you and bye to Grandma, Cara and Dylan as they watched us leave. Cara gave me a big hug and I kissed little Dylan. There were no hugs, kisses or affection from Grandma but I knew affection was never one of her strongest points, so I didn't actually expect anything different. She never really showed any emotion either, but she was harmless, and it never really bothered me. I wasn't overly good at showing emotion at times either so in reality, we were quite similar.

As I got into the car. What should have been an exciting journey was the total opposite. Dad sat quietly while he drove. It wasn't like him at all, being in the car together was usually our time, our time to listen to music or chit-chat. I guessed he was tired and didn't worry about it too much. I gazed out of the window in anticipation, wondering what was next and what our new life would be like and at that moment I began to feel my nerves kicking in. I'd had a nice time with Savannah the few times I met her, but going to live with her would be a totally different experience. We both sat in silence while we pulled up into the estate, it was a huge council estate with a massive playground in the middle, completely different to what I was used to. Dad turned off the engine and turned towards me.

'This is it, this is where you'll be staying. I'm gonna come up and stay with you for a while so you can settle in with Savannah and her family. I won't go until you're comfortable OK? And I'll come and see you as often as I can.'

I looked at his face digesting what he was saying. It was very clear what the words were, but it made no sense, I was so confused, my stomach turned, and I literally felt physically sick, like I'd been punched in the stomach.

'What do you mean, you'll come and see me? Aren't you coming too?' I asked. I actually didn't even want to hear the answer, I heard what he said loud and clear but didn't want to believe it. 'Aren't you coming too, dad?' I asked again.

He sat quietly while he looked at me. He was finding this uncomfortable, but I didn't care, I was uncomfortable, I knew it I thought, my heart pounded with rage, my body shaking with both fear and anger combined. He wasn't coming, how dare he disappear for weeks and then bring me here to leave me alone, alone again. I was no longer safe, I was in danger again, I felt betrayed and suddenly hated him.

'You like Savannah don't you, you said you wanted to come?'

This wasn't my idea of the plan, and certainly not like this.

'I only wanted to come because I thought you were coming too,' I snapped. 'I thought we were all going to live together.'

'Well, she really loved spending time with you Nikki and I'm really glad you got on so well, you'll be happy here, honestly.'

I began to cry.

'Oh Nikki, don't cry, you'll be well looked after here, these people love you.'

'So why can't you come too?' I asked, confused.

He turned away for a minute, turned back to look into my eyes and took hold of my hands. With a long sigh he spoke.

'We didn't tell you this before because we wanted to wait to see if it would work out. I didn't know how you would react,' he said. 'There's a reason why we arranged for her to visit you so often, I wanted you to get to know her properly to see how you felt about her.'

I looked at him blankly while tears dropped from my eyes.

'Look Nikki, I know you've been wondering who Savannah is for a while.'

I looked in his eyes, desperate to hear what he was talking about.

'Savannah isn't my girlfriend, she's not really my friend either.'

I frowned as I asked, 'Who is she then?'

'She's your mother.'

He let out another long sigh and repeated, 'She's your mum, Nikki.'

* * *

In that very moment I felt like I was going to pass out. I didn't know how to feel about it, I liked her, but not enough for her to be my mum. Going to the park and having ice cream was absolutely fine, but my mum? I didn't know her enough or have enough time to decide if I wanted to live with her on my own, it was so different now. She was no longer the nice secret girlfriend, she was my mum. Did everyone know about this but me? I couldn't breathe, I tried my best to remain composed but I couldn't.

'Dad, please!' I begged. 'I don't want to go, please don't make me.'

I was so nervous, and then I became extremely angry that everyone had been lying to me all this time. If she's my mum then where was she all this time while I was going through absolute hell? Did she think a few smiles and ice cream would make up for what I'd been through? And why was dad leaving me with a stranger, again? I was so frustrated I could have screamed. I looked at his face, pleading while he lit a cigarette. I was so looking forward to our new start and he was leaving me, I wanted to scream at him, tell him how I was feeling but I couldn't. I couldn't even find the words or the breath, so I just cried, I cried and cried. It broke dad's heart to see me in that state, in fact, he'd never actually seen me cry like this before. He was completely unaware that this kind of emotional breakdown was a regular occurrence for me.

'Nikki, don't cry, please, there's nothing to be afraid of I promise. I know the last few weeks have been difficult for you, but the best place for you to be right now is with your mother. Come on, wipe your tears.'

I felt stuck to the seat, I didn't want to move. I knew once I got out of this car that would be it and I'd be on my own again.

'Come on,' he said as he got out of the car. 'It won't be as bad as it seems, I'm gonna be right by your side.'

He gave me a big hug when I finally got the courage to step out of the car.

'You'll get to know your real family, they've all been dying to meet you and trust me, your mum has been waiting for this moment for a long time.'

'Where was she before?' I managed to find the breath to ask.

'It's a long story darling, I'm sure she'll talk to you about all that in good time.'

* * *

We stood waiting at the door for what felt like forever. My legs were shaking like jelly and my heart beating so fast and hard you'd probably see it pumping through my chest if you looked close enough. A tall white woman with blonde hair and blue eyes came to the door.

'Oh my gosh, Mark you were right, she's beautiful!'

She grabbed me towards her and gave me the biggest and tightest hug that I almost stopped breathing. She kissed me all over my face.

'You're so beautiful,' she said as she continued to shower me with kisses. 'Come in, come in, Savannah's just upstairs, never thought I'd see that girl like a bag of nerves, she's changed her outfit about five times already,' she laughed. 'Come and sit down,' she said as we entered the kitchen. 'I'll put the kettle on.'

We sat at the table waiting for the kettle to boil while she lit a cigarette.

'What would you like to drink Nikki?'

I shrugged my shoulders.

'Cat got your tongue?' she asked.

I wasn't quite sure how to answer that, so I just sat there.

'She's a bit shy,' dad stepped in on my behalf. 'Just give her whatever you've got.'

'We're all so excited to have you,' she said as she planted a glass of Coke on the table and sat down. 'We've missed you so much.'

I really hoped she wasn't expecting a response from me because I had absolutely no idea what to say.

'So, how've you been Mark?' she asked. 'Still in the music game?'

'Yeah, it's all good,' dad replied.

At this point Savannah entered the room. 'Hi guys, sorry I kept you,' she said with a big smile on her face.

She didn't look nervous to me at all; to me she looked extremely confident. She went to give dad a kiss on the cheek and then she came over to me.

'Hi Nikki,' she said as she sat next to me at the table and took hold of my hands. 'I'm so glad you're here,' she said excitedly. 'Make me a cup of tea, mum,' she said to the woman.

Mum, I thought to myself, that was her mum. I was so confused.

'I take it you've met my mum then?' she said with even more excitement while she squeezed my hands.

'Erm, I didn't know who she was,' I replied.

'This is Abigail, my mum,' she said. 'Which makes her your grandmother, so I guess you can call her Nanny.'

It didn't make much sense to me, my little brain had taken in far too much for the day for me to be able to work this out.

'I don't understand,' I said shyly.

Savannah and Abigail both laughed. 'I know darling,' Abigail replied, 'I bet you're thinking who the hell is this big old white woman, eh? Well it's true darling, I'm your grandmother alright.'

I looked at dad, he nodded at me. 'She is,' he said.

Savannah could see I was still confused so she took the opportunity to explain.

'I'm half-caste darling.'

'What's half-caste?'

They both laughed again.

'It means I'm half of one race and half another. My mum's white and my dad's brown.'

I'd never actually heard the term before but I nodded my head all the same. I guessed I'd figure it out properly at some point, so I nodded again and said OK. There became an awkward silence across the table and I could see both Abigail and Savannah looking at each other and then over at me. I knew this was the moment it was about to get more serious.

'Did you bring all her stuff?' Savannah asked dad.

'Yeah most of it's in the car, I'll go and get it,' he said as he got up to leave.

My heart began to beat 100 miles an hour, I didn't know what to expect next but whatever it was, it was on its way. I wondered how it was going to pan out, were they going to start with all the questions? Was I supposed to call Savannah 'mum'? Did I have my own room? There was so much to think about.

'You hungry, Nikki?' Abigail asked. 'I've got some crisps and nuts if you want,' she said as she got up to reach for the cupboard. She pulled down bag after bag of goodies. 'We didn't know what you liked so we just got a load of stuff, you can take your pick.'

'I'm OK thanks,' I replied.

I was starving but still quite unsure whether it was acceptable to say yes. I flashed back to when we were at Maria's friend's house and what had happened because I asked for more biscuits. I decided it was better to say no, just in case, until I was at least able to suss it all out, so I sat hungry.

'Oh well, they won't go to waste,' she said and lit another cigarette.

This time Savannah grabbed one from the pack too. This was so different, it was like a completely different world to what I was used to, they both seemed so laid back.

Dad came back with my suitcase.

'I think this is everything. If there's anything we've left I'll bring it over in a couple of days.'

'Shall we give them a moment?' Abigail whispered to Savannah.

'Yes, good idea,' she replied.

'Well guys, we'll leave you to it for a while,' she said. 'We'll just be in the front room.'

As they both left, dad sat back at the table.

'Are you OK?' he asked.

I didn't reply, I could feel my eyes filling up with tears again. I was heartbroken. I didn't feel right at all.

'Can't you stay here with me?' I asked one more time.

'No darling, I've told you, I need to work and sort myself out. You'll be fine here, and I promise I'll visit as much as I can'

He came over to sit next to me and wiped my face with a tissue.

'It's all going to work out fine,' he said. 'Just try it for a while and if you really don't like it you can go back to Grandma's, how about that?'

I nodded

I began to feel a tiny bit better with a Plan B in place, as much as it was very daunting it was worth a try I guessed. He held my hand as we walked towards the front room.

'OK,' dad said. 'I'll be off.'

Savannah took my hand and pulled me closer to her. 'It's OK Nikki, we'll look after you.'

Dad gave me a hug and a kiss. 'I'll see you soon,' he said, and I stood helplessly staring at him as I watched him leave. Although Savannah had her arms around me and Abigail was standing right next to us, I felt so alone.

* * *

Savannah, or should I say 'mum', showed me around. It was a three-bedroom council flat over three floors, each room equally spacious. On the top floor was the third bedroom which I figured would be mine as we'd already seen mum's and Nanny's room.

'Is this my room?' I asked as we entered.

'No sweetie, this is Mia's room. You'll stay with me in my room downstairs,' she said. 'You'll meet Mia a bit later when she gets home from school. She's my niece, your cousin, she's looking forward to meeting you too. I'm sure you'll both get on really well.'

I felt an intense pressure of having to constantly smile and get on with people I didn't know when all I wanted to do was shut myself away from the world and cry. Savannah was chatting away as we walked back downstairs to the front room, but I had no idea what she was saying, I just wanted to sleep. As we entered the front room, I sat on the edge of the sofa and looked around the room. This was it, it was so weird. I looked at Savannah as I could feel her eyes on me. As she smiled, I looked at her differently than I had before. This was my mum. This time I really looked at her, I looked at her face, her smile, her eyes, her hair; this time round I wasn't just looking at a pretty woman who brought me ice cream, I was looking at my real mum. I'd often dreamed of her and the moment I'd meet her, but I didn't expect it to be like this, and here she was, after all these years. I always imagined my real mum as some sort of power woman who would find me and save me from all the bad things and we'd live happily ever after, but this wasn't it. It was all too easy, she knew nothing. Where was she all this time, why did she wait so long? Dad had gone, and I was supposed to be happy with this, but I wasn't.

'Are you OK Nikki?' I heard her say.

'Yes,' I nodded as she sat beside me to comfort me. She put her arm around me and pulled me close to her bosom while I uncontrollably cried.

'Oh darling, I know this is hard,' she said. 'Do you fancy a lie down?'

'Yes please,' I replied. it was all I wanted to do, my head was so heavy, my eyes were so tired, I fell asleep straight away.

* * *

I woke up a few hours later to Savannah stroking my face. The sofa felt so comfortable I could have stayed there forever.

'Hey,' she whispered as I woke.

'Hi.'

'Did you have a nice sleep?' she asked.

'Yes thanks.'

'You must be hungry by now?'

I was starving, but the way I felt, I'd never eat again if it meant I could stay alone and sleep forever.

'Abi has done dinner and Mia's home too. Why don't you go and wash your face and we'll go together?' she said.

Mia was sat at the table with her school books out while Abigail was stood at the cooker frying some lamb chops.

'Mia, this is Nikki, say hello,' Savannah said as we entered.

She looked up at me, said hi and carried on with her conversation with Abigail.

'Mia,' Savannah called out.

'What?' she replied.

'I've just introduced you to Nikki.'

'Yeah,' she said. 'I already said hi, what else do you want me to do?'

'Don't worry about it,' she replied with a huff. 'That's enough, the two of you.'

Abigail stepped in. 'Just sit down Sav, don't cause a fuss, they've got plenty of time to get to know each other.'

We all ate together while Abigail and Mia spoke about school and a boy she liked.

'You let him chase you,' Abigail told her. 'Don't chase him, you chase him, and he'll lose interest.'

I was confused at how she was allowed to chat away at the table with Abigail almost in an adult conversation, especially about a boy. I had learned to be seen and not heard. We all chatted for a bit and after dinner I went upstairs with Savannah to her bedroom. She brought my suitcase up with her for me to start unpacking. We emptied my case together, and while she hung things up in her wardrobe she told me how excited she was to have me back and how much she had missed me. I wondered if I should ask where she had been, but I didn't think I was ready to hear the answer just yet, and didn't want to upset her.

'Oh, and don't worry about Mia' she said. 'She's a spoiled little brat. Abi will always stick up for her, she'll be fine once you get to know her.'

'Who's her mum?' I asked.

'Chloe, she's another one,' she replied. 'Chloe's my crazy sister who had Mia when she was only 14. She was way too young to look after her so Abi adopted her rather than let her go into care.'

I wondered what actually happened, why I wasn't with them all along.

'Where's Chloe now?' I asked.

'Oh she's around, you'll see her someday.'

She casually analysed each item of my clothing really closely with an odd look on her face before putting them away as we chatted.

'She's a spoiled little bitch too.'

'Don't you like her?'

She sighed. 'I don't hate her, I do love her, she's my sister, but her and her daughter are both spoiled little cows. It's Abi's fault, she always favoured them over me, ever since we were little kids. Chloe gets away with everything.'

I remained silent and just listened. It was the most in-depth conversation I had ever had with anyone and I was fascinated to hear the stories. This was my family too after all, I was curious to hear about them and the more I knew about them all the better.

* * *

The next day Savannah and I went out for the afternoon to buy me some new clothes.

'I don't like any of this shit,' she said about my old clothes earlier when I was getting ready.

Surprisingly, we had quite a nice afternoon together. She brought me some lovely dresses, a few tops, a pair of jeans, cute knickers and vest sets and some new shoes. It was the first time I'd ever been clothes shopping. It made me realise I never really had any girly or pretty clothes before. Mum was right, compared to this new stuff, my old clothes were pretty dull. When we got back she made me try everything on again to make sure it all fitted properly.

'Oh, that's lovely, you're so beautiful,' she said while I tried on one of the dresses.

It felt really good to hear that she thought I was beautiful which made me smile to myself as I looked in the mirror. Between her and Abigail, they'd told me so often how beautiful they thought I was, within the space of two days, and I was beginning to believe them. I was also beginning to feel more comfortable within myself in general, they were all so laid back and easy going I felt at ease and relaxed which was nice, nice to feel like I could be myself without getting in trouble.

* * *

After about a week or so I felt so much more positive and comfortable. I felt like I actually was becoming a part of this family. Abigail was really funny, I loved hanging out with her, she totally adored me and gave me those big tight hugs and covered my face with kisses pretty much every day. I liked her. Savannah wasn't as affectionate in general, but we were bonding and becoming quite close, since we shared the same room we had no choice. We spent so much time together, we even shared the same bed and I was getting used to her very quickly. I was learning a lot about her and the family in a very short time. I still didn't feel like she was mum as such; I even started to call her mum in the hope it would feel more natural. It felt like more of a friendship but all the same, nothing bad had happened so I was cool with how things were going. Mia was 13 years old and was quite distant. She'd come home from school and either get changed and go straight back out or she'd sit in her room all evening. I only saw her at dinner time. We rarely communicated or exchanged words but I was fine with that.

Dad visited that week which was nice. My feelings towards him were, however, still quite mixed. I was happy to see him and although things were working out well, I was still overall disappointed with him for leaving me, but I kept my feelings to myself and embraced him as normal. He sat and chatted away to Abigail while she updated him on how things were going with me.

'We need to sort out her school,' mum said quite abruptly. 'She's on the waiting list for the school across the road, but I'll need money for her uniform and stuff.'

'That's fine,' dad replied. 'Not a problem, just let me know what you need, and I'll sort you out.'

She left the room.

'Oh, don't mind her,' Abigail said. 'Moody cow, she's just in one of her moods again, it'll pass, I'm just gonna pop to the loo,' she said as she also left the room.

'How you getting on darling?'

'It's alright,' I replied.

'So would you say you like it here then?'

'Yeah, it's OK, they're quite nice to me.'

'That's good,' he said. 'And what about school, do you want to stay here and go to the school your mum was talking about across the road?'

'I suppose so,' I replied.

'I think you'll be absolutely fine. It's good for you to be with your family and in time you'll get to know them better. Once you start school you'll meet new friends and feel more settled, I'm always going to be around too,' he said. 'So you've got nothing to worry about.'

I listened to everything he said and although I was still feeling a bit sad he'd let me down, I believed him. It was a chance for a complete fresh start and actually I was beginning to look forward to it.

* * *

I started school a few weeks later, which to my surprise was absolutely fine. I actually made friends very easily this time round. It was how school should be. Mum and Abigail were great, I finally got to meet Chloe who I thought was really nice even if mum didn't think so. I even got to know Mia a bit more and she was actually OK. Things were pretty good, dad visited here and there, mum and I were getting closer and I could finally say I found out what it was like to feel secure, and I was genuinely really happy.

One evening after dinner, mum was washing my hair which was finally growing back to the length it used to be. We sat together in her room while she brushed and blow-dried my hair. It brought me back to the day Maria actually cut it off, how much I cried and how aggressive she was. I began to wonder again where my own mother was at that time while I was living in real life hell.

'Where were you?' I asked.

'When baby girl?' she replied.

'When I was younger, where were you?'

She turned off the hairdryer and sat quietly for a short while and let out a long sigh.

'I knew you'd ask me this one day, I wasn't very well darling.'

'Were you sick?' I asked.

'I wasn't sick like having a tummy ache or a cold, I just wasn't very well in my mind.'

'What do you mean?'

'I wasn't very strong darling, I had to go away for a few years to get my head straight.'

'Where did you go?'

'I was in Amsterdam,' she replied.

'Amsterdam, why did you go to Amsterdam?'

'I told you I had to get away for a while that's all. I had some friends over there, so I went to stay with them.'

'Why didn't you take me?' I asked.

'Oh Nikki you were just a baby, I was too young to have a baby. I was only 17, that's only nine years older than you are now, do you realise that? I wasn't ready, doesn't mean I never loved you though, I thought about you every single day, and I'm so happy to have you back. I wanted you back for ages when you were with your dad. I tried to get you back for over a year but they wouldn't let me have you.'

She put her arm around me. 'I've got you now and that's all that matters, we can start afresh, can't we?'

I wanted to believe her – I did believe her – but I felt really sad at the same time. If only she hadn't gone, if only she had taken me with her, things would have been so different. I wondered if I told her would she even care or feel guilty, everything was actually her fault yet she was unaware. On one hand I was a lot happier than I'd ever been, but on the other, the person I was feeling so happy with was the person responsible for all the pain accrued, but for some reason I felt sorry for her, she was obviously trying her best. We chatted about other things while she plaited my hair and we both went to bed. I laid awake for a while thinking about our conversation. I wanted to blame her for the past, but I liked her and was so much happier in this life that I couldn't. I decided it was probably better to forget about the past and carry on as we were so I snuggled up to her and slowly fell asleep.

* * *

A few months later, things were slowly beginning to change. Mum and Mia never really saw eye to eye and argued quite a lot. Mainly about stupid things, little things, but the arguments would escalate and get so heated that they'd last for days.

'She's just a spoilt little bitch,' mum would say to me.

Chloe came over a few times to talk to mum in an attempt to defuse the situation, but it never worked, it actually made things worse with them ending up in huge screaming matches too. It got so bad sometimes Nanny would have to step in to stop them from going too far. I didn't know why mum disliked Mia so much. I remembered when I first arrived she didn't have a great word to say about her, but I didn't realise it was that bad. One evening mum and Chloe were at each other's throats again over something Mia had done.

'Get out of my face, you stupid bitch!' mum shouted at her and pushed her aside. 'Come on Nikki,' she said to me as she stormed up the stairs and slammed her bedroom door shut. 'I fucking hate them all,' she said as she paced up and down the room and lit a cigarette. 'I've never known such a spoiled brat in my life,' she screamed, 'and that Abi just lets her get away with it, and Chloe, I don't know who she thinks she is, she doesn't even know her own daughter, she has no idea what her precious little spoiled brat of a daughter gets up to, I hate them all.'

I sat on the bed listening to her rant and rave. I personally didn't see why she was so angry. Yes, Mia was quite cheeky but she never did anything that bad in my opinion. Chloe was just trying to make her see that and was sticking up for her, I thought it was a good thing. She left the room for a bit and came back with a bottle of whiskey. She drank glass after glass and then she pulled out a small box from her drawer and began to roll a spliff. As she puffed away she told me story after story about Chloe and how she was always Abigail's favourite as they were kids, how she adopted Mia and gave Mia everything but didn't do the same for me and her.

'I was always gonna come back,' she slurred. 'Always, she knew that, but she let you go, bitch. What if I never saw you again? It would be all her fault. It's OK, I don't need them anyway.'

I remained silent through the whole thing, watching her meltdown. I liked Mia, Nanny was cool and Chloe was quite nice too. I really didn't see the problem. She poured herself another glass of whiskey, downed it and then burst into tears.

'Oh Nikki, I hate them, I hate them all,' she cried. 'It's always me on my own. Just me, do you know that? And as for your father, he's another little shit I swear, he used me, he used me only when he needed me.'

I could just about make out what she was saying, her head was swaying from side to side, her red eyes half closed, and her words were so slurred it sounded like she was almost dying. I wondered if I should go and get Nanny to help her but I didn't want to make things worse or upset her even more. I felt like I wanted to help her and wished I knew how.

'Don't worry, we have each other now,' I said as I put my arm on her shoulder. 'You don't need to be sad because of Mia and Chloe.'

'Well you would say that, wouldn't you?' she replied. 'I'm just gonna… I'm just gonna lie down for a bit,' she slurred again as her head fell to the pillow.

She was fast asleep and snoring within minutes. I managed to undress her and put her to bed properly. I reached over for one of my books and sat right next to her reading. Every now and then I'd check to see if she was OK and still breathing until I fell asleep myself.

* * *

The arguments over time got worse and worse. It got to a point where mum would get upset with me if I spoke to Mia. Mia wasn't too bothered, she'd shout back at mum, tell her to fuck off and go out or sit in the kitchen with Nanny or go to her room. In her eyes it was never a big deal. It was mum who got so wound up and angry with her. Of course, Nanny would let her get away with her behaviour, mum was right. Mia was definitely favoured and spoiled, and yes, she was quite rude sometimes but I never really understood why it stressed mum out so much. There became quite a divide in the house. It was like it was Mia and Nanny against mum and me.

'This has got to stop,' Nanny shouted one day after another stupid argument.

Mum was going crazy, screaming at the top of her voice at Mia, and this time it got really heated.

'Get the fuck away from me you freak,' Mia shouted. 'You're pathetic, look at you.'

Nanny literally jumped in and dragged mum away from Mia kicking and screaming, knocking things over, making a mess everywhere.

'Savannah, listen to me,' Nanny shouted. 'We can't live like this anymore, this has gone on far too long. You're a grown woman, you need to take Nikki and learn how to stand on your own two feet. I won't have you in this house disrespecting us.'

'What?' mum said to Nanny. She'd finally quietened down but was still mad.

She stepped closer to Nanny. 'Are you really going to choose that bitch over your own daughter?'

'Get out of my house,' Nanny replied. 'You can come back when you've learned some respect.'

'Oh don't you worry, you won't ever see us again,' mum shouted.

I looked at her up and down in total shock at what had just happened. This wasn't the woman I knew. I'd seen her upset and angry before but this was the worst I'd seen her. She was breathing so heavily and her hands were shaking so much it seemed like she was a completely different character. The anger I saw in her was almost scary. I couldn't believe it had come to this over an argument that started over something so small. The arguments were never about anything significant or even worth arguing about.

'Then you'll be sorry, won't you?' she screamed as she turned and dragged me up the stairs.

'We don't need them Nikki,' she said as she paced the bedroom smoking a cigarette. 'They'll see, I can do this on my own, I don't need her and I certainly don't need that little bitch gloating at me every day. We're leaving, we'll get our own place, yeah that's what we'll do,' she said.

She threw my suitcase down on the bed. 'Pack your stuff,' she shouted. 'And hurry up, I need to get out of here.'

* * *

'Where are we going?' I asked her as we dragged our suitcases down the street.

'I told you, we're going to get our own place.'

'Where?' I asked.

'I don't know yet,' she snapped.

She was still so angry I decided it was better to keep my mouth shut. I didn't trust this mood she was in at all and was surprised she could even get so angry so quickly, but I thought she'd probably be much happier in our own place. We sat in the council waiting room for what felt like forever. I held on to the ticket we pulled out from the counter staring at the number. Each time a new number buzzed I counted how long the wait was since the last number. I was trying to figure out how long the wait would be until we got to 103 we were on 89 and had already been waiting over an hour. It was also a good way to kill time. I had already spent half an hour looking around at all the other people in the room from head to toe, wondering what happened to them and why they were there. Most of them looked completely helpless and others just looked really poor and desperate. Stressed mothers with their crying babies or uncontrollable children, shabby looking men who looked dirty and unwashed, single women inappropriately dressed, with messy hair and awful make-up, a family with lots of kids running around surrounded with what looked like their whole life belongings in one blue and white striped laundry bag. What on earth were we doing here I thought to myself as my head shifted from one person to another. Finally, the buzzer turned to 103.

'That's us Nikki, quick!' she grabbed me as she jumped up off her chair.

'Don't say a word OK? Leave this to me,' she said just before we entered.

It was a small square room with a frumpy woman sat behind the desk.

'Take a seat,' she said as she shuffled her papers and put them to the side. 'How can we help today?'

I looked over at mum while she so comfortably and blatantly told the woman a completely different story to what had actually happened. I watched her crying and blowing her nose while she choked out all this rubbish about her mum beating her up and throwing our clothes out the window. She was good, if I didn't know any better I would have believed it myself. After a long question and answer session between them, the woman scribbled something on a form.

'Excuse me,' she said as she got up to leave the room. 'There's water over there. I'll be back shortly.'

About half an hour later the woman returned with an envelope which she handed over to mum.

'We have a temporary room available at this address as of tonight. You won't be able to get into the room itself until 8pm this evening, but take this letter with you and they'll let you check-in at least. I've made a phone call so they're expecting you and you'll be welcome to wait in the reception until 8pm when the room becomes vacant.'

'Oh, that's brilliant,' mum replied. 'I really appreciate your help, thank you so much,' she said as she wiped away her fake tears and stood up to shake the woman's hand.

* * *

We had to get the bus to the new place, which was a bit of a struggle for us with our suitcases. It was quite a long walk from the bus stop, my arms were tired from carrying my case, I swapped from side to side until mum finally took it from me and carried both.

'Why did you lie to the woman?'

She stopped and put the cases down. 'Nikki, you saw that place, didn't you?'

'Yeah.'

'Every single one of those people in that waiting room needed a place to stay,' she explained, 'and I know for a fact the council don't have that many places to give away. I know it's wrong to lie, but sometimes in life you gotta do what you gotta do to get by.'

She picked up the cases and continued walking.

'Sometimes darling, you've got to bend the truth, especially when it comes to getting what you want.'

'Oh, I get it,' I chuckled.

It didn't seem like it was the right thing to do but, in this situation, it clearly was.

'It's called playing the game,' she said.

'So where are we going anyway?' I asked.

'It's a bed and breakfast,' she replied.

'What's a bed and breakfast?'

'It's a place where they have rooms for people like us and give you free breakfast in the mornings, kind of like a hotel but smaller.'

'Oh OK, what about lunch and dinner?'

'We have to get our own. It won't be for long, it's just temporary. We'll share the kitchen and bathroom, but we'll have our own room.'

'Share the kitchen and bathroom with who?' I asked.

'The other people,' she replied. 'Hopefully they'll be some nice people there, but for now your guess is as good as mine.'

We continued walking and what felt like an exciting new adventure for us was no longer feeling so nice. The idea of sharing a bathroom and kitchen with people we didn't know was awful. I thought about the people who were in the council waiting room, the dirty men, inappropriate women and screaming kids, and if this place was specifically for homeless people, it definitely wouldn't be the nicest of places, I began to dread the thought of it.

* * *

Mum looked at the piece of paper with the address on it.

'Yep, this is it,' she said as we walked up the driveway.

She rang the bell and shortly a chubby little Spanish lady opened the door.

'Savannah?' she asked.

'Yes,' replied mum.

'Lovely to meet you, come on in, we've been expecting you,' she said as she turned to walk us through the corridor.

She seemed quite pleasant and friendly enough.

'I'll show you around first and then we'll go to the office and sign you in. Your actual room won't be ready for another hour, so we have time.'

We followed her as she showed us around. It wasn't as bad as I'd imagined, but it wasn't exactly nice. There was the breakfast room, a reception area with a few people watching TV – as she opened that door a heavy cloud of smoke hit us – the bathroom was simple but clean and the kitchen had three cookers, three fridges, a sink and a centre workspace with a couple of kettles and toasters. Each room very basic, bland and colourless. We sat at the desk in the office while she took our full names etc. and ran through visiting hours, breakfast, cooking and bath times. There was a rota we had to adhere to, to avoid overcrowding.

When our room was ready, the lady walked us upstairs and unlocked the door to our room. It was a tiny room facing the front of the house with a large bay window, one single bed, a set of drawers and a small wardrobe. It was awful. I looked at mum to see her reaction, but she was expressionless and seemed to be fine with it.

'There's only one bed,' I said.

'No, it's OK,' the lady replied as she opened the wardrobe and pulled out a small metal-framed fold-up bed. 'See, you have this here,' she said happily, as if she'd just solved a crime or something.

'Oh,' I said as I looked down at the frail looking bed with the thinnest mattress I'd ever seen.

The lady gave mum the key and left us to it.

'Breakfast is between 6.30am and 9am. I shall see you in the morning darlings,' she said. 'Goodnight ladies.'

I smiled at her as she left. We pulled our cases in and mum sat on the bed. I played around with the metal fold-up bed trying to figure out how to open it, until I finally worked it out. Mum opened her case and started hanging things up in the wardrobe. I walked over to the window to check out the view. I stood at that window for ages watching the people walking by. This house looked like all the other houses on the street, but I knew this was the only house like this; all the other houses would probably be filled with happy families, husbands and wives with their children and cars, etc. I wondered if they knew of the disasters that were going on in this house as they walked by. Eventually I took myself away from the window to see what mum was doing. She was sat on the bed with her head in her hands. I went over to sit next to her.

'Are you OK?' I asked.

She looked up at me.

'It's not that bad,' I said to her. 'We can draw pictures to put on the walls and we can get some nice things from the shops to make it pretty.'

She smiled. 'Yes, you're right, we'll go out tomorrow and get some bits. You can sleep with me tonight,' she said as she cuddled me.

* * *

The next morning, we woke up early to use the bathroom in our given time. There was a woman with a little girl waiting outside when we finished. She smiled and said hi as we crossed paths. After we dressed we went downstairs for breakfast. The room was crowded but we managed to find an empty table and sat down. The Spanish lady came over to us.

'Good morning, my lovelies,' she said.

'Good morning,' mum and I replied together.

'Did you sleep well?' she asked.

'Not too bad,' mum answered.

'You only need a couple of days and it will feel like home,' she laughed as she playfully slapped mum on the arm.

We ate breakfast and went out to the shops. We bought pretty candles, flowers and a vase, a couple of lampshades and a few plants.

It's amazing how these little things transformed the room and put us in better spirits. We bought a few bits from the supermarket, so we could cook our own lunch and dinners for the next few days, and by the end of the afternoon we'd made the best out of a not so nice situation.

That night we went to the kitchen together to make dinner. We didn't want to stay too long in the kitchen as we didn't like the idea of cooking at the same time as anyone else.

'Quick, let's get out of here before anyone else comes in,' we giggled as we grabbed our plates and left.

'You need to get to bed early tonight 'cause you need to go to school in the morning,' she said as we ate our food in front of the TV.

I hadn't thought of school once over the last couple of days with all this going on. After dinner we went to the kitchen together to wash up our plates. The woman we saw outside the bathroom earlier was in there with her little girl. We all smiled at each other as we entered the room.

'Hiya,' she said to mum. 'I'm Lacey, this is my little girl Olivia. I see you're new here. How's it going?'

'I'm Savannah,' mum replied. 'And this is Nikki.'

'Hi Nikki,' she said as she politely looked at me.

They hit it off straight away. I could see why, they were kind of similar, they were both similar in age, they even looked alike, so much that they could almost pass as sisters. They chatted away about how the house was, how the other people who lived there were, etc. I looked at the little girl. She was cute, around three or four years old. She was sat on a chair messily eating some toast while she kicked her legs back and forth.

'We should have a drink one day,' Lacey said to mum.

'Of course, yes we should,' she replied, as we gathered our pots and plates to go back to our room.

'She was nice,' I said.

'Yeah she seems nice, doesn't she?'

* * *

The next morning after breakfast, mum walked me to school. I hated that it was such a long walk. From Nanny's all I had to do was run through the estate and across the road where the lollipop lady was.

'This is so far,' I whinged, as I dragged my feet along the street. 'Can we get the bus tomorrow?'

'There isn't a bus that comes this way,' she said. 'It's good exercise, you'll get used to it.'

After what felt like forever we finally arrived at the gate.

'Have a good day darling,' she said and gave me a kiss. 'See you later.'

I waved as I ran over to my friends. After school, mum picked me up and we walked the long walk back, had dinner, and watched TV for the evening. The next morning, we went through our usual morning routine, but after school mum wasn't there. I waited by the gates. I waited and waited until it got to 4pm and every other kid in the school was gone. I decided to start walking, thinking I'd see her walking up at some point. I walked that long journey all on my own until I got to the house, surprised I didn't see her on the way and slightly worried something might have happened to her. I ran upstairs to the room which was locked. I checked the reception room, nothing, the kitchen, nothing. I went to check the office to see if she was signed in and on my way to the office I passed a room where I could hear music and laughter. I recognised the voice straight away, it was her voice loud and clear. I knocked on the door and after a minute or so Lacey opened it.

'Hey,' she said. 'It's your daughter,' she turned around and said to mum.

'Oh Nikki, what are you doing here, you're early!' I heard my mum say.

I looked around the room. Loud music was playing, the room was filled with smoke, there was an ashtray full of cigarette butts on the table and a bottle of vodka with two glasses and half a bottle of lemonade.

'Oh shit!' Lacey shrieked. 'It's gone 5pm.'

'What?' mum replied. 'You're joking.'

'It is,' said Lacey, as she started to laugh.

Mum started to laugh too. 'Oh shit,' she said as she tried to stop laughing. 'I thought it was about 1.30pm.'

They both broke out into fits of laughter. They were drunk, so drunk. I couldn't believe it, I looked to the left of the room to see little Olivia on the floor playing with her dolls. I looked back at mum in disgust while she continued to giggle.

'Oh don't look at me like that,' she said. 'You managed to get home, didn't you?'

'I'm so proud of my baby,' she said to Lacey. 'She walked all that way on her own. Come and sit here baby girl.'

'It's OK,' I said. 'I need to go to the toilet. Can I have the key please?'

She handed the key to me. 'I'll be over soon.'

* * *

I was so disappointed in her, it was just my second day of school and she couldn't make it to pick me up, she didn't even apologise. In fact, she actually thought it was funny. I went back to the room and watched TV. By 9pm mum hadn't come back so I had a packet of crisps for dinner and went to bed.

* * *

The first thing I did when I woke up the next morning was look straight over to check mum's bed. She was sprawled out fast asleep without a care in the world. I tried to wake her, but she was completely dead.

'Mum, wake up!' I raised my voice and gave her a shove.

'What?' she murmured.

'It's time to get up,' I said slightly frustrated. I didn't want to be late for school plus I was still annoyed with her about yesterday.

'Oh, you know the way now don't you? You can go on your own, you don't need me.'

She was a mess.

'Are you sick?' I asked.

'No, I'm not sick, I'm hungover,' she sharply replied.

I wasn't sure whether to be angry with her or worried. Either way, I was starving and didn't want to miss breakfast, so I continued to get ready and went down to breakfast alone.

'Morning,' the Spanish lady greeted me as usual with her huge smile as I sat at an empty table. I still couldn't remember her name.

'Morning,' I replied.

'Where's mum this morning?'

'She's sick,' I replied.

'Oh, that's a shame, I hope she gets better soon.'

I smiled in return, as if it was the real truth, however inside I was fuming. It wasn't fair, I was the one who was left outside the school gates for ages, I was the one who had to remember the way home and walk all that way on my own, I was the one who had to see the woman I was beginning to depend on in the state she was in, I was the one who had to go to bed hungry and I'm the one who has to sit here at this table eating breakfast and go to school alone because she can't be bothered to simply 'wake up'.

* * *

Over time, as horrible as it was, life here became pretty normal and although my feelings about mum were quite mixed from one day to another, she was OK. Our relationship was more like a friendship rather than mother and daughter. She took me and picked me up from school on some days and we spent the evenings together watching TV or listening to music. And on other days, I found my own way home and knew she'd be somewhere with Lacey. I personally didn't think she was the best influence on mum, but I figured it must have been so boring stuck in that place all day while I was at school, so I understood why they spent a lot of time together. Sometimes I looked after Olivia while they went out to the local pub at the end of the road. It was never for too long so I didn't mind. Olivia was fun, we'd spend time putting mum's make-up on each other and brushing each other's hair, it was like having a little sister.

One particular evening, Lacey and mum were excitedly getting ready to go over to the pub, Olivia and I sat on the floor doing a puzzle, and through overhearing their conversation I figured out there was a man Lacey was interested in. The plan was mum would sit with her in the pub so she wasn't alone and then leave her with the man a short while after he arrived.

'I won't be too long,' said mum as they got ready to leave. 'And if you get hungry before I'm back just make yourself a Pot Noodle.'

As they left all dolled up, Olivia and I continued with our puzzle. When we finished I took her to the kitchen so I could get my Pot Noodle. I switched on the kettle and we both danced around while waiting for it to boil. Once boiled I filled up the pot and put the lid back to wait for it to settle.

'Why are you putting the lid on it? Aren't you going to eat it?' asked Olivia.

'Yeah I am, but I have to wait for it to cook first,' I replied.

'But that's not cooking!' she said.

I laughed. 'I think it cooks itself,' I replied.

'How long do we have to wait?'

'I think about five minutes.'

'Let's play hopscotch,' she said as she skipped around the kitchen.

'We can't play hopscotch,' I laughed. 'We don't have any chalk.'

I went to check my Pot Noodle which needed topping up and just as I reached for the kettle, Olivia tugged at my skirt.

'Come on, let's go get some chalk,' she begged.

I turned around and the next thing I knew, Olivia was on the floor screaming her little lungs out. It all happened so quickly. It took me quite a while to realise what had happened or how, but as she pulled at my skirt, I dropped the kettle and boiling water poured all over her bare skin. She kicked and screamed and threw herself around on the floor, her cry so loud it was frightening. I completely panicked. I tried to pick her up, but she was so strong I couldn't control her. I thought about going to get the Spanish lady, but I didn't want to leave her like this. Her screaming became louder it was terrifying. I couldn't think of anything I could do but whatever I was going to do, it had to be quick. Poor Olivia was in agony, her little body rolled around on the floor as she cried, her skin red raw with burns. Luckily, one of the other residents opened the kitchen door to see what the fuss was all about.

'What the fuck is going on in here, can somebody shut that bloody kid up?' she shouted.

'Please!' I ran to the door. 'Please can you help us?' I begged. 'I don't know what happened, but I dropped the kettle on her.'

'What the fuck?' she shouted. 'Where's your mum?'

'She went to the pub,' I said.

'Oh, my good god,' the woman shouted.

She ran over to Olivia, picked her up and ran over to the sink. She turned on the cold tap and put Olivia straight under it.

'Go and get Isobel,' she shouted at me. 'Quick!'

Olivia screamed even louder as the water hit her skin.

'Who's Isobel?' I asked, upset with myself that I was taking too long.

'The woman in the office downstairs, I need you to go downstairs and tell Isobel to call an ambulance and come back upstairs OK? Can you do that?'

'Yes,' I said, but I was frozen. I stood watching her with Olivia cradled in her arms under the cold water.

'Go!' she shouted.

I jumped and ran downstairs to tell Isobel.

'What is going on?' she asked.

I was so stressed I was shouting at the top of my voice so quickly she couldn't understand a word I was saying.

'Slow down darling,' she said as she held my shoulders. 'Take a deep breath and start from the beginning.'

'The kettle fell on Olivia and the hot water went on her and she won't stop crying,' I shouted out. 'You need to call an ambulance.'

'Oh lord Jesus Christ,' she said as she picked up the phone to dial 999.

She slammed down the phone after giving the details and we both ran back upstairs to the kitchen.

'Where's her mother?' she asked me.

'In the pub with my mum.'

'Oh, good lord,' she said. 'Do you know which pub darling?'

'The one at the end of the road.'

'OK, good girl' she said. 'Don't worry darling, you're doing the right thing.'

Moments later, mum and Lacey ran into the room.

'What have you done to her?' Lacey screamed at me as she ran over and snatched Olivia from the woman. 'What did you do?'

'Careful,' the woman shouted at Lacey. 'She's burned.'

'What?' she looked down at her daughter in her arms, and looked over at me. 'Look at what you've done to her!' she screamed. 'Why did you do this? Why, you jealous little bitch?'

She ran over to me and slapped me right across my face. 'You stupid, stupid girl' she shouted. 'Look at what you've done, she'll be scarred for life.'

'For fucks sake, you can't blame her,' the woman shouted. 'She's just a bloody kid, where the fuck were you, down the pub? Women like you disgust me, shouldn't be able to have kids, and of course, I get no thanks do I? You can deal with your own bloody bullshit,' she said as she left the room.

'Where's the ambulance?' she screamed at Isobel.

'They should be here soon, don't panic, they'll be here any minute.'

I looked over at mum for help, she hadn't said or done anything this whole time. She even allowed the slap without saying or doing anything, she was just standing there blank-faced. I understood I'd done wrong and I felt really bad, but she wasn't on my side. I couldn't believe she allowed Lacey to slap me like that and didn't do or say anything. I began to cry. I was dying for her to do something, tell me it was OK, anything. Instead she stood in complete silence, as if nothing had happened. I ran back to the room, climbed into bed and cried into my pillow. I really hoped Olivia was OK. I never felt such guilt in my life. I wished it had never happened, I wished I had never wanted that Pot Noodle, I wished they had never gone to the pub.

About 30 minutes later mum came back. I watched as she poured herself a whiskey and lit a cigarette. She stood over my bed as she blew out the smoke.

'What happened?' she asked quietly.

I sat up, my head pounding and my eyes puffy from all the crying.

'I went to make the Pot Noodle and I dropped the kettle on her by accident,' I replied.

'How did you drop the kettle on her?'

'I don't know, it was an accident. We were playing, and Olivia was pulling my skirt when I had the kettle in my hand.'

She sighed as she puffed on her cigarette. 'Don't worry,' she said. 'It wasn't your fault, it was an accident. Don't worry about Lacey either, she'll calm down eventually.'

'Will Olivia be OK?' I asked.

'We'll find out when they get back from the hospital. It wasn't your fault, if anything, it was mine OK? Lie down now, you need to get some sleep.'

* * *

The next morning, I woke up with a serious headache. Mum was still fast asleep. I got dressed and sat by her bed waiting for her to wake up. I was way too scared to leave the room to even go to the bathroom or down to breakfast without her in case I saw Lacey, so I sat watching her for over an hour until she woke up.

'What time is it?' she asked as she stretched her arms out.

'9.30am.'

'Why didn't you go to school?' she asked.

'I was waiting for you.'

'Oh well, it's too late now,' she said. 'We've missed breakfast as well, haven't we?'

'Yeah.'

'Come here,' she said. 'Come and get into bed, I'm not ready to get up yet.' She held out her arm. 'I've got a really bad headache,' she said.

'So have I.'

'Let's sleep it off for a bit together. Come on baby girl, we'll feel better after a nice sleep.'

Her voice was hoarse and her eyes were hardly open. I got in the bed and she put her arms around me while we both fell asleep. After a couple of hours, I woke up to her stroking my hair. She was staring into space with tears running down her face. Once she noticed I was awake she quickly wiped her eyes and jumped out of bed.

'Come on, let's go and get something to eat, you must be hungry.'

We went to the kitchen together to make some lunch. I was hoping the kitchen would be empty, but there were two women in there having a cup of tea. As we entered they both looked over at us with pity. Everyone had heard about last night and we knew people would be gossiping.

'Hi,' mum said as she went to open the fridge.

'What happened to the girl?' one of them asked.

'It was an accident,' mum replied.

'But what actually happened, because Lacey was in here earlier saying your daughter threw boiling water over her.'

Mum slammed the fridge door shut. 'I told you it was an accident, it wasn't her fault.'

Just as she said that, Lacey walked through the door. My heart pounded at the sight of her face.

'It was her fault,' she shouted.

She looked at me with a look that frightened me so much I quickly looked down at the floor.

'My daughter's in hospital suffering from severe burns, she'll probably be scarred for life. I hope you're happy.'

'Come on, Nikki,' mum said. She took my hand and we left the room. 'We don't need to listen to this.'

'It was an accident and you know it was,' mum said to her face as we left.

'Go on, walk away,' Lacey shouted as we left. 'You've ruined my little girl's life and all you can say is it was an accident. You haven't even said sorry have you? Well fuck you,' she shouted. 'Fuck the both of you, you make me sick.'

'Don't listen to her,' mum said as she dragged me down the corridor. 'She's just a lowlife bitch.'

* * *

We went back to the council that afternoon with another dose of mum's Oscar-winning sob stories, begging for them to house us quicker. We were just about coping with life at the bed and breakfast, although things had gotten pretty awkward. The rumour throughout the house was that I had thrown the water over Olivia on purpose in a jealous rage and mum put me up to it. That was the story Lacey was telling everyone and they were all stupid enough to believe her. She had managed to turn almost the whole house against us. To avoid all the negative attention, we decided to skip breakfast and have cereal in our room and we used the bathroom and kitchen either really early or really late.

Three weeks later I made my way to the school gate after school wondering if mum would be there or not which was a daily occurrence and today she was.

'Hi mum,' I said as I skipped towards her.

She gave me a big hug and kiss on the cheek which was a first in a while. She was definitely in a good mood. I told her about my day while we walked down the street but noticed a few minutes later we were heading in a different direction.

'Are we going to Nanny's?' I asked.

'No,' she said with a smile on her face.

'Where are we going then?'

'It's a surprise,' she said excitedly.

I instantly guessed we might have got a place.

'Have we got our own place?' I asked almost jumping for joy.

'Oh, you're too smart for your own good you are,' she said as she took my hand.

'Yes!' I shouted out loud. 'I knew it, where is it, what's it like?'

'Calm down baby girl, I haven't even seen it myself yet. I just collected the keys an hour before I came to get you. Here's our bus,' she said as she stuck her arm out.

We jumped on the bus and once we got there we walked around with wide eyes and open mouths. The flat compared to the tiny little room we had been in for the last few months felt like a palace, it was huge. We were like two kids in a sweet shop rushing around each room pointing the obvious out to each other. It needed so much decorating, but I wouldn't have cared if it was just as it was – it was ours, we'd have our own rooms and we wouldn't have to hide anymore or see Lacey ever again.

* * *

Over the next few days we eventually moved ourselves in – compared to the bed and breakfast this really was a palace. It definitely was in my eyes. It was split over three floors with two big bedrooms, a huge living room, a big kitchen and a decent-sized bathroom. We spent the following weeks doing everything we could to brighten it up. We didn't have much of a budget, so we spent the weekends stripping wallpaper, filling, sanding, hanging paper, painting, the works. We'd put music on and dance around to our favourite songs which made it feel a lot less like hard work.

After a couple of weeks we had it just the way we wanted. Things were really good, mum was in a much better mood, it was nice to see her happy again which made me also feel better. I started a new school again which was quite far, but the only school that had a spare place midterm. Mum took me in the morning a couple of times at the beginning, but after that I went on my own.

'You're nearly ten now, you don't need me to be taking you to school. You're a big girl, you can go on your own,' she said.

It was a bit daunting the first few times, but as she said, I was a big girl and I began to believe it. School was fine, it took me quite a while to make friends because I'd started in the middle of term and all the kids already knew each other, Luckily about a week or so later another new girl started so the teacher made her sit next to me and we instantly became friends. Her name was Luana, a petite Portuguese girl with a shoulder-length bob who would sometimes get stuck with her English. We got on so well we were inseparable. Mum had gotten herself a job in an office meaning she got home quite late in the evenings. I took full advantage of this and went to Luana's house after school to hang out and I'd get back just before 7pm when mum got home. She didn't actually like her job or the people and told me stories about her day. She called them all idiots and said it wasn't even worth working for the crap money she got. Eventually she quit, which didn't surprise me.

School was cool. I had Luana plus I'd made a few friends who lived on the street. I absolutely loved having my own room and best of all, I finally got to see dad. We hadn't seen him at all while we were at the bed and breakfast. Mum told him where we were but suggested it wasn't the best place to visit. I think deep down she was just embarrassed and didn't want him to see her living in those conditions. One evening after a visit I asked her if they'd ever get back together.

'Oh trust me, I've asked him over and over darling but he always turns me away. I'm just not good enough for him,' she said. 'Your dad was the love of my life. I loved him so much but he never really wanted to be with me. We were young I guess,' she said. 'Gosh I love that man, Nikki, but I also hate him.'

'Perhaps if you're nice to him he might like you,' I said.

'Nah,' she replied. 'He'll never want me. I'm nowhere near good enough for him.'

* * *

Months later, although mum wasn't working, she was hardly home. She told me she had a part-time evening job with flexible hours, so I never actually knew when she'd be home. I'd either hang out at Luana's house after school or I'd rush back to hang out with the kids on the street. Amongst the group there was a boy named Kirk who lived at the other end of my road. Over time we became a lot closer than the rest of the kids. His dad worked nights too so we'd hang out alone after everyone else went home. We'd sit in the park and talk for ages, or hang out at his house watching TV or listening to music. Mum was home less and less and some evenings she wouldn't come home at all. Some mornings I'd see different men in her bedroom, or in the bathroom, or on their way back from the toilet and they genuinely had no recognition of who I was or didn't even seem to care. She was a beautiful woman, so I could understand the attention she'd get from men, but this was extreme. They came in all different cultures, shapes and sizes and never lasted. I never questioned her about who they were, and she never said anything either, it just became the norm. There was one, however, that seemed to be a favourite of hers. I actually saw this one quite a few times and eventually she got rid of the others and made it official with him. His name was Frank and the whole thing made no sense to me at all. He was a huge, tall, fat and bald black guy with quite an aggressive looking face that was permanently fixed, even when he smiled. I had no idea why she even liked him, until I learned that he had money, and a lot of it. I learned very quickly that she was just using him. He gave her money, took her out to dinner, brought her clothes, jewellery and shoes. I didn't take to him at all and he didn't take to me either which was cool. It made it a lot easier for me to just avoid him. I stayed out with Kirk or stayed in my room when he was around, just so I didn't have to see his horrible face. I looked at him like he was a monster and he looked at me like I was an irritating fly. It was quite sickening to watch mum pretend to like him. I don't know how she did it and definitely couldn't understand it but she had this idiot eating out of her hands. The worst part of it all was having to listen to them at night having sex. It was awful – her screams and his grunts, the bed banging against the wall, so disgusting. I'd put my headphones on and still be able to hear it, wondering if she was really enjoying herself or was she still acting. Was it that great even if the man was a monster or was it just an easy sacrifice for the high life.

* * *

I was at Luana's house one evening after school. We claimed we were doing homework together, but it always ended up with us chatting about all sorts and gossiping instead. When I got back mum was home. I hadn't seen her home this early for a while, so I was looking forward to having a chat with her.

'Hi mum,' I said as I walked down to the kitchen to get a drink.

She had a bottle of whiskey and her weed box out on the table.

'You're late,' she said.

'I was at Luana's house doing homework.'

'Homework? What homework? Show me.'

I looked at her trying to figure out what kind of mood she was in.

'Are you alright?' I asked.

'Yes I'm bloody alright. Show me your homework, I wanna know what you've really been up to, you little whore. I bet you've been with that boy.'

I quickly took my school books out of my bag and shoved them in her face.

'There you go.'

She grabbed a book, opened it, and threw the books down on the floor.

'Good girl,' she slurred and continued to pour herself a drink.

As I knelt down to pick them up she pushed me over.

'Move, get out the way,' she said. She was drunk, again, in the middle of the day.

'What's wrong with you mum?' I asked.

She ignored me and sipped her drink.

'Where's Frank?' I asked.

'Oh just go away, girl,' she said. 'I don't want to talk to you or Frank or anyone. Go on, get out of my face, you're getting on my nerves.'

I went upstairs to my room and shut the door. It was horrible when she was drunk. Even though she'd just pushed me and called me a whore, I knew she didn't mean it. I wondered what made her get into these moods where she had to get so drunk. She'd get so drunk one day and the next she'd be absolutely fine. Frank hadn't been around for a while, so I guessed she was upset about that.

Later that evening I went downstairs to see if she was OK. She was passed out on the beanbag snoring like a bear.

'Mum,' I shook her to wake her up. 'Mum, come on, you should go to bed.'

'What, what time is it?' she asked as she woke up.

'It's 11.30pm.'

'Oh, yeah, I'm so tired,' she said.

I helped her upstairs and put her to bed.

'You're an angel,' she said. 'Did you know I was going to call you Angel?'

'No.'

'Well I was going to, but your stupid dad wouldn't let me.'

'Well I quite like Nikki,' I replied.

'Did you have anything to eat?'

'No,' I replied.

'You should have made something to eat.'

'We've got nothing in the fridge.'

'Oh shit, yeah there's no food,' she rolled over. 'I was waiting for Frank to give me some money, but he's gone and fucked off,' she said.

'We don't need him anyway,' I replied.

'Yes we do,' she said. 'We need him baby girl, we need him to give us money.'

'But what about your job?'

'What job?'

'Your job, you can go back to your night job,' I said.

'What are you talking about?' she asked.

'Your job mum.'

'Oh yeah,' she said. 'My secret job, yeah I can do that. I don't need Frank, he's an idiot, go to bed darling, I'm tired.'

I got up to leave her.

'Are you gonna give me a kiss?' she asked.

I turned to her. She looked a bit of a state but I gave her a kiss on the cheek and said good night.

As I went to turn off the light I whispered out, 'Don't forget, we don't need Frank OK?'

'OK, baby girl,' she replied and I switched off the light.

I went to my room hoping she'd feel better tomorrow, hoping Frank was gone for good. I came to the conclusion that she'd be fine now it was just us again without Frank. However, that didn't last long at all. By the weekend he was back again.

* * *

One afternoon I got home from school to find the house empty as usual. The next morning, I checked her bedroom, it was empty. I went to school as normal thinking she'd be home later, but it was the same again the next night. She never stayed out two nights in a row which made me worry slightly. The following morning there was still no sign of her, so I didn't go to school. I called Nanny to see if she'd heard from her, but she hadn't.

'Oh you know your mother,' she said. 'She'll turn up in her own time.'

I wanted to call dad, but I didn't have his number. I sat home all day so worried and by the evening I was convinced something had happened to her. As much as we had ups and downs, the thought of something happening to her was terrifying. I was so worried I just cried. I cried all evening thinking the worst, wondering what I was going to do without her and after a few hours, she casually walked through the door. I jumped up and rushed to the door.

'Oh my god mum, where were you?' I asked.

'Oh, don't ask,' she said as she went to the kitchen to get her bottle of whiskey.

'No honestly,' I said. 'I was really worried, where were you?'

She was in the same clothes she had on three days ago and looked a total mess.

'Don't worry, Nikki, I'm fine,' she said. 'I'm fine. It's not the end of the world, I'm home now aren't I?'

I couldn't believe she was so blasé about this as if it was normal. I had been so worried for three days and she didn't even ask how I was, if I'd eaten or how I'd been.

'You can't just leave me on my own for three days,' I shouted. 'I didn't even know where you were, you didn't even call me.'

'Oh, shut up will you?' she snapped back. 'I've got a headache and you're making it worse. You're living and breathing aren't you? Leave me alone, your face is irritating me.'

I went up to my room angrier than ever. This was not OK, not normal or by any way fair. My friends at school had normal mums and dads, mums who took them and picked them up from school every day, mums who made dinner every night. I hated that my worry for her outshone my anger. I hated that she didn't even care and decided the best way deal with her was to stop caring myself.

The next day after school I went over to Kirk's to hang out. He smiled at me as he came to the door and we chatted for a while about school and what secondary school we wanted to go to. I felt so rejected by mum I needed a hug and when he hugged me we both realised we liked each other a bit more than friends.

'Have you ever kissed a girl?' I asked.

'Yeah once,' he said.

'When?' I asked, surprised at his answer.

'I kissed a girl once when I was on holiday with my dad.'

I coughed a slightly jealous cough, hoping he was going to say no.

'Was it good?' I asked.

'It was alright. Have you kissed a boy?' he asked.

'No.'

He laughed. 'No?'

'It's not funny, I just haven't.' I laughed.

I'll show you how it's done he said. I suddenly felt nervous as he came closer to me, took my face in his hands and kissed me. We literally kissed for hours and I wished I could stay with him in this moment forever. When I left to walk home. I thought about mum getting everything she wanted from Frank for her exchanges of love and how fake it really was. Being with Kirk was the first time in ages I actually felt good and it was real. How mum could pretend so easily, and sacrifice herself was a mystery which made me look at her differently. I realised she clearly couldn't care about me, she didn't even care about herself. She was becoming more transparent to me by the day, and when I got home, the house was empty.

* * *

School finished for the year, and Kirk and I lived in our cocoon right through the six weeks' holidays. We spent all of our time together, until eventually, the inevitable happened. We were so young and inexperienced, I don't even think we knew what we were doing. There was certainly no screaming or bed shaking and it was over pretty quickly, but we thought it was perfect and for us it meant everything. I thought he was amazing and really thought I'd be with him forever. He even pretend proposed to me with a ring made out of daisies which was so sweet. Whatever happened with mum didn't matter so much since Kirk and I were in love. I dreaded the holidays ending as we'd have to go to school and our time would be cut short. The last week of the holidays came around so quickly and as usual, I went over to his house to hang out, but this morning he wasn't home, so I left a note for him to knock for me when he got back. But he didn't come. The next day was the same, I tried every day that week with no luck, which was devastating, and I think my heart broke a little bit each day without him.

On the Friday evening I was chilling at home when the door buzzed.

'Kirk!' I screamed and ran into his arms as he stood at the door.

'Where'd you go? I was worried.'

'Me and my dad went out of London for the week.'

'On holiday?'

'No,' he replied. 'We went to Southampton. My dad didn't even tell me we were going.'

'Southampton? What's in Southampton?'

He sighed. 'We're moving to Southampton, Nikki. This weekend.'

'No way!' I said. 'Why?'

'Dad thinks it'll be a better life down there for us. I'll go to a better school and get a better education, and he won't have to work nights anymore.'

'Oh my god,' I said. 'Really, this weekend?'

'Yeah,' he replied. 'I've seen the school and everything. Dad's been sorting it out for ages and I never knew.'

My heart completely sank. I couldn't have Kirk leave, I didn't know what I'd do without him.

'I hate this,' he said.

'I hate it too,' I finally replied. 'I'll write you letters,' I nodded as he got up to leave. 'Aren't you gonna stay for a bit?' I asked.

'I can't, we only got back this afternoon and I've got to pack my stuff tonight. I had to beg my dad to let me come and see you. We're going to stay with our family in East London tomorrow and on Sunday we're gonna drive down to Southampton from there.'

I was so angry, but I knew I couldn't be angry at him, it wasn't his fault. I'd only actually met his dad once because he was always working so I understood his reasons. We shared our last hug and kiss goodbye. I was devastated, it was all happening really fast, there wasn't even any time to digest it. He was going and that would be it, I'd be alone again. I stood outside my front door and watched him for ages while he ran down the street. Every now and then he'd look back and wave, and sadly that was the last I ever saw of him.

* * *

The big day was ahead, I was starting secondary school on Tuesday and was both nervous and excited at the same time. Luckily Luana got into the same school so at least we'd have each other. Mum stayed home all of that weekend and although I was still sad about Kirk leaving, I was looking forward to a fresh start. On the Tuesday morning mum and I both woke up really early, I proudly put on my new uniform and we went together on the bus. It was nice to have her take me, for once it felt like she actually gave a shit. We got off the bus and walked towards the school. The palms of my hands were sweating, I felt hot and bothered and couldn't wait to find Luana to help me calm down. We walked down the street towards the gate but there was no one else around, no other kids around and no parents dropping them off. As we got to the gate it was locked.

'What's wrong?' I asked mum. 'Why is it closed?'

'I don't know,' she replied and tried to pull the gate, although it was obvious it was locked.

'You've got the wrong day ladies,' we heard a voice shout out.

There was a caretaker watering the grass at the front.

'The school don't open till tomorrow.'

I looked at mum who at this point was shuffling around in her handbag. She eventually pulled out a scruffy piece of paper.

'See,' she said, 'he's talking rubbish. 7th September, look.'

She held the piece of paper close to my face and pointed at the date.

'7th September,' she said again.

I sighed. 'Mum, today's the 6th.'

'No, no it isn't, it's the 7th.' I sighed again. 'Mum today is the 6th of September.'

'Really?'

'Yes, it's the 6th.'

It annoyed me how many times I had to say it before she believed me and even then, she still didn't listen,

'What's today's date?' she shouted over to the caretaker.

'6th, love,' he shouted back.

'Oh, darling I'm so sorry,' she said. 'I really am.'

I shook my head in disappointment. She couldn't even get the date for my first day at school right. She was pathetic, adding nothing good to my life, totally useless. She wasn't inspirational as a mother, all that build up for nothing. We turned and went back home like idiots, and for the rest of the day I sat in my room not speaking to her. The next day we got the bus again for school. This time I felt nothing, I was completely embarrassed by her as I looked around at the other kids on the bus with their mums feeling nervous and excited, exactly the way I had felt yesterday.

'Have a good day,' she said as I went to go through the gate. I gave her a weak smile in return and went inside.

* * *

It was indeed very nerve-wracking. I wondered the corridors looking for the new starters' room and searched around for Luana until I finally spotted her. We got through the day together which wasn't as bad as expected. After school we stood by the gates waiting for our mums while we talked about the day. Luana's mum arrived after about five minutes and they both waved as they drove off. I waited for what felt like ages outside that entrance with no sign of mum. There was no discussion of her picking me up or how I would get home. I had just assumed she'd be there, but I knew by now she wasn't coming. My stomach knotted and I felt so sick I could have easily thrown up I was so angry. This was my first day at secondary school, surely it wasn't that hard for her to just pick me up, even if it was only one day. I was so angry with myself for expecting anything different. Luckily, because of yesterday's screw up, I remembered where the bus stop was and luckily I hadn't spent all my money and had the fare to get home.

When I arrived home, she was just there, sat on the beanbag reading a magazine.

'Oh, how was your day?' she asked as I walked in. 'Tell me all about it.'

I stood for a minute and looked at her. 'Is that it?' I shouted. 'How was my day? I thought you were going to pick me up.'

'Really, I didn't say I would, did I?'

'No, you didn't but I just thought you would. Luana's mum came, and all the other kids' mums or dads came, so why didn't you come?'

'Well for a start that Luana's a bloody posh kid ain't she and her mum's probably got nothing better to do with her life.'

'But you're not doing anything either,' I shouted back.

'Nikki, you're 11 years old. I've told you, you're a big girl, anyway, what's the problem? You've been going and coming home from school on your own for ages, what's the difference, you knew the way didn't you?'

'Just about,' I replied.

'Anyway, I've got some chips in the oven for you. You hungry? You can tell me all about it when we eat. Go and take that uniform off, your chips will be done in about ten minutes.'

* * *

My 12th birthday came and went. Mum was still inconsistent with her moods and those whiskey moments became more and more regular. At times, she was as nice as pie and at times she was a demon. Frank had disappeared for good and every now and then there'd be a new one around. I was settling in at school OK. Luana decided she didn't want to hang around with me anymore. I think her mum had something to do with that. I used to tell Luana everything and all my secrets and although she always promised she wouldn't tell her mum, I knew she did. I could tell by the way her mum looked at me after school from the car window she disapproved. I wasn't that bothered as I had made a new friend named Kaila. Kaila's mum and dad had just got divorced, so she didn't like her mum very much either. She blamed her for everything that made her dad leave so we had a lot in common and talked for hours every day on the phone after school. We became very close very quickly and were inseparable. I was happy I'd met Kaila as quite frankly, Luana was a bit of a goody-goody and had become quite judgemental. Kaila's mum seemed quite soft and let her do anything she wanted. She spoke to her mum with such disrespect and her mum just took it.

At weekends I'd stay at her house and her mum would take us to school on Monday mornings. Mum was now never at home and there was never anything in the house to eat. Kaila would pretend she needed hair clips or sanitary towels and asked her mum for extra money so she could give it to me to pay for my school dinners. That way I could use my own dinner money to buy food later. Her mum had gotten a big pay out from the divorce so money wasn't a problem for them.

If it wasn't for Kaila, I wouldn't even turn up to school. I thought it was a complete waste of time. I never actually learned anything, I found it really difficult to concentrate. There were all sorts of crazy stuff going on at home it was easy for me to stay distracted in school. One afternoon I got home to find the place completely smashed up. As I opened the door there was glass everywhere. I was 100 per cent sure we had been burgled. My heart raced as I crept through to the front room on tiptoes which was in complete darkness. I turned on the light to see her, sat in the middle of the room on a beanbag, surrounded by mess, strangely rocking backwards and forwards. The TV was smashed, and on the floor all the pictures from the walls were shattered and all over the place. I stepped down into the kitchen – all the cupboards were open, plates, cups and cutlery were smashed and scattered on the floor.

'Mum!' I shouted. 'What happened?'

She ignored me while she continued rocking on the beanbag, not even acknowledging me.

'Mum!' I shouted again as I kneeled in front of the beanbag to get a look at her face. She was crying. 'What happened mum? Talk to me.'

'Fuck off!' she screamed. 'Just fuck off, I'm sick of you, I'm sick of hearing your voice. God, I wished you'd never been born, get out of my face.'

As much as I was totally hurt by her words I still needed to know what happened.

'Mum what happened? Were we burgled, are you OK?'

'Of course I'm OK, nothing happened,' she said. 'Just piss off.'

'So, we didn't get burgled?'

'No we fucking didn't,' she replied. 'I did it, OK? I did it. Happy now? Now fuck off and get out of my face.'

I got up and looked down at her, my eyes welled up at the sight of her, yet I wanted to smash her face in. I was so tired of her I honestly could have killed her.

'Why would you do something like this, and why would you say such hurtful words to your own daughter?'

She completely ignored me, like I wasn't there. I shook my head and I went upstairs, I literally changed my clothes and left the flat. I had nowhere to go but I couldn't face being there another minute so I walked around the streets until really late to avoid her.

* * *

We never spoke of what I called 'the burglary night' and as usual, she was on good form for a while until the next incident. This time I woke up to her screaming on the phone to someone in the middle of the night. I opened her bedroom door to find her frantically stuffing clothes into a bag,

'What are you doing?' I asked her.

'I can't stay here,' she replied. 'I have to get out now.'

'What's happened now? It's the middle of the night.'

'Baby girl,' she said, her voice trembling, 'you'll be OK, it's fine. You're a big girl, aren't you? You'll be fine, just go back to bed and I'll be back tomorrow.'

She was all over the place, pacing back and forth looking for her belongings, her arms shaking as she filled her bag.

'I need to go,' she repeated. 'I need to go now.'

She rushed passed me and ran down the stairs. 'I'll be back tomorrow,' she shouted up. 'Just go to bed and whatever happens, don't answer the door.'

Within seconds she was gone. I tried to go back to bed but I couldn't sleep. I couldn't help but wonder what could be going on, what was so bad at this time of night that she had to leave at 2.15am. As I lay in bed with my thoughts, I was suddenly awakened by loud banging on the door. I held my breath in fear, wanting to go downstairs to see what or who it was, but I couldn't move. The banging continued, it sounded like someone was trying to kick down the door. I then heard a man's voice.

'Savannah, open this fucking door.'

I sat up and held the covers over my head. I daren't move or make a sound. I then heard another bang which sounded like the door had been kicked in. Afraid to even breathe, I stayed still with the covers over my head while I listened to the footsteps walking through the flat. Completely frozen I remained silent as I heard the footsteps coming up the stairs and stop as they entered mum's room. My heart pounding while trying to hold my breath at the same time, I then heard the steps coming up the second flight of stairs towards my room. I said a prayer and prepared myself for the worst, the door opened. I sat completely still with the covers over my head, trying to control my breathing. The footsteps moved closer towards my bed, I closed my eyes thinking I was about to die. I clammed up as I felt the covers being pulled away. I held my arms up to my face and squeezed my eyes shut tight as I heard the person's breath come close to my face. Whoever it was chucked the covers back over me and left the room. I let out a deep breath and cried under the covers. I heard the person leave but I was so scared, I was too afraid to move. I tried to sleep but I couldn't switch off. I felt completely violated and totally overwhelmed. I hated this life, I hated her, it made no sense that she could even think of leaving me in an environment that she so badly had to escape from.

* * *

I woke up the next morning with the events of the night imprinted in my head and prayed it was all a dream, but as I slowly crept downstairs the evidence was there. The front door was broken and had dents in it where it had been kicked so much. Mum wasn't home so I decided not to go to school. After a few hours she arrived. Half of me wanted to run down the stairs into her arms for comfort and the other half wanted to slap her. I slowly walked downstairs in anticipation, not quite sure if she was OK or what mood she'd be in.

'Oh, you're here,' she said as I entered the front room. 'What happened here?' she casually asked.

'Are you joking?' I screamed. 'Mum, do you realise a man came here and kicked the door down?' I shouted. 'Do you realise I thought I was going to die, you left me here to deal with that all on my own. Do you know a man came into my room while I was hiding under the covers? Do you know how fucking scared I was? No you don't, do you, because you don't actually care. You fucking left me here, knowing full well something was going to happen and that's why you ran out. What is wrong with you? I fucking hate you and your stupid dramas.'

I was screaming at the top of my voice. I hadn't meant for it to go that far but I couldn't help it.

'I'm so sorry baby,' she cried. She came over and hugged me while she cried. 'You're my baby girl, my little baby girl, please don't hate me, I should never have left you. I'll never do anything like that again I promise.'

As we hugged and cried in each other's arms I couldn't help but feel slightly better.

'We'll get the door fixed and I'll call the police,' she said. 'I'll report it so nothing like that can happen again. I'll take you out for a pizza tonight to make up for it, how about that?' she said as she wiped my tears with her hands.

I sighed, once again I put my anger to the side.

'Are you OK?' I asked. 'What happened to you, where did you go?'

'It's nothing baby girl,' she replied. 'Nothing for you to worry about.'

'Will he come back?'

'No darling, he won't. You must be tired,' she said. 'Why don't you go and have a lie down and I'll bring you up some toast and hot chocolate.'

Just like that, it was like nothing happened, no explanation, no nothing, just a cup of hot chocolate and toast for dinner and everything was supposed to be OK.

* * *

The next morning I went to school, but as usual I couldn't keep focused. I was angry that I hated her one minute then forgave her the next. I was so confused about my feelings for her it drove me insane. I spent most of my day staring out of the window daydreaming of a different life. I paid no mind to the teachers as they tried to get me to pay attention. I literally daydreamed all day long, my thoughts drifting from one subject to another. I thought about mum when I first met her, how pretty and nice I thought she was, how I was so looking forward to being with her and dad. She wasn't looking so pretty these days. I wondered where she went at night and what could she have done that was so bad for that guy to kick the door down. I thought about Claire and wondered where she was and what life would have been like if I was still with her and the boys. I thought about Rashid and wondered if he'd even remember me.

I snapped out of my daydream with a loud clap in my ear. The teacher was stood right over me.

'Nikki Johnson,' she shouted, 'are you listening to me?'

'Sorry miss,' I replied.

'What is the difference between latitude and longitude?' she asked.

I looked around the class, all eyes on me as I sat trying to think of something to say. I looked up at her. She was stood over me with her arms crossed waiting for the answer. I tried to think long and hard, but in truth I had no idea.

'I don't know, miss,' I replied.

I heard the giggles from the other girls in class and in complete embarrassment, I packed up my books and ran out of the class in tears.

After school Kaila and I hung out in the park for ages on the swings talking about everything that had gone on.

'But your mum seems so nice,' she said.

I slowed down my swing, looked at her and paused for a minute. 'Yeah she does, doesn't she?' I replied.

We both laughed and that was the moment I realised to be careful, the moment I realised that everything in life wasn't always what it seems.

* * *

During the six weeks' holiday I became restless. Kaila had gone on holiday to Miami with her mum and auntie, so I had no one to hang out with. Mum had a new boyfriend, again, some Dutch guy named Alfred who hardly spoke any English. Mum actually knew a little Dutch from when she was out there before, so somehow between them they managed to communicate. He was OK, much better than Frank, still a little sleazy but of course, he had money, so she was happy.

One afternoon she came home quite early looking tearful.

'Hey baby girl, what you been up to?'

'Nothing,' I replied. 'What's up with you?'

'I'm fine, I just got back from the airport. Alfred had to go home today so I'm feeling a bit sad. Anyway, I'm glad you're home because we need to talk, come and sit down.'

She grabbed a beanbag next to hers and I sat down wondering what the hell could this be.

'You know I've been the happiest I've ever been with Alfred, don't you?' She said this about Frank too, but I nodded all the same. 'And he really loves you, do you know that?'

'Does he?' I asked.

'Of course he does, he loves you lots and so do I.'

'OK,' I replied. I'd seen the guy twice so how he could possibly love me was a mystery.

'Well he's invited us to go and live with him in Amsterdam. He told me he can't live without me and if we go, we can have everything and anything we want, it will be amazing.'

She was so excited, and I could tell she wanted me to be just as excited too, but I couldn't be.

'But we don't know him.'

'Oh darling, stop being such a spoilsport, of course we know him. I've been with him for months. Honestly, he'll look after us, it'll change our lives and Amsterdam's lovely, you'll love it. I told you I was there when you were with your dad, it's so beautiful.'

I looked away.

'There's nothing here for us,' she said.

'Yes there is,' I replied.

'Well I've booked a flight for Friday that he's paid for and he's arranged to pick us up so we're going and you're gonna love it, I promise.'

* * *

Alfred picked us up from the airport as promised and we drove the long drive to his home. After about half an hour of small talk I pretended to fall asleep, just so I could avoid it. He seemed pleasant enough, but I wasn't in the mood. His English wasn't that great, and his accent was so strong, you had to really concentrate to understand what he was saying.

'Here we are,' I heard Alfred say as he pulled into a driveway.

He carried our cases to the front door.

'We will leave suitcases, I will show you apartment and then I will take you beautiful women for a nice meal,' he said.

Mum kissed him lovingly on his lips. 'Thank you darling.'

She looked down at me with an excited grin on her face and whispered, 'See I told you he'd look after us, he's great, isn't he?'

We entered the apartment which was very modern inside and totally spotless. It wasn't huge but it was lovely and very minimalistic. After we settled our cases we went out to a really nice restaurant. Despite my reservations, I was feeling OK, the food was amazing, Alfred and mum drank wine while he told us about all the great things to do in the city. That evening I learned that Alfred was actually quite cool and I could see why mum liked him. Over the weeks, we worked out a routine that worked for all of us. Alfred worked during the day and every morning he left money on the kitchen table for us to go out and explore the city. We'd get home in the evening when Alfred came home, and we'd go out for nice meals and at the weekends we'd go on road trips to a new town or visit museums together. It was fun. We were all genuinely happy and having a great time, but unfortunately this didn't last very long as usual.

One evening, I heard mum and Alfred arguing about something. She was crying and at one point I heard him call her a prostitute. After hours of arguing she crept into my room and shoved herself in my bed. I was wide awake but pretended to be asleep. Whatever happened, I knew her so well that I just knew she'd messed something up, she couldn't help herself. The next morning Alfred left for work as normal but left no money on the table, and unfortunately, no food in the fridge. We spent the whole day in the apartment watching TV, eating biscuits when we got hungry.

'Is Alfred gonna take us out later for dinner?' I asked.

'I don't know, we'll see what happens when he gets back,' she replied.

Only he didn't come back until after 10pm.

'What's the matter with you?' she shouted as he came home. 'We've been stuck here all day with nothing to do and nothing to eat.'

'It is not my responsibility any more,' he said quietly as he left the room.

'For fucks sake I have a child,' she screamed and followed him out. 'You promised to look after us, I came here for you.'

'Well I changed my mind, it is not my fault, it is yours. I don't want to have a woman like you in my life,' I heard him say. 'I will leave money for you in the morning to eat for some days and I want you to go by the end of this week.'

I knew this whole ordeal was too good to be true. We should never have come here. How on earth did she trust this would be OK?

'What happened to you and Alfred?' I asked as we got ready for bed.

'Nothing, it was just a stupid argument.'

'So why doesn't he want us here anymore?'

'I don't know,' she replied.

Fed up with her lame excuses I asked again. 'What did you do?'

'Nothing,' she snapped back. 'What makes you think it's me?'

'Well you must have done something,' I snapped back angry at her pathetic answers and excuses.

'It's not that serious,' she replied.

'Well what is it then? Because he wants us to leave at the end of the week and we have nowhere to go.'

'He's just an idiot.'

'But you said you loved him?'

'Yeah well, I did love him, and now I don't, you heard what he called me,' she said.

'So, what are we gonna do?'

'We'll figure something out,' she replied.

'Are we going back home?'

'No, I won't let him spoil this for us. We came here for a new life, we'll just have to meet someone else who can take care of us properly. We just need a few days and I'll sort it,' she said.

I got in bed and thought about everything that had happened and everything she said.

I had to ask. 'So one minute you can love someone so much that you move to another country, and the next minute the love's gone?'

'Nikki, it's late, I'm not talking about this now,' she replied. 'Go to sleep and we'll talk in the morning.

* * *

We obviously had nowhere to go at the end of the week and couldn't move out. We had very little money for food and spent our days lounging around or walking around the city looking for work for mum, but nothing ever came up. We both lost so much weight and when Alfred was home it was murderous with explosive arguments so we'd stay out on the streets as long as we could to avoid him.

'Why don't we just go home?' I asked while we walked around the town another afternoon. 'We have no money for food and Alfred doesn't want us there and I'm so bored of walking around every day,' I whined.

'Baby girl, we'll move out soon,' she said, 'but I'm not going home. I'll find work soon, I promise, it's gonna work out, we'll be fine. I just need more time that's all.'

I was tired, hungry and hated her for this stupid life that was supposed to be so great and just wanted to go home. I was fed up with her stupid ideas, and ability to screw absolutely everything up. On our way back to the apartment, I felt weak. We hadn't eaten since breakfast and had no money for a cab or even a bus, so we walked. We walked for what felt like forever until I couldn't walk anymore. I suddenly felt light-headed, short of breath and really dizzy.

'Mum, can we stop for a minute?' I asked.

'What's wrong? Are you OK?'

Just as I was about to respond I felt myself blacking out, white spots appeared in front of my eyes and the next thing I knew, I was passed out on the floor. I eventually opened my eyes to a crowd of people huddled around me. I sat up confused.

'Slowly darling,' I heard mum say, as she knelt down and held me up.

'What's going on? Why is everyone staring at me?'

'You fainted darling,' she replied. 'Here, sip some water.' She handed me a bottle.

The crowd began to move away and within a minute or so we were left alone, sat on the floor in the middle of the street.

'Stay here,' she said. 'I need to get you some sugar to bring back your energy levels.'

She ran off towards the shop while I sat there on the floor. What were we doing here I thought, there was no point in this at all. I had fainted because we weren't eating enough, yet she was still too proud to simply go back home. She came back with a bag of sweets and a can of coke which I quickly ate and drank and eventually I began to feel better. We slowly walked the rest of the way back to Alfred's and I got straight into bed and went to sleep. I woke up after a few hours to find mum in the bathroom putting on her make-up.

'What are you doing?' I asked.

'I'm going out tonight,' she replied. 'I'm tired of looking for jobs all day. Today was such an eye-opener, I need to figure out a way to make some money. We need to move on and we need to get out of here. I'm going to a club I used to go to years ago,' she said. 'I know the owners and some people there who might be able to help me with work.'

'What about me?' I asked.

Even though Alfred came home very late, if at all, I wasn't comfortable being there alone.

'It's up to you darling, you can either stay here or you can come if you want,' she replied as she brushed her cheeks with blusher.

'Can I really come?'

'Yeah,' she replied. 'Come, it'll be fun. I'll have to find you something to wear and I'll do your make-up when I'm done here,' she said.

'Cool,' I replied, excited at the idea of going to a club.

We went through her clothes and found a silver off-the-shoulder top that almost fitted me. I was nearly 13 and although I was quite tall, I was very skinny, so it was quite hard to find something that actually fitted.

'You can wear that with your black skirt,' she said as I looked in the mirror.

I rummaged around in my suitcase and found the skirt she was talking about. Luckily, we both wore the same size shoes, so she threw over a pair of heels and I put them on too.

'You look beautiful,' she said as she admired me in the mirror. 'Come and sit down so I can do your make-up.'

I sat down and let her paint my face with her fancy products.

'I need to do this, so you look a bit older,' she said as she brushed mascara on my eyelashes. 'You look amazing,' she said. 'All grown up, all you've got to remember is if anyone asks you, you are 16, OK?'

'OK,' I replied.

I'd totally forgot it was only a few hours ago that I'd fainted, but the excitement kept my energy levels up. We walked the long walk back to the city, which was quite a struggle for me in the heels, but I managed OK. As we entered I looked around at all the people dancing to the loud music or sat at tables drinking and laughing. A cloud of thick smoke filled the air and the whole place was quite dingy. I was expecting bright lights, beautiful women with sparkly dresses and men in suits like the movies, but this place was really sleazy. We walked through the crowd towards the bar, so mum could ask for the people she knew, but the bar staff hadn't heard of them.

'No not this club,' the guy said as she repeated the names.

'I guess it was years ago,' she shouted in my ear. 'Let's go and sit over there and see if we can get someone to buy us a drink.'

We pushed through the dancefloor over to a seating area and sat down in a booth while I watched the people dancing. After a short while we were approached by two guys.

'What are you two lovely ladies doing sat on your own?' one of them said.

'Come on let's dance,' said the other guy as he took my hand.

I instantly pulled it away and quickly turned to mum for help. Although I felt and looked like I was 16 years old, I was still only 12 and this was not an environment I was familiar with at all.

'Go on,' mum said. 'It's just a dance, go and have fun.'

She almost shoved me off my seat.

'And tell him we're sisters!' she shouted in my ear.

I looked up at the guy. He was quite attractive and obviously a lot older than me. He took my hand and led me onto the dancefloor. I swayed from side to side as he danced in front of me. He laughed at my lack of movement.

'You're very shy, aren't you?' he shouted.

'Yeah, a bit,' I replied.

'I like that,' he said.

I smiled and looked over towards the booth. I noticed mum and the other guy were also walking towards the dancefloor hand in hand.

'What's your name?' he asked.

'Nikki,' I replied. 'What's yours?'

'Jason,' he replied.

'Nice to meet you.'

He laughed and shook my hand. He seemed nice, quite short but definitely good-looking with an American accent.

'Do you want a drink?' he asked.

'Yes please.'

'What shall I get you?'

'Coke please.'

'Don't be stupid,' he said. 'Let me get you a real drink.'

He went off to the bar and returned with two drinks.

'I got you a vodka and coke.'

We said cheers and continued dancing. This was the first time I had ever drunk alcohol. I didn't like it at first, but I ignored the taste and drank it until it actually tasted quite nice. After a while we went back to the booth to sit down for a chat where we could hear each other. I looked to see if mum was OK and there she was in the middle of the dancefloor with the other guy, snogging his face off.

'I'll be back in a minute,' I said to Jason.

I went over and tapped on her shoulder.

'I need to go to the toilet,' I said as she turned around.

She seductively whispered something in the guy's ear and we both shoved our way through the crowd to the toilets.

'He seems nice,' she said referring to Jason. 'Do you like him?'

'He's alright,' I said. I could feel the alcohol kicking in.

'He's really good looking isn't he,' she giggled. She stepped back and put her hands on my shoulders. 'Aww look at you, my baby girl all grown up like a real woman. Has he tried to kiss you yet?' she asked.

'No,' I shyly replied.

'Well if he does, just do it,' she said. 'Have fun, they live quite close by in a complex and if they like us they'll let us stay there with them,' she said as she gave me more lipstick to put on. 'Did you tell him you're 16?' she asked.

'Yes,' I nodded.

'Good girl. I've been kissing my one, but he's a bit of a slob, isn't he?' She laughed.

'Don't you like him?'

'Oh god no. Well, he's alright but we just need to nail this OK?'

I looked at her closely to see if she was drunk but it didn't seem like she was. I'd seen her drunk many times and knew what she was like.

She was actually fine. This was classic mum on one of her missions. She knew when she wanted something and wouldn't stop until she got it, especially when it came to men.

'You're lucky your one's good-looking so it's easy for you, just make him like you even if you have to kiss him OK? Now go back and I'm gonna go back to mine.'

She went to the dancefloor and I went back to the booth.

'Welcome back pretty lady, you good?' Jason asked as I returned.

'Yeah, I'm fine,' I replied.

He put his arm around me. 'You're so pretty.'

I smiled at him as he leaned in to kiss me and I went along with it. I thought about mum's plan and the mission we were on and felt like I had to do it.

'I'm so glad I met you,' he said. 'You're lovely, where you staying?'

'With my sister and her friend,' I replied.

'I really want to see you again, how can I see you again?' he asked.

'I don't know, I'll ask my sister when she comes back.'

'OK beautiful,' he said. 'But just so you know, I'm not letting you go, at least for tonight,' he said as he kissed me again.

I felt bad for him, he actually really liked me. I had no idea how old he was, but he was definitely way too old. Eventually mum and her guy came back to sit with us with more drinks and we all chatted and laughed away until the early hours of the morning. I learned mum's guy was called Donald, he was 42 years old and Jason was his 21-year-old son. They lived in the complex together and worked together selling cars. As the club lights turned on and the dancefloor emptied, mum and I went to the toilet again.

'You've done so well baby girl, I'm so proud of you.'

'So can we stay with them?' I asked.

'Well we can't actually stay with them just yet because of security in the complex, but we can go back to their car lot tonight to hang out a bit more and if things work out we'll probably get to stay with them in a couple of days,' she said as she reapplied her lipstick. 'You don't have to do anything you don't want to tonight,' she said, 'but if you're comfortable then go for it.'

I knew exactly what she was talking about, but even in my vodka-driven haze, I knew there were limits, and she was going too far. We got in their car and drove to the car lot she'd talked about and hung out in the office with more drinks for a while until mum and Donald disappeared to find a car to chill out in alone. I looked at Jason and I could see on his face we both knew exactly what they went off to do. Things must have looked different in the light because Jason could now tell that something wasn't right with me.

'How old are you really?' he asked. 'Because I can see you're not 16.'

'What do you mean? Yes I am.'

'Come on, I'm not stupid, look at you. You're a beautiful girl but look at you, be honest with me. I won't be angry, I just want to know the truth.'

I looked away worried I'd spoiled the plan and worried he'd kick me out for lying.

'I'm 12,' I whispered.

'What?' he shouted as he jumped out of his chair. '12?'

'Yeah,' I nodded. I couldn't look at him.

'Oh my god, I knew you were younger but 12. I feel sick,' he said.

'Why? What's the big deal?'

'You're 12 years old,' his voice raised. 'You're a fucking child.'

'It doesn't matter, I've done this before.'

'That's not the fucking point,' he said. 'Why did you lie?'

'So, I could get in the club.'

'I can't believe this shit. I actually feel so fucking sick. Listen, you are a child OK? This shit will get me arrested.'

'I'm sorry, I didn't mean to lie to you on purpose. I don't want you to get arrested, she told me to say it to get me in the club that's all.'

He stopped pacing and looked at me. 'OK I get it,' he said. 'You're lucky my dad likes your sister and you're only 12, otherwise I'd kick your arse out on the street.'

'What shall we do now?' I asked.

'Well I'm pretty pissed and tired so I'm just gonna sit here and shut my eyes for five minutes.'

He sat on the chair opposite me and literally fell fast asleep. I was so tired myself and felt really guilty, my head was so fussy from the vodkas and I was worried I'd messed up the plan. I couldn't sleep. I wondered how long mum would be, so I could warn her, but eventually the alcohol took over and I fell fast asleep.

* * *

I woke up to Jason watching over me.

'Morning,' he said.

'Morning. Did my mum come back?' I asked, totally forgetting she was supposed to be my sister. I realised the mistake just as the words came out of my mouth.

'That's the thing about lies,' he said. 'Your mum? Oh my god, this just gets better and better.'

'Please don't say anything,' I said. 'She'll blame me for ruining everything.'

He knew this wasn't my fault or my idea.

'Let's just forget about the whole thing,' he said. 'What's done is done. I don't want to think about it anymore, my dad will be back soon, and we'll probably never see you guys again.'

Two minutes later the door opened and in walked Donald and mum. I looked at her knowing what she'd been up to and felt totally embarrassed by her. The vodka had worn off and I saw everything more clearly. She looked a mess, her hair was all messed up and her make-up from the night before was smudged all around her eyes.

'Hey sweetie, are you OK?' she asked with a look to see if I'd done anything.

I looked at Jason, he looked away.

'Yeah,' I replied. 'I'm fine.'

'Right,' Donald said as he shuffled around in one of the office drawers. He pulled out some money and handed it to mum. 'You ladies go wash up, change clothes and get whatever it is you need from that place and I'll see you back here this evening. You can get a taxi from around the corner.'

Mum thanked him, kissed him on the cheek and we walked around the corner to wait for a taxi. It was so embarrassing to see her using Donald just like she'd used Alfred and Frank. She didn't particularly like any of them, it was all a game to her. I used to think she was so powerful in these situations, I used to watch her use her beauty and charm to get what she wanted, but now I was realised she wasn't the powerful one at all. In fact, it was the total opposite. She was the one losing her power, giving herself, allowing men to control her at whatever cost she decided she was worth. In this case, it was somewhere for us to sleep tonight. We were in this mess because she allowed Alfred to convince her he'd look after us and we'd be totally fine in his world, which changed when his world no longer accommodated us and now we were here. What will happen when Donald decides we no longer fit into his world either? Will we continue to go around selling ourselves for pieces of somebody else's world? How was she happy living like this when we could easily just go home? At this point I knew I would never let myself get into a position like this. At this point I knew, no matter what it took, I wanted my own world and never just a piece of someone else's. We arrived at Alfred's and quickly packed our cases, mum shoved the key in the letterbox and off we went. There was no note left, no goodbye, no thanks, nothing. I guessed that was the last we'd ever see of Alfred and that apartment and just like that, he would become a distant memory. It all felt so familiar, leaving in a car with a packed suitcase not knowing what was ahead.

* * *

We arrived back at the cabin. I looked over at Jason and he gave me a wink. I knew this meant he was OK and we'd never need to speak about last night again. We hung around the cabin all day, mum helped out with incoming phone calls, I walked around the forecourt analysing all the different cars, my favourite a silver Mercedes sports car. I sat inside it for hours pretending it was my own, daydreaming about driving away one day from everyone and everything, choosing my own destiny. I pictured myself one day being able to afford a car like this, but the thought felt so out of reach considering how life had turned out so far. However, I enjoyed the moment while I imagined. At the end of the day we all piled into Donald's car and he took us to where they were staying. It was some complex where a bunch of Americans stayed, kind of like a housing estate. It was like a whole new world, you'd think you were in America itself. There were American-style shops on the complex, burger joints, milkshake parlours and liquor stores. There were families with children playing in the basketball court, everything you could think of.

We arrived at the small apartment with a kitchen area in the corner of the reception and a single bed in the other – this was where Jason slept – and one bedroom to the left where Donald slept, so I wondered where I would sleep.

'Oh, we hardly sleep here,' Donald laughed as I asked the question. 'But don't worry, we'll set you up over here on the floor.'

We all sat around a small table for dinner. I watched as mum flirted with Donald while they ate. If you'd have seen them you would have thought they were a married couple. They eventually disappeared to the bedroom and I made myself as cosy as I could on the floor with a few blankets and a pillow.

The next day panned out exactly the same, however, by the end of the night history repeated itself once again. Unaware of what happened as usual, we were out again.

'Come on Nikki, we have to leave,' mum said as she dragged our cases towards the front door. I was chilling at the table with Jason when she came out of Donald's room with the cases. It didn't make any sense. Yesterday Donald was completely smitten with her and now he was kicking us out. I wasn't surprised to be honest, it was the story of our lives. I knew it would always be like this while she relied on men to validate her life.

'What's going on now? Why have we got to leave already?' I asked as we waited for the lift.

'Fuck him, he's an idiot.'

'But mum, seriously, do we really have to leave?'

'Yes, Nikki we have to leave. Why did you have to tell Jason your real age, because that's why we're leaving. He found out your age and found out I'm your mother rather than your sister and wants nothing to do with me.'

'I didn't tell him, he guessed, he guessed it all.'

'Well I wished you hadn't told him, otherwise we'd have been fine.'

My initial reaction was to feel bad and responsible for this screw up, but as I looked at her, I realised it wasn't my fault at all. She was the one who took me to the club, she gave me the outfit, the make-up, the shoes; she pushed me to lie about my age and tell them she was my sister, it was all her stupid plan, there was no way I was going to feel responsible for this.

'That's the thing about lies,' I said under my breath, remembering what Jason said.

'What?' she asked.

'If we didn't lie it wouldn't have happened like this.'

She looked down at me with a look like she wanted to slap me, but knew she couldn't.

'Whatever, I don't care anymore,' she said.

I turned away, unable to even look at her. There was nothing more to say, and she had nothing more to say either, we both stood waiting for the lift in silence, we were back on the road again. The only problem was, it was the middle of the night and we had nowhere to go.

* * *

We wandered the streets with no plan or clue of where we were going until we eventually came across the train station. I couldn't bring myself to talk to her, I was so angry I couldn't even look at her face. We sat on a bench in the train station with our cases in front of us, no money, no food and no idea where we were going.

'Stay here a minute,' she said as she got up and walked towards the telephone box.

She came back with a look on her face as if she'd won the lottery.

'The good news,' she said, 'I have an old friend Rachel I used to hang out with years ago. I just spoke to her and she'll let us stay with her for a few days. The bad news, there are no trains until the morning.'

'So what are we gonna do now?' I snapped. I didn't care about her stupid friend. 'We've got no money, where are we gonna sleep tonight mum, where?'

'Don't be upset with me, I need you on my side, I can't deal with this with you whining about it every minute. I'll sort something out, we'll take a chance on the train in the morning, it'll be really early so hopefully there won't be any inspectors.'

'But what about tonight?' I asked again.

'I don't know,' she shouted back. 'I need to think.'

'Well think then,' I yelled.

We were both so stressed but, in my opinion, she had no right to shout at me at all.

'I've got some change on me, come on, we'll go find a cafe or something and get a hot chocolate. We'll figure something out after that.'

We began wandering the streets again, dragging our cases in the night. It was cold, I was tired, hungry and ashamed. I slowly walked behind her, my head hung towards the floor as I followed on, worried at the fact we had nowhere to sleep. It was after 1pm and the train was leaving at 6.50am, that was more than six hours of walking around in the streets. I couldn't bear the thought of it, everywhere was shut, there were no cafés open, the streets were dark and empty, it was hopeless. We spotted a bar open and tried to get in, but were turned away by the bouncers. A few doors down we spotted a restaurant open, but it looked quite expensive and we had no money. We continued walking around looking for I don't even know what, something.

After a while we got tired and stopped at a bus stop bench to rest. I looked down at my feet in dismay, I could have cried but it was too cold. We sat in silence as I kicked my feet trying to keep warm. I looked on the floor to the left and saw a bundle of paper wrapped up. I stared at it for few seconds trying to focus, it looked like a bundle of money, but the way things were going I thought I was hallucinating. I ran over to it anyway just in case, picked up the bundle and looked at it in my hands. I looked at it for a good minute or so trying to process it in my mind. My heart literally skipped a beat when I figured it out.

'Mum!' I literally shouted at the top of my voice. 'Look!'

'What?' she replied in a panic. 'What's wrong?'

I ran over to her proudly with the notes in my hand.

'Look, look what I just found!'

'Oh my god!' she screamed as she took the notes from my hand and began counting it.

'Where did you get this?' she asked.

'It was just there on the floor,' I replied as I pointed to where it was.

'Did somebody drop it?' she asked.

'No, nobody was there, I just saw it on the floor.'

'Quick,' she said. 'Come on, let's get out of here before anyone sees us.'

She stuffed the money in her pocket, we grabbed our cases and shuffled away in the hope that no one would spot us and claim back the cash. We hurried towards the restaurant we saw earlier and sat down to eat. The waiter came along and said something to mum in Dutch and she replied. It was 1.25am and the place was due to close at 2am, the kitchen was closed but she managed to persuade him to serve us some chips and hot chocolate. Finding that money definitely lightened the mood between us and was definitely a godsend. We ate our chips while she told me about Rachel and the times they shared together years ago until we had to leave the restaurant. Although finding the money was a huge blessing, it wasn't enough for a hotel or a room for the night, so we ended up back at the train station again. We sat on the bench in the station for hours waiting for morning. I lay my head on mum's lap trying my best not to fall asleep. My emotions were mixed. Here we were, cold, vulnerable, sitting on a bench in an empty train station in the middle of the night with nothing but our suitcases and a few pounds. She had got us into this mess yet again but for some unexplainable reason, I felt sorry for her. I knew she was unhappy deep down, I knew it was why she acted so irrational, and although the thought of sleeping on a station bench was unimaginable, and it was always all her fault why we were in these horrific situations, I couldn't help but think she needed me on her side and I forgave her, yet again.

* * *

The hours went by so slowly. I looked up at that big clock in the station almost every 15 minutes until it reached the time we could finally board the train. Rachel was at the station waiting for us. Mum and Rachel embraced each other with a long hug while I closely studied her. For some reason I didn't get the best feeling about her at all. She said hello and I gave her a smile and said hi back. We walked a short walk to her apartment which was a small one-bedroom flat. It was planned that mum would sleep with Rachel and I would take the sofa. It was only for a few days so it didn't seem that bad. We settled in and all sat together for lunch while mum and Rachel drank wine and chatted about what they'd been up to since they last saw each other. In the evening they began getting ready for a night out. I guessed they wanted to go out and catch up properly and was quite looking forward to them leaving so I could have some time to myself. They drank more wine, got changed, did their hair and make-up and off they went. I happily stayed alone in the apartment watching MTV videos and movies before falling asleep on the sofa. The next morning both mum and Rachel slept all day, this became the general pattern each day and in fact, a lot more than just a few days had passed but I never really got the chance to talk to mum about anything as she was out every night and slept all day which was beginning to get a bit boring.

One night while they were getting ready I asked her for a moment in the kitchen.

'What's wrong baby girl?' she asked while she brushed her hair.

'Do you have to go out every single night?' I asked.

'I'm just hanging out with Rachel. Rachel's been good to us, she just wants some company when she's out. It's the least I can do for her.'

'Yeah but why every night?' I snapped. 'I'm so bored when you're gone mum, it's so boring, why can't you just stay home with me sometimes?'

'Oh baby girl,' she said as she came over to give me a hug. 'This is only temporary darling, it won't be forever.'

'When can we go home?' I asked. 'I'm stuck in this place all day and all night with nothing to do.'

She looked at me while I pushed her away from me. 'I just need a couple more weeks. In a couple of weeks I'll have what we need to move on and everything will be OK.'

She had tears in her eyes.

'Why are you upset?' I asked.

'No reason.'

'So why are you crying?'

'I'm not crying,' she replied. 'It's my make-up.'

I watched her and Rachel leave with their faces all dolled up, but this evening I noticed they actually had on their normal clothes and carried rucksacks. I crept into the bedroom the next morning while they slept and grabbed both their bags. I sat in front of the TV and quickly rummaged through. In one bag I pulled out a long blonde shiny wig, a sequined bra, a pair of bright pink high-heeled stilettos, loads of make-up, a packet of condoms and a load of cash. I quickly moved on to the other bag, and saw some sort of shiny one-piece that looked like a swimming costume, loads of costume jewellery, cigarettes, and again condoms and loads of cash. I searched through every single zip of each bag until I found one last thing, a small see-through bag filled with white powder. Although I was young I knew what it was, I also knew exactly what they were doing every night and felt sick. It now made sense that she needed a few more weeks, it made sense that she was almost crying, she was obviously unhappy with what she was doing. Feeling disappointed with her wasn't an unfamiliar statement; this time, I was beyond disappointed. I quickly stuffed everything back in the bags and returned them to the bedroom, I looked over at the bed where they were both dead to the world. With one glimpse they looked so innocent while they slept and with another, so trashy. It was after 1pm in the afternoon and I was tired of sitting in this apartment all day and night with nothing to do while she fucked her life up with Rachel. I knew that woman was bad news from the moment I saw her.

* * *

That same evening, I watched them in disgust as they prepared themselves for their drug-filled strip night. I had no proof of whose bag the drugs were in and who was taking them but the fact that they were there was enough. I hadn't spoken to mum all day and she didn't even notice. They drank wine and giggled as they got ready. The thought of another night of this boredom was insane. I looked on the coffee table at the empty glasses and ashtray, there was a box of cigarettes and a lighter on the side. I took the cigarettes and the lighter and hid them in my coat pocket. I waited around an hour after they left and reached for the cigarettes, slowly took one out of the box, lit it and inhaled. I don't really know why I did it, it was my entertainment for the night, or just simply something to do. The first puff obviously made me choke but I got the hang of it very quickly and within a couple of hours I'd smoked five cigarettes. It seemed pointless, but I was killing time, rebelling, trying to feel like an adult. I didn't even know the reason, but whatever the reason was, it was making me feel better for that moment.

* * *

This routine carried on for around another week or so, stealing cigarettes here and there to fill my evenings while they were out. I even began drinking the wine and whatever alcohol they left around. While they were out doing whatever, I was having my own little party too. It wasn't long before things started to fall apart between Rachel and mum. One particular morning I heard them chatting in the bedroom which sounded kind of heated. I tiptoed to the door to hear more.

'It's your own fault,' I heard Rachel say. 'You got too ahead of yourself. I brought you in and you overstepped the mark.'

'This is ridiculous,' mum replied. 'Of course I'm gonna do way better than you, it's not my fault I'm prettier than you.'

I held my breath while I moved closer to the door so I didn't miss anything.

'You bitch,' Rachel shouted and from what I could hear slapped her. 'After everything I've done for you and Nikki, this is how you repay me. I want you out of my house! Go on, get out of my room!' she shouted.

I quickly ran back to the front room, jumped on the sofa and pulled the covers over my head. Two minutes later mum came in the room. I tried my best to control my breathing under the cover after my mini sprint, but I couldn't, so I sat up and looked over at her. She was staring into space with tears falling down her face.

'Morning,' I said.

She looked over at me, got up and walked over to the sofa, squeezed herself next to me and hugged me while she cried.

'I'm so sorry,' she cried. 'I'm sorry for dragging you out here, I'm sorry for letting you down, I've been such a bad mother. I tried to find us a better life but I just keep getting it wrong. I don't know what's wrong with me.'

I wanted to hug her back, but I couldn't.

'We're finally going home, baby girl,' she said as she clung on to me. 'There's nothing left here for us, we'll leave tonight when Rachel goes out. Are you happy now?'

I wished I could have told her I heard the argument, that I knew we were leaving because we'd been kicked out, again. She was acting like it was her decision.

'Yeah, I'm happy about that,' I replied. 'Really happy.'

* * *

We arrived home and everything looked exactly the same, yet everything was different. I was different, it was the end of November and although I'd only be 13 on my next birthday, I felt like I'd grown up so much. I'd actually missed so much school and was looking forward to seeing Kaila to tell her everything. I continued to steal mum's cigarettes to smoke at night and was taking a swig of alcohol here and there whenever the opportunity arose. Mum and I never talked about Amsterdam, or anything that happened there ever again. We hardly spoke at all in fairness. Although I missed school, I felt quite anxious at the idea of going back after everything. School felt like the last place I wanted to be. I'd missed the beginning of term and knew I'd struggle. I dreaded the first morning back which was just as I expected – loads of questions regarding my whereabouts, behind in all the classes as usual, low concentration levels. I looked around all morning for Kaila but there was no sign of her.

Later that evening I tried calling, but our phone had been cut off while we were away as mum hadn't paid the bill. I asked one of the girls in my class the next morning.

'Kaila left ages ago, she never came back after the school holidays.'

That was it, no Kaila, another best friend gone and it hurt. I sat through the rest of the lesson not paying any attention to anything. Kaila was the only person I could talk to about everything and tell where I really was, and now I had no one. Instead of going to my next lesson, I blatantly walked straight out of school, took my dinner money, went to the shop and bought a box of cigarettes. I went to the park, sat on the swings and smoked the whole box, one after another until I felt sick.

When I got home, I searched through the kitchen cupboards, found half a bottle of whiskey and drank it. By the time mum got home from wherever she had been, I was passed out on the floor. I woke up to her kneeling beside me shaking me and calling my name. My head was spinning, and I could hardly see properly.

'Oh my god you're drunk,' she said. 'What the fuck have you done, you stupid girl?'

Once I heard her call me a stupid girl, I lost it. After everything, she had the audacity to call *me* stupid. I jumped up and attacked her. I slapped and punched her while screaming at her at the top of my voice.

'I fucking hate you!' I screamed. 'You're a fucking embarrassment, you have no idea of what I'm going through do you?' I shouted. 'I'm so ashamed you're my mum, you've fucking ruined my life.'

With every word I cried and with every slap or punch I became weaker and weaker. I then slumped on a beanbag and sobbed. She ran over to me, dragged me by the arms off the beanbag and across the room. She was also screaming but I had no idea what she was saying. She dragged me so hard I could feel the carpet burning my legs.

'You're such an ungrateful little bitch,' I finally heard her say. 'I gave up my life to have you back and you're so ungrateful. You've been nothing but a hindrance to my life; you always think everything's about you don't you? Well I've had enough of you, it's your fault my life's a mess, did you ever stop to think that? I only kept you for Mark and he doesn't want me so there's no need for you in my life. I wish you hadn't even been born,' she shouted.

Whilst she dragged me across the room she was also slapping me in my face until I no longer felt pain, I just heard the words. I somehow managed to gain some strength to break away from her and began to punch her legs. I was on the floor, on my knees, while we thrashed out at each other, both of us hysterically screaming and in tears, fighting like animals. I crawled over to the door in an attempt to get away from her and she slammed my head between the door and the door frame. I fell to the floor and blacked out for about ten seconds. I wanted to lie there and just cry, it was all way too emotional to handle but there was something in me that said no more. I found a burst of energy from god knows where, got up, ran across the room, grabbed the empty bottle of whiskey and threw it in her face.

'You're a fucking disaster,' I shouted. 'I fucking hate you, and actually I wish it was you who was never born.'

I ran upstairs to my room and slammed the door shut thinking she'd come after me, but she didn't. I got into bed feeling so broken. I wanted an end to everything but couldn't think of how I could stop it. I'd cried myself to sleep many times and was tired of it, there had to be a way to get out of this mess. I couldn't believe I was feeling like this again, desperate to escape with no way out. My head hurt from earlier and when I looked in the mirror I had scratches and a bump on the side of my reddened face. I held my hand up to my face and thought, my mother did this, my own mother. I'd just had a full on physical fight with my own mother and it actually felt good. It was a build-up of all my mixed emotions towards her, a build-up of wanting to kill her so many times before, a build-up of hating the fact that I always put her feelings before mine. I was so happy I was able to fight back for once and surprised at how good it felt. I was no longer going to allow myself to become a victim of anyone's behaviour ever again and although I started it, if she or anyone else came at me any other time, I would do it all over again.

* * *

Over the next few months things were pretty calm, but nowhere near normal. I hardly went to school, mainly because mum gave me no money to get there. We lived in the same house, but we were like ghosts, non-existent to each other. She ignored me most of the time and I ignored her. She had recently become best friends with my cousin Paul's mum auntie Laura and at the weekends we'd spend the day there while they went out in the evenings. I was glad for the change of scenery to be honest and I was happy to hang out with Paul. They'd typically drink wine while getting ready, and leave me Paul together for the weekend alone. Paul and I became really close. He was a few years older than me and from what he told me, his mum, auntie Laura was similar to my mum and he hated her too. She was an alcoholic and had also put him through some really difficult situations. We'd sit in his room for hours talking about all the things we had been through. Sometimes we'd lighten the mood and play Luther Vandross records and dance around together, and sometimes we'd just hang out watching TV or playing video games. Paul also smoked and drank so he'd go to the shop to buy cigarettes and we'd stand on the balcony smoking and drinking together. At the end of the night, I'd sleep in his bed and we'd cuddle each other through the night. There was an inexplicable love and understanding between us because of what we'd both been through. I felt safe telling him my secrets and so did he.

Unfortunately, it wasn't seen like that by auntie Laura who wrongfully judged our closeness. One night, mum and Laura came home from one of their nights out. Paul and I were wrapped up in each other's arms in bed. She turned the light on which woke us both up.

'Oh my god,' she shouted. 'Savannah, look at this shit!'

Paul and I sat up rubbing our eyes.

'What the fuck are you two doing?' Laura shouted.

'Nothing Paul replied. 'We were sleeping, what's wrong?'

'Get out of that bed,' she screamed as she grabbed his arm and dragged him out of the bed to the floor. 'What have you done, what the fuck have you done?' she shouted.

'Nothing mum, for god's sake we were just sleeping.'

'Do you think I was born yesterday?' she screamed and shoved him to the side.

'Mum, stop!' he shouted. 'You're drunk and you're acting like a psycho.'

I felt sorry for Paul. I'd seen this irrational behaviour so many times with mum and although we'd talked about it, it really wasn't nice to see someone else go through it.

'Come on, Laura,' mum eventually stepped in. 'Leave it, it's nothing, they're cousins, what do you think they were doing?'

'You would say that, wouldn't you? Look at her, she's a slut. Look at her, she's not even wearing a nightie.'

It was the truth, mum hardly did any washing, so I was in my knickers and vest.

'Oh shut up Laura,' mum said. 'You're overreacting, they're just kids.'

She went to see if Paul was OK, he'd cut his arm somehow.

'I'll go get you a plaster,' she said, 'and don't worry, your mum's just a bit upset, don't mind her.'

'Upset?' shouted Laura. 'Are you joking? Your slut of a daughter has probably been fucking my son this whole time.'

'Laura, they're cousins,' mum shouted. 'You're sick in the head. How can you even think that low?'

I sat in bed with the covers held right up to my face, watching while mum and Laura continued to lash out at each other. I couldn't tell if mum was sticking up for me for once or whether she just didn't like the way Laura was acting. The argument went on for ages and from what it sounded like, Paul and I were long forgotten and they were at each other's throats about all sorts of other things that had happened between them in the past. Paul sat back on the bed and put his arm around me.

'I'm so sorry,' I said.

'There's nothing to be sorry about,' he replied. 'Look at them, they're idiots, they don't even know what they're arguing about.'

We looked at each other and back at them, disappointed and ashamed of both our mothers acting like clowns. I felt sad, sad for Paul and sad for us, because deep down I knew exactly what was going to happen. Mum and I would leave in a rage, and we'd probably never see either of them ever again. It was the story of our lives and just like I thought, on this occasion, it was the exact truth.

* * *

'See,' mum said in the cab on the way home, 'I told you you were a burden to my life. I probably won't see Laura ever again because of you.'

I ignored her while she ranted about everything being my fault. She blamed me for dad not wanting her, for burning Olivia and spoiling her friendship with Lacey, for making her skint, for Donald kicking us out. She said it was all my fault and she was fed up of having me around.

'I should have left you where you were and not bothered,' she said.

I listened to her words as a tear fell down my cheek. I was too tired to react and had no energy to argue.

After that day, whenever we crossed paths we never spoke, and she never even looked at me. I went to school on the odd occasion if I had money to get me there, if not, I'd sleep all day or hang out with the kids I used to hang out with when Kirk was around. Mum eventually opened a bank account for me and arranged the child benefit to go direct to my account. It was something like £15 per week which wasn't much, but I had a cash card and my own money with freedom to do whatever I wanted with it, so it suited me fine and meant we didn't have to speak at all. She was hardly home which didn't faze me, but after two consecutive weeks of not seeing her at all, I began to worry. Luckily, I had my child benefit money, so I managed to buy food to get by. However, the money I used for food didn't leave me with any spare to get to school so I hung out at the flat all day. Deep down, I was kind of scared something might have happened to her and when it got to the third week, I just couldn't be bothered to worry about her anymore. She obviously wasn't bothered about me so I put it to the back of my head and carried on. I used my child benefit money for cigarettes and alcohol and most nights the guys would come back to the flat to chill. We'd have mini parties till the early hours of the morning, drinking, smoking and having a laugh.

One morning I woke up to knocks on the door. I jumped up thinking it could be mum, grabbed my dressing gown and ran downstairs only to see the downstairs neighbour through the peephole.

'Where's your mother?' she asked as I opened the door.

'She's at work,' I replied quickly.

'When will she be back?'

'I don't know.'

'I've heard a lot of people coming and going late at night,' she said, 'and the loud music is really disturbing me.'

'Sorry,' I replied, 'they were my friends.'

'Well I've heard it a few nights in a row now, and I'd rather it didn't happen again.'

'It won't happen again.'

'Can I come in?'

'No,' I sharply replied. I could see her trying to look behind me to see if she could see anything.

'Well when your mum comes back from work, will you ask her to come and see me?'

'Yeah sure,' I said, and shut the door.

For the next couple of days, I stayed home alone, mainly to keep the neighbour off my back and honestly, I wasn't in the mood to see anyone. I went to the supermarket that evening and stole a bottle of whiskey, I listened to music, smoked cigarettes and drank the whiskey glass after glass. I danced around the room and turned the volume up louder and louder the more I drank. I danced and danced and in my own head I was happy, I was in a different place, in a dream land, until I was disturbed again by knocks on the door. Again, thinking there was a chance it could be mum, I stumbled to the door. It was her again, the woman from downstairs.

'Hi,' I said as I opened the door. 'Do you wanna come in? I'm having a party.'

'Is your mum home?' she asked again.

'No, I told you before, she's at work,' I said as I swayed behind the door.

She shoved past me and stormed into the front room. As I stumbled behind her and watched as she looked in disgust around the room, she switched off the music.

'What on earth is going on?' she said. 'Look at the state of you! Look at the state of this place! It's after midnight and your mum's not home, she hasn't been home for ages, has she?'

I tried to think of something to say, but in my drunken haze I couldn't think of anything. I could feel my eyes welling and began to feel my head spin and for a minute I couldn't breathe. The next thing I knew I'd vomited all over the floor.

'Oh you poor thing,' I heard her say. She came over to comfort me as I continued to vomit all over the place. 'Where's your mother, darling?' she asked as she held my hair.

'I don't know,' I managed to say as I burst in to tears.

'You're coming down with me,' she said. 'Have you got a key?'

I nodded.

'We can deal with this tomorrow, you need something to eat and a good night's sleep.'

I learned her name was Julia and she was a nurse. She worked shifts and was home during the days sometimes which is how she knew mum hadn't been around. She was very sweet and of course really concerned about what was happening. After cleaning myself up, I sat at the table while she made me a sandwich and a glass of juice. While I ate she began firing the questions.

'How long has your mum been away? I know she hasn't been around so there's no point in covering for her darling.'

I shrugged my shoulders.

'Well from what I can figure out it's been about three weeks,' she said.

I nodded. 'I've got my own money and I can look after myself,' I said.

'Do you have any idea where she is?'

'No.'

'Have you called the police?'

'No, she goes away sometimes, it's normal.'

'It's not normal darling,' she replied with a sympathetic smile on her face. 'What about school? You haven't been going, have you?'

I shook my head.

'You poor little thing,' she sighed. 'You can stay here with me tonight, OK?'

She gave me a smile and I half smiled back. She brought out a blanket and a couple of pillows for me and I comfortably curled up on the sofa and fell straight asleep.

The next morning, Julia went to work early, and I went back upstairs to have a bath and change my clothes. After last night, reality hit me. What was I going to do? I couldn't go on like this for much longer. I felt like I could handle it but it was clear I needed help. I thought about calling someone, but I'd lost my address book ages ago in Amsterdam and didn't know anyone's number. I thought about calling dad or auntie Chloe, Nanny, anyone. I frantically searched the flat looking for a phone book, a diary, anything, but found nothing.

Later that evening Julia came home with the police and a social worker. I answered all their questions and they said they'd be in touch within 24 hours while they investigate.

'Is it OK if Nikki stays with you again for tonight until we get in touch?' the policeman asked Julia.

'Of course,' she replied. 'It's the least I can do.' She smiled at me as they left. 'Everything's gonna be just fine,' she said. 'You're in good hands.'

I was numb, tired and quite scared of what was going to happen or where mum really was. I thought the worst and had visions of her lying dead in an alley somewhere. Julia made me something to eat and we watched TV together until I fell asleep again on the sofa.

The next day there was a knock on the door quite early in the afternoon and as I looked through the peephole, it was Chloe. I was surprised to see her but got a sense of relief thinking everything was actually OK. She gave me a half-hearted hug as I opened the door and walked straight into the front room.

'Come and sit down Nikki, I need to talk to you.'

'Do you know where mum is?' I quickly asked.

Completely ignoring my question, she went on to mention she'd spoken to the police that morning and she thought she'd come to speak to me before they did.

'Chloe what's happened?' I asked.

The way she was behaving, I knew something was wrong and imagined the worst.

'What is it?' I yelled. 'Just tell me Chloe, what's happened?'

She took a deep breath.

'Is she dead?'

'Oh gosh, no,' she replied. 'No, she's not dead, she's just not here.' She began to cry. 'I'm so sorry, Nikki, but your mum isn't in the country. She's in Amsterdam.'

I sighed. 'Why is she in Amsterdam?' I quietly asked.

'She was struggling, Nikki.'

'Struggling with what?'

I quickly realised she knew she was going to do this all along from the way she was acting in the cab that night. It was why she opened my bank account and switched the child benefit to me.

'You know your mum isn't the strongest of characters. She couldn't handle it anymore, she couldn't handle you, she just had enough. She feels she'll have a better life in Amsterdam.'

I thought back to our trip in Amsterdam, there was nothing great about it so how the hell had she left me to go back there for a better life. I watched Chloe while she wept as she told the story.

'Why are you crying?' I asked, irritated by her behaviour.

'I feel really bad.'

'Bad for what?'

'I was supposed to check in on you a lot sooner, but I didn't get around to it.'

'How long have you known about this?'

'Just over a month,' she replied.

'So, you knew she was going?'

She nodded her head. 'I took her to the airport,' she whispered.

I sat completely still for about a minute, taking in what I'd just heard.

'Why didn't you tell me, or come to help?' I asked. At this stage, I felt so angry I could have punched her right in that pathetic face of hers, but I somehow managed to remain calm.

'She didn't want you to know she'd left you.'

'Well that doesn't make any sense, does it?' I said. 'When is she coming back?'

She shook her head. 'She's not coming back, Nikki.'

'How can you not have told me? How can you even know that information and do nothing? Why would you not come to see me knowing she was gone?' I was screaming at her. 'Do you know what I've been going through for the last few weeks?'

'I'm so sorry,' she cried. 'Honestly I am, she told me your dad knew everything and you were going to stay with him. Today was the first day I heard you were on your own when the police called, we all thought you were with him.'

I sighed, it didn't surprise me that she'd lied. We hadn't heard of or spoken to dad for years. I remembered her bad-mouthing him in one of her drunken outbursts because she never knew where he was.

'We haven't heard from dad in years, we don't even know where he lives.'

My head began to hurt. I was relieved there was finally an explanation for all of this. As much as it was killing me that she'd just upped and left, I was relieved that she wasn't dead in an alley, and then I began to think of what was really happening here. What did I do to her that was so bad? Then I realised it wasn't me at all, it was her, she was so weak, it was obvious she wasn't cut out for motherhood right from the beginning. I knew I was a burden to her and her ridiculous idea of what would make her happy in life but I still couldn't believe she had just gone.

'So what happens now?' I asked.

She was still stupidly crying, but not once did she ask if I was OK. I got more sympathy from Julia who was a complete stranger.

'Well the social workers and police are trying to locate your dad, but they haven't found him yet. In the meantime I told them you could stay with Mia.'

'Mia, why Mia?'

'You can't stay with me, and Nanny's getting too old. It'll only be for a couple of weeks, until they find your dad.'

'And what if they don't find dad?'

'They'll find him,' she replied. 'They can do all sorts these days. I spoke to Mia this morning, she knows everything, she's looking forward to having you.'

I hadn't seen Mia in years and we didn't have the best of relationships even then. She was 18 now, had two kids and lived in a council flat. I wasn't overly happy about going to stay with her, but I guessed I had no choice.

'I'll take you there now, go and get a few things,' Chloe said.

I went up to my room and sat on the bed trying to digest everything. I sat there staring into space wondering what was going to happen. I found my rucksack and slowly began packing some things and dragged myself back downstairs.

'Why can't I just stay here until they find dad?' I asked. 'Julia's really cool, I'm sure she won't mind.'

'It's the law, darling,' she replied. 'You can't stay alone without parental or family supervision. They wanted to take you away and put you in a home, so this is the best option. Is that all you need for now?' she asked making reference to my bag.

'Yeah,' I replied slowly.

'Come on then, let's make a move. Mia's expecting us.'

* * *

We walked together in silence to the bus stop. Chloe and I never communicated for the whole journey. We sat on the bus and as usual, I gazed out the window, thinking about everything that had happened since I'd been with mum. I tried to hold back, but the tears began to fall. I felt so disappointed. I remembered when dad and I were in the car the moment he told me she was my mum and convinced me everything was going to be OK. I wondered where he was and what he was doing. He'd promised he'd take me back if it didn't work out, but now he was nowhere to be found. I wondered if he even thought about me. I felt really sad and actually I felt really stupid to have believed him. I had to quickly wipe my tears, so Chloe couldn't see when we finally got to our stop and quietly walked with her until we reached Mia's. She was surprisingly very welcoming, her kids were so cute and also ran to the door behind her. Her boyfriend Scott was in the kitchen cooking dinner and welcomed me with a big hug and a kiss on the cheek.

We all sat down for dinner and I watched while Mia, Scott and Chloe chatted away and attempted many times to get the girls to eat without making a mess. Sahara was three years old and Lexi was two, they were adorable but certainly a handful.

Mia turned to me and said, 'You're quiet this evening. How've you been? I can't believe it's been ages since I've seen you. What've you been up to?'

'I've been fine,' I replied. 'Nothing much.'

She didn't really know how to respond to my bland response and continued to feed the girls. We'd all run out of small talk and continued to eat in silence.

'So do you rave?' Scott finally asked.

'Rave?' I repeated. 'No, I don't rave.'

'Oh you don't know what you're missing out on girl,' he said with a huge grin on his face. 'What music do you like?'

'All sorts, really.'

'Do you like house?'

'Yeah, a little bit.' I didn't, but I couldn't be bothered to go into anything with him. I appreciated their efforts, but I was tired and just wanted to go to bed.

After dinner, Chloe said her goodbyes and left. Mia put the girls to bed, and we all sat in the front room chilling. Mia and Scott sat together on the sofa, smoked a spliff and drank beer while I sat on the floor watching TV.

'Where will I sleep?' I asked.

'You'll sleep in here,' Mia answered. 'I've got a blow-up bed over there.'

She could see the disappointment on my face which I could tell annoyed her, but she was also trying to remain cool.

'The kids get up around 6am to watch cartoons, but that's cool, you'll be getting ready for school anyway won't you?'

I hadn't even thought about school. I hadn't been in ages but I agreed to keep the peace.

About an hour later Mia and Scott were both stoned and pretty tipsy. They cuddled, kissed and giggled together while wrapped around each other on the sofa. At this point I was so mentally exhausted I just wanted to be on my own.

'Do you mind if I smoke?' I asked.

'You smoke?' Mia shrieked in shock.

'Yeah.'

'Oh my gosh, my little cousin's a big girl now,' she laughed.

'Yes,' Scott shouted and chucked me a cigarette. 'You're definitely ready for raving!'

'Don't be so ridiculous,' Mia said as she playfully slapped him in the chest. 'She's only 13.'

'13's the age man, start them young.'

They both fell in each other's arms laughing. As I looked over, Scott gave me a wink, I looked away and continued to smoke my cigarette hoping they would just go to their room and leave me in peace.

The next few days I settled in. I'd collected most of my stuff from the flat and made myself as comfortable as I could. Mia was actually pretty chilled out, she kind of left me to my own devices. We never really spoke about anything in any depth, it was mainly just general chit-chat. She always cooked a meal for dinner, and wanted us all to eat together with the kids. Scott was out more than he was in; he'd come home from raves pretty drunk, singing and dancing while raiding the kitchen. I found him quite funny, but for obvious reasons Mia wasn't always impressed.

'You've been out all night again,' she said to him one night when he came home singing and dancing around as usual. 'And shut up will you, you'll wake the kids.'

'Stop moaning,' he replied. 'Lighten up girl, life's too short to stress babe.'

He dragged her in an attempt to dance with her while she struggled to get away from him.

'Honestly Scott, I'm sick of you going out all the time, leaving me here with the kids,' she said.

'The kids?' he replied. 'You mean, your kids, your kids that I pay for and look after. I'm entitled to a night out every now and then, don't you think?'

'I can't talk to you when you're like this,' she said and went to leave the room.

'Oi,' he shouted, 'where do you think you're going?'

'Away from you!' she screamed.

'I don't think so,' he replied. 'Come back here.'

He dragged her back into the kitchen. I was sat at the table watching it all.

'Dance with me babes,' he said as he draped himself all over her. 'Stop stressing, don't you wanna dance with me?'

He was so drunk he nearly fell over as he dragged her around.

'No I don't,' she replied trying to get away. 'I can't believe you called my kids stupid, Scott, that's so rude.'

'Fuck your kids,' he snapped back and pushed her away from him. 'And fuck you, you frigid bitch.'

'You make me sick Scott, you're such a fucking bastard sometimes,' she shouted back. 'How can you even say something like that?'

'What'd you call me?' he shouted back.

'A bastard,' she shouted.

'Yeah, I'm such a fucking bastard aren't I?' he replied. 'Watch how much of a fucking bastard I can be.'

I jumped as he punched her right in the head.

'You don't fucking talk to me like that, I've told you this before, haven't I?' he punched her again, in the face this time.

I gasped, wanting to do something, say something but I completely froze. I didn't see that coming at all. Mia grabbed a cup and threw it at him.

'I want you out of my place,' she shouted. 'Just get your stuff and get the fuck out of here. I mean it this time, Scott.'

'Oh, you want me out do you, you weren't saying that last night when I was fucking your brains out. I can't believe how fucking stupid you are, it's the same old story. I'll go tonight, then you'll cry all night and beg for me to come back tomorrow. It's boring, you're boring, you stupid fucking cow,' he shouted as he left and slammed the front door.

Mia sat at the table and cried. I had no idea of what to say or do but I definitely felt really sorry for her. Scott was quite a big guy, so those punches must have really hurt, let alone the way he spoke to her. I got up, made a cup of tea and sat with my arm around her while she sobbed and told me how shit he was when he's drunk, but how good he was with her and the kids when he's sober. She told me he'd done this sort of thing a few times before, and swore this was the last time, but tonight she swore he was no good for her and the kids and he was gone forever.

* * *

That was until the next day. Scott was 100 per cent right. I'd been hanging out with friends and got back to Mia's quite late to find them both snuggled up on the sofa watching a movie. I stood at the door appalled at what I saw. I reluctantly hovered by the door, dreading having to sit in their company waiting for them to go to bed.

'What you doing out there?' Scott shouted out. 'Come in, I won't bite.'

I pushed the door open and slowly walked in. Scott was in his usual playful cheeky chappy mood which I took as arrogance. He had his arms gripped tightly around Mia's shoulders. As I glanced at him, he looked me right in the eye with a sly smirk on his face and gave me a wink. I glanced over to Mia who quickly looked away. I sighed to myself, sat in the corner and lit a cigarette.

'You alright Nikki?' he asked. 'How was your day?'

'Fine,' I replied, and for the rest of the evening, not one word was said between the three of us while we watched TV. In fact, not a word was ever said between us about the previous night.

* * *

It was quite an unusual dynamic living with Mia and Scott. Everything and everyone revolved around Scott's mood. If Scott was happy, everyone was, if Scott was in a bad mood, everyone was. Mia was definitely on eggshells and tiptoed around him. You could sense her desperation to keep him happy, which was quite sickening to watch. I'd hear the arguments, the fighting and things getting smashed; the girls would get upset and turn to me for comfort. There were a few times I could feel the tension brewing and took the girls out for a walk to buy sweets to avoid them seeing or experiencing what was going on. Although I thought nothing of him and showed it with my facial expressions, he never treated me or spoke to me the way he did Mia. At times he spoke to her with so much disrespect I couldn't understand why she even had him in her life. With me he was always respectful and quite pleasant. I could almost say we got on quite well despite my thoughts about him. Regardless, I never really felt comfortable living there and was constantly waiting for the next explosion to take place, which wasn't that far away.

It was around midnight, we'd all had quite a nice meal together earlier and the evening was as good as it could be. Scott was on good form and the girls were in bed. Mia, Scott and I hung out watching a film and all went to bed around 11pm. The next thing I knew the front room door sprung open with Mia in her dressing gown hovering over me.

'What's up?' I asked.

She kneeled beside me.

'Has he touched you?' she quietly asked.

'What, who?' I sat up rubbing my eyes.

'Scott, has he touched you?'

'No, no he hasn't,' I replied, and got up to turn the light on. 'Why? What's happened?'

'Don't worry it's fine,' she said as she got up and left the room.

I went back to bed wondering why she would even ask a question like that, hoping she was OK, and about ten minutes later I heard the loudest scream and bang coming from their bedroom. I jumped up and ran across to the room to find Mia on the floor with Scott on top of her literally punching her face from side to side. Blood flew from her face and mouth with every punch.

'Of course I would fuck her, she's fucking better looking that you are. You can't tell me what I can or can't do. How many times have I told you, huh?'

This time I had to do something. I ran over to him, jumped on his back and locked my arm around his neck.

'Get off her, leave her alone,' I screamed.

He completely ignored me and continued punching her. All I could think in my head was he's gonna kill her. I had to stop it. I dug my nails deep into his skin and scratched his face from his cheek to his ear which finally distracted him. He shoved me off him and got up to face me. I stood up, held my shoulders back and looked right back at him. I wasn't afraid at all. What could he do? Hit me too, punch me like he'd just done to Mia? Whatever was coming, I'd probably had worse and was ready for it. I breathed heavily as I continued to stare into his eyes and finally nodded my head to give him the go ahead. I saw the scratches on his face which were quite deep and blood poured down the side of his cheek. He stepped closer towards me.

'Come on then!' I shouted. 'Come on!'

I was shaking, so angry I didn't care about the consequences. I wanted him to hit me. He was such an arrogant coward I was desperate to have it out with him.

He leaned his face in close to mine and whispered in my ear, 'She should have been more like you darling, if she was she might have had a chance.'

He weirdly kissed me on the cheek and walked away. I exhaled, I couldn't believe he didn't do anything. He'd hit Mia so easily so many times and to be honest I was expecting it. I was even ready for it but for once it didn't happen. I leaned down to help Mia up. Her face was cut, her lip was busted open and I could tell she was going to get a black eye. Her poor face was a mess. I helped her up and out to the kitchen where I got some TCP to wipe her cuts. Scott was in the bedroom shouting out all sorts of abuse to both of us while he packed his stuff. I didn't even register what he was saying, I just needed to help Mia.

Moments later the front door slammed. He'd finally left, for good I hoped.

'Thank fucking god for that,' I said under my breath as I wiped blood away from Mia's face.

She burst into tears. 'I can't believe he's gone,' she cried. 'He won't come back this time, I know he won't.'

I stepped away from her. 'I'd like to hope he doesn't,' I said. 'He's a monster.'

'But I can't live without him,' she cried.

'What?' I said in complete shock. 'What on earth are you saying, Mia? Are you seriously upset that he's gone after what he's just done to you?'

'It's my fault,' she cried. 'It was me, he's done nothing wrong and I provoked him.'

'Are you fucking joking?' I said. 'You seriously think he's done nothing wrong? Look at your face! Imagine if the girls had woken up and seen that.'

I put the kettle on to make us a cup of tea and took two cups out of the cupboard.

'What happened anyway? Why'd he do this to you?'

'I don't want to talk about it,' she replied.

I became suddenly offended. I'd almost risked getting battered myself for her, so I needed to know.

'OK, well I'll call the police then shall I? And you can tell them,' I said quite angrily.

'No,' she quickly replied. 'I can't call the police, it'll make it worse.'

'OK, so tell me.'

She held her head down.

'Has it got something to do with me?'

She sighed.

'I don't get it,' I said. 'Nothing's happened between us, Mia, and it never would have, even if he'd tried.'

'I know,' she said. 'I told you it was my fault, I was jealous.'

'Jealous of what?'

'Of you.'

'Why?'

'Because he fancied you.'

'No he didn't.'

'Yes, Nikki, he did. He told me, he told me he'd fuck you all day long.'

I felt sick.

'Well he was probably lying,' I said. 'And how did it get to him beating you up like that?'

'I don't know,' she replied. 'You know what he's like, he just gets so angry. I did accuse him though, and I pushed so I got what I deserved. I see the way he looks at you and I hear the way he talks to you.'

I shook my head. 'That's stupid Mia, I'm your cousin.'

'I know you wouldn't do anything. I don't want it to be awkward between us, it's not you, it's him. Anyway I don't want to talk about it anymore,' she said. 'I'm tired, I just wanna go to bed.'

* * *

I got up really early the next morning, mainly because I couldn't sleep thinking about the previous night. I first went to check on the girls and was so glad that they had managed to sleep through last night's events. Luckily, they were still fast asleep. I walked across to Mia's room and gently knocked on the door. As I heard no response I slowly opened the door slightly to check she was OK. She was lying on top of the bed wide awake.

'Morning Mia, how you feeling?'

She turned her head, looked at me and looked away.

'Go away Nikki,' she said, 'just get out.'

'What's the matter?'

'I don't want to talk about it, and I don't particularly want to see you either.'

I figured she was just feeling a bit upset about everything, so I shut the door and left her in peace. She came into the front room about an hour later and sat on the edge of the sofa. I shuffled up to make space.

'You alright?' I asked.

She nodded. 'Nikki, I want you to leave.'

'What?'

'I'm sorry, but I want you out of here.'

I looked at her for an explanation.

'This would never have happened if you hadn't come here,' she continued. 'I know it's not your fault, but we were fine before you came. We all know he's not got the best temper in the world, but he loves me. I need him in my life and I can't have you here when I get him back.'

I was absolutely disgusted with what she was saying. This guy almost killed her, and all she could say was she needed him in her life. She was putting that animal before her own flesh and blood, not to mention the fact that she would even allow someone so unpredictable and dangerous around her kids. I had absolutely nothing to say, and in truth I was desperate to get away from her and her stupidity as fast as I could. She wasn't even worth a response. As I looked at her, I no longer saw Mia, my older cousin, I saw a pathetic little girl who had no respect for herself. I couldn't sit there any longer and literally packed my bags and left her to it.

* * *

I had no money to my name whatsoever. I'd used the last pound I had for the bus fare and a packet of crisps. I went to the supermarket looking for small items I could pocket and settled for a couple of tins of tuna, a small bag of rice and few packets of biscuits. It was actually quite a nice feeling to be back home. I sat on one of the beanbags with a packet of biscuits thinking over the last couple of months, wondering what would happen next. The thought of what could be ahead scared the living daylights out of me, and suddenly I became really upset. I laid flat on the floor with my arms out and stared up at the ceiling, paralysed, unable to move, tears falling down the side of my face. The room went from light to dark as I remained in the same position for hours. Eventually, extreme hunger motivated me to peel myself up and make something to eat. The plan was to cook the rice and tuna I'd stolen earlier, but I felt so tired I just ate the cold tuna out of the can, closed the curtains and went upstairs to bed. As much as I tried to sleep, I couldn't. I couldn't clear my head, so I laid awake with my thoughts until I heard the door knock. I quickly jumped up. No one even knew I was there. The door knocked again, and I heard the voice.

'Hellooo!'

I recognised the voice straight away. It was Julia. I was surprised at how relieved I felt and ran down the stairs as quick as I could to go and see her.

'Nikki, what are you doing here, darling?' she asked.

I wanted to tell her everything, but had no idea where to even start.

'How did you know I was here?'

'Well I came home from work and noticed the curtains were closed. They'd been open since you left so I thought I'd check. I certainly didn't expect it to be you.'

I was about to say something, but instead I just burst into tears.

'Oh Nikki, what's happened?' she said as she hugged me.

She was just what I needed in that moment. She gave me a big hug and took me downstairs for a cup of tea and I told her everything. She immediately got on the phone to the social department to see if she could find out what the situation was, but because it was so late no one could help. I stayed with her that evening and peacefully watched TV on the sofa while she cooked dinner. It was so nice spending time with her, she was actually one of the nicest people I'd ever met and wished there were more people like her in the world.

After dinner we snuggled up on the sofa together watching TV until bedtime. In the morning, Julia went off to work while I lounged around doing nothing much. I'd just made myself a toasted cheese sandwich when the phone rang. I knew it wasn't my place to answer her phone, but I thought it could be Julia checking to see if I was OK, so I answered. It turned out it was social services wanting to speak to Julia about me since she'd left a message last night. I explained who I was, why I was there and asked them to let me know the situation. Eventually, after a long list of questions to confirm I was who I was, they mentioned they'd been in touch with my father. They'd been trying to get hold of Chloe but had no luck. They arranged a date for a meeting with myself and dad, accompanied by a social worker, to take place next week at his home address. I confirmed I'd be available and put the phone down. I looked down at the piece of paper I wrote the address on for ages. I thought I'd be really happy to finally know where he was, but I wasn't. I sat on the sofa and looked closely at the address trying to imagine what type of house it was. I began to wonder what he was doing in life, what he did from day to day, what car he drove, everything. I began to remember the good times, how he made me feel when I was with him, and as much as I felt angry, I also missed him and couldn't wait until the following week.

* * *

The next few days flew by and before I knew it, it was the day to meet dad. I packed a few things and nervously waited with Julia for the social worker to arrive. Julia had been amazing over the last few days and in truth, I wished I could just stay with her. She gave me a huge hug and wished me the best in life as we left. I sat in the car with the social worker not knowing what to expect. I had no expectations anymore, no ideas of happy endings, nothing, but I did, however feel extremely nervous. My legs shook as we rang the bell and as he came to the door I literally froze. I felt like I was about to cry but did my best to hold it back. I looked at his face and he looked at mine. I wanted to run to him and give him a hug and I wanted to scream at him at the same time. He looked exactly the same and no matter what I was thinking, it was still good to see his face. He attempted to give me a hug, but I stood stiff which made it a bit awkward, so he turned and invited us in.

We all sat down in the front room while the social worker went through details of some document he had to sign. There was no discussion about anything else or about what happened or where mum was, so I was completely out of the know of what he knew. They finished up and dad walked her out while I sat on the sofa nervously looking around the room, anxious of how we were going to figure this out and what the future was going to hold this time. Dad came back in the room and sat down next to me.

'You hungry?' he asked.

I shook my head.

'Want a drink?'

'Yes please.'

I watched him from behind as he went to get the drink. I thought about when he said dads and daughters stick together. That statement was one of those that never left my head, but we hadn't stuck together, so it felt like a lie. He came back with the drink and sat back down.

'I'm really sorry your mum did what she did.'

I nodded. We both sat quietly for a while before he went over to his turntable, put on a jazz record, sat back down and built himself a spliff.

'You smoke, don't you?' he asked.

My head immediately raised as I looked at him to see his expression. He was completely chilled. Not sure of what to expect, I didn't reply.

'The woman already told me you smoke, Nikki, so here's what's gonna happen from now on. Me and you are not going to have secrets, and I don't want you doing anything behind my back. It's gonna take some time and it starts from here.'

He lit a cigarette and put it in the ashtray.

'Smoke that,' he said.

I looked at him with the most confused look on my face and wondered what the hell was happening. I was 14 years old and my long-lost father was sat in front of me telling me to smoke a cigarette. I understood what he said about no secrets, but this was extreme. If I picked up that cigarette I was absolutely sure he was going to slap me around my head or something, so I left it there to burn, and he lit another.

'Trust me,' he said. 'I ain't gonna be upset with you, smoke it.'

'Is it a trick?' I asked.

'No darling, it's not a trick. I just want you to feel comfortable that's all. If you're a true smoker, you must be dying for a cigarette right now.'

He was right, I really was. I decided to go for it and if he slapped me around my head I'd expect it. I took the cigarette out of the ashtray, took a drag and waited for the slap. I looked over at him to see his reaction. He opened a can of beer, took a sip and leaned back in the chair, relieved there was no slap. I shyly continued to smoke the cigarette.

'Good,' he said. 'That's our first barrier broken. I can see now you've been smoking for a while haven't you?'

'How?'

'By the way you held it, by the way you inhaled and exhaled, the way you put it out, everything.'

I didn't realise he was even watching.

'When did you start?'

'12,' I replied.

'Damn,' he said as he took another sip of beer. 'Did your mother know?'

I shook my head.

'What made you start?'

I shrugged my shoulders. It was too much questioning and I didn't really want to have to explain anything, so I shut up and stopped responding.

'You still into music?' he asked after a while.

'Yeah.'

'What you listening to these days?'

'All sorts really.'

'Go have a look through those records over there and pick out anything you want me to play.'

Dad had a lot of records when we lived with Rashid and Maria, but now there were thousands, literally thousands, and they were all over the place. There were shelves all down one wall full of them, and piles and piles all over the floor. I went over to where the turntable was and began to flick through. I was clueless as to what any of them were so just picked out the ones with cool album covers. We spent the rest of the evening playing the records I picked; he asked why I chose them and if I liked the songs or not, it was fun. I felt a lot more relaxed than earlier and it allowed us to chat together about the music while he educated me on who was who and the different genres. Surprisingly, I enjoyed the evening; it was the best evening I'd had in ages and dad was so chilled, it made it easy to enjoy his company.

I went to use the bathroom and sneaked around to get a cheeky look around the rest of the flat. It was quite a small flat in general, but done up really modern. I nosily tiptoed around but noticed only one bedroom.

'Where's my room?' I asked as I went back to the front room.

'In here for now. I got us a sofa bed, so you'll have to sleep here until I get a new place at some point later. I've started looking but I'm gonna need some more time.'

'So I haven't got a bedroom?'

'Nope, it's cool,' he said. 'We'll just need to make do for now.'

I nodded and sat back down. I wasn't sure how I felt about not having my own space, in fact it made me feel slightly uneasy. But if that's how it had to be, I'd have to get used to it. We ordered a Chinese takeaway and after a couple of hours it was time to call it a night. He helped me pull out the sofa bed, said goodnight and closed the door. I sat on the bed thinking about how the day went, surprised it went so well. I waited for about an hour to be sure dad was asleep, smoked one of the cigarettes I secretly stole out of the box earlier and went to bed.

* * *

It was quite a challenging time for the both of us trying to figure out how to live together when we were so far apart mentally. I could tell for him it wasn't as easy as he'd expected, and half of the time my moods were so up and down, he didn't quite know what to do with me. His main focus for the time being was getting me back to school and after a few conversations with the head teacher and a couple of meetings, he managed to get me back in. I looked forward to going back, yet dreaded it at the same time. I wanted to get back to normality and feel like a normal kid again, but I knew my life had been so far from normal I wasn't sure if I'd be able to fit in. When the time came, it wasn't as bad as expected, everyone was extremely accommodating, the teachers had all been informed to let the classes know that I'd been on an extended holiday due to a family crisis which made things a lot easier and it was great seeing all the girls again. The downfall was realising how behind I was in every single class. Outside classes I was having the best time hanging out and having a laugh with the girls, and during class I was under so much pressure I couldn't even explain the levels of stress I felt. I knew absolutely nothing and everything seemed so alien to me. I couldn't pay attention for longer than 15 minutes without feeling completely lost, which often led to me drifting away into my own little world.

Dad was a smart guy so I hoped he'd be able to help me catch up, but that wasn't easy either. He worked shifts so we didn't get to spend much time together. He was a computer programmer and worked four nights on and three nights off. I'd be alone in the evenings and he'd come home about an hour before I woke up in the mornings, so when it came to homework, I never did any of it. The evenings dad was home, he'd ask how I was getting on and I'd say fine.

'I don't believe you haven't got any homework,' he said one evening. 'This is an important year for you, I thought they'd be giving you extra stuff to catch up with?'

I shrugged my shoulders, way too embarrassed to tell him I actually had homework every night but never understood any of it.

'Let me see your books.'

I felt so hopeless as I took my books out of my bag and handed them over. I watched anxiously while he slowly looked through the books one by one. I was waiting for it, waiting for him to shout at me for lying, shout at me for all the unfinished work, but he said nothing. Instead he put the books down, got up and went to get his coat.

'Come on, let's go get something to eat, I'm starving.'

I got up, grabbed my coat and followed him out. We went to the Chinese shop at the top of the street, ordered a load of food and went back home to eat.

'Did your mum ever help you with your homework?' he asked while we ate.

I frowned and shook my head.

'Did she ever look at your books or ask how you were getting on?'

I wanted him to stop with the questions, but didn't know how to say it, so I sat uncomfortably biting my nails.

'Well?' he asked.

'Shut up,' I shouted. 'Stop asking me questions, stop asking me about her, she's gone. It doesn't matter what she did or didn't do anymore.'

I saw his reaction to my crazy outburst, so confused as he looked at me not knowing what to do or say. I felt so bad for shouting at him, but I couldn't breathe. I grabbed my coat and ran out of the door.

'I'll be back in a minute,' I said on my way out and slammed the door.

I ran down the road to the park, sat at the top of the slide and cried my eyes out. I was so lost. If he knew anything that happened, even one thing, he'd probably send me away. I sat in the park for hours contemplating what to do. I felt sorry for dad and knew he was trying to tread as gently with me as he could, but I didn't trust him enough to tell him anything. I decided I'd never tell him anything and would just try to be good so everything would be OK. I'd try really hard to catch up with my schoolwork and it would all work itself out in the end. I finally felt a bit better, jumped down from the slide and went home.

I quietly walked through the door, still quite ashamed about my outburst. Dad was leaning back on the sofa with a beer in his hand, jazz music playing in the background. He turned towards me as I entered the room and nodded his head. I nodded back and sat on the floor beside the sofa. We both sat in silence, however the chilled music was certainly helping my mind to relax and I generally felt a lot better.

'I'm sorry,' I eventually said.

'It's cool,' he replied. 'You needed space.'

'How did you know that?'

He shrugged his shoulders exactly like I would have done.

'You're my daughter, aren't you?'

'Weren't you worried?'

He took a sip of his beer, looked at me and gave me a wink.

'Nah, I've got faith in you girl.'

I smiled and without discussing anything further, we'd just formed an understanding with each other.

* * *

We grew closer over time as we worked out a routine that suited us. When he was off work, he'd pick me up from school in his sports car, which was always so funny because the older girls were smitten with him. He was charming, good looking, well dressed and a lot younger than most dads. He knew the attention he got while he waited for me with music blasting out and purposely speed off at full speed when I got in to cause a scene and we'd laugh together while they watched. We'd get a takeaway on the way home, have dinner, chit-chat and listen to music while he had a couple of beers and a smoke. He managed to help me out with my schoolwork when he was free which gave me so much more confidence. The three days of the week I spent with dad were amazing, but for the four days he worked it was horrible. He was totally unaware of how I felt because I hid it really well, but the contrast was an emotional roller coaster for me. When we were together it was great, but when he worked I couldn't help but feel vulnerable and lost again. When I was on my own I felt a need to fill the time with attention elsewhere, and since I always got a lot of attention from boys, and due to the freedom and spare time I had, I began to act freely with them without a care in the world. I had a sharp temper which I couldn't control and got myself into all sorts of crazy situations. I became so short fused, I'd lash out very easily and very quickly and would be the first to start an argument or a fight. I got off the bus one day and some guy actually tried to rob me for my trainers which I was not about to accept at all. My limited edition Air Max that dad and I searched high and low for, and this guy was trying to bully me into taking them off in the street. I completely lost it and lashed out on him so badly he was bleeding all over his t-shirt and ended up running off. I didn't even care, I was afraid of nothing and when it came to bullies, I was not receptive at all.

I'd become really good friends with the Turkish guy at the kebab shop near my house and he'd give me free food and money for a cheeky kiss or a fumble here and there. He called me his future wife – really he was just filth, but I knew that and didn't care. I was shoplifting a lot more than I did before, just for the thrill of it. I was an absolute nightmare, but at home I was daddy's little princess. I tidied up, cleaned, washed and ironed his clothes, I was good as gold, two completely different people which mirrored my emotions when I was with dad and when I wasn't. I became very disruptive at school, pretty much at the centre or the main cause of most, if not all misdemeanours. I'd get sent out of classes and had detentions almost every day. Most teachers no longer believed in me and left me to do whatever I wanted. I gave them hell, backchatted them, shouted at them, and called them names. When one of them reacted and told me she felt sorry for my parents, I got so angry I actually grabbed an apple from a girl's lunch box and threw it at her head. If I had my way, I wouldn't even go to school, but the good side of me wanted to make dad proud; proud of what I didn't quite know because I wasn't actually achieving anything. But I wanted him to at least know I was making the effort to attend.

I believe the school had tried to contact dad at home on many occasions to discuss my behaviour, but of course he was either sleeping or at work, so they could never reach him. It all came to light when I got suspended for fighting on the school grounds. Some girl started some gossip that I was flirting with her boyfriend so she was going to beat me up after school. I'd hardly even spoken to this girl, yet she'd spread this message right round the school about this fight that was apparently due to happen at 3.45pm in the park. I didn't even know who her boyfriend was. He may have tried to talk to me, but loads of boys did and half of the boys I had encounters with, I didn't even know their names. But if she wanted a fight she could damn well have one I thought. In fact, I was excited about it. I wanted to kick her arse for calling my name.

I walked through the corridor after my last lesson to hear all the girls chatting about it, ready to go to the park to watch this fight, so I decided to leave via the back entrance, so I didn't have to see anyone or talk to anyone beforehand. I just wanted to turn up, get this over with and go and see my Turkish guy from the kebab shop. But as I walked towards the gate, I saw the girl also making an exit through the back. I ran right up to her and tapped her on the shoulder. She was a lot taller than me and actually quite a big girl.

'What you doing here?' she said as she turned towards me.

'I heard you wanted a fight?' I said.

'Yeah,' she replied, 'but not here, at the park.'

'Do you want a fight or not?'

'Yeah, are you stupid or something? I said not here.'

The fact that she called me stupid was it, enough for my temper to kick in.

'OK,' I said. 'If you wanna fight, let's do it.'

And with that same sentence, I jumped up punched her in the face, grabbed her hair and dragged her to the floor. I didn't think twice, and before we knew it, we were in full fight mode and within seconds, there was a crowd of girls around us shouting 'fight, fight, fight!'

I saw no faces, just bodies while I continued laying into this poor girl. Minutes later, a couple of teachers ran to the scene to drag us apart. I heard one of the teachers got punched in the face in the interim which I had no knowledge of. I hardly knew what was going on, but what I did know was I'd be in deep trouble, but I didn't care. After an intense lecture with the headmistress, I waited outside the staff room for what felt like forever while the head of year, Mrs Fisher, spoke to my dad on the phone. She'd forced me to give her his work number to make sure she got hold of him and I knew she'd take the opportunity to talk about the other stuff I'd got up to. She smiled at me as she came out of the staff room and handed me a suspension letter.

'Your father's expecting this,' she said. 'I need you to get straight home and don't try any funny business on the way.'

I smiled a sarcastic smile and walked away with the letter. I got home, called dad to tell him I was home, and went to see my guy at the kebab shop and told him all about it. The next morning, I woke up really early, worried about how dad was going to react. I'd been suspended for a week which was pretty bad. Dad had done so much to keep my place in school and I knew I was messing it up. I put the sofa bed together, got dressed and patiently waited for dad to wake up. I psyched myself up to talk about it all and was prepared to take whatever punishment was to come. He finally woke up around midday and carried on as normal.

'Have you eaten?' were his first and only words said to me. I'd probably prefer him to scream and shout at me and be done with it, but the mystery was worse.

'No,' I replied.

'OK, gimme a minute and we'll go and get something to eat.'

I couldn't work him out.

'Don't you wanna ask me about school?' I said.

'Nope,' he replied while he put his shoes on.

'Don't you want to know what happened?'

'I know what happened,' he replied as he left the room to get his coat. The suspense was killing me.

We went out to the cafe for lunch, went to the record shop, went to his friend's house and everything was fine. We engaged in conversation throughout the day as if nothing had happened. In the evening we got a McDonald's, he dropped me home and went off to work.

The next morning, he woke up again around midday. We had no food in the house so went to the supermarket to do a food shop. Still no mention of anything about school, which was like a form of torture itself. In the evening we went out for dinner and chatted as normal about general stuff. At this point I assumed he was OK with everything. We enjoyed our meal, went home and chilled out, he put some music on, had a couple of beers, and just as I thought everything was cool…

'So, what happened with this girl?' he asked.

The question came out of the blue and caught me right off-guard. Everything I'd prepared in my head two days ago was gone.

'What do you mean?'

'Simple question, what happened?'

I thought about lying for a second to make out that it wasn't my fault, or she started it but when I looked at him, I realised I didn't want to lie. Once I'd finished telling the story he opened another beer, rolled himself a joint and sat in silence while he smoked his spliff. I also sat in silence wondering how he was going to react.

'I think you did the right thing,' he finally said.

I let out a sigh of relief and grabbed a cigarette out of his box to take the edge off.

'I've told you before not to let anybody take the piss out of you or bully you. No one is better than you, remember that.'

I nodded.

'I don't condone violence as you know, but you gotta be smart about these things. You were right to kick her arse, but what you should have done was kick her arse outside the school, so you wouldn't have got caught. That's where you were stupid.'

'So you don't think it was bad that I had a fight?' I asked.

'Look,' he replied. 'I'd rather you weren't fighting at all, but if this girl was coming for you like you said, I'm glad you stood up for yourself, and by the sound of it, you got her good.'

I laughed at his response, but still felt quite uneasy.

'So, what about the other stuff? Your general behaviour at school? They told me you're a bit of a distraction, what do you think they mean by that?'

I didn't quite know how to respond and felt ashamed he knew what I was getting up to.

'Well?'

I shrugged my shoulders. I didn't know why I behaved the way I did, so there was no way I was about to or even know how to explain. He looked at me waiting for an answer or some sort of explanation. I began to tear up, ashamed of myself and ashamed of showing him my emotions. I got up and left the room. I couldn't handle letting him down and needed to get away. I locked myself away in the bathroom, embarrassed by my actions, and cried for about half an hour before I pulled myself together to face him. He was chilled on the floor with his back to the sofa as I entered the room. He held his arm out to me.

'Come here, come and sit with me.'

He put his arm around me as I sat behind him and drew me closer.

'Don't worry about it for now, we'll talk about it later.'

I nodded my head as I blew my nose.

'You know you can tell me anything, don't you?' he said. 'I want you to feel comfortable talking to me, I'm not the enemy you know.'

I totally believed him, but I don't know why I found it so hard. We sat in silence for a few minutes while we appreciated the music.

'Back in a sec,' he said, as he got up, went to the kitchen and came back with a bottle of champagne and two glasses. He sat back down, opened the bottle and poured the two glasses. He picked a glass and handed it to me.

'Taste this,' he said.

I nervously took the glass and took a small sip. I wondered what was going on in his mind, why he offered me this drink.

'Sip it slowly, don't drink it all at once.'

He picked up his glass, toasted with me and took a sip. I automatically felt better after a couple of sips and although I was supposed to be drinking it slowly, I couldn't help myself, and within a few minutes I'd drank the whole glass. He topped up my glass and again, and I happily sipped away. We began chatting about general stuff, and after about an hour he went to get another bottle. I felt merry, but nowhere near the way I felt when I drank whiskey. That whiskey got me so heavily drunk, but this was a lighter kind of feeling. We were deep in conversation while the music played in the background. I was beginning to appreciate the different styles of music he'd play; he educated me on who it was, where it was from and where and when it was released. It was fascinating to know how much he knew about every single record he had and there were thousands.

'So how do you feel about your mum leaving?' he randomly asked.

'Dunno,' I replied.

'Do you miss her?'

'I hate her.'

'Hate?' he repeated. 'That's a strong word darling, why do you hate her?'

'I just do.'

'But she's your mother.'

'So?'

'You must have had some sort of love for her at some point?'

'Not really, she's pathetic, so stupid and I hate her.'

'Woo!' he said as he topped up our glasses. 'Take it easy. I'm not sure how I feel about you talking about your mother like that.'

'Well it's the truth.'

'What did she do to you, apart from leaving, to make you hate her so much?'

'Loads of stuff, stuff I can't even explain.'

'Try, I'm aware your mother isn't the most stable person in the world, but it couldn't have been that bad?'

'It was bad.'

'Drink up,' he said as he took a sip of his drink.

I took a sip too. I took a cigarette out of the box to smoke, took another sip of my drink, and began telling him the stories. We were up for hours while I talked about some of the things that happened. It was the first time I'd ever spoken to anyone about what had ever gone on between mum and I and he listened carefully and closely, asked questions, asked me how I felt, what I thought, and with the influence of the alcohol, I wasn't holding anything back. I saw the shock and pain in his face as each story unfolded, his reactions so strong it made me realise how wrong it all was. I'd become so used to her and her ways, it seemed normal, but dad's face told a story in itself.

'None of what you've told me is OK, do you hear me? None of it.'

I was desperately trying to hide my emotions but the moment he said none of it was OK, I stopped to think about it. If he thought that was bad he didn't know the end of it. I took a deep sigh and looked down at my nails.

'I don't want you to ever think that any of that was OK or normal.'

My eyes filled with tears.

'If it wasn't normal, then why did it all happen?' I shouted as I burst into tears.

'Come here, darling,' he said as he pulled me closer and wrapped his arms around me. He kissed my forehead. 'You're OK now, you're with me, I'm not gonna let anything like that happen to you ever again.'

We sat on the floor with our backs to the sofa while he held me for what felt like forever, until I fell asleep in his arms.

* * *

The next morning, I felt a little fuzzy due to the champagne, but felt a lot better that we'd spoken about things. I wanted him to know everything and he wanted to know more. We had breakfast together and carried on the conversation. It was a lot easier to talk to him now the ice was broken; I no longer felt embarrassed or stupid, and it became clear to him why I acted the way I did. Conversations with him became so intense and he cleverly dug deeper and deeper until he got me to bare my raw feelings. He was very persuasive and had a way of making me feel comfortable; he told me how beautiful he thought I was and told me stories about when he met mum, and how beautiful he thought she was. He said I was much more beautiful than her, and would grow up to become a much better woman because I had beauty and brains too. I was learning to trust him a lot more, but it was still bothering me why he left me in the first place. Life could have been just like this without all the drama. I needed to know why he did it.

'If you knew what she was like, why did you leave me with her?' I asked.

'I'd never have left you if I knew what I know now. She told me she'd changed, and I believed her. It was a time when things weren't going too well for me, and I thought you'd be better off with your mother.'

'Well it wasn't better was it? It was a mess, dad. You even said you knew she was unstable!'

My voice raised and my eyes filled again with tears. I went to the bathroom to get some tissues and took myself back into the front room and sat on the floor.

'How you feeling?' he asked.

'Fine,' I replied.

'What do you want to do today?'

'Nothing.'

We hardly spoke all day, and if he asked anything, I gave one-word answers. We'd literally gone ten steps forward and ten steps back. I didn't even stop to think how difficult it must have been for him, I was so up and down from one day to the next, it must have been really difficult.

Later that afternoon he popped out to the shops and came back with some food and a couple of bottles of champagne. He poured himself a glass and looked through his records to find something suitable.

'Want a glass?' he asked as he sipped his.

I shrugged my shoulders. He left the room and returned with another glass.

'You got cigarettes?' he asked.

'No.'

He took out a cigarette from his box and chucked it over to me. We sat together in an uncomfortable silence drinking our drinks for a while until he poured us a second glass.

'You talking to me yet?' he eventually asked with a smile on his face.

I shyly smiled back. I couldn't resist.

'Yeah.'

'Good,' he said. 'So now you can tell me about all this shit that's going on at school.'

'I told you about the girl,' I said.

'Yeah, I know about the girl,' he replied. 'But what's all this about you being a distraction and backchatting teachers?'

'They're idiots,' I said.

'Yeah, they might be in your eyes, but in my eyes they're heroes.'

'Heroes?' I repeated.

'Yep,' he said. 'They gotta stand up there all day and deal with a bunch of unruly loudmouth kids like you, and they choose to do it because they want to make a difference.'

I listened as he spoke. I never saw it like that, they were just teachers to me.

'You choose what you want to take from them, but if you don't want to take anything from them, you don't have to. But they don't deserve to be disrespected. If you don't want to listen, don't listen, if you don't want to learn don't, but that's your choice not theirs.'

He was right. I was giving these teachers such a hard time for what? Because I was behind, or I didn't really understand anything or because I was in a bad mood.

'I know it's not all down to you, you missed a lot of school 'cause of your mother,' he said, 'but that Mrs Fisher sees so much potential in you, you can catch up, you've got time, you're smarter than you realise, you just need to want to.'

I nodded.

'Do you want to?' he asked.

'Yeah.'

I didn't really care about school in all fairness, but I cared about what he thought of me and I wanted to make him proud.

'Good,' he replied as he changed the record.

He handled those records so delicately, like they were a piece of fine jewellery – it made me laugh.

'What would you do if there was a fire?' I asked, 'Would you save me or the records?'

He turned to me with a pretend serious look on his face.

'Boy, I don't know you know, it might have to be the records,' he joked as we both laughed.

He put the record on and sat beside me.

'Of course I'd save you,' he said as he kissed me on the cheek. 'You're my little princess.'

I looked up at his face and wanted to know more. I wanted to tell him everything, there was still so much unsaid.

'Do you know what mum was doing in Amsterdam?' I asked.

'I heard all sorts, darling, but I wasn't around so I can't say.'

'What did you hear?'

'It ain't very nice stuff, Nikki, not really worth talking about.'

'Yeah, that makes sense,' I said.

He looked at me knowing I had something to say so I told him all about Amsterdam as he listened in complete disgust. He got up and sat me on his lap.

'If I'd have known any of this, I would never have left you. I can't believe I let this happen.' He was almost in tears, hurt so much by what I was telling him.

I'd pretty much told him everything about life with mum, but the worst times were with Maria. I knew this was the time to bare all. If we were going to move forward, he'd have to know everything and I wanted to know what he knew. The timing was perfect. I could now ask the questions I needed the answers to years ago.

'What about Maria?' I asked.

'What about her?' he replied surprised I'd brought her up.

'Do you still talk to her?'

'Why darling?'

'Just wondering.'

'I have to talk to her, to deal with Rashid.'

'Is Rashid OK?'

'Yeah, he's good. I'll get him over here soon, so you can spend some time with him.'

I nodded.

'What's all this about Nikki?'

'I just want to know if you still like her,' I repeated.

'Like her in what way?'

'Any way.'

'Maria and I were over a long time ago, and no I don't particularly like her, but I don't hate her either. She's the mother of my child. I have a certain level of respect for her if that's what you want to know.'

I moved from his lap and sat facing him on the sofa.

'Why, what's up?' he asked. 'Do you want to see her or something?'

'No,' I snapped.

'That was harsh,' he replied. 'No matter what happened between us, I still respect her. She had a hard time with her family for taking you on, do you know that? Her friends and family went against her for ages because they felt she shouldn't have done it. For that reason you should always have some sort of respect for her.'

It made even more sense why she hated me so much, but I'd never have respect for her.

'Have respect for her?' I said. 'Never. I'd be happy if I never saw her again.'

'Woo double harsh! What makes you say that?'

'She did bad things too,' I said under my breath.

'Really, what'd she do?'

'You know, don't you?'

He frowned. 'Know what?'

I was interrogating him as if he was a criminal.

'Did you know about anything she did to me?'

'Nikki, come on baby, spit it out. How am I supposed to know if you won't tell me?'

He took hold of my hand.

'What did she do?'

At this stage I realised he really didn't know. I looked back into his eyes and began. I slowly told him everything, taking deep breaths as I went from one story to the next. Five minutes into the story a tear fell down the side of his face. He said nothing, he didn't ask questions like before, he just listened and when I got to the part where my legs were cut, he left the room. I saw the state he was in as he re-entered, he was so distressed. His eyes were blood red from crying, his hands shook as I watched him open a beer.

'Are you telling me the truth?' he asked.

'Of course I am, why would I lie?' I responded with my voice raised.

'I don't think you're lying darling, but I just can't believe what you're telling me.'

He held his head in his hands and wiped his eyes. 'I just can't believe it.'

'Yeah, it's pretty hard to believe,' I said, 'but it happened. I'll show you.'

I stood up and pulled down my trousers to show him the scars. Four large slashes at the top of my thigh which are still apparent to this day. He looked at my scars, looked up at me and looked back down. He gently stroked his fingers across them in disbelief. His tears slowly dropped to the floor. I'd never told anyone about the past and had no idea how difficult it would be. I cried uncontrollably as I realised how hurt he was.

'So you didn't know?' I asked him through the tears, my voice shaking.

'Of course I didn't.'

He stood up and held me close to his chest while we both cried.

'You do believe me, don't you?' he finally asked.

'Yeah,' I managed to answer.

'I had no idea, if only I was home more.'

'Doesn't matter,' I whispered. 'It wasn't your fault.'

He sighed. This was a woman he once loved; he couldn't believe she was even capable of doing such things.

'You must be tired, you need some rest,' he said. 'You can sleep in my bed tonight.'

I was exhausted, my eyes were sore and puffy from crying so much and my head felt heavy from the champagne, so I agreed and quietly went to bed. I fell asleep as soon as my head hit the pillow, while dad stayed up for hours, in his thoughts before coming to bed. I heard him come into the room and as he got into bed he literally hugged me so tightly I couldn't get comfortable and couldn't sleep, but it didn't matter. I'd finally got what I wanted from him for so long and was happy enough with that.

* * *

The following morning, we both slept until after midday. The evening was so intense we were obviously drained. It was Saturday, dad had taken the week off work to spend this time together. As usual I woke up first, absolutely starving, and as usual the kitchen was empty.

'I'm starving,' dad said about an hour later as he finally woke up.

'Morning, so am I.'

'Didn't you eat?' he asked.

'Nope, and just out of interest, what would I have eaten exactly?' I asked jokingly.

We both laughed together.

'Come on, get ready, we need to eat, and then we're gonna do some serious shopping.'

I jumped up to get ready, looking forward to the day. Whatever we did was always fun, even if it was just food shopping. When dad was in a good mood he was extremely funny and had me in stitches all day. We went to get a McDonald's for breakfast, or lunch considering the time it was, and went shopping after. I generally thought he meant food shopping because we had no food in the house and didn't realise his plan was to shop for me, but we went to Oxford Street and bought loads of new things – clothes, two coats, a pair of Kickers and a new pair of trainers. I had so much stuff I couldn't believe it. I felt so spoiled. We'd been shopping for new clothes a couple of times before, but never as much as this.

'New start,' dad said. 'New start, new you, we're gonna throw out all of your old stuff. We're gonna replace all that shit and we're gonna move forward.'

In the evening, we rented a couple of movies for the rest of the weekend and ordered a Chinese takeaway. We snuggled together on the sofa filling our faces with Chinese food while watching movies. Before bed, I folded up all my new clothes and put them in the spare drawer in dad's room. Previously all my clothes were stuffed in a black bag in the corner of the room, but these clothes were way too nice to be shoved in a bin liner. It was definitely challenging the two of us living out of a one-bedroom flat, but we managed to work with it. We learned to accept it for what it was and made do. We mucked in together and in all fairness, I was so happy with how things were going with us it didn't bother me one bit.

* * *

The weekend flew by and before we knew it, I was back to school and dad was back to work. I wished I could have stayed at home with dad forever, the thought of going back to school and seeing everyone after the fight was nerve-wracking. I imagined all the going around while I was off and prepared to be hated, but I had my new coat on and my new shoes and was ready to face whatever was to come. I was completely right. The fight had been the talk throughout the school, but not in a negative way. Apparently I had become a bit of a legend and was commended for standing up to someone who had given loads of people hell for ages. Girls thanked me for teaching her a lesson and told me stories of what she'd done to them, and within that week I'd become Miss Popular. I went from the awkward troubled girl to suddenly cool which actually made school life more easier. I remembered what dad said about the teachers and behaved much more respectfully towards them and paid more attention in class. I was still very behind, but because the teachers were more patient with me, I was slowly beginning to catch up.

I was now 15 and hit puberty. My periods started and the thought of talking to dad about it was horrifying and not even an option. I was so embarrassed about what was happening to me and my body and had no idea it was something natural for a woman. I didn't even think he'd know what it was. If it wasn't for my friends, I wouldn't have known what to do. I couldn't bring myself to ask dad for money to buy sanitary products so I'd either go without lunch or better still, steal them. My breasts were growing, and I needed bras, but again I was way too embarrassed to ask, so I had to steal them too. I was changing, and I didn't understand it myself, let alone be able to talk to a man about it. I had to just work it all out. I hid it all from him really well and avoided him like the plague when I was on my period, and wore baggy clothes to hide my breasts. I wasn't proud of the fact that I found shoplifting so easy, but I thought it was the only option. He wasn't short of cash at all and gave me good pocket money, but I felt bad to ask for anything from him.

On those time of the month days, I'd stay out after school at friends' houses or out and about until really late to avoid him, which began to cause tension between us. He gave me a time to be home but which never happened. He tried talking to me and I'd agree and promise to come home on time, but then it'd happen again. He tried punishing me which didn't work either. It caused a real strain on everything we'd built, and after everything we'd been through, he felt I was just taking the piss. The bond we'd worked so hard to build was slowly falling apart. I couldn't just tell the truth and the longer I'd left it, the more I couldn't say. I was in my own head again and after everything, I couldn't help but want my mum. I hated the idea of wanting her and was so upset with myself that I did, it drove me insane. I felt bad for dad that I wanted her instead of him after he'd done so much more for me than she'd ever done, so it was easier to just avoid the whole situation and hide away from it. It was a nightmare for him to deal with, but I didn't see it from his eyes. Sometimes I wouldn't even come home until the next day. Dad tried so hard to discipline me, but I was so blasé about things, I'd just walk out of the house and not come back. It got to the point for a while where he stopped saying anything to avoid the conflict and stop me from disappearing for days. I was spiralling out of control and he had no way of managing me. I knew by the way he looked at me he wasn't impressed and I looked at him the same. I had absolutely no idea of the disrespect I was showing him or that my behaviour was hurting him. I had no idea his silences were because he was on edge and didn't know how to handle me. He was unaware of the changes I was going through and that this whole disconnect stemmed from the innocence of puberty which felt like hell – it was a complete disaster. I wanted things to be how they were before, but I had no idea how to get back there. I wasn't his little princess anymore; I didn't know who I was, or who I was even becoming.

* * *

I sadly began bunking off school again. I'd tried really hard at school, but it was so much easier to save the embarrassment and just not bother. I couldn't face the teachers who'd tried so hard with me and been so patient. I was tired of pretending that I could catch up because I couldn't. One afternoon, to avoid a maths test, I left school to go shoplifting, only this time I wasn't as lucky as I'd always been. I happily filled my bag with all the things I needed but wouldn't ask for, and as I was leaving, two men grabbed me on each side of my arms.

'Security, come this way.'

They dragged me up to a room and emptied all the items from my bag. I sat in complete denial while they made a list of all the items and added up the cost.

'If it was just one item I'd let you off with a caution, but this, this is hundreds of pounds worth,' he said. 'Bloody shocking.'

I didn't answer.

'Well darling, I've got no choice. I'm going to have to call the police.'

After an hour or so the police came and escorted me to the station. They took my fingerprints and sat me down for questioning. When asked who my next of kin was, I panicked at dad finding out so I lied and said no one. They asked and asked but I stuck to my guns thinking I'd be able to hide it and they'd just let me go. But they didn't. They put me in a cell and told me I wouldn't be able to leave until I gave them an adult's name and number to contact. I stayed in that cell for hours thinking over and over about everything, and for some reason I thought about what I was doing and how it had ruined everything. I suddenly felt so sorry for dad. Once again, he had no idea where I was and would probably die if he knew I was sat in a police cell. I thought about how good he was with me when I told him my stories and how much he cried at hearing them. I thought about the times he'd go to every effort just to make me laugh, the times we'd sing songs in the car while he drove too fast to make it fun.

The cell stunk of piss, was filthy and really cold and in that moment, a tear dropped down the side of my face as I realised how much we'd destroyed our relationship. When an officer finally came to offer me some water, I gave in and gave him dad's number. My head dropped with embarrassment and the pain hit me so hard knowing I'd gone too far when I heard the words. 'Is that Mark Johnson? This is Croydon police station, we have your daughter here in custody.'

Within an hour I saw dad's figure at the front desk, and was totally ashamed. I realised the only way out of this mess was to come clean. I was going to tell him everything I was feeling and going on in my mind, and he'd understand like he always did. It was the only idea I could think of that could fix it. We walked to the car in silence, drove home in silence and although I had my plan, I couldn't bring myself to say anything. I could see he was so annoyed with me by the way he looked at me in the police station, so I decided I'd wait till we got home. He'd have a beer and a smoke, and I'll talk to him then.

When we got home, I sat uncomfortably on the sofa thinking about how to bring it up, but he went straight into the bedroom and shut the door. I went to peep my head round the door.

'Do you want a beer?' I nervously asked.

He was sat on the bed rolling a joint.

'What?' he replied.

'Do you want a beer?' I repeated.

'Are you fucking joking?'

Stunned at his reaction, and me being me, I went right into defence mode. I was so angry he'd dismissed my efforts. That was the first time he'd ever sworn at me it and it got my back up so much I couldn't help my response.

'No, I'm not fucking joking,' I repeated in the exact tone he had, but with a bit more attitude.

He jumped off the bed, stormed up to me and slapped me across my face.

'How dare you!' he shouted. 'Do you have any idea what you are doing? You haven't got a fucking clue, have you?'

I stood in shock, not believing what had just happened. The man who once promised nothing bad would ever happen to me again had just slapped me in the face. I stood still like stone, frozen, I couldn't move.

'Do you know how selfish you are?' he continued. 'Do you know how much stress you've been putting me through?'

I instantly burst into tears, I couldn't handle that pressure. I knew I'd been a nightmare but not to this extent. He hit me, were the words that repeated over and over in my head. My safety net gone, and it was all my fault. I left the room and tried to go to sleep, but I couldn't settle. We were supposed to be having one of our nice evenings with drinks and music. I was going to tell him everything and he was supposed to understand. We were supposed to be getting back on track, but now he'd done this. My trust that he'd understand and my trust in him in general disappeared with that one slap. I hated him, I hated everyone. I couldn't live here anymore was the only thought my brain could comprehend. I'd be better off on my own I thought, and eventually drifted off into a deep sleep.

* * *

The next day I went to school thinking of how I could live somewhere alone, somewhere where there was no one to hurt me and I could just be me. Mrs Fisher called me to her office to ask why I missed my maths test and with all the events of last night I completely broke down. I told her everything about the shoplifting and why I was doing it. I told her about my period starting and needing bras and how awkwardly ashamed I was about it. I told her how crap it was living out of a bin liner with no bedroom or privacy. I told her that dad slapped me and that I couldn't live there anymore. I was crying so much I didn't realise how much I was actually telling her. She was warm and endearing and knew the right questions to ask to keep me talking.

'I can't live there,' I cried. 'I need to go somewhere else, please help me,' I begged.

'Your father is a good man Nikki,' she said as she tried to console me. 'I've had numerous conversations with him about the circumstances you're both in and he's doing his best. It's not easy for either of you, but I know you can come through this. I'll talk to your dad,' she said with a smile on her face. 'You're a bright girl Nikki, we all believe in you, but you just need to believe in yourself. I'm going to call your father and we're going to sort this out, everything's going to be fine,' she said. 'Trust me.'

She picked up the phone and began dialling. I nearly died when I heard her speaking to dad, but she had this way about her, she was calm and controlled and made light of the story as if it wasn't as bad as it really was. She winked at me while she spoke which gave me comfort, and within a couple of hours dad was at school to pick me up.

My head hung down the minute I laid eyes on him.

'Come here,' he said.

I could see the guilt in his eyes as I looked up, but I couldn't go to him.

'Come here,' he said again as he pulled me close to him.

He wrapped his arms around me and gave me a huge hug. I sunk into his body and cried.

'I'm so sorry,' he said as he held me.

'I'm sorry too,' I replied.

I managed to get a glimpse of Mrs Fisher as she watched us with a sympathetic yet proud smile on her face.

'Can I have a word?' she asked dad once we let go of each other.

'Of course,' he replied.

'You sit here for a minute, Nikki,' she said. 'We won't be long. I just need a chat with your dad, OK?'

I nodded as I sat outside the room. When he eventually came out he smiled at me with a smile that told me everything was OK. He looked exhausted and I felt guilty that I'd caused him so much stress.

'Come on,' he said as he put his arm around me. 'Let's get you home.'

When we got home we sat down together and he apologised. I was just as sorry as he was, and deep down I knew it was probably more my fault than his. I felt awful but knew from the way we hugged each other earlier we'd be able to work it out. He got out a bottle from the fridge and I felt a massive sense of relief knowing we were about to sort this out.

'Nikki, I can't apologise enough for putting my hand on you. I know I shouldn't have done it.'

I knew he didn't want to hurt me, and smiled at him trying to put him at ease.

'I knew this wouldn't be easy,' he said, 'but I am trying. You know that, right?'

'Yeah.'

'I know you need more from me, but I've got to work to get us out of this situation to build a better home.'

I listened patiently as he spoke. It was nice to actually hear how he felt about things.

'This is all new to me. I know I'm not the perfect father – I'm trying to figure it all out – but you've got to talk to me. I need us to be in a place where we understand each other, we're gonna get nowhere if you keep things from me.'

I nodded as I took a sip and lit a cigarette.

'Why didn't you tell me you started your period?'

I clammed up with embarrassment.

'Don't know.'

He sighed. 'I'm not a monster, I'm your dad. I know you probably feel like you want your mother in these situations, but she's not here. It's just me and you.'

'I know,' I replied.

'How am I supposed to deal with what I don't know?'

I shrugged my shoulders.

'It's me and you darling, we ain't got no one else so we've gotta make this work. We can't fail, do you hear me?'

'Yeah.'

'I know I'm a man and you feel embarrassed, but trust me, there ain't nothing you're going through that I don't know about. I know women, don't forget,' he said with a slight chuckle and winked at me.

I giggled too.

'And one more thing,' he said quite humorously. 'I've had my run-ins with the police in my time and they ain't my favourite people.'

He was laughing as he spoke.

'When I got that phone call I was like, for fucks sake, I gotta go deal with these fuckers. I'd had a few drinks and I was kinda stoned too. It'd have been me they'd arrested if they knew the fucking state I was in.'

We both laughed. I loved dad when he was like this.

'I'm sorry,' I said.

'It's cool darling, we'll deal with this, me and you yeah?'

He topped up our drinks.

'And please promise me one more thing, whatever goes on between us, don't go telling the school. I don't want them people in our business. I want us to be able to handle our shit together, OK?'

'OK,' I replied.

'And don't make me have to go deal with no police again,' he laughed. 'Me and police ain't friends.'

He was right. We only had each other, and had to figure it out. That night we stayed up till all hours talking about everything and nothing. We'd totally forgotten about all the crap previously and went back to how we knew each other at our best; so tired and slightly tipsy by the time we decided to go to bed, we couldn't be bothered to pull the sofa bed out so we comfortably slept together in his room.

* * *

I went to school the next day completely exhausted, wondering how I would get through the day, but I was so happy dad and I were back on track. I sat in class daydreaming about me and dad versus the world, until I heard my name on the tannoy requesting me to go to Mrs Fisher's office. I slowly walked to her office thinking she wanted to talk about yesterday, but as I entered there was another woman sat behind the desk.

'Nothing to worry about Nikki,' she said. 'This is Janet. Janet is from the Children's Society and just wants to ask you a few questions.'

I sat down in anticipation and looked at Janet with the dirtiest look on my face.

'Hello Nikki, I'm just going to ask you some questions about your home life, OK? Just answer as honestly as you can, you're not in any trouble and I want you to know that I'm here to help you.'

'Help me with what?' I asked rudely, while she took out a notepad and a pen.

'So, how are things with you?' she asked.

'Fine.'

'Mrs Fisher tells me you were quite troubled yesterday. Do you want to tell me about that?'

'I'm fine.'

'Mrs Fisher tells me you live with your father, is that correct?'

'Yes.'

'And how would you describe your relationship with your father?'

'Fine.'

She scribbled on the notepad as I answered. I thought about the conversation with dad last night and believed dad and I could deal with anything on our own.

'Am I correct in saying you don't have your own bedroom?' she asked.

'Yeah, but it's only until we get a new place.'

'So where do you sleep?'

I knew exactly what she was trying to do, and it pissed me off.

'I sleep on the sofa bed,' I replied bluntly.

'Every day?'

'Yes.'

'Has there been any night you slept in your father's bed?'

I looked at Mrs Fisher. I had already told her I had, but I needed to protect dad and our relationship.

'Only a couple of times.'

'And why would you say you slept in your father's bed on those occasions?'

'Only if it gets too late to get the sofa bed out.'

'How do you feel when you spend the night with your father?'

'Fine,' I snapped.

'Do you and your father have a cuddle when you spend the night together?'

'No, we just sleep,' I replied in the same patronising tone she was using. 'We just sleep, and it's only been a couple of times when it's late.'

She continued writing in her book. I looked at Mrs Fisher for help. She knew how it was. Mrs Fisher gave me a nod as if to say it was OK, but I decided I'd had enough of this rubbish and wanted to end the conversation there and then. She had no idea about us, or anything for that matter, and would never understand what dad and I had.

'You can stop writing what you think you know in your stupid book. Me and my dad are fine, there's nothing wrong, and if you actually think something's going on you're sick. So just leave us alone.'

'It's OK, Nikki,' Mrs Fisher intervened.

'No it's not OK, she's trying to make out like something's wrong,' I screamed.

I knew she understood, she respected the position dad and I were in and admired him for his efforts with me. I even think she secretly fancied him. I wouldn't have blamed her if she did.

'These are just routine questions,' she said. 'We have no intention of upsetting you. You're doing really well Nikki. Janet is just doing her job.'

'Fuck her, her stupid job, and her stupid questions,' I screamed and stormed out of the room.

I ran to the cloakroom in tears, worried there was a possibility I could have said the wrong thing. What she was implying made me sick to the stomach. I sat in the cloakroom for a while wondering what to do, but all I wanted to do was get home to dad. I jumped over the school wall and rushed home as quick as I could, but by the time I got there it was too late. Janet was already there sat with dad on the sofa with her stupid notebook asking the same questions.

'I already told you everything was OK,' I snapped as I entered the room.

'It's alright Nikki.' Dad turned to me and said, 'Janet's done with her questions.'

He was just as angry as I was.

'She's leaving,' he said, as he stood up and ushered her to the door.

'We'll be in touch,' she said and stuck out her hand to shake his.

He looked down at her hand, ignored her gesture and opened the door for her to leave.

'What's gonna happen dad?' I asked as he came back to the front room.

'Nothing,' he replied. 'I've just got to get us a new place a bit quicker and get these fuckers off my back that's all. They don't like our living situation, but it's OK, I've explained everything.'

'What about our living situation?'

'They don't like the fact that you haven't got your own room and that you sleep in my bed sometimes.'

'So what? It doesn't matter, does it? You've told them how it is, haven't you?'

I was naive to what was really going on and how it looked to an outsider.

'Yes darling, I have but if I don't change it soon they'll want to take you away until I can sort it and I can't have that.'

He slumped back into the sofa and rubbed his face.

'I'm sorry dad.'

'No darling, you have no need to be sorry. It's not your fault. I told you, we're gonna deal with this shit. It's cool, we'll sort it.'

* * *

Since then we both made such an effort to respect each other and things with us were good again. I spent my free time trying to catch up with school work, or listen to music. Amusingly, I wasn't actually allowed to touch dad's records or the turntable, but I'd watched him do it so often, I knew exactly how to master it without him knowing and spent hours going through all his records. I never heard anything again from Janet and even if dad had heard from her he never told me. He was working more hours to save for a new place, so I spent a lot more time than usual alone. It was part of the plan for us to move so it made it a lot easier to deal with; as much as it was boring or lonely, I felt it was my contribution towards achieving our goals. The love/hate relationship I had with school remained the same – some days were good and some bad – but as far as I was concerned, as long as I turned up and tried what in my opinion was my best, I had done my bit. I sat at the back of maths class which was the norm for me; I sat at the back of most classes with the other bad girls messing around, gossiping, and getting up to no good. There was always something crazy to distract us, and this particular time we'd figured out that sniffing Tipp-Ex thinner gave us a buzz. We giggled while we poured drops of it on our ties and inhaled. We laughed at each other as our heads spun and we became more and more spaced out. I could hear my name being called by the teacher, but couldn't actually focus on where she even was which we all found hilarious. Within minutes she was hovering right over my desk shouting all odds, and that short fuse I had kicked in. I stood up.

'Get the fuck away from me!' I said, but she ignored me and continued shouting. 'You better step away from me!' I shouted as she came close to my face.

She was way too close for my liking, so close I could feel and smell her breath under my nose and I literally pushed her out of my face.

'I told you to get away from me!' I shouted as she stumbled backwards.

'You pushed me!' she said in shock, holding her face. 'You'll be in big trouble for this young lady. Get out of my class you animal.'

The whole class gasped as she said the words. Silence filled the room in anticipation. I heard the word 'animal' and wanted to kill her. I looked around the class, all eyes were on me; my fists clenched and my heart pounded so fast. I contemplated what would happen if I hit her and as much as I wanted to, I knew I would have gone way too far and restricted myself from punching her right in the face. Instead I picked up a chair and threw it at the wall as I left the room.

'You're gonna be in serious trouble and you're banned from my class,' she shouted out as I slammed the door.

I didn't care. In honesty, I was glad for the opportunity to leave. I sat in the cloakroom for hours. In my anger, in my confusion, not understanding anything, it seemed everything would be easier if I just disappeared for a while. I wondered what was going to happen to me as I got older and if one of those teachers was right. I'd end up working in Woolworths. The future terrified me and the way it was going, I wouldn't be able to achieve anything. I sat there in my thoughts, unable to move, school was over yet I still sat there, alone. Eventually, I felt the silence; everyone had gone but I was still sat there. I wandered around the corridors, not ready to go home. I wandered round looking in the empty classrooms where so much and nothing happened, until I reached the maths room that I'd got kicked out of earlier. I stood in the room where flashbacks of the afternoon's events came back to me

– the Tipp-Ex thinner, the laughter, the teacher calling me an animal. I looked at the blackboard which had instructions for today's homework on it. I ran to the board, grabbed the board rubber and rubbed it all off, my arms spread all over the board like windscreen wipers on a car. I then grabbed a piece of chalk and began writing. The sound of the chalk screeched as I wrote. It was like I was hypnotised, I didn't even think about it, the words just came out. *I hate my life, I hate everything, I hate school, I hate teachers, I hate my mum, I hate everyone, I want to die, somebody please kill me!* I stood back and admired what I'd written, took a deep breath, and found my way home.

The next day, while sat in geography at the back of the class as usual, paying absolutely no attention, I heard my name being called over the tannoy.

'What have you done now, Nikki Johnson?' the teacher said as I got up to leave.

'I dunno,' I replied and made my way to the headmistress's office.,

I knocked on the door as I arrived and was greeted by the headmistress Mrs Greystone.

'Nikki, come in dear.' Her face was stern. It always was, but she was trying to be nice by smiling which didn't suit her at all. 'Take a seat,' she said

Mrs Fisher was in the room and some other woman. I assumed it was a social worker again wanting to fish about me and dad.

'What now?' I said with attitude. 'Who's this and where's Janet?' I said.

'Janet's not here today, Nikki,' Mrs Fisher explained. 'This has nothing to do with Janet, it's a different matter altogether.'

'We're here to discuss an incident which took place yesterday evening,' Mrs Greystone interrupted. 'An incident with the blackboard in the maths room. Can you tell me about that Nikki?' she asked.

'No,' I replied.

She sighed, 'Nikki, we're here to help you, my dear, so why don't you just tell the truth? Tell us how you're feeling right now.'

'There's nothing to talk about.'

'We know it was you who wrote those things on the board,' Mrs Fisher said, 'and we just want to help. It's not a witch-hunt I promise, please just trust us. This is Mrs Brown, Mrs Brown is going to ask you some questions and run some tests with you.'

'Just some routine tests that will help us in our analysis,' Mrs Brown said. 'The comments you wrote on the board were very strong comments, Nikki. We just need to ask some questions, so we can get an understanding of where they came from.'

Mrs Brown was a child psychologist and was there to see if I actually had mental issues or if I was about to really kill myself. After a long list of questions which I felt I answered appropriately, she pulled out a number of visual cards and continued with the questioning.

'Which colour do you see first? How does this image make you feel? Can you write down the first word that comes to your mind? What do you see in this image first?' She watched intensely as she slowly placed each card in front of me and waited for my answers.

Once she finished with her cards she began asking about dad.

'I didn't mean what I wrote, I was just angry.'

'That's understandable, Nikki,' she replied. 'From what we know you've had a very troubled time, everything seems in hand, but I need to ask if you've ever had any real thoughts of ending your life before?'

'No,' I answered.

'What is it you look forward to on a daily basis?'

'Being with my dad,' I replied.

'Well that's good,' she replied. 'I'm sure your dad looks forward to spending time with you too. Would you like your dad to be proud of you?' she asked.

'Of course,' I replied.

'Well I think that would be a good start. Let's focus on making your dad proud,' she said. 'You're a bright girl, Nikki. I'm sure your dad is very proud of you. We'll just focus on one step at a time. I'll need to have a couple more sessions like today with you over the next month,' she said as she smiled at me, 'just to be sure we're making progress.'

I smiled back and nodded. 'What happens now?' I asked, still slightly worried there was more to it.

'That's it for now, Nikki,' Mrs Brown said. 'You're welcome to go back to class.'

Mrs Fisher jumped up and followed me out of the room.

'Can I have a word Nikki?' she called out as I was halfway down the corridor. 'I just want to check everything's OK,' she asked.

'Yeah, fine thanks.'

She smiled at me and stroked my arm. 'You're a beautiful girl Nikki, I know things have been really tough for you, but I want you to know you can achieve anything you want. But you need to stop treating school like it's a youth club and try to get the best out of it.'

'Yes miss,' I replied.

'Can you do one thing for me?' she asked.

'Yeah.'

'If you start taking school a bit more seriously I'll help you.'

'How?' I asked.

'It's not impossible for you to catch up, but it's going to be hard for you to get the results you would like in your GCSEs, so how about we focus on your creative side?'

I shrugged my shoulders.

'You're good at art, aren't you? And you're good at music, you're even good at English, you just don't put the work in. If you can show me that you can do well in these lessons I'll help you. I think you'll be great at modelling.'

'Modelling?' I repeated in surprise.

'Yes,' she said. 'You'll make a great model, you're a beautiful girl, and underneath everything I can see you're a determined little thing too.'

I looked into her eyes which were full of enthusiasm and wanted to see exactly what she saw.

'I've got a couple of contacts in the industry and can put you in front of the right people. I'm going to speak to your dad and see what he thinks about it, but I just want to let you know I'm on your side, OK?'

'Yes miss,' I replied.

'Now go back to class and do your best for me. I'll only help you if I can see you're doing your best,' she winked at me and gave me a smile.

'Yes miss,' I said as I happily went off to class.

I felt grateful for Mrs Fisher. I always thought she was being nice because she fancied dad, but realised she generally cared. I appreciated her and secretly wished dad fancied her too.

* * *

Dad was on nights that evening, but I wanted so badly to tell him about Mrs Fisher's idea about modelling. I got home, threw my stuff down on the floor and grabbed the phone to call him at work but he wasn't there.

'He left around two hours ago,' his colleague said.

I put down the phone and slumped on the sofa waiting for him to come home. Hours later when there was no sign of him I began to worry. Once it was past midnight with no sign of him or no phone call, I really began to worry and although I'd long gone to bed, I couldn't sleep. I was terrified something could have happened and panicked at the thought of losing him. I got out of bed and passed the room, crying, thinking the worst, that I'd be alone again. The thought hit me so hard in my stomach I began to vomit. I'd got myself into such a state and then I heard the door slam. I ran to the front door to see dad taking off his coat in the hallway.

'Dad!' I screamed. 'Where were you?'

He looked tired, but noticed the state I was in straight away.

'What's wrong, Nikki?' he asked. He cupped my face in his hand. 'Have you been crying?'

'Yes,' I sniffed.

'Why?'

'Because you didn't come home, and you weren't at work.'

'Sorry darling, I didn't mean to scare you.' He put his arm around me as we both walked to the front room. 'I'll never leave you Nikki, I've told you this.'

'I know, but I was still scared that something might have happened to you.'

'Nothing's going to happen to me, you need to stop thinking that. How did you know I wasn't at work?' he asked.

'Because I called. Did Mrs Fisher call you?' I asked.

'No.'

I stopped for a minute and realised something was bothering him.

'Is something wrong?' I asked. 'You look upset about something.'

'Truth is, darling, I won't be at work for a while,' he said as he opened a beer. 'My contract has ended, and they haven't renewed it.'

After he explained how contracting worked, I understood what it meant for us and our plans.

'Then can't you just get a new one somewhere else?'

'Yeah, I should do,' he replied. 'But it's not a good time to be without work. People aren't employing much these days.'

After he explained that we were in a recession and what it meant, it made sense, but dad was kind of a superhero in my eyes.

'You'll get another job?'

'Yes darling, I should do. What did Mrs Fisher want?' he asked. 'What have you been up to now?'

'Nothing.'

'You sure?'

I giggled. 'Yeah, I'm sure. Do you like Mrs Fisher?'

'Yeah, she's a good girl.'

'But do you *like* her?' I asked again.

'She's alright, she looks pretty good for a white woman, don't she?' he cheekily said as we both laughed. 'Go on,' he said. 'It's late, you've got school in the morning. Go and sleep in my bed, I'm gonna stay up for a bit.'

I kissed him on the cheek.

'Goodnight dad.'

'Goodnight darling.'

I climbed into bed feeling stupid for thinking the worst. I hated that my emotions were so up and down, but I couldn't help it. I figured out that I would try to think more positively about things, after all, dad was smart and was easily going to get a new job. Before falling asleep, I prayed he'd get a normal job so we could be together more and prayed he'd end up marrying Mrs Fisher.

* * *

The next few months were going great for me, but for dad they were testing times. I did the best I could in the lessons and kept my promise to Mrs Fisher. In return, she stuck to her word and had managed to get me on the books of a modelling agency who booked me quite a few jobs. Modelling was cool. I was nervous at first, but after the first shoot I knew what to expect and it became quite natural to me. Dad was really proud of what I was doing and because he was at home now, he was able to help me with my school work and make sure I was on top of it. I continued with my meetings with the child psychologist who in the end confirmed they were happy with me and my progress. However, the social were still on dad's case about getting a bigger place. This was a problem as dad's employment situation hadn't changed, he was struggling to secure a contract and we were living off the savings he had put aside for the new place. Months later it became really difficult and dad was now looking for permanent work which would have meant a lot less money, but even that was hard. The country was deep into recession which was challenging for all. The mortgage hadn't been paid for months and where the interest rates had gone up to 14%, it would prove almost impossible to catch up on the payments. There was an outstanding £15,000 he was supposed to fork out for maintenance which he hadn't paid either. He had tried to keep it away from me to not worry me, but it had got to the point where action was going to be taken. So he sat me down one evening and explained it all.

'If I can't come up with the money we'll be evicted,' he said.

I sat quietly listening to what he was saying.

'I've got 30 days to come up with the money or I'll have to declare myself bankrupt and we'll have to leave.'

'Are you joking?' I said.

I heard what he was saying, but my mind couldn't comprehend it. We didn't deserve this, we'd both been through so much, we needed a break.

He sighed. 'I don't know what we're gonna do. I can't afford to lose this place, but we might have to if something doesn't come up.'

My heart broke for him. He'd tried so hard to get work, but it was just not happening. I watched him remain so strong, even though he probably felt so defeated. We would lose our home and as much as he'd been keeping so calm about it, deep down he was devastated it had come to this. I wanted to help, but I couldn't think of how. I just had to pray he'd get a job in the next couple of weeks and come up with the money.

* * *

Two weeks passed and nothing changed. If anything, it got worse. Absolutely no one was employing, dad hadn't even had an interview in that time and every day was becoming closer to us becoming homeless. After school one evening I noticed he was a bit quieter than usual.

'Is everything alright?'

He was sitting on the sofa, no music, no cigarette, no spliff, no beer. This wasn't like him.

'Dad, you're worrying me, what's wrong?'

'I've got to show you something.'

He went into the bedroom, came back with a box and shoved it in my hands.

'Here,' he said, 'they're yours.'

I sat on the sofa and opened the box. I recognised the handwriting straight away, letters from mum. I looked back up at dad.

'I'm sorry darling,' he said. 'She started sending them a few months ago. With everything going on, I didn't want to upset you.'

'Have you read them?' I asked.

'No, you can read them now with me if you want or you can read them on your own, it's up to you.'

'I'll read them now,' I replied.

I felt nervous, not knowing what to expect, but I wanted dad with me for support. I slowly opened the first letter by date and began to read. The content angered me as I read the pages, complete fluff about what she's been up to in Amsterdam – she found a job, a new place by the lakes, a new boyfriend blah blah blah. Dad and I had gone through hell and back, and she had the audacity to write to me to tell me how great her life was going. I threw the letter over to dad to read while I opened the next. It explained how settled she was with the guy and that she won't be coming home, suggesting I'll be better off with dad permanently. She explained auntie Chloe had been looking after the flat while she'd been gone, and to ask her for the rest of my belongings. I ripped this letter up and went for the last one. The third one I guess was her apology. I'll always love you, you'll always be my baby girl, I'll never forget you and so on. I handed it to dad and watched him scan through it. I tried to hold back the tears, but I couldn't. I literally covered my face with my hands and burst into tears. That was it, I would never see her again; she was choosing this new life over me. I cried out so loud that dad came over to the sofa to console me. He held me in his arms while I wailed out abuse about her.

'I hate her dad,' I cried. 'How could she do this to me?'

My heart was literally broken. Although it was clear she left, I didn't expect this; I didn't know what to expect to be honest, but it wasn't this. I always thought she'd come back for me at some point, but this had made her feelings about me very clear, she really didn't want me.

'It's OK,' dad said as he held me while I cried. 'It's not your fault, it's hers. You've done nothing wrong.'

'I must have!' I shouted. 'How could she say she loves me, but abandon me like that?'

'I know,' dad said firmly. 'We can do this without her.'

I looked in his face wanting to feel better, but I didn't. I wanted him to take the pain away like he usually did. He was right, she'd done way too much to hurt me and if she didn't want me then I didn't want her either. I'd have to learn to live with that and forget about her very quickly. I decided she no longer existed and although the thought of that hurt quite deeply, I knew it was the only way I'd be able to accept it and move on.

* * *

I slept in quite late the next morning through exhaustion after the previous night. It was Saturday afternoon, dad was in the kitchen making breakfast, screaming because the frying pan was on fire while he attempted to fry bacon. This was typical dad at his best and I couldn't help but laugh.

'This is the best breakfast you're ever going to have in your life,' he laughed and continued to battle with the frying pan.

'You need to turn it down, dad,' I giggled.

'I've got this little girl,' he responded. 'Go sit your pretty little arse down and breakfast will be served shortly.'

I laughed to myself as I went to sit down in the front room and switched the radio on and in that moment I knew we'd be fine without mum. We now knew that this was it, things were going to be hard, but we'd get through it. Moments later he came in with our breakfast, burnt bacon sandwiches – smoked crispy bacon sandwiches he called them. Either way, I happily ate them, just for his efforts alone. We used to eat out for breakfast or lunch and usually got a takeaway in the evenings, but money was tight so we had to start cooking between the two of us. It was always quite eventful to say the least.

'Shall we go and get your stuff from the flat today?' dad asked while we ate.

I shrugged my shoulders. I didn't care about getting anything, and couldn't think of what was there. I'd been with dad for nearly two years and was nearly 16. In my head there was nothing I needed, but thought I might as well go have a look, and then I had a massive brain wave.

'Dad!' I screamed with my mouth full. 'We could live there.'

'Where?' he asked.

'The flat, I've got the key and it's two bedrooms. Mum said Chloe was looking after it in the letter didn't she?'

He slowly smiled and nodded his head. 'Good idea. Well done girl, that's not a bad idea, could be a good plan for the time being while I sort myself out.'

We got dressed and drove down, but when we got there my key didn't work so I rang Julia's bell. We embraced with a massive hug.

'How are you, sweetheart?' she asked.

'This is my dad,' I said proudly.

'Oh lovely,' she said as she shook his hand. 'Nice to meet you, your daughter's a lovely girl.'

'She is indeed,' he politely replied.

'How've you been my lovely, are you doing well?' she asked. 'You haven't been here for a long time.'

'I'm good, but my key doesn't work,' I explained.

'We may need to stay here for a short while,' dad continued.

'Oh, I see,' replied Julia. 'I don't think that'll be possible right now. Someone else lives there, I've never met them, but I do hear them.'

I looked at dad, devastated.

'Might be one of your mum's friends or something,' he said.

'Mum didn't have any friends,' I said.

Julia laughed. 'Well I don't know what to suggest,' she said. 'I can let you in this door, but that's about it.'

'That'd be a great help,' dad said. 'Thank you.'

'You're welcome,' she replied. 'Good luck and good luck with everything.'

She gave me another hug, shook dad's hand and left.

Dad and I tried the key and knocked with no luck. The locks had definitely been changed and no one was home. Disappointed, we both left and got in the car.

'Shall we go to Chloe's?' I said.

'That's exactly what I was thinking, but you know I don't like that woman and don't really wanna ask her for nothing.'

I understood his logic, but we had no choice.

'We have to. I have a right to the flat more than she does.'

He took a deep breath and started the car.

'Come on then, can't believe I'm doing this but fuck it,' he said. 'It's about me and you, not her.'

'Yep,' I replied as we drove over to her place.

* * *

Chloe didn't live too far from us. Luckily, I remembered exactly where it was from the train station. I hadn't seen Chloe since the day she took me to Mia's. We patiently waited as we knocked on the door.

'Oh my gosh!' she said as she opened the door. 'Nikki!' she called out, 'how are you? It's been like forever!'

She gave me a rough kind of hug and looked over at dad.

'Mark Johnson,' she smiled as she called his name. 'What a nice surprise, I haven't seen you in a long time. You look really well,' she said.

'Yes, so do you as always,' he replied.

'What can I do for you?' she asked as she stepped closer to him.

I looked her up and down and watched her body language. She looked drunk to me, which wouldn't have been a surprise.

'Can we come in?' I asked, slightly irritated she was giving dad more attention than me – borderline flirting, which was quite embarrassing.

'Oh, you wanna come in?' she asked.

'Would be nice,' dad replied.

'I wasn't expecting visitors, but yeah, come on in.'

Dad and I followed her into the front room and sat down. She offered dad a drink as she poured herself a glass of wine.

'I'm sorry Nikki, I don't have any coke or anything.'

'It's fine, I'll just have water thanks.'

Dad and I gave each other the look as she left the room to get the water. Without words we both knew what we were thinking.

'This'll be interesting,' I whispered while he laughed.

'So, how've you both been?' she asked as she returned.

'Fine,' I replied.

'Your mum told me you'd get on well with your dad.'

I nodded my head. 'Yep, it's cool.'

'And how are you getting on, Mark?'

'Yeah, it's been brilliant,' he replied. 'We've had our challenges, but I wouldn't have it any other way.'

'Oh, that's good,' she said. 'Well, you look well, but you always looked well didn't you Mark?' she smiled.

Watching her behaviour was sickening. I'd had enough of her pathetic attempts at flirting, and butted in.

'We need the keys for the flat.'

'What flat?'

'Come on, Chloe,' I said, irritated by her stupidity. 'The flat.'

'I can't give you the key, I'm looking after the place.'

'Yes I know that, but we need to stay there for a while.' Dad politely interrupted. He could tell I was irritated by her and my tone wasn't the most engaging. 'Look,' he said, 'I'm in a bit of a situation Chloe, you know. It's hard times right now with the recession and everything, I've been out of work for a while, so we just need somewhere to stay for a short while until I can sort something out. It's nothing long term.'

'I can't do that,' she replied.

'What do you mean, you can't do that?' I jumped in.

She scowled at me with a look that could have killed. 'Don't you question me, little girl,' she said.

'OK, I'm a little girl, whatever, but we need somewhere to stay so we need the key,' I said again quite sharply.

'Didn't I just tell you, I can't do that?'

We were both getting heated.

'What's the problem?'

'I rent it out, so you can't stay there.'

'Does mum know?' I asked. 'Because she never said anything about that. Actually she told me to ask you if I need anything, so now we need something you need to just give us the key and everything will be fine.'

'Don't you dare talk to me like that,' she shouted.

'Oh so now you're angry?' I shouted back. 'What the fuck have you got to be angry about? Me and dad are about to be homeless, do you understand that? Does mum know you're making money off that flat?'

'It's none of her business,' she shouted back.

I simply couldn't believe what was going on here. I had to calm myself down a bit and try a different approach, this wasn't working.

'Chloe,' I said calmly. 'Dad and I are getting kicked out in exactly two weeks. Can't you tell the people to leave and then you can get someone else after?'

'And why would I do that?' she snarled.

'Because I'm your niece,' I shouted out in complete shock at her reaction. 'You know, family, you owe me.'

'Fuck family,' she said. 'What the fuck have family ever done for me? I don't owe you anything,' she said. 'You don't know anything, you stupid girl. I don't know who you think you are.'

'Woooo,' dad stepped in. 'Take it easy, that's my daughter you're talking to.'

'I don't give a shit,' she said. 'You lot come to my fucking house asking me for shit, disrespecting me in my own home, you can both fuck off,' she said. 'Go on, get the fuck away from me.'

'We're not disrespecting you,' I said quite firmly. 'We just need you to help us, Chloe.'

'I told you to get the fuck out of here, didn't I?' she replied.

At this stage I realised it was obvious she wasn't going to help. I sat back in the chair and shook my head.

'Wow, you're just like her,' I said.

'What did you just say?' she snapped.

'You heard, but I'll happily repeat it for you just in case. You are just like her – selfish and ugly,' I said.

'I've had enough of you!' she shouted. She got up and grabbed my arm. 'Get the fuck out of here! Go on, run off with your little daddy.'

'Get off of me!' I screamed as I struggled to get her hands off me.

'Come on, Chloe,' I heard dad say. 'That's enough, let go of her.'

And just as dad got up to step in she slapped me across the face.

'You need to learn some respect, little girl,' she shouted.

I gasped as her hand struck my face. It all happened so quickly. Dad managed to get her away from me, but it was too late, the slap had already happened, and that was it, I saw red. My whole face heated up with rage, I ran over to her and slapped her five times over and five times harder across her face.

'How dare you touch me after everything!' I screamed. 'You think I'm a stupid little girl, well not anymore,' I shouted. 'Keep the fucking flat, let's see how far you get with that. We don't need your fucking help. I hope it makes you happy. Come on dad,' I snapped. 'She ain't helping us.'

I looked over at dad who was stood with a proud look on his face and he gave me a wink. He turned to Chloe, who was slumped on the sofa holding her face. He nodded his head at her.

'Chloe, it was a pleasure,' he said as we both left.

I cried with both frustration and anger as we walked towards the car. I couldn't believe she wouldn't help us for a start, and secondly, I couldn't believe she hit me, in front of dad. How the hell did she think that was OK?

'I can't believe it, dad. I can't believe she won't help,' I cried.

'You did good,' he replied as we got in the car. 'Don't cry over her darling, she's not worth it. Look at the state of her,' he laughed. 'She's a mess, she ain't gonna get nowhere in life, is she?'

Still upset, I managed to laugh too.

'Honestly Nikki, I'm really proud of you, you handled yourself really well.'

'Really?' I asked. I personally thought I'd gone too far.

'I thought I was gonna to have to step in, but you handled it. I don't condone violence as I've told you before, but when she slapped you, Nikki, believe me I wanted to kill her, but I'm a man and I can't hit a woman, so when you done her, trust me, I was kind of glad,' he laughed. 'She actually deserved that.'

'Do you think?' I asked feeling quite guilty about what I'd done.

'Yeah man, you just did what I couldn't do. I wouldn't live there now if she paid me. We'll sort something out.'

I was glad dad stood up for what I'd done. I actually felt a bit bad that I gave her so much attitude and of course hitting her, she was still my aunt. I gazed out of the window while we drove home trying to calm down, I was still so blown away and in shock by it all, I thought she would jump at the chance to help us. She was just as messed up as mum, I thought to myself. Dad was right, we didn't need her help or the flat for that matter. There were so many bad memories there it wouldn't have felt right anyway. I had no idea what we were going to do, but I knew we'd figure it out somehow.

* * *

I was still optimistic over the next two weeks that something would come up, but unfortunately nothing did. I felt for dad, he was trying his hardest to remain positive but the pressure he was under was so intense I could feel it. Regardless, he still tried his best to keep in good spirits. We'd been packing over that last few days to prepare for the move that Friday. At times I'd glance over and notice his expression and realised he was finding it tough. He was so ambitious, and such a proud man yet here we were, ready to flee from everything we were working towards. Money was never an issue for him previously, he was always a high earner, so this was a very difficult time. We were so busy that week, it flew by and before we knew it, it was time to go. That last evening we shared a drink together and chatted while we sat on the floor boxing up stuff in shoeboxes. Midway through the conversation he just stopped and called my name. I stopped what I was doing and looked into his eyes. He took my hand.

'Nikki, please, I want you to promise me one thing,' he said.

I nodded while I stroked his hand.

'I promise.'

'Please make sure when you're young, that you do good with your money. Make sure you do something with it, don't do what I did.'

His tears dropped as he spoke and I held his hands tighter nodding my head.

'I've spent money like crazy, I've brought cars, clothes, champagne, bullshit really, and now look at me, I've got nothing to show for it. Make sure you set up your future, 'cause money comes and goes darling, and nothing lasts forever, do you understand?'

I nodded my head and smiled at him. He was saying this while trying his best not to break down. It killed me to see him cry. I sat next to him and put my arm on his shoulder.

'Yes dad, I promise.'

'I mean it Nikki, 'cause this ain't no joke, look at us.'

I quickly nodded, trying to hold back my own tears.

'I know dad,' I sniffed. 'It's OK, I still love you and we'll be fine.'

He looked at me and stroked my hair.

'Of course darling, we're gonna get through this, as long as we have each other we'll be fine.'

We continued to pack up way into the early hours of the morning, both so exhausted I could have fallen asleep on the kitchen floor I was so tired. But my loyalty to dad kept me awake, there was no way I'd bail out on him, so we kept going. We wanted to be long gone before the actual eviction took place to avoid the drama and embarrassment, and planned to leave first thing. We managed to get a couple of hours sleep and were ready to go at 7am. We planned to stay with Grandma for a while until we figured out what was next. The flat was completely empty; it looked so different and lifeless when it was empty. We'd hired a removal van to take the records and bigger items into storage and we had a few black bags and a couple of suitcases in the car. We stood together in the front room looking around and at each other. It was sad to leave, to have to walk away from our home. So much had happened in that time, dad and I had been on such a roller coaster. Great times and really challenging times, but at the end of it all we were where we were that day which was unbreakable. The journey to get to this place was so eventful yet so rewarding, it felt such a shame to leave the place where it had all happened.

'Life moves on,' dad said. 'Nothing stays the same forever.' He took my hand. 'Come on little girl, let's go.'

I took one last look around and once we shut that door, that was it, the end of another era.

* * *

We were at Grandma's and tried to make the best of it. Grandma would have dinner ready for us in the evening, but it was nowhere near the same as when it was just dad and I alone. It was a completely different dynamic; most evenings after dinner we all just sat staring at the TV. I could tell dad wasn't himself and wasn't comfortable with the situation. Gran didn't allow smoking or drinking in the house, which annoyed him, plus he missed his music. It became obvious after a few days when I came home from school one evening to find he wasn't there. He called later to let me know he was staying with a friend and he'd be back at the weekend. He told me he couldn't deal with living with his mother as a grown man. I missed him intensely and wasn't overly comfortable myself at Gran's either, but I was grateful and definitely understood how he felt. A part of me felt incredibly uncomfortable with the fact that I was separated from him, but I knew it had to be that way for now. He called every night for a chat which I looked forward to every day.

Gran was OK, but we were never the closest, so most of the time I sat alone in the same room I'd stayed in years ago. Summer holidays arrived which made the days even longer and lonelier. Gran had me doing chores, cleaning the house, shopping, ironing, I hated it. She was a real traditional woman who believed a girl should learn these things in life to find and keep a man. The thought of my life revolving around finding a man and doing boring chores to keep him made me feel sick, but I guessed it was just her generation. I spent a lot of time during the days with my headphones on daydreaming, of how things will be in the future, dreaming of having everything I ever wanted and everything working out in the end. I spent a lot of time wondering why things had gone so bad for me in general and some nights I'd even cry myself to sleep at the thought that life could get in the way of achieving my dreams. As a 15-year-old girl, I'd experienced more bad things in life than good; I'd cried so much over time it felt easier to cry than being happy, but I knew no matter what happened, I had to find a way to achieve my dreams.

* * *

A few days later dad came over. I hadn't seen him in a while and was happy to see him, although he looked tired.

'Go get ready,' he said. 'We've got to go somewhere.'

I quickly changed and grabbed my coat.

'Where we going?' I asked.

'I'll explain in the car.'

As we drove he explained that he'd been trying to figure things out, but it wasn't easy while he still had no job.

'This is our last resort,' he explained. 'It's not the nicest of places, but it's the only option we've got right now.'

We arrived at the council.

'I've been here before,' I said as we walked in.

'Have you?'

'Yeah, with mum.'

'Oh I see, so you know how it works?'

'Yeah, mum made up this crazy story about us being homeless, she cried and everything.'

He laughed to himself. 'OK, well we're gonna have to do exactly the same thing.'

We took a ticket and sat in the waiting room. It was exactly like before, screaming kids everywhere, people with their life belongings in black bags, a man shouting at the woman at the main counter, people that really were desperate and homeless. And then there was dad and I who seemed to be the only visually conventional people in there. This whole ordeal was massively knocking his pride internally; this wasn't the place for us, but as he explained earlier, it was the only option we had. We both sat people-watching for what felt like forever before our number got called. Dad was miles away.

'Dad, it's our turn!' I said as I nudged him. 'Quick before they call the next number.'

We jumped up and went to the booth which flashed our number. The woman looked us both up and down as we took our seats.

'How can I help you both?' she asked.

I looked at dad, he looked at me, he looked behind him. He wasn't as comfortable as mum was in this situation.

'Have you got a private room?' he asked.

'I'm sorry,' the woman replied, 'you need to state if you want a private room on your arrival. You'll need to get another ticket and wait again if you want a private room. It's about a two-hour wait, as they're limited.'

Dad sighed. 'I need some help,' he said quietly.

'What kind of help?' she asked.

He shuffled in his seat. 'We've got nowhere to stay,' he whispered.

'Can you tell me how you have come to being homeless?' she asked.

She scribbled on her notepad while dad explained how he'd struggled to find work for almost a year and how we'd lost our home.

'Can I ask where the child's mother is?' she asked.

'She's not around.'

'What about any other family members?'

'Look, this isn't easy for me,' dad replied. 'I've been trying to do the right thing by my daughter since her mother left and it's been bloody hard. I can't leave her with anyone else, I'm not prepared to do that to her, she's got to be with me,' he said. 'It's not been easy and I really feel like I'm failing.'

His voice trembled as he spoke and his eyes welled up, he was a hero in my eyes.

'I've got to protect this little girl and I'm struggling,' he continued. 'I'm all she has and I need to give her a decent chance.'

He managed to hold his tears back, but to hear what he'd just said, with so much emotion, completely set me off and I cried my eyes out. He was always so strong, I never for one minute thought he was struggling as much as he was, and now it was clear to me how much I, and all this, meant to him. I even think our story broke the woman's heart. It would have been hard to have not.

'Bear with me one minute,' she said as she left her desk.

I looked through my bag for a tissue and blew my nose. I remembered the last time I was in this position with mum, how she played the woman so well with her story, but this was real and dad wasn't playing here. I'd never seen him like that and as much as it made me sad, it gave me comfort to know he'd do anything to keep us together.

The woman eventually came back.

'I've been trying really hard to find a solution for you both,' she said, 'but if you can understand sometimes it's not that easy. We see hundreds of homeless people a day needing our help. There's nothing I can do for you immediately, but if you can find yourselves somewhere to stay for the next couple of days, I'll have an option that will work for you.'

'Really?' dad asked.

'Yes, my love,' she said. 'You're a good man; you don't come across men like you every day,' she said with a smile on her face.

I watched closely as the woman continued talking to dad. I watched her body language, her facial expressions, her tone, it was clear she had a soft spot for him, and I wondered if she'd have done as much as she could if she didn't. But it made no difference really, it was just interesting to see how women behaved around him. He was like a magnet for women. I don't know what it was, but they were always so fascinated by him and having me made it even worse. He had quite a few female friends that admired him for being a single father and would help out by inviting us over for dinner or doing our washing; some of them even brought presents for me and always tried to get involved more to impress him, but he saw through them and never let any of them get close which I was thankful for.

* * *

After a few more days spent with Gran we were ready to move into our new place. It was temporary accommodation until the council could find us something permanent. I didn't care where or what it was, as long as dad and I were together again. It wasn't such a bad place, quite spacious, but really dated, and filthy. The kitchen and bathroom were old and filled with grime, there were damp patches on some of the walls, the carpets were worn down to the floorboards in some places, the whole place had an indescribably bad smell throughout and the curtains were old and stunk of smoke. Dad and I looked around as we arrived. He absolutely hated it but I saw the potential. I looked at dad's face as he wandered around the place.

'It's not that bad,' I said. 'We can clean it up, get some new curtains, get some plants to hide the walls. It'll be fine.'

Luckily, over the last couple of days he'd also secured a new job. It wasn't a contract but a full-time job which meant he'd accepted a salary much lower than usual. I spent the next few days cleaning and scrubbing the place while he went to work, and at the weekend we went shopping to buy some cheap furniture, plants, curtains and a couple of rugs. Within a week, we had the place looking and feeling like home.

* * *

We comfortably fell back into our familiar living style. I was back at school and dad worked so we were together in the evenings and spent our nights with candlelight to create a better atmosphere. It was my last year at school, and although I was feeling generally better overall, the pressure of upcoming exams killed me and we went through some really challenging times with a lot tears and tantrums. Sitting exams was tough, even though I felt I did the best I could possibly do, they were all too hard. I'd tried so hard to catch up over the last couple of years, but I had missed way too much and my school life was so sporadic it was impossible. I cried to dad each night of those exam weeks and told him how crap I'd done and how I felt like I'd failed; and every night he cuddled me and gave me pep talks.

'You know there's never an end,' he said one night.

'What do you mean by that?' I asked.

'You did your best, didn't you?'

'Yeah, kind of.'

'Well that's all you could have done. As long as you know in your heart you did your best then that's it, you're not at the end darling, there's never an end unless you say it's the end.'

'I don't get it,' I said.

'Are you gonna give up?'

'No,' I sniffed.

'Have you said it's the end?'

'No.'

'Well then, whatever happens you're going to keep on going, aren't you?'

I nodded.

'Good girl.'

It made sense. Everything dad said made sense. And I joked that his words sounded like music to my ears, like lyrics from songs that stayed in my mind forever. I felt better that he supported me no matter what the outcome would be, he always knew how to fix things and was so good at it. I peacefully sunk into his chest while we watched a movie together.

* * *

A few weeks later it was results' day and I woke up feeling so stressed. This was it, my future dependent on these results; my whole school life over with whatever these results would be to show for it. I felt sick.

'Just remember, it's never the end,' Dad shouted out as he left for work.

I believed him, but still couldn't get that sick feeling in my stomach to go away. I knew I hadn't done well, but prayed I would at least get a decent grade on the exams I actually managed to finish. School had been a roller coaster for me. There were times it was my escape and times it was total hell, and now it was over I felt sad, sad that I wasn't given a fair chance, sad because deep down I wanted to achieve and couldn't see how to do so. I walked through the corridor towards the board where the envelopes were pinned up. I stood back and waited a while and once there was a free moment, I searched for my name and grabbed the envelope. I stepped back with the envelope in my hand and watched as some of the other girls opened theirs. I looked at the smiles and faces while I clenched my envelope. I took a deep breath and ripped it open. I sighed to myself as I stared down at the piece of paper – I'd only passed one exam, a B in art and design, the others Ds, Es and Fs, and a couple of unclassifieds. I stuffed the paper in my pocket and rushed to leave.

I got home and got into bed, devastated, my chances destroyed. I had dreams of showing mum I didn't need her and showing dad I could become something. I wanted to show him that his efforts and hard work with me had paid off, and I'd make him proud. I was tired of feeling like a lost cause all the time. I beat myself up so much in my head and wondered how I could become better. I was the girl that attracted bad things, and although I was beginning to feel better about myself generally, this knocked me right back to my worst and I felt stupid and inadequate. Why I even expected different was beyond me. I believed good things didn't happen to girls like me. I was used to it and although I had dreamt of become something or someone different, I had to face reality that it wasn't me, it would never be me. I believed I was a burden on dad and believed he'd lost his home because of me. He'd made so many sacrifices for me I believed he'd probably be better off without me. Dad told me it was never the end, but it really did feel like the end, I even wished it was. If I was going to continue through life feeling like this then the end felt like a good option. I peeled myself out of bed and went to the bathroom to wash my face and as I looked in the mirror I stared at the reflection looking back – a pretty face with no emotion behind the eyes. I stared in the mirror for ages at the face, but I didn't see myself, and when I looked even closer I saw mum's face. Dad always said it was terrifying how much I looked like her and how much my mannerisms resembled hers and looking in the mirror that evening, seeing her reflection in me made my stomach turn. A slow tear rolled down my cheek as I stared deeper at the reflection. It scared me that I saw her face so clearly and felt if I was like her, I was definitely doomed. I didn't know what I was seeing, but it wasn't my face. It was like my mind was taken over by something, and in that mind I felt I was looking at something evil. Evil had always got the better of me and I wanted it to end. It was my lowest point, memories of everything that had happened in the past came flooding back where I couldn't see anything else, my brain so occupied with all the bad things that happened. And failing my exams was a result of it all. I was exhausted with the constant battle. I opened the cabinet cupboard and picked up a packet of paracetamol and began popping the pills out of the packet and swallowed them one by one. I swallowed each and every tablet, feeling that it would all be over. I continued looking in the mirror as I'd swallowed all the tablets looking for the change, waiting to close my eyes and peacefully drift away. But nothing happened. I waited, still fixated on the reflection but nothing. I reopened the cabinet searching for more tablets, but there was nothing apart from a few plasters and some cough medicine so I took that out and downed the whole bottle thinking that would do it. Moments later I felt sick, my stomach knotted and turned. I sat on the floor in a cold sweat, shaking, my stomach turning and although in severe pain, I was sublimely happy it was working, I began to vomit and it really did feel like I was dying, I tried to get up to get to the toilet rather than continue vomiting all over the floor, but when I got up I somehow lost my balance and fell back down. I couldn't move, I had the biggest stomach cramps ever, my head spun and my eyes were blurry. I lay there shivering in my own vomit, with my head on the floor hoping something would happen. I closed my eyes wishing they wouldn't open but they did, it hadn't worked. I laid still on the bathroom floor staring up at the ceiling, hoping any second now I'd fall into darkness. I stared up at the blue lampshade which was turning from blue to green to black in my haziness, hoping my eyes would eventually close, and moments later I heard dad's voice calling my name. I slowly moved my head in the direction of where he was.

'Nikki, what's happened?' I heard him say as he kneeled beside me. He pulled my head up off the floor, and looked into my eyes. 'You've been sick, have you eaten something, what did you eat?' he asked.

I couldn't answer, my body felt so weak, my head fell back as he tried to hold me upright.

'Nikki, talk to me, what's going on?' He looked around the room and noticed the medicine bottle and the paracetamol packet. 'Oh my god, Nikki!' he shouted. 'Have you taken these tablets? Answer me, did you take the tablets?'

I just about managed to nod my head.

'Oh my god, Nikki, why?'

He held my head up in his arms and quickly stuck his fingers down my throat which made me vomit again. He ran to the kitchen, got a glass and forced me to drink loads of water. He then ran to call an ambulance.

'Darling, what have you done?' he said as he held me up and forced me to drink more water. 'Why would you even think of doing this?'

I was numb, weak and still unable to talk. Why had I done it, I thought. I didn't want to be here but looking at the stress in dad's face made me feel guilty, sad and really selfish. If this had worked, he would have found me unconscious or even dead and wondered how could I have even thought of doing that to him. I felt terrible, even worse than before. I vomited again while dad held me over the toilet rubbing my back. My head continued to spin and before I knew it, there were a bunch of doctors hovering around me hooking my arm to a drip, shining a torch in my eyes, giving me injections. One was in the corner talking to dad. I just about made out the conversation and overheard that it wasn't serious or threatening, but they felt I should go to hospital for stomach pumping just in case. When it became clear to me that it was obvious I wasn't going to die, I wished I had so I wouldn't have to face the consequences or have to explain why I did it. The doctors lifted me on to the stretcher and escorted me to the ambulance. Dad was right by my side and held my hand as he walked with me.

'I'm sorry,' I managed to say. I couldn't stop crying. 'I'm so sorry,' I repeated over and over.

'Stop apologising,' dad replied. 'Let's just focus on getting you better.'

I was in the hospital for around four hours before being released. We got a cab back and I sat staring out of the window. I couldn't say anything. I didn't have any energy to talk and didn't want to either; I just felt really sad. Dad also remained quiet, knowing him he would have been trying to figure it all out in his head, plus we were both so exhausted. When we got back, I had a quick shower and got straight into bed. Dad sat by my bed and stroked my forehead. There were no words said but I could feel how sad he was. I closed my eyes while he continued to stroke my face and hair.

'I'm really sorry,' I said again.

'Don't mention it,' he replied. 'You need to sleep, just sleep darling.'

* * *

The next morning, I woke up feeling a lot better. I opened the curtains to let in the daylight and opened the window for fresh air. I couldn't help but think of how different things could have turned out last night. There was a chance I wouldn't be here looking out of this window, looking at the sky, watching and hearing the birds chirp as they flew from tree to tree or breathing the cool air into my lungs. I felt grateful for that moment and realised how stupid I'd been. I went to the kitchen to make something to eat and noticed dad was home. He was waiting for the kettle to boil.

'Morning,' I said as I entered.

'Morning darling,' he replied. 'How you feeling?'

'Fine,' I answered.

'Tea?'

'Yes please, haven't you got work?'

'Nope, I took the day off to hang out with you.'

He finished making our tea and we both went to the front room. He took a sip of his tea.

'What's going on?' he asked.

I looked down at my feet for ages, not knowing what to say. My thoughts and feelings were so strong and apparent last night, but now they felt invalid. I couldn't think of a way to explain it without sounding stupid.

'I don't know,' I replied.

'What's on your mind?' he asked.

'I don't know, I just felt like shit.'

'Why?'

I looked at his face and again in his eyes. I saw how concerned he was and realised he must have been so worried. I didn't want to talk about it, but he deserved something from me, he deserved to know I was OK and wasn't going to do it again.

'It just feels like everything goes wrong, like things never work out for me. I'm tired of everything being so hard.' I cried as I spoke. 'I tried so hard with my exams and I've got nothing, it's not even my fault, it's hers, all hers. I try to forget about her, but I can't. She's gonna affect me forever, I'm never gonna get anywhere and I'm never gonna be OK.'

'Of course you are,' he said.

'I'm not!' I shouted. 'I'm like her! I just felt like life would be better if I wasn't here, and if you didn't have to worry about me.'

'What are you talking about?' he replied. 'Come here,' he pulled me closer. 'First of all, you're nothing like your mother, do you understand? You're ten times a better woman than she is, do you hear me? And secondly, having you in my life has been the best thing that's ever happened to me. You give me a reason to breathe every single day.'

I blew my nose and wiped my eyes as I listened.

'Yes, you've had a difficult start, but that doesn't mean you've failed. You're a bright girl Nikki, so bright you don't even realise. You just haven't had the right chances yet.'

'I failed all my exams dad, all of them apart from one.'

I left the room to get the scrunched-up piece of paper and shoved it to him.

'See, look at this, it's shit.'

He looked closely at the paper for a while with no expression.

'OK,' he said, 'So we just need to focus on what's next.'

He put the paper down and lit a cigarette.

'Look darling,' he said. 'We gotta figure this out. I can't have you feeling like you did last night. Yes you failed most of your exams, but what does that mean? Does it mean you're done? No, you've got a long way to go. Does it mean you failed? OK, well yeah in this moment it feels like it. It doesn't mean it's the end does it? How many times have I told you it's not the end unless you say so?'

I sat quietly taking in everything he was saying.

'When you give up, then yes darling, it's all over, but that ain't you is it? So if you don't want to change this situation, you can go and work in a supermarket like that teacher said you would, or you can meet some guy, get married and have kids which wouldn't be hard for you to achieve, or you can fight this and try to achieve what you really want. What is it you want?'

'I want to make something of myself,' I answered.

'OK then, what are you gonna do about it?'

'I don't know,' I answered.

'Do you think there's nothing you can do, or is there something you can do?'

I shrugged my shoulders.

'Think about it, what can you do?'

I thought long and hard.

'I could do re-takes I guess, but that's embarrassing.'

'Embarrassing to who?'

'My friends.'

'Darling, your friends are not gonna help you with your life, your friends are not gonna put money in your pocket and pay your bills are they? So, what do you want to do?' he asked.

'I want to do well in life,' I responded.

'Well the only person who can make that happen darling is you.'

I began to feel slightly better. It now felt like there were options to turn it around.

'Right,' dad said. 'So we're gonna look into doing your re-takes yeah?'

'Yes,' I said.

'Good, now I want to hear what made you actually think you needed to take those tablets, and please don't say you don't know.'

I smiled to myself because that was exactly what I was going to say. It was my easy answer to everything. I took a deep breath.

'I just wanted it over,' I said.

'Oh Nikki,' he said. 'You've got to be strong darling. Life will throw things at you that are difficult, but you have to stay strong. Nothing lasts forever and nothing ever stays the same, whatever you're feeling at one time will always be different after a few days. You feel different today compared to how you felt yesterday don't you?'

'Yeah, I do actually.'

'Exactly, no feeling lasts forever, emotions change every day and the best feeling is when you conquer those dark moments and come out the other side. And as for your mother, wouldn't it be a good feeling to show her you did OK without her? To kill her with your success?'

I was listening to his words like my life depended on what he was saying, and I guess in truth it did. This was a huge turning point for me in life, this was the moment I began to see things differently, this was the moment I knew I could find strength in me to be better, the moment I became mentally stronger. The anger and insecurities I carried for so many years immediately turned into an aggressive determination; it was like there was a trigger switch in my brain that had just been turned on. Dad and I had some really deep conversations over the years, but this was the one that changed everything.

'Last night you were at your lowest point,' he said. 'Probably the lowest point you'll ever be at. There's nowhere to go now apart from up, and please don't forget, I need you.' He smiled. 'Remember, it's me and you.'

I looked up at him. I loved him so much I cried. He was my life. If it wasn't for him I don't know what would have happened to me. He was my protector, my strength, my rock, a diamond, and on this very day, in this very moment, he literally saved my life.

* * *

Dad was right, nothing stayed the same. A few months later we had moved into a new house. We were so lucky the council actually found us a three-bedroom Victorian house in a pretty decent area. I'd started college to do my re-takes, which was a complete fresh start. No one knew my history, teachers treated me like normal, the head teacher actually said it was very courageous of me to sit my re-takes and take them so seriously. I listened, took notes, did my homework on time. It was so refreshing to start over and do things properly. Dad was getting used to his 9–5 job and it was nice for the both of us to have the extra space and privacy we needed. Dad felt more comfortable entertaining at the weekends, and had friends over for drinks. These were some of the most interesting and fascinating times ever. I'd literally sit on the sofa pretending not to listen while a bunch of men sat together having a drink and a smoke, setting the world to rights. Half of the time they'd get so drunk there were no boundaries when it came to their conversations. I heard it all and was fascinated, fascinated to hear men's point of views, how men saw the world and especially how men saw, spoke about and treated women, which a lot of the time was the main point of discussion. I learned so much – the things women did they liked or hated, things they wanted them to do, things they argued about, the way they dressed and looked. It was priceless. Hearing them talk so openly was teaching me what kind of woman I'd like to be and what kind of woman I would definitely not want to be. There were certain points made that were discussed so graphically, I told myself I would never want a man to talk about me in that manner. It was amazing, and without even realising, the influence of those conversations were slowly moulding me. I began to dress better, keep my hair neater and kept my room tidier. I tried to be at my best at all times, not because I wanted to serve a man, but because I wanted to be the best woman I possibly could be.

* * *

We were having the best time ever, but things were actually quite tricky financially. His job paid half of what he was used to before, but the way the economy was, he was lucky to have that job. We pinched the pennies wherever we could to make it work. He found it tough but to me it was fine until I noticed some of the bills were not getting paid. The thought of him struggling to pay bills, or even having to worry about how to pay them pulled on my heart strings. I was 16 and decided I was ready to help. I was finally old enough to get a job. We were in this together and I was now able to do my bit to help and was quite excited. I was aware of the lifestyle he'd given up for me and always felt quite responsible, so when he came home I made him a nice dinner and brought him a cold beer.

'What's going on?' he asked as he sipped his beer. 'What you up to?'

He knew me so well it was scary.

'So,' I said as I took a deep breath. 'I decided I'm gonna get a job.'

'Oh really? What makes you want to do that?'

'I want to help us, and I saw the electricity bill.'

His face dropped. I knew I wasn't meant to have seen that bill, it was a final warning threatening to cut us off in 28 days. I knew he wanted to protect me by not telling me how skint he really was, but we were now shopping at lower budget supermarkets, we hadn't bought any new clothes or shoes or anything nice in months, it was obvious. He sighed and held his head in his hands.

'And I want nice clothes and make-up too,' I quickly said to lighten the mood.

He looked at me with that proud look in his eyes.

'We're in this together right?' I said.

He smiled. 'You're a good girl Nikki, but you don't have to get a job darling. You've got to concentrate on passing your exams.'

'It'll just be a Saturday job, and I can study in the evenings. I want to pay for my own clothes dad. I want to buy make-up and get my hair done, plus I want us to have nice dinners and drink champagne again. Please dad?'

He sighed and gave me that stern dad look which secretly made me laugh.

'I'll do well in my exams and if it gets in the way of my work I'll quit.'

He laughed at my enthusiasm. 'Well well well, look who's all grown up?' he said sarcastically. 'Well, since you're so enthusiastic about it, and as long as you promise your exams come first, it's fine.' He put his hand on my shoulder. 'You go girl, go get yourself a job. Saturdays only, OK?'

'Yes!' I screamed. I jumped up, hugged him and did a little dance. '*I'm gonna get a job,*' I sang, '*I'm gonna make us rich.*'

Somehow, in the middle of my crazy dance and song, I managed to trip myself up and fell to the floor. We both hysterically laughed so much we were in tears and our stomachs hurt.

* * *

As with everything in life, getting a job wasn't as easy as it seemed. I had no idea where to start or even what to do. The first thing I did was ask dad.

'Dad, how do I actually get a job?' I asked the next evening.

'If you want to get a job then go get a job.'

I looked at him blankly, disappointed even.

'What do you mean?'

'If you want a job then get one,' he repeated.

This wasn't helping me, I looked closely at his face to gauge his mood.

'But you're supposed to help me.'

'Yes darling, I am helping you.'

'No, you're not,' I said, slightly irritated.

'Yes sweetheart,' he said again, 'I am helping you. There are times you're gonna have to stand on your own two feet. I want you to start learning how to do things for yourself, you started this whole idea, so I want to see you follow it through. You can't come up with an idea and expect someone else to do it for you.'

I gave him a cheeky dirty look because he was right, again.

'You gotta give me something,' I said. 'I haven't got a clue where to even start.'

'Where do you want to work?' he asked.

'In a shop.'

'OK, what type of shop?'

'Any shop.'

'If you wanted to look up a phone number, or an address of a shop where would you look?'

I thought about it for a few seconds. 'Yellow Pages!' I excitedly replied.

'That's a start, isn't it?'

I rushed to the cupboard under the stairs where the Yellow Pages was and started to look through it. Addresses and phone numbers of every shop in London was listed in that book, I was bound to get a job.

'What now?' I asked.

'Pick up the phone and ask.'

'Phone who?'

'Phone them, innit?' he laughed.

'I can't phone them,' I giggled.

'Why not?'

'I don't know what to say.'

'Say what you want, you want a job, don't you?'

'Yeah.'

'Then ask for one.'

At this stage we were both in stitches, laughing at how simple he made it sound. The content of this conversation was so basic it was hysterical.

'Just pick up the phone, dial the number and ask if they have any jobs. The rest will come after,' he eventually said once we'd caught our breath.

I looked through the Yellow Pages and searched for a number. I picked up the phone and dialled the number. My heart was beating so fast. The phone connected, and I quickly slammed the phone down.

'What did you do that for?' he asked.

We were both laughing so much we could hardly breathe. I don't even know why it was so funny, but it was. The combination of being so scared, and it being so funny at the same time made the moment priceless.

'I got scared.'

'Scared of what?'

'I don't know,' I laughed.

'Scared of asking someone a question?'

'Yeah.'

'It's just a bloody question!'

I was almost on the floor with laughter.

'OK, I get it,' I managed to say. 'I'm gonna do it tomorrow. I can't look at you when I'm doing it, you're making me laugh too much.'

'I ain't doing nothing.'

'You are,' I jokingly shouted and we both fell into fits of laughter.

I loved moments like this, we had so much fun sometimes it was ridiculous.

The next day after college I sat on the floor with the Yellow Pages and began calling, and after a few weeks of hard work, I finally got myself a job. Unfortunately, it wasn't a glossy shop on the high street, I'd got myself a job at McDonald's and was so proud of myself, proud as I'd followed it through all by myself just like dad said. It was my first ever achievement and although it was just McDonald's, it gave me confidence that I could actually achieve something if I put my mind to it.

* * *

I absolutely loved working and the financial benefits it gave me. I hated it at first as they made me sweep the floor and empty bins. I wanted to walk out so many times but as usual, after talking to dad, he encouraged me not to give up. Of course, he was right as always. On my next shift, I looked at the guys on the till and drive-through taking it easy and having a laugh while I was out in the lobby cleaning up, emptying used trays and bins, and said to myself that this day would be the last day I would empty another bin. And that's exactly what happened. I found this crazy sense of competitive behaviour, which was a learned behaviour that carried on throughout my working life, a kind of determination that could almost be described as aggression when it came to work. But I had a focus, I was determined to get what I wanted and was going to try my damn hardest to do it.

* * *

I managed to get better GCSE results. I didn't exactly set the world on fire, but did a lot better than the previous year and was genuinely happy with my passes. I was learning that hard work and determination paid off and the feeling of achievement was like a drug to me. I was at a new college studying art and fashion. College was great, I was doing something I really enjoyed, I made a bunch of cool new friends, I brought myself nice clothes and shoes, I started taking driving lessons because dad told me I can't hang around waiting for buses for the rest of my life. I even got myself a mobile phone. I started having fun with the boys again. In truth, I'd always been quite popular with the boys but never took any of them seriously. Overall, I was happy, things were going pretty well. One afternoon, after spending my lunch hour in the record shop, I was frantically rushing to get back to college in time for my next class. It was coming up to dad's birthday and I wanted to buy him the latest Tribe Called Quest album. I grabbed the bag from the girl at the till and dashed to the shop across the road to quickly buy a card and some wrapping paper. I rushed out of the shop so fast I accidently bumped into a woman, almost knocking her over.

'Oh gosh I'm so sorry!' I said as I continued to dash off.

'Nikki, is that you?' I heard as I was halfway down the street. I stopped still, I recognised the voice straight away. I stood still for a few seconds, took a deep breath and slowly turned around. As I was turning, I thought to myself, it can't be, but when I finally saw the face it was. She stood staring at me with a huge smile on her face.

'Well aren't you going to say hello?' she said.

I stood frozen, looking at her, she wasn't supposed to be here.

'Well can't you say hello to your mum, I'm not that bad, am I?' she laughed.

'What are you doing here?' I said.

'I've been here a while,' she replied. 'I've been writing to you. I've been dying to see you, but you never responded.'

I stood still, staring at her, unable to answer.

'Didn't you get my letters?' she asked.

'Yeah,' I replied.

'So you knew I was coming back then?'

'No I didn't.'

'But you said you got my letters, I've been sending them monthly.'

'I don't live there anymore,' I quietly said.

'Oh I see,' she replied. 'Where do you live now?'

'Doesn't matter,' I replied.

'Are you still with your dad?'

'Yeah.'

'How is he?'

'Fine,' I snapped. 'Why are you here?' I asked again.

'I came back for you,' she answered.

'No you didn't,' I quickly responded.

'I did baby girl, I missed you so much. Look at you, you're beautiful.'

She came close to hug me but I stepped back.

'Oh come on,' she said. 'Don't be like that, you're still my baby girl.'

'No I'm not,' I said calmly. 'You left me, remember? I'm nearly 18, are you aware of that? I haven't seen you in four years.'

'Of course I'm aware,' she replied. 'Let's not do this here, let's go and get something to eat or a cup of tea.'

'I can't, I've got to go,' I replied as I began to walk away.

'Don't go, Nikki, you can't just walk away.'

'What like you did?' I shouted back.

'I'm sorry, can I call you?'

I wanted to walk away so badly, but I knew if I did I'd never see her again. I didn't even want to see her, but there was something in me that wanted to hear what she had to say, something in me telling me there was more for me to say, so many questions in my mind I could finally ask. I ripped a piece of paper out of one of my college books, wrote my mobile number on it and reluctantly handed it to her.

'Here's my number,' I said. 'Call me later, I've got to go.'

Her eyes lit up like she'd won the lottery. I rushed back to college feeling stressed and flustered. I couldn't concentrate for the rest of the afternoon, I had all sorts of thoughts about what just happened. I couldn't actually believe I just saw her, the woman I'd hated for so long and spent the last few years pretending didn't exist. I'd programmed myself to think I'd never see her again, yet there she was. I thought about dad and what he'd say about it. I had to leave college early and go home.

As soon as dad got home he could tell something wasn't right and continued to ask throughout the evening. He pulled me and sat me on his lap.

'What's happened, darling? You're not yourself this evening, is it a boy?' he asked.

'Gosh no!' I replied.

'Phew,' he laughed. 'Because we've had enough of those dramas.'

'I know,' I replied shaking my head.

'Then what is it, sweetheart?'

'I saw mum.'

'What?'

'I saw mum,' I repeated.

'Really?'

'Yeah.'

He was surprisingly calm, a lot calmer than I'd thought.

'Where?'

'Near my college.'

'OK,' he said, 'what happened?'

I got upset with myself as I told him what happened and how I felt about it.

'It's OK, darling,' he said. 'I knew this day would come, it had to come at some point.'

'Really, you knew she'd come back?' I asked.

'Of course,' he said. 'I know your mother, remember. She always had some stupid idea, but nothing ever lasts with that woman, she was bound to come back at some point.'

'So you're not upset?'

'Of course not. You're going to want to talk to her, you're a big woman now and you're gonna want answers. I'm glad it's now when you're much older.'

'I guess so,' I replied.

'If anything, you need to do this, I think it will do you good.' He wiped my eyes. 'No more tears, OK? You've cried way too much over her, it's us against the world remember?' he said with a wink.

That had become our statement of the century. We meant it so much before, but now we used it in a more comical manner and it always made us laugh whenever we said it.

'Yeah,' I replied with a smile on my face. 'You're right.'

He was my real-life superhero, and it made it clearer how crap she was. What I had with dad was worth a thousand times more than her herself, and now, as much as I felt quite nervous about speaking to her, I was ready for her stupid call and to hear what she had to say. That evening, as I thought, she called. The conversation was brief and I gave one word answers to her questions.

'I think it would probably be better if we met, don't you think?' she asked.

'I guess,' I replied.

'Yes baby girl, we should meet. It will be better for us, we can talk face to face.'

We agreed a time and a place for the following day and ended the call. I went downstairs to talk to dad and tell him how it went.

'It'll be interesting to hear what she's got to say for herself,' he said. 'I wanna know what she comes up with.'

* * *

I slowly sipped my cup of tea while I waited in the cafe where I'd arranged to meet her. I had rehearsed what I was going to say over and over all day to a point where it was embedded in my head. Like dad said last night, I was so looking forward to hearing what she'd have to say after all these years. I wanted to know if her reasons would justify what I went through, what dad and I went through. Half an hour passed, and I began to get irritated. I hated waiting for people at the best of times, but this was taking the piss. I checked my phone to see if she'd called or texted – nothing. I waited another half an hour before I accepted the fact that she wasn't coming. I couldn't even explain how disappointed and angry I was. I couldn't believe I allowed her to do this to me, again. I should have learned a long time ago never to expect anything from her. Her behaviour was typically predictable and deep down, I had a tiny feeling she wouldn't show. I paid for my tea and went home.

'How'd it go?' dad eagerly asked when he got home.

I shook my head. 'She didn't come.' I replied trying my best not to cry.

'I knew she'd bail,' he said as he cuddled me. 'God that woman will never change. Try not to get upset darling,' he said. 'You did the right thing by giving her a chance, it's her loss not yours.'

'I know,' I replied. 'I just wanted to speak to her.'

'I know you did, you gave her the opportunity and she hasn't taken it so that's on her.'

I nodded.

'You may never get the answers you want darling, but at least you gave her a chance. She'll have to live with the guilt, not you.'

I agreed with him, he was right as always, but I couldn't help but feel upset about it and for some reason I couldn't get her out of my mind. It was easy to forget about her whilst she was in another country, but now she was here it was much tougher.

* * *

About three weeks later I randomly received a text from her. I sat on my bed reading the text again and again – an apology for not showing, and begging for another chance. I wanted to delete the message, but I couldn't. I still wanted the answers dad said I may never get so I texted her back and rather than meet her in a public place, I arranged to go to her home. It was a small little flat she was renting short term as she wasn't sure where to settle. I looked around the place while she made a cup of tea.

'You've really grown up beautifully,' she said as she sat down.

I sipped my tea with no response.

'So how's things with your dad?'

'Yeah good,' I said.

'He's a good man, your dad.'

'I know,' I replied.

'He was always a good man.'

'Yep,' I nodded.

She didn't need to tell me about dad, I knew everything about him and it irritated me.

'He's done such a good job with you, but at the end of the day, you're my daughter. I'm back now so you can come and live with me.'

I nearly choked.

'Live with you? Why would I want to live with you? You left me!'

'I know baby girl, I was all over the place then, but I'm in a much better place now. I'm gonna get a job and I'll get a bigger place. It will be like before, me and you baby girl, we need to be together, we've been through so much, I need you with me Nikki.'

I felt so confused. I didn't trust her but her words sounded so sincere. All the questions I had disappeared and I was completely clouded by what she was saying. I didn't even realise I hadn't even asked why she left. I looked in her eyes and in that split second I saw the sweet woman who took me to the park when I was staying with Grandma. I knew there was some good in her somewhere, there had to be.

'What about dad?' I asked.

'You can see your dad whenever you want,' she said. 'He's a good-looking young man, I'm sure he could do without the responsibility to be honest.'

I'd never thought of it like that, but she was right, I was a burden on him. He liked to go out, have a drink and a smoke, have friends around, stay up late, have women over. If I lived with mum he could enjoy his life a bit more without having to worry about me, I thought, and he could see me at weekends or whenever we wanted. It actually sounded like a good idea.

'OK,' I said reluctantly.

It didn't feel 100 per cent right, but I wanted to believe it was the answer. If it worked out well it could be the best thing for all of us, so I was willing to give it a try, and if it didn't work I could always go back to dad.

* * *

I ordered a takeaway and waited for dad to get home so we could eat together and I could tell him everything. I felt I was doing something good for him by giving him some freedom back, and felt I was doing good by giving mum a second chance.

'You OK dad?' I asked as I dished out his food.

'Yes darling, I just had a shit day at work, and I've got a massive headache.'

He'd been complaining about headaches for quite a while now, sometimes they were so bad I'd find him sat in the dark.

'I've got something to tell you,' I said excitedly thinking the news would cheer him up.

'Go ahead, I'm intrigued.'

'I finally saw mum!'

He looked at me surprised. 'Really?'

'Yeah, I saw her this afternoon, I went to her house.'

'Oh,' he frowned. 'You didn't say anything.'

'I know,' I replied. 'It happened really quickly. I went to hear what she had to say.'

'And what did she have to say,' he asked.

'She wants me to go and live with her.'

'Oh, does she now?' he asked.

'Yeah, I think it's a good idea.'

'What makes you think that?'

'Well, if I go and live with her it will be better for everyone.'

'Better for who?'

'All of us,' I replied.

'I can't believe this,' he laughed. He stood up and walked towards the door. 'If you want to go and live with her, go, take your shit and go, and once you leave don't ever step foot in this house again.' He walked out and slammed the door.

I sat staring at the door with my mouth wide open. That was not the response I expected. My heart sank to my stomach, I had no idea why he'd said that and now I was so confused. My head couldn't deal with what he'd just said, but I didn't understand why he was so angry. I didn't want to hurt either of them, but making a decision like this would hurt one or the other. I went to bed without eating. With my head hurting so much, I couldn't sleep. I tossed and turned all night at the thought of rejecting one of them.

In the morning I had to speak to dad to clear the air. It had been ages since we'd had an awkward moment and I didn't like it. I made him a cup of tea and took it to his room.

'I couldn't sleep,' I said as I put the cup on the side table.

He sat up in the bed. 'Neither could I,' he replied.

'Are you angry that I saw mum?'

'No, I'm not angry at that. I told you, I always knew this was going to happen.'

'So why are you angry?'

'If I'm totally honest, I was disappointed.'

'Why?'

'Think back, Nikki, think back at what she did, think back at how you felt when she left.'

I sat on the edge of the bed and looked out the window as he spoke.

'Think back at everything we've been through to get you to the person you are now, think back to all the tears, the tantrums, when you went to the hospital, the late nights, all the hard work we've put in to get to where we are now, the sacrifices we've made for each other. And you wanna give that all up and go live with her?'

My eyes began to well up. He was speaking with so much passion in his voice, I could feel every word in my heart and I couldn't move my face away from the window. I was so embarrassed, I cried as I thought back to all those times we went through, and how much I loved him. I didn't see it like that and felt stupid to have to be told. After hearing his point of view, it made my idea sound pathetic and nowhere near valid. There was no question about it, I wasn't going anywhere.

'I'm so sorry, dad,' I cried as I crawled in the bed next to him.

He put his arms around me. 'It's OK darling, don't worry, I can see why you thought it would work out. She is your mother at the end of the day, you're always gonna feel like you need her at times. But you've got to remember, she's the type that will fuck things up over and over, she'll do it again and again darling. I'm sorry I snapped at you like that last night, I shouldn't have reacted like that.'

'It's OK,' I sniffed. 'I'm sorry too, I won't leave you,' I said.

'And I won't leave you,' he replied.

'Promise?' I asked.

'Promise,' he answered.

'Good, 'cause we're in this together remember?' I said sarcastically with a smile on my face knowing it would make him laugh.

'Oi, that's my saying!' he said and hit me over the head with a pillow.

'It's mine now,' I giggled as I hit him back.

He playfully got me in a headlock and bashed his pillow over my head while I screamed out laughing.

'Who's saying is it now, huh?

'OK OK OK!' I laughed. 'It's yours!'

'Good girl,' he jokingly replied and proudly sat back. 'How about this, how about it's *our* saying?'

'Yeah, I can deal with that,' I laughed and snuggled up next to him.

* * *

Everything was generally good. I was busy with work and college and doing all things a normal 17-year-old girl should be doing. Dad was working as usual and feeling less pressure financially since I was able to help out and pay for my own clothes and necessities. He had been in a relationship with a woman for a while, but kept it very separate to ours although we'd talk about it sometimes. He was generally in good spirits apart from the odd headache here and there. Some evenings he would sit on the floor between my legs and I'd massage his neck and temples.

'It's probably because you sit at a desk in front of a computer all day,' I said one evening.

Over time the headaches got worse and turned into neck aches and pain in his shoulders. He'd been to the doctors who said it was down to stress and muscle tension and suggested regular massage to relieve the pain, which he did, but he still struggled with it. We decided it could also be bad posture and brought a new sofa to give more back support which seemed to help, since I never heard him complain again. A couple of months later, he came home quite late one evening while I was up working at the table.

'Hi dad,' I said without looking up. He stood at the table staring at me. 'You OK?' I asked as I looked up.

'I need to talk to you,' he said quite sternly as he turned off the TV. 'Come and sit here.'

He walked towards the sofa and sat me on his lap.

'What's wrong?'

He looked tired, his eyes were red and his whole body language was drawn.

'I'm gonna have to leave you on your own for a while.'

I instantly panicked.

'Why?'

'I've got to go to hospital for a while.'

'What for?'

He sighed.

'What for dad?'

He hesitated for a while and then literally spat it out. 'I've got a tumour,' he said.

'What do you mean?'

'The headaches, the back pain, it's because I have a tumour,' he said.

'I don't even know what a tumour is dad, what is it?'

'It's a cancerous growth that's growing on my spine.'

'You've got cancer?' I screamed.

'Well yes, if you put it that way,' he replied.

I suddenly realised how serious this was, but I knew this wasn't about me it was about him.

'So what do you have to do?' I asked, trying to remain strong.

'It'll be OK,' he said. 'I'm going to go to the hospital for an operation and they'll cut it out.'

'OK, and will you be better then?'

'Yeah I should be.'

'OK,' I replied. 'When?'

'On Monday.'

'Monday, dad why didn't you tell me before?'

'I didn't want to worry you darling, you're doing so well. I didn't want to distract you from your work and I only found out last week. I did the tests ages ago and waited ages for the results.'

'Oh my god, dad.' I was devastated.

'Darling, it's not going to be long. I'll be out in a week or so. I'll just need some help with things when I come out while I recover, but other than that it's not as bad as it sounds.'

'Are you sure?' I asked.

'Course darling, let me go and get this mother fucker cut out of me and I'll be fine. I'll be home after a week and right as rain. You can handle a week can't you?'

'Of course I can,' I replied optimistically.

I wasn't convinced it was as easy as that at all, but I went along with it to keep the peace. I knew dad so well and could tell he was trying to play it down for my sake, and he could tell I was playing down my feelings for his sake. For the first time we were both being dishonest with each other but it was easier this way. I gave him a big hug.

'OK dad, you'll be fine, and I'll be fine,' I said.

'Yes, we will darling,' he replied as he hugged me back.

* * *

Monday came by so quickly and dad being dad, wanted no fuss and went to hospital alone. That evening I went to the hospital to see him after college. The operation was due the next morning, so he was on good form. I sat by his bed for hours while we chatted away.

'Are you scared?' I asked.

'Nah, I'll be out of it. Won't feel a thing and you shouldn't worry either.'

I left him that evening feeling fine, that it was all very simple. I'd see him the day after the operation and everything would be fine. Two days later after the surgery, I excitedly went to the hospital, but he wasn't on the ward he was in previously. It frustratingly took about eight nurses to finally let me know where he was which was the ICU unit. I followed the signs towards the unit and entered. It was hard to recognise anyone in the beds as I walked through due to all the tubes, wires and equipment attached to people. I hadn't seen anything like it, it was horrible. Some of the beds had curtains drawn so it took me a while to actually find him until I finally spotted Gran in the corner with dad's girlfriend deep in conversation. I walked over and said hello. They both stopped talking and acknowledged me, but something didn't seem right.

'How's dad?' I asked.

'Not too good,' dad's girlfriend Phoebe responded.

'What's happened?'

'There were some complications with the surgery, so he needs extra care for his recovery.'

Phoebe looked at Gran. 'Perhaps you should tell her,' she said.

Gran shook her head as if to say no you tell her. I looked at both of them, back and forth.

'What's happened?' I asked.

'Well, your dad didn't respond well to the surgery and we nearly lost him,' Phoebe explained. 'He's OK now, but he's really weak and needs a lot of support to recover.'

'What do you mean we nearly lost him?'

'They lost a pulse for a while, but he's doing really well now. He's a fighter, you know that don't you? He's gonna be fine, it's just going to take a bit longer than expected. Why don't you go over and see him? He can't talk right now because he needs support breathing, but I'm sure he'll be happy to see you.'

I looked at both of them, blank-faced, confused.

'Why didn't you tell me?' I directed my question at Gran who didn't actually respond. I looked at Phoebe as if to ask the same.

'It wasn't my place to say,' she responded with a sympathetic look.

I shook my head and slowly walked over towards the bed. Seeing dad in the state he was in was excruciatingly painful, he was literally a vegetable, tubes stuck all over his body, in his nose, his mouth, there were tubes everywhere. I stood over the bed and put my hand on his head.

'Hi dad.'

I was quite choked up but tried my best to remain composed. He nodded his head and gave me eye contact to say hi back. He looked so vulnerable it scared me to death. I wanted to ask if he was OK, but knew that was a stupid question so instead, not knowing what the hell to say, I just stood there. A nurse came over to take his blood pressure.

'Hi, are you Nikki?'

'Yes,' I quickly replied.

'Lovely to meet you,' she said as she fiddled around with him. 'Your dad's a very brave man.'

'Is he OK?' I asked.

'He had a close shave, but he's doing really well. He's responding really well to the medication and with time and some regular physio we'll have him back on track in no time,' she said as she smiled at me. 'Hi Mark,' she said to him as she continued to take his blood pressure.

'You were right, your daughter's a lovely girl. I bet you're happy to see her, aren't you?'

He nodded his head which made me feel instantly better.

'Is there anything you want to say to Nikki?' she asked.

He nodded.

'Let me get you a fresh piece of paper and you can let Nikki know what's on your mind.'

I stood staring at him, staring at the machines, staring at the tubes, feeling completely numb. The nurse went away and returned with a piece of paper and a pen and handed it to him. He struggled to hold the pen properly in his hand and after much effort he managed to write *are you OK?* and *don't worry*. I couldn't hold my emotions in any longer and burst into tears. As I looked in his eyes I noticed a tear falling down the side of his face which I wiped for him.

'I'm fine,' I said as I wiped away my own tears. 'I'll be fine, just get yourself better.'

He nodded and attempted to write on the piece of paper. *You should go now* he wrote *I'm tired*. I didn't want to leave him at all. If I had my way I would have sat there with him all night, but I was respectful of his wishes. I knew he was saying it for my own good. I had college in the morning and was in the middle of my exams, plus he needed all the rest he could get. I kissed him on the forehead and began to leave and as I left the room I saw Phoebe and Gran in the waiting room.

'How's he doing?' Gran asked.

'He's tired,' I said. 'So we should go home.'

'You should go home,' Gran replied. 'I'm going to stay.'

'Yeah, so will I,' said Phoebe.

I stopped for a minute and looked at them both. There was no acknowledgement for me or how I felt. Dad was my everything and they acted like I was completely irrelevant, no one even asked if I was OK. I stood for a second longer waiting for something from them, but when I received nothing I turned and went home.

The next evening I figured I'd go later to spend some alone time with him. I wasn't in the mood to see Gran, Phoebe or anyone else for that matter, I just wanted to be with dad alone. I didn't understand why no one understood how this was for me. When I finally arrived, I felt relieved to see that my plan had worked and he was alone. I hurried right over to his bed, excited to tell him about my exams and that I'd tidied the house. I wanted him to know how strong I'd been and that I was handling things, but when I got there he kept his head straight, his eyes were open but he didn't make eye contact, and I automatically felt a bit uncomfortable.

'Hi dad,' I said enthusiastically, still no eye contact. 'Are you OK?' I asked.

I saw that tear rolling down the side of his face again, but he still made no eye contact at all. I went outside to ask one of the nurses for a pen and paper so he could write something, and when I presented him with it, he slowly wrote *go home*. I couldn't breathe for a minute, he hadn't even looked at me.

'Dad it's me,' I said as I took his hand.

He pulled his hand away and wrote again on the paper *go home*. There was nothing I could do, he'd written it twice, it was no mistake, he didn't want me there. I felt like my whole world had crushed right under my feet. Everything I thought about our relationship had changed. Had I got it all wrong? I thought to myself. I stood looking at the piece of paper for ages, breathing heavier and heavier. I was heartbroken and so confused, there was still no eye contact, and when I realised I wasn't going to get it, I left, I was crushed. I'd felt a hell of a lot of hurt over the years, but this topped it by a mile. I didn't need him I thought, I didn't need anyone. I was working, I was nearly 18, I'd get my own place and I'd handle life by myself. When I got home, I noticed a message on the answer machine. I listened as the message played. It was Gran telling me not to go to the hospital because dad didn't want to see me.

'It's too late for that now,' I said out loud to myself as I deleted the message halfway through.

I decided I wouldn't talk to her or Phoebe ever again. As much as it hurt, I put my feelings aside and made a decision to focus on myself and college, so I could figure things out and make plans to support myself on my own.

* * *

The next day I went to my friend Sabrina's house after college. I'd met her at McDonald's and we'd become really good friends over time. She knew everything that was going on with dad and her family also knew the situation and felt quite sorry for me. I spent the following few evenings at her house; it was nice to be in a different environment where I didn't have to think about dad. Her mum and dad were lovely and most evenings I'd sit with them all for dinner. Sabrina didn't live too far away so most nights I got the train or bus home, and a couple of nights I was lucky enough to get a lift with her dad who went to a dominoes' club near my house. One evening I sat on the train on the way home from Sabrina's, reading a book. I was always quite into reading and hadn't read a good book in ages and since everything was so up in the air, I saw it as a great distraction. I had my face deep in my book when a guy sat next to me and asked what I was reading. I looked up at him, not even noticing he was even there. He had a cute smile on his face and the moment I looked up, his eyes caught mine and he winked at me.

'Well?' he asked, 'what are you reading?'

'*Flowers in the Attic*,' I replied.

'I've heard about that book,' he said. 'Got no idea what it's about though,' he laughed.

I managed a small smile.

'That's better,' he said. 'So now you can tell me what the book's about.'

'It's about a woman who locks her kids in the attic pretending they don't exist, so she can win over her dad's love and get written into his will.'

'Oh my god, that sounds intense.'

I laughed at his response.

'There's more to it than that.'

'I'm sure there is.'

He was cute, a little bit shabby, his outfit wasn't the best and his trainers looked quite old, but he had a nice face and I couldn't resist his smile. We began talking small talk and coincidentally, we both got off at the same stop. We walked around for ages talking, and in that time we learned we lived quite close to each other. I told him briefly about the situation with dad and that I was spending most of my time alone. We talked for so long we didn't realise the time, it was past midnight so he walked me home. We swapped numbers and arranged to meet the following day. From that moment we were inseparable. His name was Aiden, he was a bit of a street boy who had no job, but he was kind and sensitive and understood me. I'd messed around with so many guys previously but never trusted any of them and never took them seriously, but something was different with this one. Within days we'd fallen for each other so much we couldn't be apart. He lived with his mum, dad and little brother and they all adored me. I spent most of my time between his house and Sabrina's, which was nice. I hadn't heard anything from Gran or anyone about dad and, in my mind, I was better off without them. Both Sabrina and Aiden's parents accepted me and treated me as their own and I was equally comfortable in both environments.

One Sunday afternoon, I left Aiden's to go to Sabrina's for Sunday dinner. We spent the afternoon doing her hair and gossiping about boys and the relationships we were both in and later in the evening we all sat down together, had a lovely dinner and watched a movie. After the movie we played a game of monopoly. I never actually liked the game but it was just fun playing together as a family. The evening was so much fun all round, I had no concept of the time. Aiden called a few times to see how I was and was happy to hear I was fine and we agreed I'd stay home that night rather than at his. At the end of the evening Sabrina's dad offered to take me home. I happily gathered my stuff and said my goodbyes as we left. We chatted on the way, and as we arrived outside the house we carried on talking for a while.

'So how's your dad doing?' he asked.

'Fine,' I replied. I didn't want him to know I didn't actually know.

'It must be really hard on you, such a beautiful young girl all alone.'

'I'm not alone,' I replied. 'I've got a boyfriend.'

'Oh, have you?' he said. 'How old is your boyfriend?'

‘Eighteen.’

‘Oh he’s a boy, he can’t do nothing for you, you don’t need a boy you need a man,’ he said.

‘He’s fine,’ I replied.

It was weird talking about this with my friend’s dad and found it quite uncomfortable. It was friendly but borderline inappropriate, so I attempted to wrap it up and get out.

‘Well, thanks for the lift,’ I said.

I went to open the door and he grabbed my arm.

‘There’s no need to leave just yet,’ he said quite sternly. ‘We’re talking, aren’t we?’

‘Yes,’ I said uncomfortably.

‘Well let’s talk.’

I sat clenched up, not really knowing what to do. My instinct was telling me to get out, but my mind was telling me to be polite and carry on. I didn’t want to offend him so I sat still and continued.

‘So what does this boyfriend of yours do for you?’ he asked.

‘I don’t know, he’s just really nice. Anyway, I’ve got to go now,’ I said. ‘Thank you again for the lift.’

At this point I really was uncomfortable with the way the conversation was going and just as I attempted to leave again, he grabbed me. I struggled as he tried to touch me. I could feel his hands all over my body and when I tried to scream he held his hand over my mouth.

‘You know you want this,’ he said, while his lips slobbered all over my face. ‘If you can fuck around with that young boy, you need to learn how to fuck with a real man that knows how to give it to you good.’

I struggled as one of his hands held my mouth shut and the other began opening his trousers. I knew exactly what he was planning, but I knew I couldn’t let it happen, I just couldn’t. My brain was working a hundred miles an hour to figure a way out as I watched his manhood appear from his trousers and his body come closer. I felt him yanking at my belt and for one second I almost felt defeated, like giving up and letting it happen. He was a lot stronger than me and I felt stuck, but something inside me said no, I was not going to let this happen. It was all a blur, but somehow I managed to find some strength out of nowhere and got free from him. I kneed him in his crotch and slapped him round the face.

'You fucking bastard!' I screamed as I jumped out the car, my top half way over my head, my chest exposed, my trousers undone.

I ran to my front garden, picked up the dustbin and threw it at the car.

'You messed with the wrong fucking one this time!' I shouted.

I was hysterically shaking, I picked the bin up again and smashed it multiple times on the car the front window shattered.

'You think I'm some stupid little girl?' I screamed. 'You have no fucking idea!'

I wanted to kill him, and that short fuse I used to have when I was younger came right back.

'Come on then, you fucking arsehole, come and get me now!' I screamed. 'Come on, what's stopping you?'

A neighbour came out to see what all the noise was about.

'Are you alright love?' she shouted over. 'Do you want me to call the police?'

The moment he saw the neighbour come out he sped off.

'It's fine!' I shouted back as I threw the bin to the floor and went inside.

I paced up and down the corridor thinking of what to do. I had so much adrenaline in me I didn't know what to do with myself. It was late, I was upset, I was angry, I was hurt, confused, my head spun round and round thinking what I could have possibly done to allow him to think he could put his hands on me in that way. I wanted my own dad so badly but had to remind myself very quickly that he didn't want me.

Eventually the adrenaline wore off and I slumped myself on the stairs and sat there staring into space. I held my knees to my chest and rocked from side to side wondering what to do. I contemplated calling the police, but because he was my best friend's dad, it felt too complicated, and even though what he done was a huge disrespect, he didn't succeed with his plans so I decided against it. The easiest option for me would be to sit there and cry or cry myself to bed and god knows I really wanted to, but this time I knew I was going to have to handle things on my own from now on. I had to learn how to deal with things rather than cry. I picked up the phone, called Aiden and told him everything. His first reaction was to go straight over there, but after much persuasion he agreed to come to mine in a cab. Once he arrived we sat in my room while I told him the story in more detail. We sat up for hours sharing our stories, our pasts and our dreams, and as much as I felt like shit that evening, I was so glad I had Aiden. I wouldn't have known what I'd have done if it wasn't for him. When it got really late, he put me to bed, wrapped himself around me and cuddled me until eventually we both fell asleep.

* * *

I avoided Sabrina the next day and went over to Aiden's after college to spend the evening with him and his family. I told his mum and dad over dinner what happened and as much as they were both disgusted by the story, they insisted I stay with them for a few days rather than staying home alone.

'Go and get your stuff and come and stay with us,' his mum said. 'You shouldn't be on your own, we'll be happy to have you.'

I happily welcomed the offer and went home that evening to collect a few things. The home dad and I lived in that was once such a happy house, felt cold and empty. There was no food in the fridge, the heating hadn't been on in ages, so it was cold, and it felt completely lifeless. Once I filled my bag with a few things, I took a wander round the house and soaked in the memories. I wandered over to dad's room and stood looking at the bed remembering times we'd spent cuddling or play-fighting. I looked inside his wardrobe, held his clothes to my face and breathed in. His scent was so strong it brought visions of his face to my mind. I missed him so much, but each time I thought about him, I had to think of that piece of paper with the words *go home* written on it to bring me back to reality. I looked at the bottom of the wardrobe and spotted a box I'd never seen before and before I could even think of what it was, I was on my knees going through it. There were old bills, his passport, old birthday cards, photos, and just loads of bits and pieces. I looked through the photos and came across a few of him and Phoebe on holiday. I'd only known about Phoebe quite recently, but these photos said 1992 on the back, and when I thought back to that time, it was when we were homeless, and I stayed at Gran's. He'd been with her and kept it a secret all this time. I felt a massive lump in my throat. I thought we told each other everything. The fact that he had this secret changed it all. I didn't even think it was possible for him to keep something like that from me. I flashed back to around that time, the times I was so bored at Gran's, and he was running around having an amazing time on holiday with her. The disappointment in what we were, what I thought we were was the biggest to date. I continued to rummage through the box further and came across a birthday card from her. I read the words inside *Happy birthday my darling, I love you so much and can't wait for the day we can be together properly.* I read the words over and over, *can't wait for the day we can be together properly*. I realised I was a hinder to their relationship, the reason they couldn't be 'properly' together. I felt like a fool, I believed for so long dad was my hero and did everything for our benefit, but I wasn't his main priority like I believed. I didn't mind that he had a girlfriend at all, but it was the lie that he'd kept for so long that broke me and confirmed I was doing the right thing by moving on. I put everything back in the box, closed the wardrobe, grabbed my stuff and confidently walked straight out the house.

* * *

I stayed at Aiden's for a lot longer than a few days, and the longer I stayed, the more we all bonded. Aiden and I were as loved-up as ever and his mum and I had grown very close. We talked for hours every day, we cooked together, went shopping together, she told me how nice it was to have a girl in the house and having me around was like having the daughter she never had. His dad was a cabbie and worked long hours, so he was happy she had me as company. Apparently, before I came along Aiden was never in the house and his little brother sat in his room most of the time, and now we were all hanging out together, eating together, watching movies, just spending time with each other, it was nice. I only needed to go home every now and then to get more stuff and it had gotten to the point that being at Aiden's felt like such a better option.

I went home one afternoon to pick up a few more things, and surprisingly heard the TV upstairs coming from dad's room. I crept upstairs and opened the door to his room, he was lying in bed watching TV.

'Hi dad,' I said.

'Hi,' he slowly replied.

'How are you, are you OK?'

'A bit tired, but OK.'

I was really happy to see he was better and home, but I couldn't get out of my head how I felt about everything else. I thought about the fact that I was alone for so long and no one even bothered to check in on me. He was unaware of everything that had happened while he was in hospital, including the drama with Sabrina's dad. I wanted to sit and chat with him, but my heart wasn't feeling right.

'I've been home for days,' he said with quite an angry tone. 'Where've you been?'

'I was at my friend's house.'

'What friend?'

'Just my friend from work.'

I wasn't ready to tell him about Aiden, it wasn't the right time. It was such an icy conversation considering we were usually so close, but I couldn't bring myself to say more.

'OK,' he said and turned to go to sleep.

I stood watching him for a minute while he literally ignored me.

'OK, I'll leave you to get some rest,' I finally said as I hovered in the doorway, hoping he would say something, but he didn't. 'See you later then,' I said, still feeling slightly awkward.

'OK,' he replied.

It was such an uncomfortable conversation you would have thought we were strangers. Even though things at Aiden's were great, I didn't feel right about this at all. I still wanted to know how he was, but I guessed it would be best to find out later once everything had settled and decided the best thing to do was keep my distance until we were in better moods, so I left.

In the meantime, I had been ignoring Sabrina's calls for days and figured I couldn't avoid her forever, and arranged to meet her. We met at her house and went round the corner to sit on the wall while I told her what happened. I looked in her face for some kind of sympathy, an apology, something, but instead she completely turned.

'No,' she said. 'You're lying.'

'Why would I lie, Sabrina?'

When thinking about it, I could understand why she didn't want to believe it.

'No,' she said. 'No way, you must have provoked him, or you must have tried it on with him, my dad wouldn't do something like that.'

I thought about if it was the other way around and quite frankly, I'd probably do the same, but I wanted her to know the truth about her dad, even if it wasn't for my benefit but for hers.

'I'm not saying this to cause trouble,' I said. 'It's the truth.'

'You're lying, Nikki,' she repeated, 'and I don't even know why. I'm sorry you don't have a family and your dad's sick, but that's not my fault.'

I looked at her in disbelief, regardless of what I was saying, she knew how I felt about dad, but I understood she was trying to hurt me, and at this stage I knew there was no point in carrying on the conversation. She was never going to believe me over her dad.

'Well, I didn't mean to upset you,' I said. 'I just wanted you to know. I understand if you don't believe me, but I wouldn't be saying this for no reason would I? My brain doesn't work like that Sabrina.'

She looked to the floor and shrugged her shoulders.

'You finished?' she asked.

'Yeah, I'm finished.'

She jumped down from the wall and walked away. I sat on that wall for a short while thinking about the conversation. I'd lost a good friend just like that and wasn't even sad about it. I wasn't sure if I was becoming emotionless or immune to loss, either way, I wasn't bothered. I knew the truth and that was all that mattered to me. I jumped down from the wall, went home to Aiden and told him all about it.

* * *

A few days later after a lovely Sunday dinner with Aiden and the family, I couldn't keep myself from thinking about dad. I felt guilty that I was so close to this family, yet I had my own dad that I hadn't seen for ages. We couldn't not speak forever I thought, this couldn't be the end of us, after everything we'd been through. I decided to go home and confront the situation. I was nervous at the thought of it, but knew I had nothing to lose. As I got there, I went upstairs and heard voices in his bedroom. I knocked on the door and popped my head round. Both Phoebe and Gran were sat on his bed. I said hi to everyone, Gran kind of grunted some sort of word and looked away, Phoebe said hi with no enthusiasm and dad completely ignored me. I couldn't understand why they were all so distant. I slammed the door shut and went to my room to gather up more things and leave. As I was packing, Phoebe came in to the room with Gran behind her.

'What's wrong with you?' she asked.

'What do you mean?' I replied with attitude and carried on stuffing my bag.

'Don't you know your dad's sick?' she shouted. 'Where have you been all this time? How can you just leave your dad like that, after everything he's done for you?'

She was shouting at the top of her voice, I couldn't get a word in. I'd hardly even spoken to Phoebe and here she was in my room shouting at me. I didn't realise he was still sick and her shouting at me the way she was got me so angry. Emotions were running so high for the both of us we ended up having a massive argument, but she didn't listen to one word I was saying when I tried to explain. She just went on and on.

'That's no excuse,' she shouted.

I tried to explain that it was his decision, that he didn't want to see me and how upsetting that was.

'No, I'm not buying that,' she shouted. 'Your dad's bedridden, Nikki, and all you can think about is yourself. You've done nothing to help, you should be ashamed.'

'I thought he was better!' I shouted back. 'No one's even bothered to speak to me or tell me anything.'

We were back and forth shouting our views louder and louder, getting absolutely nowhere. In my mind this was the last straw. I was so angry with her I literally could have hit her to shut her up and get her to listen, but it was useless, her mind was made up and she wasn't having any of it.

'Gran, tell her to leave me alone!' I screamed. 'It's none of her business.'

'She's right,' Gran replied. 'You should be ashamed of yourself, I told you not to go to the hospital and you went against my word,' she said. 'I told you not to go, didn't I?'

'No, you didn't, none of you have even spoken to me.'

'I left you a message.'

I sighed and remembered the voicemail I deleted half way through.

'I deleted that, and for the records, leaving a message isn't talking is it?'

'I knew you would let your dad down,' she said. 'I always told him you're a troubled girl and you'll let him down eventually, and now look at you.'

I can't explain the anger I felt as I looked at her, but knew I was getting nowhere with either of them. I honestly thought because he was home, he was better. I had no idea he was bedridden. If I had known, of course I would have helped, but no one said anything.

'Well you won't have to worry about me ever again,' I shouted. 'Get out of my room!'

They both looked at each other with disappointed looks on their faces.

'Are you going to apologise?' Phoebe asked.

'No I'm not,' I said. 'I'm leaving so you can have him all to yourself, just like you wanted, and none of you will have to worry about me ever again.'

I gathered the rest of my clothes and stormed out of the house. That was it, I said to myself, I was done with them all, I was never going back and from that moment on, I was on my own.

* * *

That night was the night I officially left home. I was nearly 18 and felt ready to face this on my own. I had Aiden, I'd get a better job and we'd save for our own place. I had it all worked out and luckily Aiden's parents were happy to have me on a more permanent basis and willing to support us until we worked things out. I left McDonald's and got a better job in a clothes' shop. I only had a few months left of college and had already secured a full-time position for when I finished my exams. Aiden and I were good and looking forward to working towards the plan. He wasn't as well put together as me and struggled to get a job, but he made money here and there and was more than capable to contribute to our savings. When I finally passed my driving test, he surprised me with my first car, a battered Mini Metro that used to overheat and smoke up after 30 minutes of driving. He'd got a good deal from one of his mates and was so happy to get it for me I went along with it and understood his intentions were good. It got me from A to B as long as it was a journey shorter than half an hour, but it was the thought that counted and it made me laugh so much that he thought it was brilliant. When I asked how he made his money he told me he was doing odd decorating jobs for cash-in-hand and couldn't talk about it too much because he was also claiming benefits. Everything was pretty normal and I'd become accustomed to this new life and looked forward to our future plans.

* * *

After six months of absolutely no communication with either dad or anyone in the family, I received a voice message from dad. *Nikki it's your dad, I think it's about time we talked, come over to the house when you're free, see you soon.* My heart jumped with both fear and excitement at the thought of seeing him, but I knew I had to go. I called back straight away to see if he'd be free that evening. I was too impatient to wait and knew it would play on my mind and I'd start overthinking things if I waited. I was looking forward to it, looking forward to telling him what I'd been up to and letting him know how capable I was dealing with things on my own. I took a deep breath, opened the front door and quietly shut it behind me. Dad was in the front room watching TV.

'Hello,' I said as I slowly walked in the room. If I felt comfortable enough I would have run over and given the biggest hug ever, but I remained calm and sat beside him on the sofa. 'You OK?' I asked once I'd sat down, realising he hadn't actually greeted me yet.

'Yep,' he said in quite a cold manner. 'What you been up to?' he asked.

I happily chatted away, telling him about my new job, my driving lessons, my new car and the overheating, while he quietly listened.

'So where are you staying?' he asked.

'With Aiden,' I eventually replied.

'Who's Aiden?'

'My boyfriend.'

'How long have you known this guy?'

'About eight months.'

'And you think that's OK to just go and live with him?'

'We're saving for our own place.'

'And what happens when it all fucks up?'

'It won't, he's really cool dad.'

'Who does he live with?'

'His mum, dad and brother.'

'Are his mum and dad happy to have you live with them?'

'Yeah, they really like me,' I replied.

'What do they like about you so much?'

'I don't know, they just do.'

'It doesn't make sense to me, what do they know about you?' he asked.

'What do you mean?'

'What kind of mother and father take in a young girl just like that after a few months?'

I didn't think of it like that, but realised there was some truth in what he was saying.

'So what's the story with this guy then?'

I shrugged my shoulders. 'Nothing, he's just a nice guy.'

'Does he have a job?'

'Not really, but he does decorating sometimes.'

'So what's gonna happen when there's no decorating jobs and he's got no money?'

I sat biting the side of my lip, the interrogation was awful, and I hadn't thought about any of this and definitely wasn't expecting this grilling.

'Do you want me to come home?' I asked, secretly hoping he would say yes.

'Come home?' he laughed. 'Come home, nah you stay out there with your big plans.'

Taken aback, I frowned at his response. 'I thought you'd be proud of me,' I said.

'Proud of you?' he said. 'You actually disgust me. You've known these people five minutes, don't think that his family will give two shits about you when you and the guy mash up. What you gonna do then?' he snapped.

'Why are you being so horrible?'

It felt like he was purposely trying to hurt me, and he was succeeding.

'Horrible,' he snapped back. 'You're lucky we're even having this conversation.'

I looked at him with the most confused look on my face, so hurt that he was talking to me the way he was.

'I don't understand dad,' I said. 'I don't understand why you're being so mean.'

'Do you know I nearly died?' he asked.

'Yeah, but I thought you were OK now?'

'Now,' he said. 'Just about. Do you know it's taken me six months to learn how to walk again? And even now I can only walk a short distance. When I came out of hospital I couldn't do anything for myself, I couldn't go to the fucking toilet without help, I had to piss in a bucket. You did absolutely nothing, and now you want to sit there and tell me about this family who are so fucking cool. I couldn't get down the stairs when I was hungry, I couldn't do nothing for months and you didn't even ask how I was!'

There was absolutely nothing I could say. I sat in silence taking deep breaths as my heart pumped so fast at what I was hearing, it felt like my heart was literally breaking. I looked up at his face. He'd never looked at me the way he looked at me then. I felt like he hated me.

'I had no idea,' I embarrassedly replied. 'Honestly, I had no idea.'

'You didn't even ask, after everything we've been through Nikki. We've been through some tough moments over time, but this,' he said, 'this is the worst and I'll never forgive you for this.'

Those words cut my insides in pieces.

'I thought you were better when you got home,' I cried. 'I thought the hospital only sent people home if they were better.'

'But you didn't even ask when you realised I was home, you didn't even offer me a cup of tea, nothing. Why Nikki?'

'Because I was upset,' I replied.

'Upset about what?'

'I was going through a lot too,' I shouted. 'I was by myself and stuff happened to me too, but when I came to see you, you told me to go away.'

'I was fighting for my life,' he shouted. 'Do you think I wanted you to see me like that? I was protecting you.'

'I thought you didn't want me,' I cried.

He rubbed the side of his face while I wiped my tears and blew my nose. It was so clear we had both got this so devastatingly wrong and the consequences of our misunderstanding/miscommunication had bought us to this. We both sat in silence for a while. I couldn't control my tears I was so distressed. I wished we could go back in time, I'd have happily done everything I could to help him. I'd spent my whole teenage life wanting to please him and give back something for all his efforts with me, this was my one opportunity to actually give him as much as he'd given me, and I'd fucked it up. I couldn't believe this was happening between us.

'I would have helped you,' I said hoping he'd believe me. 'I really would have dad.'

He nodded his head. 'Well, it's done now,' he replied.

I knew nothing I could say right now would fix this, but I hoped he understood my side of the story.

'What now?' I asked.

'Nothing,' he replied. 'You go back to the family that love you so much, and I'll carry on.'

I stared at him in disbelief. Even if he couldn't forgive me, I hoped he would have understood it wasn't intentional, but his words were so sharp. I didn't realise he was just as hurt, if not more than I was.

'OK,' I said. 'Yeah, I'll do that.'

I got up and walked towards the door.

'See you soon,' I said as I looked back at him.

'Yep,' he replied.

My eyes were so filled with tears I could hardly see. The way he looked at me, I knew there was no going back, so I did what felt like the easier option and left. That was the most heart-destroying situation ever. It tore me apart knowing the truth about him. I was disgusted with myself and didn't blame him for feeling the way he did. I'd never ever wished life could go back in time, but in this case I'd have done anything to go back and change it. I'd lost my dad and there was nothing I could do. I sat in my little red car crying my eyes out. Prior to today I was proud of myself and my plans, but now I felt stupid with no plan at all. I'd lost him, I knew it, and this time it was my own fault. I'd have no choice now but to make it work out there on my own. I composed myself and drove back to where I now called home.

* * *

Aiden's family took me in full time and accepted me as their own. I spent a lot of time with his mum who was lovely. I think she enjoyed spending time with me as much as I did her. We'd been to the supermarket together one evening and we chatted in the kitchen while putting the food away.

'I can't believe we've met such a lovely girl like you,' she mentioned out of the blue. 'We are all so happy you came into our lives.'

'Aww thanks,' I replied.

'No you don't understand,' she continued. 'Our family went through a really hard time before you came along.'

'That's OK, all families go through hard times, it's pretty normal,' I said jokingly.

'Darling, we went to hell and back with that boy.'

'Who, Aiden?' I asked in shock.

She put down the box of cereal and leaned on the kitchen worktop.

'I shouldn't say anything, but I'm scared it's happening again.'

'What are you talking about? Aiden's fine.'

She shook her head. 'I don't think I can lie to you anymore.'

'Lie about what?' I asked slightly worried. Everything seemed absolutely fine to me, but obviously, from what she was saying, something wasn't right or as it seemed.

'Don't you worry when Aiden comes home late?'

My tone changed as I shut the cupboard door. 'No, he's working.'

She looked at me as if to say that wasn't true. 'He is,' she sighed. 'I hope so.'

'Why?' I asked. She'd started something and now I needed to know what she was going on about. 'Why?' I asked again, slightly sterner this time. I went over to her and held her arm. 'If something's wrong with Aiden I need to know.'

'Aiden has a problem with drugs, Nikki.'

'No he doesn't,' I quickly responded.

'Darling, believe me he does. He just came out of rehab when he met you.'

I pulled my hands away from hers while I stood in shock.

'Really?' I asked.

I thought back to when I visited dad, he was right, again. To him it didn't make sense why the family accepted me so quickly and easily.

'Yes Nikki, it's the truth,' she said, 'and now that he's out every night again I'm scared he might be relapsing.'

'No, I don't believe that,' I said. 'He would have told me, we tell each other everything.'

'It's not something you'd want to talk about exactly is it, especially when it got really bad?'

'How bad?'

'He stole from us, he stole money from me, our TV, jewellery, he'd walk right in and out with something to sell and there was nothing we could do about it. We had to change the locks which was so hard, darling, but we had to. We couldn't take it anymore. One time he disappeared for ages, we never saw him and then he actually broke into his own home and tried to steal our passports.'

'How did you know it was him?'

'His dad caught him. That was the night we took him to rehab.'

'Really?' I asked in shock. 'That's awful.'

The story didn't sound anywhere near the truth, but I could see she wasn't lying.

'Nikki, he stunk, he lost weight, his clothes were filthy, when I looked in his eyes it was not my son looking back at me,' she explained while she cried. 'And do you know, that boy hit me, his own mother.'

I didn't know how to take this information, it didn't make sense to me. Aiden and I told each other about all our dark times and secrets, he'd told me some real heavy stuff previously which is why we got on so well. I felt really stressed, but I knew Aiden, and he was fine.

'What happens at rehab?' I asked.

'Well they treat you for your addiction until the drugs are out of your system and the habit itself is gone.'

'So he's better now then?'

'He's been so good since he met you,' she said. 'He's been at home a lot more and off the streets.'

Now I knew why they were so happy to let me stay, so they could keep tracks on him, it wasn't for him, or me. I suddenly felt really upset and quite betrayed. Had I known the truth before, things would have been so different, especially with dad.

'Well, I'll speak to him later,' I said as I went to leave the room.

'Are you upset with me?' she asked.

I was upset but there was no point in letting her know.

'No, I'm OK,' I replied.

'Good,' she said, 'but don't tell him I told you. Please promise me you won't say anything, he'll go mad at me and I don't want him to have any excuse to go back to that life.'

I thought about asking him, but if what she was saying was true, I didn't want to cause any discomfort to start for him again either. But I had to speak to him about his whereabouts, and what he was doing in the evenings, just to hear it for myself.

We were on the bed later that evening chatting, and I dropped each question in as conversation. He answered so easily it all sounded true to me. I smiled as he hugged me, happy that if it was true, it was the past and still in the past, it was too late to judge him on that now. No one in the house ever mentioned the situation again, it was like the conversation had never even happened, until one Sunday afternoon. It was a normal Sunday just like any other, Aiden's mum was singing in the kitchen preparing Sunday dinner, I was in the front room with Aiden's brother playing computer games, Aiden's dad was home but asleep and

Aiden was chilling upstairs. Everything seemed absolutely fine until I heard banging upstairs and Aiden's mum shouting hysterically at the top of her voice. I ran upstairs to see what was going on.

'Aiden, this isn't fair!' she shouted. 'Open the door now!'

'What's going on?' I asked.

'He's been in there for ages and I need to use the bathroom.'

'Just leave him,' I said thinking she was causing a scene for no reason. 'He'll come out when he's ready.'

'You don't understand,' she snapped. 'He's been in there for over an hour.'

She ran into her bedroom and woke up his dad.

'You need to try and get him out,' she said. 'He won't listen to me.'

'Aiden!' his dad shouted as he knocked on the door, his voice deep and croaky from his sleep. 'Aiden! Come out of there!'

'Maybe he's in the bath. The more you bother him, the more he's gonna ignore you,' I said.

I knew Aiden pretty well and that would have been classic behaviour of his.

'Leave him alone for a bit, he'll come out when he's ready,' I said and went back downstairs.

About an hour later Aiden's mum barged in the room. 'Nikki, I've had enough, you need to go and sort him out, he's still in there and he told me he'll only open the door to you.'

'OK,' I finally replied and confidently went upstairs and knocked on the door.

'Are you on your own?' he asked as I knocked.

'No, your mum and dad are here.'

'Tell them to go away,' he said.

I looked back at both of them and gave a hand gesture to go away.

'They've gone. What's going on?' I asked.

'I'm embarrassed,' he replied. 'I love you but I'm too embarrassed.'

'Embarrassed about what, are you sick?'

'You could say that,' he replied.

'Just let me in.'

'I can't, you don't understand.'

'Don't be silly, if you're sick I'll help you. Are you in the bath?'

'No.'

'Are you on the toilet?'

'No.'

'So what are you doing, Aiden? You're scaring me, open the door.'

He didn't respond.

'Well now you're pissing me off, so if you don't open the door I'm gonna leave you to it. I haven't got time for this.'

'No wait!' he shouted back. 'Wait please, Nikki, I'll open it in a sec just wait. Don't leave me.'

I could hear the distress in his voice so I sat outside the bathroom door and told him I'd wait until he was ready.

'Are you still there?' he eventually asked.

'Yeah.'

I heard the lock turn and jumped up to see what was going on. I slowly peered round the door, worried about what I was going to see. In my head I imagined him sitting in a pile of sick or something, but when I actually set eyes on the scene, I was totally appalled. He was sat on the floor with this desperate look on his face staring up at me, his eyes red, his top was off and I quickly scanned his body for a wound but saw nothing. On the floor next to him was half a bottle of water with a hole in it, foil wrapped round the top with an elastic band, a spoon, a small bundle of small white rocks bundled together on a rough piece of ripped newspaper and his lighter. I stood in the doorway unable to move. My eyes darted from one item to the other and back at him about 15 times over. I knew it was drugs, but this wasn't a world I knew about so my brain couldn't take in what my eyes were looking at.

'Shut the door,' I finally heard him say. 'Quick, before mum and dad come up.'

I shut and locked the door behind me and kneeled beside him.

'Aiden, what's going on? What's all this?' I asked.

'I need help, Nikki,' he leaned into my chest and cried. 'I need help.'

'What is this, Aiden?'

'This is me,' he replied. He sat up and looked into my eyes and took my hands. 'This is me Nikki, it's heroin, I've been lying to you.'

'I don't understand what you mean,' I replied. 'What is heroin, and what the fuck is all this stuff for?' I asked as I brushed it all away. 'Talk to me!' I yelled.

He dived to gather everything back and held the items tight in his hands. I watched him, shocked at his desperation to keep all this stuff safe.

'I wanted to show you because I can't lie to you anymore. I love you and you're the only one who I can trust. I need you to understand it, so you can help me. I need you to see what it does to me.'

How I felt in that moment was indescribable. I looked again at the way he held the items so tightly like his life depended on it, his eyes were like someone else's, his stare so hazy I didn't even recognise him.

'I need to stop this Nikki, so if I tell you about it and show you then you'll know, and you'll be able to help me.'

I sat in silence, not responding to his words. He slowly began to show me exactly what he was doing. I wanted to grab the stuff and throw it all down the toilet, but I knew from the way he was so precious about it that it wouldn't be a good idea. So I reluctantly and curiously watched as he began to burn one of the white rocks on the spoon and broke it into small pieces. He rested them on top of the punctured foil on the half-filled water bottle, lit them with his lighter and inhaled the smoke. I couldn't believe it, it didn't feel real and I couldn't shift my eyes away from what he was doing. It was so calculated. Where did he even learn this from, I thought. He inhaled a few more times and leaned his head back on the toilet. It was one of the most disturbing things I'd ever seen. He was completely out of it and I just watched, unable to do anything. I tried to shake him to get his attention.

'Aiden!' I cried. 'Look at me, what has it done to you?' I yelled as I held his head in my arms.

He grunted some sort of response that I couldn't make out, so I just continued holding him and cried. We both sat for what felt like hours on the floor with his head in my lap. I stared at the floor wondering what to do. The fact that he trusted me to help him made me believe I could. I had to help him, I couldn't walk away plus I had nowhere else to go. I stroked the sweat away from his forehead and slowly stroked his face. I was still crying.

'Please don't cry,' he said as he opened his eyes and looked up at me.

'I can't help it.'

'Will you help me?' he asked.

I looked down at his face and wiped my tears.

'Yeah, I'll help you.'

I eventually dragged him up and out of the bathroom and put him to bed.

'I love you, Nikki,' he said as I sat on the bed with him for a while. 'You will help me, won't you?' he asked again.

'Yeah it's fine, I'll help you.'

'Do you still love me?' he asked.

I hesitated but knew I had to keep him sweet. If I had a choice, I would have run a mile but I felt stuck.

'Yes Aiden, I still love you.'

'Good, I promise I'll get off.'

'Go to sleep, I'll come and check on you soon.'

I kissed him and went downstairs to see his mum and dad.

'Is it the drugs?' his mum asked the moment I walked in the room.

I looked at her differently to how I had before, like our relationship was a lie all this time. She knew this day would come and it would be down to me to help.

'Yes it is,' I calmly replied.

'Oh no, god almighty,' she shouted. 'No, please no!' She held her head in her hands crying, 'Please dear lord help us.'

'It'll be fine,' I said while I stood watching her break down.

She ran up to me and hugged me. 'Nikki you've got to help us!' she shouted.

I stood stiff while she clung on to me.

'Please don't leave him Nikki, he loves you, he only listens to you. If you leave us, god knows what will happen.'

I peeled her away from me. 'It's fine,' I said. 'I'll help him.'

'Oh Nikki, you are an angel, let me make you a cup of tea,' she said as she eagerly left the room.

Aiden's dad was sat at the table.

'Do you know what you're getting yourself into?' he asked.

'No not really,' I replied.

I saw the sympathy in his eyes under his glasses.

'I'm sure it won't be too bad, he wants to stop, so I'll just stay with him every day until he stops.'

'If it was as easy as that we wouldn't be in this situation now,' he replied. 'But let's see what happens.'

I guess you could say I was naive to the situation. My lack of knowledge on the subject led to a lack of understanding of what was to come, but at the time I thought I had what it took to help.

'Yeah let's see,' I said.

I drank my tea and went up to check on Aiden, but when I entered the room he was gone.

* * *

Aiden hadn't been home in days and we were all equally worried. His mum begged and begged if I knew where he was or where he could be, but I didn't know. I had already called his friends to ask for information, but they knew nothing either. I hadn't been to work for days, hoping each day he would turn up, and eventually they called me to tell me they were making cutbacks and had no more hours, so I was now jobless. His parents were very supportive and said I could stay there as long as I wanted. His mum even offered to pay me a weekly allowance to get by. I thought it was them being nice, but looking back it was obvious it was a kind of blackmail to keep me there, but I accepted it all the same. I made a decision that I had to start making moves to get out of the house and away from this mess. I decided this was the time to think about getting my own place without him, so I went to the council to see if they could help. I'd done it twice with both mum and dad so I had a good idea of how it worked, but unfortunately they couldn't help me as they said I wasn't completely homeless. They explained that the best they could do was to put me on the list which could take some time. I accepted and remained where I was for the time being in the hope of getting a place very soon.

Ironically, that evening Aiden got in touch telling me he'd been helping his friend with a big decorating job and he had to stay at his friend's house so they could get there early in the mornings.

'Why haven't you called?' I asked.

'There's no phone at his house and the guy didn't pay us until today. Baby, I've missed you so much, can you pick me up in a couple of hours?'

I held the phone to my ear, not believing a word he said, but I unwillingly agreed and got ready to leave. A couple of hours later I arrived at the address he'd given me, but there was no answer when I rang the bell. I went to knock on the window, there were blinds at the window and as I leaned forward and peered through the gaps, I saw a bunch of guys sat around on the floor with all the drug shit lying around. The place was filthy and filled with smoke, you could hardly see their faces. I looked more carefully at them all individually to see if I could recognise Aiden, hoping he wasn't there, but to my dismay there he was, sat on the floor with his legs crossed passing that water bottle to one of the guys. My immediate reaction was to just get him out of there, so I banged on the window so hard it almost smashed, and within a minute or so he came to the door.

'Babe, give me two minutes and I'll be back,' he said and shut the door before I could say anything.

I went to wait in the car and after half an hour there was no sign of him. I wanted to turn the car around and drive off but I knew I had to get him home so I went and banged on the window again. This time some other dude came to the door.

'Get Aiden for me,' I snapped.

'Chill man,' the guy said, 'he's coming.'

I pushed passed the guy and stormed into the flat.

'Come on Aiden, get the fuck out of here,' I shouted as I tried to drag his arm and pull him out.

'Oi, what the fuck do you think you're doing?' one of the guys said. 'You can't come in here like that with your shit.'

'I can do what the fuck I like,' I shouted back, 'and if you wanna try me, go ahead,' I said as I continued dragging Aiden.

The guy stood up to come at me, and in truth I wanted to smash his face in – all of theirs, they were all trampy little idiots who thought they were something they obviously weren't.

'You wanna come at me? Trust me I'm ready.'

I let go of Aiden's arm and took a step closer to him.

'This is your chance,' I said to him slowly looking straight in his eyes. 'Take it.'

He immediately looked away while I stared at him.

'Yo Aiden, get this dumb girl out of here man,' he said and sat back down. 'Dumb bitch messing with my vibe.'

'Just as I thought,' I said as I got hold of Aiden again. 'You're all full of shit.'

I slammed the door as I dragged him out.

'What you causing trouble with my friends for?' he shouted as I dragged him to the car.

'Shut up and get in,' I said and shoved him in. I quickly ran round to the driving seat so I could hurry up and drive off without him getting out. 'You think these people are your friends?' I asked as I sped off. 'You idiot, do you think they're your friends, really?'

He sat staring out of the window as I went on.

'Answer me!' I shouted. 'Tell me you think those people want the best for you! So you sat there taking that shit when you knew I was outside waiting for you, are you that addicted?' I yelled.

'Why do think I asked you to pick me up?' he shouted back. 'Because I knew you'd get me out. I don't want to do this, I've told you I don't.'

'So why have you been there all week?' I screamed. 'Especially after the conversation we had?'

'I don't know,' he replied.

As angry and stressed out as I was, his response made me realise that he really didn't know. I begun to understand it a bit more. He was an addict, it wasn't his fault, this drug was stronger than him. We drove the rest of the journey in silence while he cried, and I tried to get my head round it all. We arrived home and his mum hurried down the stairs.

'Oh lord Jesus Christ, thank you so much,' she said as she hugged him tight. 'Where in god's earth have you been?' she asked.

'At his friend's house,' I quickly jumped in.

I didn't want her putting more pressure on him, I'd already done that and we had to make life comfortable for him so he wouldn't disappear again.

'He's tired,' I said. 'We're gonna go up to bed.'

'OK Nikki, thank you,' she said. 'I'll bring up something to eat for you both in a little while.'

We both went upstairs and got into bed.

'Will you promise to help me?' he asked.

'Will you promise not to leave again?' I said as I wiped his tears.

'I promise,' he said.

'Then I promise too.'

I thought he actually believed what he was saying, yet I knew he wouldn't be able to do it but agreed just to keep him happy, while all the time in my head, I was planning my way out.

* * *

The next couple of weeks were manageable, but challenging at the same time. I was under so much pressure to keep Aiden from going off the rails it was unbearable, especially as I wanted to go to the council again. If I went to a friend's house he came with me, if he went to see family or friends I went with him, we spent all day every day together and it was getting on top of me. I had no job and felt like I couldn't get one because of the situation. I had no money other than the £30 a week his mum gave me, and felt completely stuck. I decided to sign on so I could get some money of my own. It would also give me an excuse to go out for an hour or so every two weeks without Aiden which is what I did. It was the perfect opportunity to go to the council straight after, to tell them what was going on so they could bump me up the list. I felt bad lying to Aiden and his family, but I had to do what I had to do. Having my own secret plan was what kept me going and level-headed. I felt like mum back in the day when she was brave enough to put her life in the hands of a man she never knew. I remembered thinking I would never let that happen to me, yet here I was, doing exactly the same. I had to change it.

One evening we were in bed watching TV when I surprisingly received a call from dad. The moment I heard his voice I crumbled and realised how much I actually missed him, but after a couple of minutes of small talk, I realised he was just calling to tell me he was moving and wondered what to do with my stuff. He told me he and Phoebe had bought a house and gave me the address, so I knew where they were.

'Throw away the stuff, keep it, it's up to you,' I said and put the phone down.

He called straight back. 'What's going on, is everything OK?'

I took deep breaths as I tried to compose myself. I wanted to scream at him for breaking his promises.

'Everything's fine,' I finally responded.

'Why don't you come over next week? We're moving on Friday, so give me the weekend to settle and come over, any time after seven.'

'Yeah OK,' I said. 'See you soon.'

'See you soon,' he replied.

I held the phone, hesitating for a few seconds, wanting to say more, before putting the phone down. I then thought about the house. Once he left that house, there would no longer be an us, it was well and truly over. He was buying a new house with Phoebe and was leaving me behind. We said so many times in the past that we'd never leave each other, but somehow we couldn't sustain our promises. I suddenly felt sick. I went downstairs to sit on my own for a bit. My head pounded, I felt cold and then hot within seconds. I became short-breathed and my whole body began to shake, my eyesight became distorted and out of nowhere, I picked up the vase on the table and smashed it against the wall. I picked up the next thing I saw and smashed that too. I grabbed the curtains from the window and dragged them down to the floor. At this stage Aiden came running in.

'Nikki!' he shouted. 'What the hell are you doing?'

I looked over at him and realised how angry I was with him and wished I'd never met him. I ran over to him and started punching him. He tried to restrain me, but I didn't stop. Whatever was happening to me, I was too strong for him to manage and then I fell to the floor.

'I can't take it anymore!' I screamed, as I continued to punch his legs.

Aiden tried his best to hold me and get me to stop, but I carried on. I cried and cried out so loud until I eventually calmed down. Aiden pulled me up from the floor and held me.

'Breathe, Nikki, breathe! It's OK, I've got you,' he said.

I slowly began to catch my breath.

'What happened?' I asked.

'I don't know,' he said.

I looked around the room at all the mess. 'Did I do that?'

'Yeah,' he replied. 'Don't worry about that, I'll sort it. Let's just focus on you for a minute.'

He sat me on the sofa and went to get some water. I slowly sipped it while he sat with his arm around me. My body was still shaking and I was sweating all over.

'Lie down here for a minute, I'm gonna run you a warm bath. I'll sort this shit out before mum comes home and we'll go to the doctor's tomorrow.'

I nodded my head.

'Now it's my turn to look after you,' he said with a smile on his face and went upstairs to run the bath.

I sat in the bath holding my knees up to my chest, still crying while Aiden cleared up downstairs and fixed the curtains. He eventually came back upstairs and put his hands in the water. It'd had gone stone cold without me even realising. He released some of the water and ran the hot tap again. He began washing my body, and I finally felt a lot calmer. He got a towel, wrapped me in it and carried me to the bedroom, where he dried me, put my pyjamas on and put me to bed while giving me kisses and telling me how much he loved me. We stayed in our room all evening, had something to eat and talked about how I was feeling. I told him the truth about my fears with him and the drugs.

'You've got nothing to worry about anymore, I'm never gonna touch that shit again. I've got you, haven't I? We're gonna get married and we're gonna have our own little family. I promise Nikki, just give me some time to sort myself out and we'll do it.'

I couldn't tell him I hated the idea and that was never going to happen. I didn't have the energy and was too exhausted to even think, so I said nothing.

* * *

The next day Aiden was just as attentive as he was the previous night. He made breakfast and brushed my hair.

'I want you to feel good about yourself when we go to the doctors,' he said.

I smiled. As much as I embraced the pampering and attention, I couldn't help but think he was thriving off the fact that I was vulnerable for once. It proved even more to me that this wasn't where I was meant to be. I still felt so trapped and knew at some point I'd have to figure out how to get out, but I put that aside for the moment and went with the flow. We sat together in the doctor's waiting room and when they called my name we both got up.

'I want to go in on my own, Aiden,' I said slightly irritated.

'It's OK babe, we can go together.'

'It's fine,' I snapped. 'You're here aren't you, I won't be long, just wait here,' I said and dashed off into the room before he could say anything.

I literally poured my heart out to the poor doctor who only asked 'what can I do for you today?' Everything came pouring out, from my mum, to dad being sick, to Sabrina's dad, leaving home, to losing my job, the pressure with Aiden and the drugs, everything. She took my blood pressure which was sky high, took my temperature, weighed me and looked in to my ears and eyes with that little torch.

'I believe you may have suffered a mild nervous collapse,' she said and started tapping away at her computer.

'What's that?' I asked, quite worried at the sound of it.

'Don't worry, it's nothing serious or as bad as it sounds, and in a lot of cases it'll probably never happen again in your life. You've had a lot of stresses and pressure over the last few months for someone of your age, it seems everything just got on top of you.'

I nodded, happy that she understood what I was going through, and happy I wasn't going crazy.

'I need you to get as much rest as possible. I'm going to give you a course of Prozac which are just calming tablets. You shouldn't need another course after this, but come back when the course is finished and we'll assess you then.'

'OK, thank you,' I replied as I got up to leave.

'Hold on!' she called out. 'I'm not finished, I'm going to write you a letter to take to the council stating your current state of health and position. Hopefully this will help you when you next see them.'

She scribbled on a piece of paper, stamped it, looked over her glasses at me and smiled. She gently took my hand and gave me the letter.

'Off you go darling, and do come back and let me know how you're getting on,' she winked at me as I thanked her again and left the room.

I felt like that woman was my guardian angel sent from heaven. I'd just won a ticket to getting my own place and felt so much better I smiled from ear to ear. I folded the piece of paper, put it in my back pocket and went down the corridor to the waiting room.

'How'd it go?' Aiden asked as we left. 'What did she say?'

'She said I had a mild nervous collapse and gave me some tablets.'

'Oh shit, that sounds really bad.'

'No, it can happen once in a while with stress, it's nothing to worry about.'

He grabbed my hand. 'What do you want to do today? Do you want to go to the park or something?'

'That'll be nice,' I replied.

I didn't care what we did that day, I could have spent it in a dungeon and I'd have been happy. I had my golden ticket and was on my way out of this mess.

* * *

I had about five days to wait until I needed to sign on which was the only chance I could get some time alone to get to the council, but I was happy to wait. Aiden was doing his best to make me what he thought was happy by never leaving my side. I knew he meant well, but really I was suffocating. I told Aiden in the morning that I'd agreed to see dad at the new place and he insisted on coming with me. I had no choice but to give in. I figured I'd get it out of the way, and once I was out of there, I'd be free to do whatever I wanted. Dad smiled at me as he came to the door which was a response I wasn't expecting. It felt so nice to see him looking healthy and happy. We went inside and he gave us a tour around the house. Once we settled in the front room, I got upset with myself and sat quietly while dad and Aiden chatted about football. I looked over at him while he continued talking to Aiden, and he caught my eye. He winked at me and got up to leave the room.

'Aiden, give me a minute,' he said and gestured to me to come with him. I followed him into the kitchen and he poured us both a glass of champagne. 'What's happening?' he asked as he handed me a glass.

'Nothing.'

'Nikki, I know things aren't right. Aiden told me about last week.'

'How did he tell you, you don't even know him?'

'He took my number from your phone. I also asked him to take care of you and let me know how you're doing. I asked him to bring you here just in case you wouldn't come.'

'Oh, I see,' I said. I now understood Aiden's behaviour since the incident.

'I wasn't sure about the boy, but he's alright, he really cares about you.'

I nodded my head.

'So what's going on, what made you feel like that?'

'Nothing, I was just a bit stressed about not working.'

'Are you in trouble?'

'No.'

He put his new landline number in my phone. 'Call me when you're free.'

'I will,' I replied and downed the glass of champagne.

We went back to the front room, continued small talk for a little while longer before leaving. It felt really weird visiting dad like we were long distant acquaintances, sitting together on our best behaviour, engaging in small talk, but dad and I were different now, I had to accept that. He was moving on with his life and I had to do the same. I decided I wasn't going to call him until I'd got everything sorted out and was in a better place.

* * *

My golden ticket certainly worked out well for me the next time I visited the council. They finally assigned a temporary place for me available from the next evening. I was definitely excited for the opportunity, but felt really bad about telling Aiden. He was his usual affectionate self, pretty much smothering me. I looked at his little face while he kissed me, knowing I was going to devastate him, and worried the news would send him off the rails, but I had to do this for myself.

'Aiden, I need to tell you something,' I said as we lay together on the sofa watching crap TV.

'What's up, bubs?'

I turned the TV down. 'I'm gonna leave.'

He sat up. 'Why, bubs?'

'I need my own place.'

His face dropped.

'I can't live here forever, Aiden, I need to move on.'

'But that's what we're saving for,' he said confused.

'I know but I need to leave sooner and actually get my own place. I don't want to get a place with you anymore.'

'But I thought we had this all planned?'

'I haven't been myself for ages, I haven't achieved anything since I left home and I don't feel like I'm going to being here. I need to do this in order to move on with my life.'

He smiled at me and gave me a kiss.

'I understand,' he said. 'It's cool bubs. When you get your place, I can move in with you.'

I looked at him stunned.

'I can move in, can't I?'

I slowly shook my head. 'No, I'm going on my own.'

'What you saying, Nikki?'

I decided I'd figure out the break-up part once I was out, but for now, I just had to make it easy enough to get out simply.

'Just let me do this and we'll see how it goes.'

'OK, I can help you.'

'It's fine, I've sorted something out.'

'Sorted what out? When?'

'Stop with the questions,' I replied. 'I'm going tomorrow. I really don't want any dramas, let me just go and we'll figure the rest out after.'

He reluctantly nodded his head in agreement. 'I'm just gonna miss you that's all, I'm with you all the time, it'll be weird without you here.'

'I know, but we'll get used to it.'

His mum was in the kitchen so I left the room to go and talk to her.

'I can't believe you're leaving us. What about Aiden, is he going with you?'

'No, not for now.'

'What's he going to do?'

'I don't know, but I want to thank you for everything you've done for me. I just need to move on now.'

'I understand you've got to live your life for yourself and move on Nikki, but Aiden needs you.'

I rubbed the side of my temples. I wanted to scream at her for being so selfish and forced myself to remain calm.

'He'll be OK.'

'But what if he relapses?'

'He'll be fine, and with all due respect, his issues and choices have got nothing to do with me.'

I tried to be as polite as I could, although I was pretty pissed off. She wasn't happy at all, but she knew she couldn't stop me.

'Is there anything I can do to change your mind?'

I looked at her and smiled, 'No.'

She sighed and gave me a hug. 'You will keep in touch, won't you?'

'Of course.'

'You've been like a daughter to me and I'll really miss you, we all will.'

'I'll miss you too, and I'll keep in touch.'

'You'd better,' she joked.

'I will.'

* * *

Aiden helped me pack the car the next evening.

'I'll call you once I get there,' I said as I kissed him goodbye and drove myself to the hostel.

A young guy invited me in, took my details and showed me to my room. I sat on the edge of the bed and looked around. If I saw it for how it was, I'd probably have broken down but I had to see it as my first step to getting my own place and it wasn't going to be forever. I couldn't sleep at all that night, the walls were so thin I could hear voices and doors slamming throughout the night. My room faced the street and the traffic noise was constant. The next morning, I went out first thing to get a few bits. I had £40 to my name and spent that on a new Walkman and some food for the week. When I got back, I went to check out the common room, where the TV was and where everyone hung out. Everyone seemed around my age, it had the same vibe as a college common room with less people. I sat on my own for a short while before one of the girls called me over.

'Hey, new girl!' she shouted over. 'Come and sit with us.'

I went over said hi to everyone while they all shuffled around to give me space to sit down. There were five of them in total and she was obviously the ringleader. Her name was Chivon, a tiny mixed-race girl, quite pretty and very outspoken. She asked a string of questions one after the other.

'It's quite cool here,' she began telling me once she was satisfied with my answers, and for the rest of the evening they all began telling me what it was like, who was who, who to look out for, and how to get around the rules.

All these girls had a sad story and were all pretty much from the streets or broken homes and families. I could relate to them because of my past, and although I'd had my moments, I'd changed so much since then and felt that I wasn't on their level, but they didn't have to know that. Aiden called a few times and I purposely ignored his calls.

'You've got a mobile!' one of the girls screeched out as it rang.

'Yeah,' I replied, forgetting that having a mobile was a big thing in those days.

'How come you're here if you've got a mobile and a car and you're dressed so well?' she asked.

'I used to work in a clothes' shop,' I quickly replied.

'Oh OK,' she said, with a look of approval.

Ten o'clock was the curfew in this place, the time the common room shut and officially bedtime. I said good night and went to make my way to my room, while they all stood around giggling.

'What's wrong, have I got something stuck on me?'

'No,' Chivon replied. 'Are you really going to bed?' she asked.

'Yeah, we have to, don't we?'

'Yeah, but we never do,' she laughed. 'Every night we hang out in a different room, it's Jade's room tonight. Come, it's a laugh and the boys will be home in a bit. Everyone has to be in by 10pm so you'll meet them too.'

'Oh, cool,' I replied as we giggled and made our way to Jade's room.

Chivon was right, over the next few minutes a bunch of guys came up, and we spent the night into the early hours of the morning, smoking, drinking, playing cards, and having a laugh. Every day they'd all put money together, buy loads of drinks and cigarettes and hide them in whoever's room the party would be at that night. This was the norm every night and I went along with it. The next morning, I woke up with the biggest hangover and loads of missed calls from Aiden. I called him back feeling bad that I didn't call yesterday and told him how the evening went which he didn't take too lightly. We ended up in a massive argument which suited me fine to be honest, this way I didn't have to deal with him for a while.

I spent the day hanging out with the guys and of course, the party after ten went ahead, as it did, for the following two weeks. Chivon and I became quite close, followed by Jade. The rest of them were cool too, but did their own thing during the days. Chivon, Jade and I would go across the road to the pub at 6pm for happy hour and share a bottle of cheap wine. Chivon was sleeping with one of the barmen so we'd get more bottles for free as he secretly replaced the old bottles when no one was looking. We'd get back just in time before curfew and continue the party throughout the night. I understood I couldn't live like this forever, but it was fun for the time being. One of the guys, Austin, took a liking to me, but I wasn't interested in him like that. I wasn't interested in any guy and was just happy having fun and getting drunk. One night he managed to sit next to me and we ended up chatting amongst ourselves while the others played blackjack.

'You're different to these girls,' he told me. 'I don't know why but you just are,' he said.

'You shouldn't be hanging around with them.'

'They're all right,' I replied. 'I think they're pretty cool.'

'Chivon's fucking the guy from the pub across the road for free drinks and Jade's a slag, she fucks anything in sight and you think that's cool?'

I nearly spat out my drink at what he just said, but he was right. I'd heard all about Jade's encounters, but I never judged her for it, she was cool, and I'd had my moments before I was with Aiden so who was I to judge?

'You should hang out with me more,' he said smiling.

'Oh, should I now?' I laughed. He was cute, but I still couldn't fancy him like that. 'You know I've got a boyfriend, don't you?'

'I heard but I ain't seen him around.'

His persistence made me laugh as I shook my head.

'It's cool,' he said. 'I'm just looking out for you, you're a cool girl so I'm gonna look out for you anyway, is that cool?'

'Yep, cool.'

The following week, Chivon got her place and left, so I ended up hanging out with him more anyway. Jade met some guy and got kicked out because she'd missed her curfew too often, and after one drunken night Austin and I went all the way. The next morning, he acted like the cat that got the cream, but I felt otherwise.

'We shouldn't have done that,' I said as I dragged the covers over me and got out of bed.

'Why not?'

'Because I have a boyfriend remember? We were drunk, it wouldn't have happened if we weren't.'

'It happened because we like each other,' he replied. 'You're feeling guilty, but you just need to sort out the situation with this guy and end it properly, no pressure, I'll wait.'

I couldn't be bothered to battle with him, my head hurt and I knew I'd be out of there soon. From then on, I went out of my way to speak to the shift managers every day to push them into helping me with my flat. I hadn't contacted Aiden or his mum and felt bad. I hadn't called dad either, but knew I couldn't call him until things were sorted which made it more important to move on. Whilst chatting with one of the shift managers in the office one afternoon, a new guy came in. I sat and watched while he registered, but when he looked over at me he gave me the dirtiest look ever.

'Are you OK?' I asked sarcastically.

'What's your problem?' he snapped back.

'Nothing, what's yours?'

He put his bag down and came right up to my face. 'You're going to have a problem now little girl,' he said. 'Nobody talks to me like that.'

'OK,' I said. 'Whatever.' And I left the room.

His name was Ade, a tall, big-boned African guy with nappy hair and tribal marks on his face. I had no clue what his problem was but that was the start of a whole new ordeal. I went to chill in the common room with my Walkman and a magazine and about half an hour later he came in, dived straight over to me and knocked my Walkman out of my hands.

'You think you can cross me?' he said. 'You don't know me, I know stuff.'

I jumped up out of the chair and stepped up to him. 'What's the matter with you, you fucking psycho? You don't know me either,' I said. 'Fuck off out of my face, you idiot.'

I gathered up my Walkman which was so damaged the top wouldn't close.

'Look what you've done you freak, you need to pay for this.'

'No, you're going to pay,' he said.

'Oh whatever,' I replied. 'Fucking weirdo, don't come near me again.'

I could hear him roaring with laughter as I left the room and when Austin come back that evening, I told him what happened.

'Who is this idiot?' he asked as I told him the story. 'He ain't gonna trouble you no more,' he said. 'I'm gonna stick around tomorrow and show my face. The guy sounds like a prick.'

I laughed. 'Yeah he is.'

He wasn't around the next morning, but the whole house was talking about him. He'd told everyone that he was an African warrior who'd previously killed people back home. He was obviously a nutcase, but everyone seemed to be scared of him.

'Don't be stupid,' I said to one of the guys as they told us what he was saying. 'He's an idiot.'

'I don't know,' the guy responded. 'He sounded pretty serious to me.'

'Oh whatever, I don't believe any of it, he's a twat.'

And just as I said that he walked in the room.

'Oh here's the little self-obsessed bitch,' he said. 'So now you think you can talk about me with these fools, believe what they say,' he said. He roared that beastly laugh again as he came over to me, his breath stunk as he spoke. 'Don't worry, pretty girl,' he whispered. 'You won't be so pretty for too long. I'll make sure your little boyfriend here won't want you anymore.'

'Is that a threat?' I replied. I wasn't about to let him get the better of me or allow him to think I was intimidated by his bullshit.

'No pretty girl, it isn't,' he said calmly and left the room.

We all looked at each other stunned.

'See, I told you, he's a fucking lunatic,' I said to Austin who was lost for words. 'Are you scared of him?' I asked abruptly, 'Because you didn't say or do anything.'

'I wouldn't mess with him,' one of the guys said.

'Nah me neither,' another added.

'You lot are all stupid,' I said. 'Scared of him? What for, he's an idiot.'

He was actually standing outside the whole time listening and came back in again.

'You should be scared,' he shouted out.

'Oh shut up,' I shouted back. 'I've had enough of your shit, it's boring. Come on Austin,' I said, 'let's go.'

I brushed past him out the room with Austin following behind.

'He sounds kinda mad,' Austin said as we went upstairs.

'Are you seriously scared of him?' I asked.

'Nah I'm not scared of him, but it's probably best to stay out of his way. You don't know what he's capable of.'

'He's a bully,' I snapped. 'That's all, I'm not gonna let him bully me.' I said very firmly. 'Anyway forget him, let's just chill,' I said as I unlocked my door.

'I think I'm gonna stay in my own room tonight,' he said.

'Why?'

'I just wanna chill on my own tonight,' he replied.

'You let that beast speak to me like that without doing anything, and now you want to leave me on my own?'

'Babe it's no big deal, I'll see you tomorrow.'

'Well you can fuck off too then,' I said and slammed my door shut.

I chilled on my own for the evening and went to the bathroom quite early the next morning. I waited outside while it was in use and as the door opened, it was the beast. I'd nicknamed him that in my head because that's exactly what he was and how he behaved. We ignored each other and I turned away to go upstairs to use the bathroom on the second floor instead.

'You think you're too good to use the same bathroom as me?'

'Oh for fucks sake give it a rest, it's too early for your crap,' I replied and continued to walk away.

'Yeah, you carry on walking,' he shouted. 'You'll be ugly soon.'

'Yeah, yeah, whatever, it's getting a bit boring now don't you think?'

I really couldn't work out what was wrong with this guy and what his problem with me was, it didn't make sense. I finished up in the bathroom, and when I got back to my room, my Walkman and my mobile phone had gone. I quickly got dressed, ran to Austin's room and franticly banged on his door.

'What's happening?' he asked as he finally opened the door.

'He's stolen my phone and Walkman!' I yelled. 'Austin, I need you to help me with this guy, it's too much now, he's stolen my mobile, I need that phone, it's got my phone numbers in it.'

I was desperate, I couldn't take this guy on by myself, and needed Austin to step in. All I could think was how would I call dad when I was ready.

'How do you know he stole your phone, it could have been anyone.'

'Are you joking?' I said. 'Of course it was him, he did it while I was in the bathroom. He was the only one who knew I wasn't in my room at the time.'

He stood in the doorway looking at me like I was stupid.

'So you are scared of him?' I said. 'Whatever Austin, don't bother, I'll handle it on my own.'

'You think I'm good enough to fight your battles, but I'm not good enough to be your man?' he finally said.

'Oh, so that's what this is all about,' I replied as I stepped back. 'So because I won't fuck you, you'll allow this idiot to threaten me, steal my stuff and god only knows what next, really, is that what it is?'

'I didn't mean it like that,' he replied.

'Well how did you mean it Austin, 'cause that's how I heard it?'

He looked away.

'Are you gonna help me or not?' I asked one last time. He didn't move. 'Even as a friend?'

'I don't want to get involved,' he eventually said.

'Oh I see,' I said slowly. I laughed to myself. 'You're not the man I thought you were, but don't worry, I'm used to people like you,' I said and walked away.

I ran downstairs to try and sort it out myself and saw him smugly sitting in the common room surrounded by a bunch of idiots who only hung out with him because they were scared. I took a deep breath and walked up to his chair.

'I need my phone back, keep the Walkman, just give me my phone and we'll call it quits.'

'What's this stupid girl on about?' he said to his entourage. 'She must like trouble.'

'No, I don't want any trouble, I just want my phone.'

'I don't know what you're talking about.'

'I think you do,' I replied.

'Nope,' he said and shrugged his shoulders.

I knew I'd never see that phone again, but it was the principle of letting him get away with it that bothered me the most. I moved closer to him and pointed in his face.

'Do you know what?' I said. 'People like you literally burn in hell, do you know that? And while you're slowly burning, please remember this face and this moment, you disgusting piece of shit.'

I turned to leave the room and he literally jumped out of his chair and dived for me. Luckily his stupid entourage held him back.

'You just wait, I'm gonna kill you!' he shouted.

'Kill me?' I yelled back. 'Seriously, don't be so fucking stupid.'

'I will have you killed!' he shouted even louder, his arms were waving all over the place while he was being restrained. 'I will curse you, I will curse you with voodoo so you suffer a long, long time and then I will have you killed.'

'Fuck you,' I shouted and left the room.

I wanted to go straight to the office to tell them everything, but I could feel myself wanting to cry. I was trying so hard to stand up to Ade and not be intimidated by him, but really I was actually quite scared. I knew he wasn't going to leave me alone, and knew I had no one to support me. I never felt so alone in my life. I felt like I was fighting this losing battle with Ade and now I had no phone, no phone numbers, most importantly dad's. I'd been let down by my one and only friend in that place. I sat on my bed, locked my door and let out my tears. I wanted to get out of this place more than I wanted to leave Aiden's and knew I had to stay strong and make it happen.

Later that evening I went to tell the office staff what happened earlier, but all they said they could do was talk to him and reminded me I had no proof he stole my belongings and couldn't accuse him.

'But what about his threats to kill me?' I asked.

'We'll make a note of it, and if anything else happens we'll look into it.'

'That's bullshit,' I responded.

'People say all sorts of things when they're angry,' she replied. 'I wouldn't take it too seriously.'

I was annoyed with her casual attitude, but had to keep my cool. I went back to my room and chilled. I didn't even have my Walkman, I just sat there staring into space. I felt exhausted but couldn't sleep, there was nothing to do but cry, and eventually the exhaustion from crying so much kicked in and I slept.

The next morning, I went to hang out with the office staff for a chat and to try and see how they were getting on with finding me a place. I also knew if the beast saw me there'd be nothing he could do in front of them. After about an hour of chatting to the guys in the staff room, I noticed him leave the house through the window, so I comfortably went to chill in the common room for a while. One of the guys who saw what happened yesterday came to speak to me.

'Hey Nikki, you OK?'

'Yeah I'm cool, thanks for helping to hold him back.'

'It's cool man,' he replied. 'You handled him really well you know.'

'Did I?'

'Yeah man, that guy's a monster. Everyone's scared of him but you stood up to him, should be proud of yourself.'

'He's still got my phone though, so it doesn't even matter.'

'Yes it does matter,' he replied. 'You done more than most of these guys would do. He sits here all day bragging about his tribe and connections in Africa. I think it's a lot of crap to be honest,' he continued.

'I don't want to talk about him,' I said.

'Yeah, I hear that, anyway good chatting to you, we need more people like you in the world,' he said as got up and left.

I thought about what he'd just said. It was nice to hear, but it didn't make me feel any better. I sat on the sofa with my legs crossed watching TV for the rest of the evening. People came in and out, but for most of the evening I had the room to myself which was what I needed. I was right in the middle of watching a documentary when I suddenly felt my head being pulled back, my hair yanked back by my ponytail. I screamed out in a panic and when I turned around, the beast was stood with a pair of scissors in one hand, and the other hand behind his back. I screamed out again as I grabbed the back of my hair to realise my ponytail had gone. Within seconds, he'd literally grabbed my ponytail and cut it off.

'Oh my god!' I screamed. 'What is wrong with you?'

He held the clump of hair up in the air.

'Now you are ugly,' he said. 'Now I have everything I need, from now on you will feel the power of the curse.'

I couldn't take it anymore. I couldn't shout, I couldn't fight, I couldn't do anything. I touched the back of my hair again in disbelief, hoping it was some sort of joke but it wasn't. My hair was gone. I looked around the room for help, but there was no one there. I couldn't take this guy on anymore, I felt defeated. Looking at him literally felt like I was looking at the devil himself and where I'd usually run to attack him, this time I knew the best thing was to just get away. I wasn't necessarily scared of him, but I was scared of what he was capable of, and he had that pair of scissors in his hand. I was smart enough to know enough was enough, it had gone way too far and wasn't worth it.

'I'm not giving you any more of my energy to thrive on,' I said. 'Take the hair, do whatever you want with it if that's what really makes you happy, I'm not gonna let you affect my life anymore. My hair doesn't change my face or who I am, like you think it does, it will eventually grow back, but you, you won't grow at all. I actually feel sorry for you,' I said and left the room.

I heard his voice spilling out all sorts of rubbish, but I wasn't listening. I was done. I went upstairs to my room, locked the door, pulled the hair band off the remains of my ponytail and looked in the mirror. My normally long hair was now unevenly above my shoulders. I stood staring in the mirror for ages at my hair, asking myself how this happened, how was this my life, what had I done to deserve the cards I was given, everything was so hard all the time. I eventually stepped away from the mirror and sat on the floor with my legs crossed and my head held in my hands. I prayed to god to just take me away. After falling asleep on the floor for a couple of hours, I looked again in the mirror at my unevenly chopped hair and couldn't help but burst into tears again. I had no strength to go downstairs to ask the office for a pair of scissors, so I took out my nail scissors from my make-up bag and cut bit by bit trying to neaten it which took absolutely ages.

I sat on the bed going over my whole life, from the very beginning until this moment and my conclusion was, life really wasn't worth it. I didn't care about anything anymore, I didn't care if I never spoke to another person again. I no longer cared whether I got a flat or not. My eyes were puffy and sore from all the crying. I slowly got into bed and fell asleep until I was awakened by the most bizarre thing I'd ever seen. I'd suddenly jumped out of my sleep to see an indescribably bright light shining through the glass panel at the top of the door. I'd seen nothing like it, it was like a florescent bluish, kind of electric light which beamed right through the panel and seemed to get brighter and brighter the longer I looked at it, so bright it was almost blinding, like lightning, but at such a bigger volume it brightened the whole room. I then felt a sudden sense of calmness inside, and it seemed like I was being spoken too. I felt like I was literally floating for a couple of minutes, then all of a sudden it was gone and I felt normal again. I looked around me and saw nothing. I quickly jumped up from the bed, ran to the door and opened it expecting to see something or someone there, but the corridor was in total darkness. I looked behind me back in the room which was in darkness too. I switched on the light in the corridor which was a standard light bulb and lit up the corridor as normal. I looked at the time, 3.15pm. Confused as ever, I got back in bed and looked back up at the glass panel and saw the same darkness I'd seen every other night. Whether it was a guardian angel or some sort of spiritual awakening, I automatically felt calmer and a lot stronger. I no longer felt like crying or disappearing, and where everything felt so heavy earlier, I suddenly felt light and managed to sleep comfortably.

* * *

I slept deeply and peacefully way past midday and woke up on a mission. I had to get out of this place. I went to the office and told them about what the beast had done to my hair to get them to focus on helping me. After that I decided to go and see Aiden, he was the only one who had my dad's phone number. I also needed some familiarity and to get out of that house. Aiden came to the door in his underwear half asleep.

'Oh, so you finally show your face,' he said rubbing his eyes.

'Were you sleeping?'

'Yeah, why?'

'Because it's four o'clock in the afternoon, why are you sleeping in the middle of the day?'

'Nikki don't question me, I haven't seen you in weeks, you haven't even called.'

'I lost my phone and it's been a crazy few weeks.'

'What have you done to your hair, I don't like it.'

'I'll explain later, let's go inside and I'll tell you what's been going on.'

After a few icy yes and no answers back and forth, he finally warmed up when I told him I missed him which actually was the truth, even though he did look a lot rougher than usual.

'Not sure if I like the hair, but I'm happy you're back,' he said as he hugged me.

I told him I let one of the girls cut it as a drunken dare which he believed. We spent the rest of the afternoon wrapped up on the sofa watching a movie. His mum and brother came home later that evening, both extremely happy to see me and we all sat chatting over dinner until it was time for me to leave to get back by 10pm.

I spent the following week with Aiden during the day, and my nights at the hostel which made it a lot easier to handle, until at last I got news of a new place. It wasn't exactly my flat just yet, but due to the problems I'd experienced, the office staff managed to find me an alternative temporary place which was available immediately. So I packed my stuff there and then and loaded the car. There was no sign of the beast ever again. Once the car was full I went to the office to thank them all for their help, signed out, and made my way to the main door to leave. As I walked out the front door, Austin was sat outside on the step.

'Are you leaving?' he asked.

'Yeah.'

'Where you going?'

I ignored him.

'I don't need to know exactly where,' he said.

'I've got a new place, not too far from here,' I said.

'OK, nice,' he replied.

'Yeah, thanks.'

'What happened to your hair?'

I hesitated for a second as I looked at him. 'The beast cut it.'

'What?'

'Yep,' I replied. 'It doesn't matter now, what's done is done, you weren't interested then, so I don't know why you're interested now,' I snapped.

He got up and walked towards me. 'Shit, I'm sorry Nikki, I should have been there for you.'

'See you later Austin,' I said as I walked towards the car.

'Is that it?' he asked.

I turned to face him. 'Yeah, that's it,' I replied, as I got in my car and drove away.

* * *

I went to pick up Aiden to help me with the move and to see the new place. It was a high-rise block with a car park to the back, and the flat itself was on the eighth floor. A short, chubby but very sweet-looking girl came to the door as I knocked and excitedly welcomed us in. Her name was Zoya, she'd been there with her boyfriend Akeem who worked nights for about six weeks, and explained how happy she was to have a nice girl to live with. She gave us a quick tour of the flat and told us how she liked everything clean which I agreed. It wasn't the prettiest of places, but luckily, Zoya was a clean freak and everything was spotless. Once she showed us to our room she left us alone, said goodnight and told us to call her if we needed anything. The room was pretty basic as expected but it was clean, so I was happy with it.

Aiden sat on the bed chatting while I unpacked my things and from that night on, he ended up staying full time. It wasn't planned, but it was easier to have him around than not. We did the best we could to make the place more comfortable. His mum gave us a spare TV, bed sheets, towels, plates, cutlery and loads of bits and pieces we needed. She was so happy Aiden and I were back together and promised she'd help us as much as she could. Zoya was quite a sweet girl, Akeem seemed pretty cool too. We said hi and shared a few words whenever he was around, but we hardly saw him as he slept all day and worked in the night. Things remained this way for around a month or so before the cracks began to appear. Aiden and I weren't doing so well, he was home less and less, with sometimes a whole week gone with no sign of him.

It turned out that Akeem was lying about his nightshift and was seeing someone else. Night after night there were explosive arguments between him and Zoya. I sat in my room trying not to listen to all the screaming, shouting and banging. One night while they argued, I heard him hit her. I could hear it all so clearly and although I didn't want to get involved I couldn't help it. I rushed to the kitchen and saw him beating her while she was scrunched down by the fridge trying to protect her head. I thought right back to when Scott was beating up Mia, and although Zoya wasn't family, in my mind I couldn't let this happen. I rushed to the drawer, grabbed a knife and pointed it right at him.

'Stop it, Akeem stop! If you touch her one more time I swear,' I said as I held the knife to his face.

He stopped hitting her and stepped away to turn to me.

'Don't be silly,' he said. 'Don't get involved, this has nothing to do with you.'

'I don't care, you can't hit women like that, not in my presence, and trust me you're lucky I haven't called the police.'

He walked towards the sink and splashed his face with water. I sighed a sigh of relief but still kept the knife in my hand, just in case.

'The next time I see you put your hands on her I'm gonna call the police,' I said as he left the room.

I helped Zoya up and helped her back to her room. I felt sorry for her, but if I was honest I could have done without having to deal with their crap. I had my own issues to deal with and from then on, I knew I had to move on again very quickly. I'd have to harass the council myself until they gave me my own place. I literally went every single day to the council and told them stories that would hopefully help. I went so often and made such a fuss, they referred me to the housing association where it was apparently a lot easier and would guarantee a nicer place.

I did exactly the same with them until it got to the point where the staff knew me by name. One particular woman took a liking to me and I'd sit in her office for ages chatting about all the things that happened in the past while she listened and wrote notes on my file. I knew she was doing her best to help and knew it was just a matter of time before I could move on, I just had to be patient.

Aiden's mum called on the landline one evening, I'd given her the number in case of an emergency, but never actually expected her to call. She was hysterically crying asking if Aiden was with me.

'No, he's not here, I haven't seen him for about two weeks,' I said.

'He's on the drugs again, I swear he is,' she cried.

'What makes you say that?'

'Money's gone missing from the house, I thought it was me losing my mind but today I came home Nikki, and everything's gone, the TV, the stereo, the computer, everything. I thought we were burgled but there's no sign of a burglary, it's him Nikki,' she cried. 'I know it is.'

'Oh my god, I knew something was up.'

'I want to call the police Nikki, I really do but he's my son and I can't.'

'I know, I understand,' I said trying to calm her down.

'Do you know where he is, Nikki? Please tell me.'

I hadn't seen him in ages, and then it came to me that he could be at that shitty drug den I picked him up from months ago.

'I might know where he is actually, but it's a slim chance.'

'Tell me,' she desperately shouted. 'Nikki, you must tell me before he kills himself.'

'It's OK,' I said. 'I can't remember the name of the road, but I know where it is. I'll go there later and see if he's there. I'll let you know if I find him.'

'Oh thank you,' she replied. 'Do you want me to come with you?'

'No, it's fine, it's best if I go on my own.'

'Oh Nikki, you're such a good girl,' she said. 'Let me know what's happening as soon as you can.'

'I will.'

The thought of Aiden behaving like that again disgusted me, and I wanted to find him to prove to him how pathetic he really was and finally end our relationship once and for all. I got in my car and drove straight to that place. I parked up and banged on the window. No one came to the door, so I banged again. I could hear music playing, and when I looked through the blinds, just as before, I saw them all sat there in the same shit they were in last time. I couldn't actually see Aiden, but I recognised his jacket hanging over the sofa. I banged on the window until eventually someone peeped through the blind.

'Get Aiden!' I shouted.

'Yo Aiden, your girl's here.'

'What are you doing Aiden?' I said as he came to the door. 'Are you fucking crazy, you left me to come here?' I shouted. 'Here to this shit?'

'I was just passing,' he said. 'Just passing to collect my stuff.'

'Bullshit, don't give me that shit Aiden. I've had your mum crying down the phone all night. Did you steal the stuff Aiden?' I asked.

He looked guilty as anything.

'Aiden, did you steal from your parents' house?' I asked again.

He shifted from side to side. He looked a mess, his face was drawn, he'd lost weight, it was only about ten days since I'd last seen him and perhaps I wasn't paying enough attention before, but for the first time he actually looked like a real addict. I wanted to leave him there to rot in hell, but I thought about his mum, I'd promised her.

'I'm taking you home,' I said and dragged him to the car.

He was so high it was a lot easier than I thought to get him to the car. I drove off and headed to his mum's. When he realised where we were going he tried to get out the car.

'No, I'm not going home,' he shouted and opened the car door while we were driving.

'Oh my god, Aiden shut the fucking door!' I screamed as I emergency-stopped the car. 'What's the matter with you?' I said, as I dragged him back and tried to catch my breath.

'You can't take me home Nikki, I'll jump out I swear. I can't go home.'

'OK, OK,' I replied. 'We'll go back to the flat.'

I hadn't planned on taking him back to the flat at all. My plan was to get him away from that drug place and dump him on his mother to deal with, but I couldn't take the risk. I'd never seen him like this, it was awful, and at the same time really scary.

'Where we going?' he asked as he frantically looked out of the window to the left and behind him.

'We're going home, Aiden,' I said. 'Calm down, you need to calm down.'

'Stop talking to me!' he shouted. 'I'm calm.'

I ignored him and continued driving.

'It hurts, Nikki!' he cried after a few minutes. 'It really hurts!'

'What hurts?'

'Pull into here!' he yelled. 'Quick, turn around.'

'What, pull into where?'

'There,' he pointed. 'The petrol station, quick, turn around, I need to get something.'

His behaviour was so irrational it stressed me out so badly. I just needed to get back as soon as I could and put him to bed, but he insisted so much on turning back to go to the petrol station, so I gave in and turned back. I watched him closely in case it was a plan to do a runner. He picked up a couple of things, paid and came back to the car.

'Drive,' he said as he got back in.

'Of course I'm gonna drive,' I snapped back irritated with the whole situation. 'What did you need to get so badly?' I asked as I drove out the station.

He ignored me as he fiddled around in his pockets. I looked on his lap and saw he'd bought a Kit Kat, a bottle of water and a box of matches. I began to speed up dying to get back as quick as I could, yet at the same time curious to see what he was doing. He threw half the water out the window, took the foil from the Kit Kat, threw the chocolate out the window and wrapped the foil around the top of the bottle, pierced it with a matchstick, made a hole in the bottle with his lighter, took out his shit, crumbled it on top of the water bottle, lit it and inhaled. I'd seen enough in my life and although I'd also seen it that day in the bathroom, this was extreme, the fact that he couldn't even wait, the fact that we were just five minutes from home, the fact that his body was hurting so much that he needed it right there and then made reality hit home. He was a full-blown addict, and at this level it was dangerous. I wanted to scream at him but there was no point, it would make no difference, so I looked away and continued driving. I watched him as he literally got his hit, calmed right down and leaned back in the seat, and in that moment, I burst into tears. He was so out of it he didn't even notice.

I pulled up in the car park, dragged him out the car and helped him up to the flat.

'Get in the bed, Aiden,' I said and shoved him on the bed.

He was talking all sorts of crap I couldn't understand, slurring his words, talking rubbish, and then he went on to how much he loved me and how much he needed me to help him. I'd heard this all before and this time I was done with him and his bullshit bribery.

'You need to help yourself,' I said. 'Look at the state of you, it's disgusting. Are you that addicted you couldn't even wait five minutes?'

'You don't understand Nikki, I need this.'

'No you don't,' I shouted. 'You think it's only you who's had a hard life? Oh poor Aiden,' I mocked, 'you've had it easy. You've got a loving mum and dad, you've never wanted for anything, you've got a good home, and you do this to yourself, for what?' I screamed. 'To be like this, addicted to that shit?'

He looked at me with his glazed eyes and started to cry like a baby. 'Nikki I need you, please!' he cried, 'Please don't leave me, you're the only person who makes me want to stop.'

'Aiden, I can't help you anymore.' I sat down next to him and held him in my arms. I was too exhausted to carry on with the argument, and the best thing for me to do was put him at ease and get him to sleep so I could take him to his mum the next day.

He cried in my arms for a while, while I rocked him to sleep. Once I was comfortable with knowing he was in a deep sleep I put him to bed and watched TV trying to take my mind off everything. About an hour later I heard him groaning and mumbling behind me.

'Go back to sleep Aiden.'

'I can't sleep,' he mumbled while he got up and fumbled around in his coat pockets.

I shook my head as I guessed he was looking for his shit.

'Aiden, it's late, not now, just go back to sleep. We'll sort this out in the morning.'

'Didn't I just tell you I can't sleep?' he shouted, and threw his coat to the floor. 'I've got to go out,' he said and grabbed my car keys.

'Go where?' I yelled and grabbed my keys back off him. 'Are you mad? You can't even drive.'

He came at me trying to get the keys back. He began pushing and pulling me, trying to get the key from me.

'Give them to me!' he shouted.

'Are you fucking serious?' I screamed. 'You can't even drive Aiden, you'll kill yourself.'

I held my arms up in the air so he couldn't get hold of them, but he didn't give up. He was shoving and pulling, trying to drag me down by my jumper, so I quickly shoved the keys down my jeans and into my knickers. I did it so fast he didn't even see and showed him my empty hands.

'Where are they?' he yelled.

He dived around the room shoving things out of the way looking for these keys.

'They aren't here!' I cried. I couldn't compose myself any longer, I was devastated at what was happening. 'Aiden you can't go anywhere, please, it's late, just try and sleep and we'll get you some more in the morning.'

'It hurts!' he shouted. 'It fucking hurts.'

'I know it does,' I cried and tried to hold him.

'What did you do with them?' he shouted and roughly grabbed my breasts to see if they were in my bra.

I pushed him away. 'Aiden, you're hurting me!' I screamed.

'Fuck you Nikki, you're not helping me!' he shouted, as he rushed to leave the room.

I ran to the door, pushed him out the way and stood in front of the door with my arms spread out.

'You are not going anywhere tonight, Aiden,' I cried. 'I swear you're gonna have to hit me to get past this door 'cause I'm not moving.'

And in that same sentence he ran to the window and attempted to jump out.

'Oh my god!' I screamed and ran to grab his legs. 'Aiden please,' I screamed as I pulled his legs as hard as I could.

He was halfway out of the window and my heart pumped out of my chest thinking this was it, he was going to die. I screamed his name at the top of my voice begging.

'Aiden, please you'll kill yourself!'

I pulled and pulled his body as much as I could.

'We're on the eighth floor, Aiden, you'll die!'

The panic and fear I felt in that moment was the strongest emotion I'd ever felt. There was no way I was ready to watch him die right in front of my eyes.

'I will not let you kill yourself,' I screamed, and pulled his body with all the strength I could find, and with that last pull we both fell to the floor. I quickly rolled him over and sat on his stomach to keep him still.

I don't know where I got the strength from that evening, or even the guts to do what I did, but it came from somewhere. If I hadn't found that strength or thought quick on my feet, that boy would have been dead. I breathed heavily, trying to catch my breath while sitting firmly on his stomach. The responsibility of this guy's actual life was in my hands and I'd never felt such pressure in my entire life. I was absolutely exhausted and had no idea what to do next, but I knew whatever happened or was going to happen, I couldn't let him leave that room.

We remained in that position for ages in silence. I could hear the TV in the background which sounded so loud in the silence, but I couldn't move to turn it off. Aiden lay there crying with his mouth wide open, his chest pumped up and down at a speed that didn't feel normal. I put my hands on his chest in an attempt to calm him.

'Take deep breaths,' I said. 'Breathe in and out slowly.'

He curled his body into the foetus position and cried out.

'I'm so sorry, Nikki, look at what I've done to you.'

'Shhh, it's OK, just breathe,' I said.

After a few more minutes I could see he was a lot calmer. I managed to pick him up, luckily without resistance, and get him back into bed. He mumbled how sorry he was and how he had never wanted to hurt me, while I dragged his clothes off.

'It's OK,' I said in the hope of keeping him calm. 'Don't worry, you just need to sleep now.'

'Will you sleep next to me?' he mumbled. 'I don't want to be on my own, I'm scared and it hurts.'

'I know,' I said, as I undressed to get in bed.

I curled up next to him and held him close to me. I wrapped my arms around him and stroked his head.

'Mmm, that's nice,' he said.

'Good,' I said, as I carried on stroking him until he eventually fell fast asleep.

* * *

I couldn't sleep at all that night. The events of the evening went round and round in my head and I just couldn't settle. I couldn't believe what happened really happened. I looked over at Aiden as he slept, he looked so innocent it was hard to think it was the same person. The fact that he'd lost all control, enough to risk his own life terrified me and I wanted no part of it. In fact, I couldn't wait until he wasn't my problem anymore. I called his mum first thing and told her about the previous night. She was distraught by the story, but happy he was safe and with me. She tried to hint that he'd be better off with me, but I was completely done. I wasn't going to allow her to put that pressure on me anymore and said no. She was so desperate she was almost begging, but I had to stand my ground and asked her to come and collect him.

When he woke up, I made him a cup of tea and asked how he was feeling.

'Did I upset you last night?' he asked.

'Aiden, you tried to jump out that window, do you remember?'

'No,' he replied.

'Well yeah you did, you were so desperate to get out for that shit you almost risked your life.' As I spoke, my voice became sharper and sharper. I didn't mean it to come out like that, and before I knew it I was screaming at him.

'Are you that weak?' I shouted. 'To think that life is going to work out well for you, do you think it's good, something to be proud of?'

He sat looking up at me with his glazed eyes as if I was crazy. In his head, absolutely nothing happened last night. I stopped for a second and realised there was no point, there was no point in him anymore and wished his mum would hurry her arse up and get him away from me. His mum took him, along with the TV since Aiden had stolen hers, and he insisted on me giving him the car keys, which was also understandable. His mum gave me a tearful hug and wished me luck in life. We thanked each other for everything and off they went.

* * *

I was alone again, but this time it was for the best. I felt free, no hassle, no one else to think about but myself, and I was determined to make things better. I was dying to contact dad to prove I could handle shit and make him proud of me, but I stuck to my promise that I'd only call him when I was in a good place which I could feel was very soon. I updated my CV and began applying for jobs. I continued to go to the housing association to see my woman almost every day. I told her all about Aiden and that situation which she thought was unbelievable. I showed her my CV and told her I was going to get a job so I could pay my own rent. She was so impressed with me for trying to get myself together she tried to help as much as she could; she brought some nice good quality coloured paper and printed loads of CVs for me so they would stand out. After a few interviews I managed to get myself a job in a high street clothes' shop. It was perfect. I could start earning again, meet some new people, get cheaper clothes, and I could walk there in ten minutes. I was so grateful for the opportunity and couldn't wait to start working again. I rushed to the housing office to tell the woman my good news and thank her for her help. She was over the moon.

'Good girl!' she said. 'See, you really can do anything you put your mind to, can't you? I'm proud of you love.'

'Really?' I asked.

'Of course,' she said. 'You're a tough cookie you are, a real fighter.'

I grinned as I nodded my head. I loved that she believed in me so much and saw something in me that I didn't even recognise myself sometimes. Having her support at that time was very significant for me, she gave me the confidence I'd forgotten I had which allowed me to start my new job on the right path. It was so much fun working again. The people were great, the manager was super cool and I worked really hard. My manager took me out for lunch one afternoon and told me how impressed he was with my work ethic and if I continued, he'd put me forward for a promotion. Between the woman at the housing office and my new manager, I felt like I had all the support I needed and was on my way to achieving my goals.

* * *

Zoya and Akeem seemed to be on good form meaning there were no more fights, although I wasn't too sure about the status of their relationship. One evening Zoya popped her head in to tell me they were having a party on Saturday for Akeem's birthday to which I was welcome. She spent the next few days moving furniture around and cooking in preparation, so to give her space I spent my time after work at the housing association until one day they told me I'd secured a place. I screamed and jumped up and down when the woman told me the news.

'Are you serious?' I yelled as she laughed at my reaction.

'I can arrange a visit for you this afternoon to take a look, but it's due to be decorated and won't be ready to move in to for a couple of weeks.'

I didn't care, it was the best news I'd had in ages. I couldn't get there any faster, and when I got there, I couldn't believe it. The flat was amazing, a nice modern, spacious one-bedroom flat on a lovely cul-de-sac. I rushed back to the housing association to accept as quick as I could and described the flat to the woman who just sat there and smiled at me.

'You deserve it love,' she said as we filled out some paperwork and set a move-in date for two weeks later and I literally almost skipped home I was so happy.

* * *

The next few days flew by. I was so looking forward to moving and already started buying little things for the flat. Zoya was excited about the party at the weekend and told me how great it was going to be. It was perfect timing for a party and although the party was for Akeem, I kind of secretly saw it as a bit of a celebration for me too. I arrived back from work around 7pm to find the party in full swing already. I went to my room, quickly got changed and joined in. Akeem was already half gone, which was quite funny to see. Apparently, he'd been drinking all day before the party even started. He stomped around losing his balance while chatting to people, he tried to drag people away from their seats to dance, but generally he was in good spirits. Zoya was also downing the drinks, yet still managed to keep a close eye on him and she watched while he tried to pull me up to dance. I innocently laughed off his advances and told him I'd dance later to keep him happy.

'How you doing, Zoya?' I asked a bit later when she crossed my path. 'Are you having a good time?'

'I'm fine,' she snapped and stormed off.

I dismissed her abrupt tone and figured she was probably stressed out by hosting or just a bit drunk. About an hour later, a bunch of us were sat in the front room chatting when Zoya came running into the room screaming at the top of her voice.

'I knew it!' she yelled. 'I knew it was you!'

We all looked around the room at each other, wondering who she was shouting at when she pointed in my face.

'Look at me!' she screamed. 'Look me in the face.'

'What, what are you talking about?' I asked, 'what's the matter?'

'It was you all along, you've been sleeping with him.'

'Oh Zoya, don't be so stupid,' I replied brushing her off. 'You're drunk.'

She grabbed my arm.

'I've got proof!' she screamed as she attempted to drag me out of the chair.

'Zoya,' I said calmly. 'Let go of my arm.'

She continued pulling my arm so I stood up. I didn't want to disrespect her in front of her friends or cause a scene so I asked her again very nicely.

'Zoya please, let go of my arm. I don't know what you're talking about, but whatever you're thinking right now is a load of rubbish.'

'I'll show you the proof,' she shouted and dragged me towards the door.

She was literally about to attack me, but I got there first and pushed her out of the way. She was so drunk she fell into the door and back on the table knocking it over. She'd caused such a scene she actually made herself look really stupid.

'She's so drunk,' one of the friends said to another.

A couple of guys at the back of the room chuckled as she lay on the floor shouting that I was sleeping with her man.

'I don't know what she's going on about,' I said to the group I was chatting to.

'Don't worry, it's not you. She does this every single time,' one of them replied.

'Yeah, remember it was me the last time?' one of the girls said as they quietly giggled.

Akeem rushed over to her and tried to shut her up.

'Shut up you stupid woman, you're embarrassing yourself again, look at you,' he said. 'You're an embarrassment to me and you're embarrassing Nikki in front of these people.'

'Why you sticking up for her?' she shouted.

'Zoya, calm down,' he yelled. 'You're ruining my party.'

He dragged her from the floor to their bedroom while she kicked and screamed. That was my time to call it a night. It was still quite early, but it was getting out of hand too quickly and in my eyes the party was over. I went to my room, sat on my bed and put my headphones on. Seconds later Zoya burst into my room with a box of condoms in her hand.

'See, this is my proof you're sleeping with him.'

I shook my head. I was tired, I'd been at work all day, I'd had a few drinks and was not in the mood.

'Zoya, you've got it wrong babe.'

She waved the box of condoms in my face.

'I found this in your bin and he has the same empty packet in his pocket.'

'Well it's not mine. I don't know where that came from, but it's not mine.'

'You're lying!' she screamed and dived over to me. She wrapped her hands around my neck trying to strangle me, I managed to get her hands off my neck and pushed her against the wall.

'Zoya, don't make me do this,' I said as I held her arms against the wall.

She got out of my lock and pushed me back, she tried to attack me but I managed to restrain her. My gut instinct was to punch her in the face, but she wasn't a bad girl, she was just drunk and upset. A couple of guys came to the room to break us up and finally dragged her away from me and out of the room. I slammed the door shut and put my headphones back on. Akeem told everyone the party was over, told everyone to leave, and from what it sounded like, once everyone left he started on her again. He dragged her to the bedroom, hit her and told her not to come out. I felt terrible, but on this particular night I wasn't going to get involved, so I turned the volume up on my Walkman and tried to ignore what had just happened.

Akeem knocked on the door about an hour later to see if I was OK. He came in, sat on the edge of the bed and apologised for Zoya's behaviour.

'It's OK, it's not your fault, she's just drunk. Did you hit her?' I asked.

'No, I didn't quite hit her, I just pushed her.'

'Are you sure Akeem?' I said. 'Because I've seen you hit her before and you know you shouldn't hit women, don't you?'

He laughed. 'I didn't hit her I promise.'

'Good,' I replied. 'Did you put the condoms in my bin?'

He hesitated.

'Did you?' I repeated.

'Kind of.'

'Akeem,' I raised my voice, 'this is all your fault. Now she thinks we're sleeping with each other.'

'No she won't, I'll tell her the condoms are mine,' he said.

'So you are cheating on her then?'

He sighed. 'I didn't mean to cheat,' he said and began telling the whole story of how his affair started.

'Well you've got to tell her now,' I said quite assertively. 'You can't play with her feelings, and you've got to do what makes you happy.'

We sat for a few minutes chatting when I noticed the door open and shut again.

'Do you think that was Zoya?' I asked.

'Oh shit,' he replied. 'She might have heard us.'

'Well if she did it will probably make it easier for you,' I said, and just as Akeem was about to respond, she burst in the room waving a knife around, the same kitchen knife I used to threaten him with when he was beating her up.

'Oh my god!' I screamed and jumped off the bed away from her. 'Zoya!' I shouted. 'Stop, nothing's going on!'

She was crying hysterically and rushed right over to Akeem.

'You see!' she yelled. 'You're fucking her, under my own roof.'

He also jumped up and tried to restrain her and somehow, right in the middle of the rumble, she lunged at him and stabbed him in the arm. He screamed out loud.

'You fucking bitch!' he shouted. 'You fucking stabbed me.'

He went to grab her and I jumped on his back to stop him.

'Akeem no, leave it!' I shouted. 'Leave it Akeem, it's not worth it.'

He calmed down, sat on the bed and glanced down at his arm which was heavily bleeding. Zoya stood there with the knife in her hand in shock at what she'd done. I slowly walked up to her with my hands out.

'Zoya, please, drop the knife,' I asked. 'Please, just drop it on the floor.'

She dropped it on the floor and I quickly kicked it under the bed.

'Thank you,' I said. 'Now can you go back to the bedroom for a minute?'

She stood still staring at Akeem's arm, looking slightly wavy.

'Now, please Zoya,' I said.

She snapped out of her trance and went to her bedroom while I went to check on Akeem.

'I'll call an ambulance,' I said.

'No, don't bother, it looks worse than it is, it's just a scratch.'

'But there's blood everywhere.'

He pulled up his sleeve up to look at it properly. There was a lot of blood, but the wound wasn't as bad as it seemed.

'I'll kill her,' he said.

'No you won't Akeem,' I said firmly. 'You're gonna clean yourself up, you're gonna go to bed and you're gonna sort this out with her in the morning.'

'Yeah, you're right, you're not a bad girl are you Nikki? I'll sort this shit out tomorrow,' he said as he left the room, and after about 15 minutes I heard the front door slam and he was gone.

I thought about checking on Zoya but decided to leave it well alone in case it piped up again. I ran my hands through my hair, took a deep sigh and sat on the edge of the bed.

'What a fucking nightmare,' I said out loud to myself, and when I looked down at myself, I noticed I had blood all over me from when I jumped on Akeem. I shuddered with disgust and almost gagged at the sight of his blood on me.

I crept to her room as quietly as I could and slowly peeped through her door. Thankfully she was passed out on top of the bed with her clothes on snoring. I locked myself in the bathroom, took a shower and cleaned myself up. I moved my bed up towards the door of my bedroom and sat in bed awake for the rest of the night until morning. I tiptoed to her room, peeked through the door, but she wasn't there and the bed was made. I looked at the coat rail and her coat was gone. I sighed with relief that I had the place to myself for a minute. I put the chain on the front door and finally got some sleep.

The following morning, I called in sick and went to the housing office to see my woman. I explained what happened over the weekend and told her I needed to move today. Although traumatic enough, I overdramatised the situation and put the waterworks on. I told her my life was at risk if I stayed there one more night. I begged and pleaded with her and told her there was an empty place that was already mine and a few more days wouldn't make a difference if it meant I was safe. She reluctantly agreed and pulled some strings so I could move in that day. I was so grateful for that woman and so happy I could finally get away from all the drama. Although I had absolutely nothing to my name but a few kitchen utensils and a duvet set, I couldn't wait to finally move in. We signed all the paperwork, I got my keys, rushed back and began packing, hoping I could go before anyone came home. I called a cab but the amount of stuff I had couldn't fit in one journey, so I had to do two trips.

While packing the second time round Akeem came back. He came into my room and asked where Zoya was.

'I don't know, I haven't seen her since the party,' I replied while I stuffed clothes into a black bag.

'What you doing?' he asked.

'I'm leaving.'

'When?'

'Today.'

'Are you leaving because of what happened?'

'No I was leaving anyway.'

'You don't have to leave,' he said.

'Akeem, it's fine, I was due to leave today, I just didn't say anything.'

'Oh damn,' he said. 'Well I'm going to miss you.'

'No you're not, we hardly spoke Akeem.'

'Yeah, but I always thought you were a cool girl.'

I completely ignored him and continued gathering my stuff.

'Did you hear what I said?' he asked.

'Yes Akeem, I heard what you said, thanks for the compliment, but it's Zoya you should be worrying about, not me.'

'Fuck that bitch,' he said.

I shook my head as I pulled more clothes out of the wardrobe.

'You're much better than her.'

'Whatever, Akeem.'

'I'm serious,' he said. 'Look at you, you know I fancy you don't you? I fancied you the first day you came here but you were with that idiot.'

'And you were with Zoya,' I snapped.

'I told you, fuck that bitch,' he said again.

'Don't talk about her like that, it's disrespectful.'

I began to feel uneasy with where the conversation was going so I left the clothes and gathered up the last few personal bits from my drawer and put them in my handbag.

'I've got to go, I'll come back for the other stuff later,' I said and made my way towards the door.

He got up and stood by the door.

'Leaving without saying goodbye properly?'

'Akeem, move out the way please. I'm tired and I've got loads to do.'

He grabbed my hand. 'You know you feel the same way,' he said. 'The way you spoke to me on Saturday was so sweet.'

I pulled my hand away. 'We were talking about your affair remember, and I don't see you like that.'

'Yes you do, I can see it in your eyes,' he grabbed my shoulders and tried to kiss me.

'Get off me!' I shouted and broke away from him.

'Come on, Nikki, don't be scared, we've finally got the place to ourselves.'

I flashed back to that night in the car with Sabrina's dad and made a decision that this wasn't going to happen again. He was standing in the doorway with this disgusting look on his face that made me feel physically sick. I thought about hitting him or kicking him in the balls, but knew if I did that I'd provoke him into god knows what. I had to think quick.

'I need to go to the toilet,' I said to him and stroked his arm. I was cringing inside but I needed to get past without a fight. 'I'll be back in a sec,' I said and smiled.

'I'll be waiting baby,' he replied.

I went to the bathroom and racked my brain. My stuff was still there, but I had to get out.

'Nikki!' I heard him call out. 'What you doing baby?'

'I'll be out in a bit,' I replied.

I couldn't believe he actually thought something could go down with us. I literally felt sick and had to breathe slowly to stop myself. I opened the door and ran towards the house phone. He came out looking for me. I picked up the phone.

'You come anywhere near me and I'll call the police.'

'Don't be like that,' he said and came closer.

'I swear Akeem, don't come closer.'

I began to dial the numbers and he grabbed the phone from my hand.

'Now you're being stupid,' he said and tried to grab me.

I punched him in the face and ran out of the door and down the stairs. I ran out of the building and continued running as far as I could without looking back. He hadn't come after me, but I continued running to the point where I couldn't physically run anymore just in case. I crouched down by a wall catching my breath and wondered what to do. Half of my stuff was still there. I contemplated walking away and leaving it, but then I remembered a box at the top of the wardrobe with my passport, driving licence and a few other personal things. I sat on the wall completely distressed. This was meant to be a happy moment for me, and that fucker had ruined it. I thought about calling Aiden but decided that would probably make life a lot worse. I rummaged through my handbag, pulled out my address book and frantically searched for the page where I wrote down dad's number. I held the book open on the page and stared at the number for ages. I began to tear up; this wasn't how I wanted to do it but felt I had no other option. I jumped down from the wall and walked around searching for a phone box. When I eventually found one, I cried as I dialled the number. I totally broke down at the sound of his voice the minute he answered.

'I'm so sorry dad, I'm so sorry to call you like this but…' the line went silent while I hesitated. 'I need your help.'

'What's happened?' he asked as calm as ever.

'Can I explain when I see you?'

'Where are you?'

'I'm not sure exactly, but I'm not far from the high street near my college.'

'Make your way to the train station,' he said. 'I'll be there in 20 minutes.'

* * *

He pulled up outside the station 20 minutes later in his black BMW like a superhero. My heart felt warm and safe at the sight of him, yet at the same time I felt nervous as ever. I never wanted to call him like this and it looked so bad that I hadn't called before. It bothered me so much that it wasn't the happy phone call I'd waited all this time for. If I'd have known it was going to end up like this, I would have called him a hell of a lot sooner.

It was extremely awkward the first moment I got in the car. He lit a cigarette and turned the music down.

'What's going on?'

I was shivering, not knowing what to say or where to even start.

'Nikki you're shaking, tell me what's going on.'

What would have been so easy to do at one point was now so hard. I couldn't get any words out, there was so much to tell him in order for him to understand the situation, but it wasn't the time, so I just told him what happened at the weekend and what had just happened with Akeem.

'Where is this place?' he asked as he turned on the engine.

I told him the address and we drove in silence while we went to pick up my uncle and went straight to the flat. As we parked up, dad pulled a baseball bat out of the boot and hid it inside his coat. We got to the flat and luckily no one was home. I felt somewhat relieved as I didn't want any more trouble and certainly didn't want dad to have to use that bat, although there was a small part of me that wanted Akeem to know he couldn't get away with what he'd done. I went to my room to get my stuff together and when I opened the door, all the clothes I'd left in the black bag were scattered all over the floor. I went to gather them up and noticed they were all ripped to shreds. I grabbed each item one by one and held them up, they were all cut and slashed, every item. I sat on the bed staring at my stuff.

'Leave it,' dad said. 'Don't worry about it, it's just material shit, what else do you need?'

I had no energy left in me to even move, I felt so tired but then I looked at dad and my uncle stood waiting for me and pushed myself to get up and gather my other things. Dad and I dropped my uncle back and once we drove around the corner towards the new flat, I perked up and felt much better. I couldn't wait for him to see it and actually I was looking forward to spending some one-on-one time with him.

'Not bad,' he said as he walked around.

'It's cool, isn't it?'

'Yeah it's alright, well done. I've got a few things to do,' he said. 'You stay here, start unpacking and I'll be back a bit later.'

'OK,' I replied disappointed that he was leaving just like that. I wanted a hug, something, but he just left.

I had nothing to sit on so I leaned on the radiator and gazed out of the window. I wondered if he was still angry with me for all the hospital stuff, or because I hadn't been in touch until now. If so I wouldn't have blamed him, but I felt quite sad all the same. I slowly unpacked a few things, cleaned the kitchen and bathroom and then wrapped myself in the duvet on the floor and slept. Two hours later I was woken by the buzzer. I jumped up out of my sleep knowing it was dad and buzzed him in. He came to the door with a couple of fold-up chairs, two bottles of champagne and two champagne glasses.

'Looks like it's gonna be a long night,' he said as he held up a bottle.

I automatically felt so much better and smiled while my eyes welled with tears. We sat in the empty front room facing each other on the little chairs while we toasted the flat. Communication was a bit sketchy to begin with, there were a couple of awkward silences here and there, but once we got going we both opened up and chatted for hours, just like we used to before. I told him all about Aiden, the drugs, the hostel, the flat, everything.

'Why on earth didn't you just call me?' he asked.

'For what?' I replied. 'You wouldn't have taken me back, would you?'

'Of course I would, you're my child, why would you ever think I wouldn't?'

'Because you wanted to move on with your life with Phoebe.'

'What?' he said.

I told him again how I felt while he was in hospital in more detail, the night he said he'd never forgive me, what happened with Sabrina's dad, the card I saw from Phoebe, everything came out that evening, there was no holding back. There were still obviously some bad feelings on both sides over how it all went between us, we both felt neglected by each other at our most vulnerable times which hurt us equally so much. We'd missed so much of each other's lives and had been through so much individually it was a shame we weren't there for one another. It was interesting to see how we'd both changed in just a year. I was much more mature and a hell of a lot stronger than I was a year ago, and he was a lot more blasé about things and saw the world differently since his near-death experience. After all the stories, tears, questions, answers and explanations, we both promised never ever to let that happen to us again. It was finally a moment of understanding between us that was so overdue. I wished so badly we could have had this conversation a year ago but sometimes things happen for a reason and how it went was just the way it went. There was no point dwelling on the past because it was gone, it happened how it did and now we were here. I was, however, very relieved we'd managed to get it all out in the open, it was the relief I needed and deep down yearned for. I was grateful for this day. I had my dad back and in that conversation I found out if I'd have just asked, I would have known that Phoebe was an addition to his life rather than my replacement as I thought. And although he was disappointed with me at the time, I never actually lost him as I believed I had; he would have never left me to fend for myself if he'd known what I was faced with. It broke his heart to hear what had been going on and it broke my heart to know he never stopped caring and would have been there for me. Out of all the conversations and chats we'd had over the years, this seemed to be the most defining one. We were both adults now, therefore we now understood each other so much more. The level to which we communicated was like never before, and from that moment on we put everything in the past and moved forward.

* * *

I spent the next few months working hard and sorting the flat out. I became a perfectionist and wanted the best of everything, so I did nothing but work to get more money until I eventually got promoted to assistant manager which made things a lot easier for me financially. Dad was back at work and pretty much spent every other evening with me as well as weekends. He was really proud of my progress which is all I ever wanted from him. Our relationship went from strength to strength over the years and with his support and influence so did I. I became manager at the shop and treated myself to a pretty decent car. I originally wanted him to help me out with it, but dad being dad left me to it and told me to do it all myself.

'If you want a new car, go and buy one,' he said when I called him for help.

I laughed ridiculously as it reminded me of when he tried to get me to make that phone call for a job. It was just dad's way, he was very much supportive in everything I did or wanted to do, but he wanted me to do things for myself. The day we finally went to collect the car I'd managed to 'sort out' on my own, he joked about the fact that I was 21 years old, and drove out the showroom with a brand new car I'd paid for in cash, just like that. He joked that he wished he knew a girl like me when he was 21.

I decided I wanted to get the best out of my career and moved to the City for more money and recognition. In my mind, whatever was there for the taking, I wanted it. I was on a mission to finally have that chance I dreamed of as a little girl, the chance to stand out and become something I never thought was possible when I used to feel so lost. With dad's support and my growing understanding and confidence, I knew I could do it. I never wanted to be like any one of the people I'd crossed in life who messed up their own lives due to their own weaknesses and insecurities. I never wanted to make excuses for myself because of my past as to why I couldn't achieve; I wanted to be mindful of my own self-being, and I was lucky enough to have the biggest cheerleader ever in my father. He told me how amazing or smart or beautiful I was every day, he supported my goals and dreams and gave me confidence to believe I could achieve anything, he was such an inspiration and I believed in his vision of what I could become. We became the best of friends ever and shared everything you could possibly think of. He went on to marry Phoebe and had two more children who I adored. They were new blessings in his life where he was able to be who he always wanted to be in a family environment and I was over the moon for him.

I moved on to my first real city job as a sales executive and made friends with the most amazing, like-minded, and intelligent people I'd ever met. I became one of their top sales execs and travelled throughout Europe, interacting with the most senior-level people in business within the world's core blue chip companies. The fact that I didn't do well at school was a distant memory. After two years of highly achieving at work, I was financially ready to move on and buy my own place. I never forgot the conversation dad and I had when we became homeless about making sure I did something with my money while I was young. It stuck with me even to this date, and although I was financially comfortable, I spent my time closely watching what I spent from month to month and always budgeted and saved as much as I could.

I was 26 and constantly thought about my future; and if I ever had kids, I knew I'd want to give them everything that I couldn't and didn't have and knew I had to keep on achieving, and when I finally purchased my first property, it was the best feeling ever. I could only afford to buy a complete wreck to do up, and throughout that project I became obsessed with property and left my job to become an estate agent. I met the most fascinating and influential people, made the most dear friends who are in my life to this day, and again I went from strength to strength becoming one of the company's top sales negotiators. I consistently ranked top three throughout the company, winning competitions, cash incentives and holidays which eventually lead to me becoming sales manager of one of the most profitable branches within the company.

I could finally say I was in a good place. Dad and I were good, the only piece to the puzzle I felt was missing was my love life. I'd meet guy after guy over the years, but no one of any significance. After many dramas and heartaches with guys, I eventually gave up on looking for Mr Right and used guys for fun. Dad and I would talk about it over drinks and he'd tell me it would take a very special guy to be able to interest me and that he was out there.

'You're too good for these jokers,' he said. 'Don't be wasting your time with no one who isn't on the same level as you, it'll never work, and never run down no man. If a man's interested in you he'll show it, and if he isn't he'll show it too.'

I felt so lucky to get advice from one of the smartest men I knew, and everything he told me about men, I digested like a sponge. While my love life was non-existent, I continued moving forward and within the next couple of years I bought a second flat for investment and also brought myself a new house. Moving into my new house was another huge achievement for me and dad was over the moon. I was 32 years old, I had a great career, good friends, savings in the bank, a decent car, two buy-to-let investments and my own house. Dad and I sat having a drink one evening reminiscing about the past.

'Remember when you thought you couldn't achieve anything?' he asked.

'Gosh yeah,' I replied.

'Did you ever think you'd end up where you are now?'

'No way,' I said. 'Never. If it weren't for you, I'd probably have ten kids living on benefits, or I'd probably be in jail,' I laughed. 'It's all down to you,' I said.

'No it's not,' he replied, 'it's down to you.' He had a tear in his eyes as he spoke. 'Look at how far you've come,' he said. 'I can't stress enough how proud I am of you, after everything you've been through, you never gave up and that makes me so proud.'

'I nearly did give up remember, many times.'

'Yeah but you came through it fighting, didn't you?'

'I guess so,' I replied.

I sat for a moment thinking about our journey and looked at him.

'Thanks dad,' I said.

'No darling, thank you, it's been brilliant and I wouldn't change any of it for the world.'

A tear dropped down my face and I wiped it away.

'OK, let's lighten the mood shall we?' I said, as he wiped a tear from his face too.

I put on a CD and began to dance to the music.

'What do you know about tunes?' he joked.

'It's not just you that has good music,' I replied.

'Gosh, you really are my daughter, aren't you?' he said as we both laughed.

* * *

I had a 'work hard play hard' attitude and spent my spare time going out, seeing friends, drinking, partying, having a good time until I finally met someone who was kind of OK. His name was Preston and we got on really well, he was totally cool and in complete awe of me. Unfortunately, dad and Phoebe weren't doing too well with their marriage, and had agreed to separate. He'd had another operation the previous year to chip away at the tumour that had grown slightly since his first operation, so for him, it was a difficult year all round. Dad and I had numerous conversations over drinks about his marriage that he never wanted to fail, but it had got to the point where it was too broken to fix. I had a tenant in my old flat in which the tenancy was due to end, so we agreed he could temporarily move in there until he sorted himself out which worked out well for both of us. He'd settled in well and got used to single life again, but a year later he began complaining about the headaches again. He always suffered some sort of pain since his very first surgery but was able to manage it with rest and painkillers, but this time he was losing feeling down the left side of his body. Sometimes we'd be out and his leg would suddenly give way, or he'd lose his grip and drop a glass or cup. He was slowly becoming paralysed on his left side.

'I can't take another surgery,' he said one night when I told him he's going to have to get it checked out. 'I'm a lot older now and my body's a lot weaker than it was before, I'm not even sure if I can handle it.'

'You're gonna have to dad, you can't leave it.'

He agreed to go and check it out and within the next three months he'd had his scan and the results were back. I took a day off to go to the hospital for his consultation and we sat together in the waiting room. Dr Rogers eventually called us in after a long wait and pulled up the photos of his scan on the screen. He showed us both where the tumour was and how it had grown, he showed us where the tumour was pressing on his nervous system which was causing the paralysis on his left side. If left alone it would eventually paralyse him fully within a year, or there was a chance of one more surgery.

'If you choose to go ahead with the surgery, we will be able to cut away a lot more than previously due to its current size,' Dr Rogers explained.

Dad and I looked at each other.

'What do you think?' he asked.

'You've got to do it dad,' I whispered, 'or you'll be in a wheelchair this time next year.'

It was a no-brainer to me. After careful consideration, he agreed to the surgery and within a couple of weeks he had a date. He didn't want anyone other than me knowing, he wanted to be in and out with no fuss. He didn't want to alarm the kids and he certainly didn't want Gran to know. He was keeping his distance from her, as she'd previously meddled in his marriage when things were at their worst which he despised, so I kept his wishes and told no one.

On the Sunday evening we packed his things, drove him to the hospital and stayed with him for as long as I could before they kicked me out at around midnight. His surgery was taking place in the morning and was due to take 12 hours. The hospital rang that afternoon to tell me he was all finished and back on the ward, so I left work and headed straight down there.

'How'd it go?' I asked as I approached his bed.

'They couldn't do it.'

'Oh really?' I asked. 'Why?'

'They opened me up, but they couldn't touch the tumour. Dr Rogers words were "the tumour had grown so rapidly it was stuck like gum around the spine".'

'Oh my god dad,' I said. 'So what now?'

'I don't know,' he replied.

I held his hand, I wanted to cry but had to be strong for him.

'Whatever happens we'll deal with it,' I said.

'Nikki, lovely to see you, I'm glad you're here,' Dr Rogers said as he entered the ward. 'Has Mark explained the situation?'

'Hi Dr Rogers,' I replied and stood up to shake his hand. 'Yes he's explained, but I don't understand what that means for us going forward.'

'Well as discussed previously, the scans showed the tumour pressing against your dad's nerves causing paralysis, however the tumour is growing very aggressively which was not expected at the time of surgery, so we couldn't perform. We have taken scans of the tumour in its current position and will carry out studies to see if there is any other option we can consider.'

I looked at dad. 'See,' I said. 'It's not all bad, I'm sure they'll figure something out.'

He nodded, there was some hope with what Dr Rogers was saying, but he was still afraid.

'Your dad is going to need good care, Nikki,' Dr Rogers continued. 'He hasn't taken too well to this surgery. We had to open him quite deeply this time and even though we couldn't perform a full surgery, it's still going to take some time to recover from what we've done.'

'OK thanks, Dr Rogers,' I replied. 'I'll take care of him.'

'I'm sure you will,' he replied. 'You're a smart girl. Mark is lucky to have a daughter like you.'

'And I'm lucky to have a dad like him,' I replied.

We both smiled at each other as he excused himself and left the ward. The next few months were very challenging to say the least. Dad struggled to recover and was left bedridden, he was in so much pain he could hardly walk or do anything for himself. I spent my time working ten hours a day, six days a week and went to the flat after work to either cook, clean, change sheets, go shopping, wash up, wash clothes, everything, even if it was to just sit with him for company and a chat for the evening. I was physically exhausted, but I didn't care. We eventually told the rest of the family the situation, but no one really understood the severity of it, so hardly anyone visited or helped out. Gran visited a few times, but not enough in my opinion since she only lived 15 minutes away and had a car. This put an even bigger strain on their relationship, as dad felt she hadn't pulled her weight as much as she should have. She was more upset that he didn't tell her he was in hospital in the first place and in truth I think this was the general feeling of everyone else.

'It's just me and you as always,' he said one evening while explaining how upset he was with his mum.

'It's fine,' I replied. 'We'll figure it out, like we always do.'

'What if I end up in a wheelchair?'

'If you do we'll figure it out,' I said.

'I can't Nikki, I can't live the rest of my life in a wheelchair. Do you know how soul-destroying that is?'

'Dad, loads of people live in wheelchairs and they get by OK.'

'Darling, if I was born in a wheelchair it would be different, but look at me, I've got no money, my marriage has failed, I got four kids, I'm living in my daughter's flat, I can't work and all I have to look forward to is life in a wheelchair.'

He was distraught, his eyes were glazed like he was about to cry. I could actually see the pain in his eyes and I felt like I could feel his pain too. My heart felt so heavy every time I saw him, but I had to put how I felt aside and focus on him. I literally cried every night at the thought of his pain when I was alone, but in his presence I remained calm. He needed to feel free to talk about how he felt and I had to be his strength and allow him to do so.

We'd sit up at night talking about everything. I learned so much I never knew about previously, especially in his younger days and the days when he played in the sound. He told me again how proud he was of the woman I was today and confessed he was tough on me in the early days because he knew one day he wouldn't be there for me and I'd be alone. He confessed he always knew this day was coming and was indirectly preparing me for it all the time. He knew from the very first surgery he wouldn't live to 60 and the thought of him knowing that this would impact our lives so much at some point for all that time pulled at my heartstrings. He was so brave, I admired his bravery and the thought of him hurting tore me apart, but we were in this together, just as we always said, so if he was hurting then so was I and I had to deal with it. As long as he was in my life it was a sacrifice I was more than prepared to handle.

* * *

He became stronger and stronger each day until he finally got to a point where he was completely mobile and able which was brilliant. He was no longer fit for work but was comfortable enough to live a perfectly normal life managed with painkillers and medication. Watching him go through life with a smile on his face day by day, knowing he had this illness was so admirable. My relationship with Preston was up and down for various reasons and in reality, if I had more time to think about things, I probably would have ended it, but as dad was at the forefront of my mind, I left things as they were. He wasn't a bad guy, he was actually very sweet but there were certain cracks forming that I'd turned a blind eye to due to what was going on with dad.

About three months later, Dr Rogers called and suggested he'd found a solution after their studies and called him in for another consultation.

'I knew something would come up,' I said when he told me the news.

He was quite relieved too, but still very sceptical. He now walked with a full limp and had no feeling from his left shoulder down to his hand. Dr Rogers again showed us the scans on the screen and advised they wanted to perform another surgery, but this time from a different angle. We learned if the surgery was performed well it would halt the paralysis for around 10–15 years, but the downside was it was a very risky surgery.

'What do you mean when you say risky?' dad asked.

'Well the tumour is set so close to the nerves, if touched it could cause complications. It is a risky surgery Mr Johnson, but I've looked very closely at this over the months and I'm very confident we can perform with success.'

We walked to the car both deep in thought as we left the hospital. Dr Rogers had explained everything, but it was clear to both of us that there were complications with this surgery.

'You hungry?' I asked.

'Yeah, starving.'

'Let's go to the cafe,' I suggested, 'my shout.'

We sat in the cafe with a cup of tea while we waited for our lunch. We still hadn't said a word about what Dr Rogers had said. We looked in each other's eyes and both laughed a nervous laugh.

'What you gonna do dad?' I finally asked.

'Fucking hell girl, I don't know,' he said shaking his head. 'What do you think?'

'Don't ask me, I don't know, it's your decision.'

We sat in silence for a few moments more.

'This surgery could save me for what, ten years, and what happens after ten years? I'll be fucked,' he said. 'I'll be fucked for months while I recover and then I'll be fucked again in ten years. If I don't have the surgery I'm fucked, and if the surgery fucks up, I'll be fucked.'

It wasn't actually funny, but we both saw the humour in what he was saying and hysterically laughed.

'It's a tough one dad, but if the surgery goes well you'll have another ten years, possibly more. There's still so much for you to see in ten years dad, the kids are young,' I said. 'You'll get to see them grow up, you need to see me get married, I need you to walk me down the aisle, and you need to be a grandad. Ten years is a long time, and if it takes some months to recover, it'll be worth it wouldn't it?'

He stirred his tea taking in what I'd said.

'And if it doesn't go well?' he asked.

'Then you're fucked,' I said as we both laughed.

Seeing the humorous side of it, made it a lot easier for us to deal with.

'All jokes aside though dad, if it doesn't go well, then it doesn't, and if you don't have it you'll end up in that chair by the end of the year. But ultimately, the decision is yours, no one can tell you what to do and no one knows how you feel.'

'I know darling,' he said. 'You're an angel.'

We ate our lunch in silence as the reality kicked in a bit more. I was internally heartbroken for him, it was such a tough position to be in and a really difficult decision to make. He had no one else but me to talk to about it, and I tried my absolute hardest not to be biased. The final decision was his and I wanted no influence on his decision. I dropped him home that afternoon and left him to have his thoughts alone. In fact I left him alone for the next few days, so he could really make his own mind up, and when we finally spoke he told me he was ready to do it.

* * *

I took a week off work the week of the surgery. Dad put a brave face on, but really he was terrified. I sat with him all night the night before talking about all sorts. He was feeling very reflective and brought up the time we didn't speak.

'I'm so sorry it happened like that,' he said.

'Dad it's in the past, it doesn't matter.'

'It does matter, I should never have left you to go through all that. Look who's here now? Me and you, just like it always was.'

'I know, but it's fine, we both know what it was,' I said.

'I wasn't in the right frame of mind at that time, but my mum,' he said, 'my mum sat back and let that happen, that should never had happened.'

I agreed with him, but it was too late to start pointing fingers now.

'I think she is a lot to blame for that you know,' he said.

I personally didn't have much to say on the matter. I had my ups and downs with Gran over the years, and although I saw truth in what he was saying, I felt it wasn't my argument.

'How could my own mother watch that happen to us?'

I shrugged my shoulders and shook my head. 'Well it's done now,' I said. 'No point in going over the past.'

He was right though, thinking back she could have done more to help. In fact, it was partly her behaviour that added to me leaving in the first place.

‘I have to tell her about the surgery dad,’ I said.

‘Tell her when I get out,’ he responded.

That was typical dad and I giggled as he said the words. We spent the rest of the night going over his plans if the worst happened, his finances and wishes.

‘It’s gonna be fine, but yeah, I’ll handle it if anything happens.’

‘Good, ’cause your my next of kin darling, I know you’ll handle whatever it takes accordingly.’

‘Yep,’ I replied as I took a deep breath.

It all felt really serious, but I tried my best to stay positive for the rest of the evening until the nurses asked me to leave. I drove home that night feeling very uneasy. I had to pull over a couple of times to compose myself. It was a 21-hour surgery which felt like forever. I rearranged my wardrobe and cleaned the house, until I finally got the call from Dr Rogers who said the surgery was a success. I excessively thanked him and made my way to the hospital straight away.

‘Hey dad,’ I said as I approached the bed and took hold of his hand. ‘How you feeling?’

‘I need help,’ he said.

‘OK, what is it? Do you want me to call the nurse?’

‘I can’t move.’

‘What do you mean?’

‘I can’t move my body, I can’t feel anything.’

I looked at his hand while I held it tight in my hands. ‘Can you feel this?’ I asked as I squeezed his hand, he shook his head.

‘No I can’t feel anything.’

‘Can you move your legs?’

‘Nope, I don’t know why but I can’t move my whole body.’

‘Right, I’m gonna find Dr Rogers and find out what’s going on,’ I said calmly and left the ward.

I leaned back on the wall for a minute trying not to worry. I managed to find Dr Rogers who explained he managed to do what he set out to achieve with the tumour, and due to the intensity of the surgery, it would take some hours for his feeling to come back but should slowly return within 48 hours. Satisfied with the response I went back to tell dad.

'Yes I know, that's the same thing he told me earlier, but something isn't right, they're hiding something.'

'Nah you're probably imagining it dad, they can't hide anything from you, surely.'

'I'll believe that when I can bloody move,' he replied.

* * *

That evening one of the nurses called to tell me dad had taken a turn for the worse and had been taken to ICU. I got to the hospital the next morning to find out what was going on. I rubbed my hands with sanitiser as they buzzed me in and directed me to where he was. My heart dropped as I saw him lying there with all the machines and tubes attached to his body.

'Hi dad,' I said weakly as I approached.

He smiled and nodded his head.

'What happened last night, why are you in here?' I asked, he didn't respond. 'Dad,' I asked again. 'What's going on?'

I saw his eyes trying to communicate with me, but he wasn't saying anything. He shifted his head and eyes towards the nurse in which I understood he wanted me to ask her.

'You must be Nikki? she politely asked as I approached her and confirmed. 'Your dad had a turn last night with his breathing. He's unable to breathe on his own and needs assistance. We've fitted a tracheostomy but unfortunately it affects his speech.'

'Can he talk?'

'No he won't be able to talk I'm afraid.'

'Oh my god, how long for?'

'Well it all depends on how well he recovers, but we can't tell at this stage.'

I pretty much stood staring at the nurse for ages, my mind completely blank.

'I know this can sound very disturbing initially, but it sounds a lot worse than it is.'

I stared at her while she spoke, like it was nothing, but to me, this was a big deal.

'Can he move yet?' I interrupted.

'No not as yet. We've arranged for a physiotherapist to visit him twice a day to work on his movement so hopefully we'll see some progress soon.'

I looked over at his bed.

'So he just lies there all day?' I asked quite abruptly.

'Well yes, but he's in really good hands. We're doing the best we can to keep him comfortable.'

It was tragic, agonising, to know how frustrated and scared he must be. I could have burst into tears right there and then at the thought of what he could possibly be thinking, but I promised myself I would be his support and crying wasn't in that job specification, so I did my best to stay strong. I sat with him for the rest of the day trying to communicate with him. It wasn't easy but we both persevered and managed some sort of dialogue between us.

* * *

I was back at work working till 7pm, rushing straight to the hospital after to sit with him until they kicked me out. I was getting home after 11pm every night and most nights I wouldn't even eat, but somehow I handled it. This situation went on for weeks with absolutely no progress so I set up a meeting with Dr Rogers to get some answers. He confirmed that after weeks of physio, there was no change and there wouldn't be. He also confirmed that the surgery had left him permanently paralysed from the neck down and his internal organs were breaking down. It was the most traumatising news I'd ever heard. He was going to live the rest of his life like a vegetable.

'Can't you do something to make it better?' I asked, unable to control my tears.

'The only thing we can do is do our best to make him comfortable.'

'Is that it?' I shouted. 'So that's it? Seriously, is that all you've got to say? You do an operation and then you just leave him like that?' I shouted.

'I promise you we've tried everything we possibly could, but we are in a position now where we have to look at the facts. I'm very sorry, Nikki, we'll do our best to make him comfortable from now on.'

'Comfortable?' I said. 'He's shitting himself every day, do you think that's comfortable? No one can understand what he's trying to say, do you think that's comfortable? He's one of the smartest people on this planet, yet he lies there stuck all day knowing he isn't going to get better, what's comfortable about that?'

I was livid, I'd been holding my emotions in for so long and completely lost it. Dr Rogers left the room and came back with a cup of water.

'I understand this is a lot to take in, and if you have any questions about his physical state please contact me, I'll be happy to answer them. Other than that he's in good hands with our ICU team who will also make steps towards his future care. The hospital offer a lot of support, and I will organise a meeting for you to find out about all the facilities we have in more detail. Once again, I'm very sorry Nikki.' He looked at his watch. 'I must leave as I'm due in surgery very shortly,' he said.

He shook my hand and left the room, that was it. I sat in that room for about half an hour, digesting what I'd just heard. I wasn't stupid, I knew what was going on. He wasn't gonna make it, not even to a wheelchair. I began to feel really hot and light-headed, I drank the water and sat staring into space. Is that it, I kept thinking to myself, were they allowed to just screw someone's life up just like that with a 'difficult' surgery and just shake my hand after? It wasn't enough, I wanted more but that really was it, there was no more, there was no other explanation. My head felt heavy, my breath became short, my body swayed back and forth and moments later, I was vomiting all over the floor. I held my head in my hands for a minute or so after and caught my breath. They can bloody well clean this shit up themselves, I said to myself as I finally found the strength to get up and leave.

* * *

The next couple of months were indeed all about keeping him comfortable, whatever that meant. A speech therapist worked with us to help him with demonstrating his words a lot clearer, and for me to learn how to lip read. We were finally able to understand each other so much better and managed to hold proper conversations. I spent as much time as possible at that hospital, so much time that all the nurses got to know me on a personal level. The rest of the family visited here and there, but no one understood what was really going on. I'd sit with him after work and at weekends, trying to think of good things or fun things to tell him or talk about to cheer him up, but it was tough. Sometimes he'd embrace me, and other times he didn't. It was unimaginably so hard for him, and his moods were understandably up and down. At times the drugs messed with his mind so much, he thought the nurses were vampires and were trying to kill him, and sometimes he just cried. Whenever I left that hospital, I'd look in his eyes which now told so much more than they'd ever told before. I'd cry all the way home, never wanting to leave but had no choice. He was at an all-time low and one particular evening while sat with him rubbing Vaseline on his feet, he told me he knew he was facing death and how scared he really was. He told me that he lay there all day looking back on his life wondering why he'd ended up like this, wondering what life was all about. It was one of the saddest conversations ever. His tears fell to the pillow as he communicated how he felt. My eyes welled up too but I managed to hold back. I held his hand and stroked his face.

'I wish I could do something to help, it breaks my heart to see you like this,' I said.

'You can do something,' he mimed.

'I'd do anything to help, but I don't know what will.'

'Pull the cord,' he said.

'What?'

'Pull the cord,' he darted his eyes towards the machine. 'Pull it,' he said.

'Dad, I can't do that.'

'Please,' he begged.

I could see in his eyes he really meant it, he really wanted me to put him out of his misery. I wished I could have or found some other way to help him, I really did, but I also knew he wasn't thinking rationally.

'Dad I can't do that,' I said, 'it's murder.'

He nodded his head as if to say I could.

'I'll go to prison dad, for killing you, do you understand what I'm saying?'

He turned his head away and continued to cry. It was so heart-breaking to see the man who was my inspiration cry tears of such agony; knowing there was absolutely nothing I could do destroyed me. I knew him so well that I knew in my heart we were losing him, I could feel it, and now he'd given up mentally. It was inevitable it was only a matter of time.

* * *

I somehow managed to continue life outside of work and the hospital. My relationship was OK, there were a few issues behind closed doors but for the sake of this challenging time, we were both adult enough to put it all aside and actually he ended up being a great support. I'd fallen out with Gran over an argument about dad. He never communicated or even attempted to when she visited him, which bothered her intensely. He'd completely ignore her when she turned up and on one of his bad days, he told her he didn't want to see her ever again. She called me, stressing that she didn't know why he ignored her, yet he spoke to me all the time. Her tone was quite sharp which I dismissed because I actually felt quite sorry for her. I felt if I told her why he was upset with her, she'd understand and have a chance to rectify their relationship, but she took it the wrong way and wasn't having any of it. She took it as if the words came out of my mouth. She screamed and shouted at me, told me I was disrespectful and rude. She reminded me that she was his mother and she was more important in his life than I was because she gave birth to him. I retaliated at first until it got to a point where I found it quite pathetic and couldn't be bothered to argue.

'Oh well,' I said, 'I've tried to help you, you told me you didn't understand why he ignores you and I've told you why – his words, not mine by the way – if you don't want to rebuild your relationship with your son before he dies, that's up to you.'

'You see how wicked you are, you want your father to die.'

'Are you stupid?' I replied. 'Of course I don't want him to die, but he's going to, so you can be angry with me, or you can go speak to him,' I said and put the phone down.

She wound me up so much, but as far as I was concerned I'd done my bit. Whatever she did or wanted to do was up to her now, and when I saw her at the hospital, which wasn't often, we completely ignored each other.

It was a tough time for everyone all round. I was like a walking bag of nerves, wondering if each day was the day. With everything going on, I still managed to somehow keep composed until one particular evening, I'd just got back from the hospital and poured myself a glass of wine. Preston and I were chatting about how the day was when I got an alert on my phone. It was a Facebook messenger alert which I never used, and when I opened the message I was stunned. I looked at her profile picture to be sure and it was her. She looked exactly the same, I took the plunge and read her message:

You're looking good Nikki, check out my profile, anyway it would be great if you got in touch. Nanny would love to hear from you as well. How's your dad, love mum xxx.

I read the message over and over. She hadn't even asked how I was. She'd obviously gone out of her way to search for me on Facebook, she should have been desperate to hear how I was. I suddenly got really annoyed and responded:

Dad's fighting cancer in intensive care at the moment, not looking good.

I kept it brief purposely to make a point that I wasn't interested in engaging in friendly conversation. I read her reply.

I'm so sorry about your dad, but he told me years ago that he wouldn't get much older than 50. I would like to visit him one last time, we went through a lot together, did each other wrong but he was the love of my life. If the family wouldn't mind too much could you let me know if I could visit him? Please stay in touch mum xxx.

Again, I read this response over and over – love of her life, he hated her, what about me, her very own daughter? I could be married, I could have kids, anything yet all she had to say was dad was the love of her life. Bullshit, I said to myself, her crap wasn't even worthy of a reply or my energy, so I put the phone in my handbag and carried on with my evening.

'Perhaps it's happened for a reason,' Preston said. 'Don't you think it's a coincidence she's got in touch now while you're almost losing your dad, it could be a good thing.'

'A good thing,' I repeated. 'Trust me, there was nothing good about that message, you don't know her like I do.'

I remembered what dad said about her when I was little, and he was right, she was emotionally challenged, and I wanted nothing to do with her. The next morning, I woke up to another message:

I really need to see your dad, to say goodbye, here's my number. I've rung the hospitals today. It would help if you text with the details, please don't leave it until it's too late mum xxx.

I found it extremely offensive that she had the cheek to call herself mum and add kisses to the messages, and seeing these stupid messages pop up on my phone when I had other things to think about pissed me off so much, and once again she was making it all about her. I was done with even seeing her name pop on my phone. My emotions were already running high and the last thing I wanted was to have her adding to my stresses, and it annoyed me that she was taking up space in my head. I sent her what in my mind was a final reply hoping she'd get the message and back off.

It's best you don't contact or visit the hospital, he doesn't want to see you so can you leave it please? I have your number and if anything changes I'll contact you.

I had absolutely no intention of contacting her, it was intended to keep her quiet in the hope that she'd stop bothering me. But this was my mum we were talking about, she never did what was morally correct, so it didn't surprise me when I received another message from her two weeks later. What did surprise me, however, was the content.

So what's happening Nikki? This suspense is not funny because it's not a game! I'm beginning to wish you hadn't bothered to contact me. I certainly don't know why you did, do you? Perhaps it was a spontaneous thing and you acted before engaging your brain. I can understand that but I can't understand why you're not keeping me up to date, chances are he won't want to see me anyway and I'll have to do my goodbyes from afar, but if he's still in ICU will he even care who visits or who doesn't? Or maybe he's at home now, or maybe he's not that ill, or maybe it was a joke, or maybe you said it to wind me up, or maybe it's all in my head, or maybe it's payback time for something, oh I know, being a bad mother???!!!

I slowly read each sentence very carefully and became angrier as I read the message again and again. I was in total shock that a human being could write something so disrespectful and discourteous to another, let alone mother to daughter. If I was face to face with that woman I swear I would have killed her. I must have read that message over ten times taking in every word. Half of me felt she wasn't even worthy of a response, but the other half of me said no way, she doesn't get to write something like that to me and get away with it.

How dare you! In case you forgot, you contacted me. Stupidly I thought it some sort of sign that you got in touch. Yes it may have been a spontaneous reaction to respond to you but I thought it would be rude to ignore you. You're right, I shouldn't have bothered. Have you stopped to think that you are not at the forefront of my mind right now? I told you I would let you know if there were any changes, there haven't been. Have you any idea of what I (your daughter) am going through? No, but here you are making out that I'm the bad person. It's funny how you're so desperate to see him yet you haven't given one thought to your own flesh and blood. For you to even think, let alone write those comments is outrageous and confirms everything I have always thought about you. Do you really think the ethics of that message portrays a caring person? Do you think what you have said deserves any respect? Why the hell would I make up something like this just to 'wind you up' or play a joke on you, trust me you are not that important. Damn, you are either messed up or sick. Let's just leave this here, you and I are never going to get on or see eye to eye. Dad may have been the love of your life but don't forget you left our lives a long time ago. I'm not a kid anymore, held to ransom with your shit, I'm a grown 33-year-old woman with my own mind and opinions and will not be bullied or disrespected by you anymore and no this is not payback it's the truth.

There was so much more I could have and wanted to say, but this was enough to get my point across. That evening I told dad about it all and showed him the messages. He raised his eyebrows in shock and then shook his head. I knew exactly what he was thinking.

'You don't want to see her, do you?' I asked.

He frowned and franticly shook his head. I laughed at his reaction which was so clear even without words.

* * *

Over the next two weeks I knew something was different. I couldn't describe how, but it was like my mind was in his head and I could hear his thoughts. I could read his face and his eyes spoke to me, and somehow I knew he was going. It was like he told me he was ready. That evening I made sure I called every single member of the family to tell them I didn't think he had very long, even Gran, and whatever they decided to do with that information was up to them in my mind. I understood it may have sounded crazy and it was only my personal opinion, but as far as I was concerned, I'd given the warning.

Each day we lost a little bit more of him and it broke a piece of my heart every day. Grandad spent quite a lot of time with him in the days which was nice and sometimes we'd crossover, almost like shifts. I'd turn up in the evening while he was preparing to leave. Grandad was a very intelligent, honourable and logical man, he was extremely funny and well-loved within his circle. We hadn't spent much time with him over the years as he travelled quite a lot with his wife and since we got talking quite a lot at the hospital, I grew closer to him and spent quite a lot of time getting to know him better. He felt it would be nice to get the family together for a meal and invited us all over on Sunday for dinner. The plan was to get there for 4pm, but the moment I woke up that morning I felt like I was getting sick, my head hurt, and my temperature was sky high. I called Preston to double check times to meet etc. for the dinner and told him I didn't feel too well.

'You might feel better when you get some fresh air and a good meal inside you,' he said. 'You've been so stressed recently you were bound to get sick at some point.'

'Yeah, you're right,' I replied and jumped in the shower to get ready.

Whilst getting dressed the phone rang. I looked at the unknown number flashing and knew straight away it was the hospital.

'Hi Nikki, it's Karen from ICU.'

'Hi Karen, is everything OK?'

'We wanted to call you to tell you that your dad isn't responding and think you should come and see him.'

'Not responding to what?' I asked.

'He's just not responding,' she repeated. 'He's been in and out of consciousness all morning and he's asking for you, are you able to come down?'

'Yes, sure, I'll be there soon.'

I put the phone down and immediately called everyone to tell them what the nurse said and rushed down there. When I got there, Karen rushed up to me.

'Oh Nikki, we're so glad you're here,' she said.

'How is he?' I asked.

'He's holding up, he seems a lot better now, but he's had a really difficult morning. I'm sure he'll feel better for seeing you, he's been asking for you all morning.'

'OK thanks Karen, I'll go in,' I said.

'Oh and by the way,' she called out as I walked on. 'We had your grandmother on the phone all morning.'

'Really? What about?'

'She wanted to know what was going on, so we suggested she came down as we did with you.'

'OK,' I said. 'Thanks.'

'I feel really bad saying this, but she gave us a bit of a hard time.'

'Why?'

'She was upset that we didn't call her first this morning.'

'Oh just ignore her,' I said. 'She gets like that sometimes.'

'No,' Karen said, 'it was quite serious. She shouted at us and told us she won't stop calling until we change the first point of call to her. She said we shouldn't be calling you first.'

'Oh really?' I said, not surprised.

'We're not allowed to change a next of kin without your father's permission, but she went on so much we had to, just for now, is that OK?'

I wasn't really fussed, I just wanted to see dad and was more embarrassed that she was causing the nurses so much stress when they had more important things to deal with.

'I'm so sorry,' I replied. 'She gets herself upset sometimes, but she's harmless. I'm sure it doesn't matter if you have her number as well.'

'Thanks Nikki,' she replied. 'I'll let the front desk know.'

I was totally shocked when I saw dad's face. He looked completely different. I'd seen him getting weaker and weaker on a daily basis, but today was different. His skin colour was different, his breathing was unregulated, and he struggled to keep his eyes open. It took him quite a while to figure out it was me sitting beside him, and when he did he attempted to tell me something. His breath was so short and he was so weak he could hardly move his mouth in order for me to read his lips. I just about managed to understand he was asking for the rest of the family. I told him I'd called them and they were coming soon. I also told him about the dinner at Grandad's which he seemed to be happy about. He then asked for the kids.

'Oh they're fine,' I said. 'I'll look after them, I'll make sure they're fine.'

He nodded his head and tried to say something else, but I couldn't make it out. He tried so hard, but I just couldn't get it which got him agitated. The machines went crazy and I could see the stress was a strain on his body.

'It's OK dad,' I said. 'Don't worry, everything's OK, the kids are OK, everyone's fine. Don't worry about anything, you just need to sleep.' I kissed his forehead and put my hand on the side of his face to keep him calm. 'Everything's OK, I promise. You're tired, please, just sleep.'

I kept one hand on the side of his face, and the other on his chest until I could tell he was calm. I sat with him for about an hour until he fell asleep and left to go to Grandad's. On the way, I flashed back to the night I tried to overdose and he'd said exactly the same to me. I knew he felt at peace when I told him to sleep, just like I did on that night, and even though I usually hated leaving him, I felt comfortable on this occasion.

* * *

We had a lovely dinner with Grandad and his wife. It was a lovely afternoon overall, great food and good company. Grandad was on good form, entertaining us with fascinating stories, making us all laugh. Phoebe took the kids home around 8.30pm, and the rest of us sat drinking wine, enjoying the rest of the evening. We were in full conversation when my phone rang.

'I wouldn't usually answer that,' I said, 'but I think it's the hospital.'

Grandad turned down the TV as I took the call.

'Nikki, it's Karen from ICU.'

'Hi Karen,' I said and waited to hear what she had to say.

'Nikki where are you? We've been waiting for you for hours.'

'What do mean? I was there earlier, you saw me, has something happened?'

I felt the pressure as looked around to see everyone looking at me, the room was quiet, and all eyes were on me.

'Nikki, your dad died at 4.42pm this afternoon.'

'OK,' I said calmly. 'I'll be there soon.'

I put the phone on my lap and looked around the room. My heart was beating a hundred miles an hour and I felt physically sick. I looked around the room for about a minute wanting to say something, but couldn't get any words out. I attempted to speak, but it was like I'd forgotten how to. I think my reaction spoke a thousand words but no one said anything, the room remained in silence, in anticipation and I was stuck. I had to do something, I had to get there I thought to myself, but I also had to say the words.

I counted to three and just said the words, 'He's gone.'

'Noooooo!' I heard auntie Cara scream as she fell to the floor.

'It's not true. Nikki, it's not true,' she cried.

I looked at Grandad who had his head in his hands. Grandad's wife was trying to console Cara. I looked at Preston who was sat in disbelief, and I sat looking around the room from left to right expressionless, watching the reactions, the crying, the screaming. If anything, I was relieved, relieved he had been put out of his misery, relieved he was no longer suffering and so grateful the kids were not there to see this.

'We've got to get down there,' I suddenly said, as I snapped out of my trance. 'I'll see you there,' I said to everyone, and nodded to Preston to leave.

He attempted to give me a hug as I stood up, but I brushed him off, I didn't want the sympathy hug to start me off or trigger any emotion. I knew I was going to have to remain strong to see or deal with whatever I was going to be faced with. I couldn't think of anything else but to just get there and get this over with.

We went ahead of everyone else and I made the relevant phone calls on the way to tell the rest of the family he had passed. I don't even know how I managed to make those phone calls, I can't even remember the words used. The hospital was about a 40-minute drive from Grandad's but it felt like forever. My legs and hands were shaking.

'Hurry up,' I said. 'Why is it taking so long?' I snapped to Preston.

'I'm doing my best babe, without getting us killed,' he said light-heartedly. He was trying his best to keep the mood light and I appreciated how uncomfortable it was for him so I apologised.

We walked down the corridors toward the unit which also felt like it took forever, and once we got to the ward I saw Karen rushing towards me.

'Nikki I'm so glad you're finally here,' she said.

'Well I'm here now,' I replied slightly irritated.

'Where were you? We thought we would have seen you earlier.'

I looked at my phone, it was 9.50pm.

'I got here as quick as I could, I physically couldn't have got here any quicker.'

Karen stepped back, I could see by the look on her face there was something else she wanted to say.

'Nikki we called your grandmother at 3.30pm this afternoon to tell her we thought we were losing him, didn't she tell you?'

I looked at her and in that moment we both knew exactly what had happened. She had made that huge fuss about being the first point of contact earlier. In my mind, it was the most self-centred and unforgivable behaviour that she took that call and did nothing. The sounds surrounding me became muted, my vision limited to almost nothing, I heard and saw nothing around me, everything went black, I felt faint yet anger rushed through me like electricity keeping me standing, I felt like screaming, yet a darkness ran to my brain allowing no words. My vision slowly became more apparent, as I finally saw the general motions of the ward, and then I spotted my grandmother at the end of the corridor walking towards me.

'She's here?' I screamed out. 'How long has she been here, Karen?'

'A few hours I think,' she replied reluctantly.

'Are you joking?' I shouted. 'She was here?'

'Nikki, don't do this now, please,' Preston said. 'This isn't the place.'

He knew how angry I was and knew about the phone call this morning. He took my hand, but unbeknown to me I was gripping back so tightly my nails dug into him piercing his skin.

'Oh you're here?' she said as she approached me.

'I've got nothing to say to you,' I said as I shoved past her. 'Where's my dad, Karen?' I shouted as I dashed round the ward searching for him.

She rushed to grab my arm and directed me to where he was.

'Take as much time as you need,' she said and left me with him.

I opened the curtain and looked at his still body. He looked so peaceful, like the pain he'd been suffering was no longer there, like the man he was before he was sick. I stroked his face like I had earlier as my tears dropped onto his chest.

'It's over dad,' I whispered and kissed his forehead. 'It's over.'

I stood over his body stroking his face for ages as I felt at peace. I flashed back over so many moments and memories of him and smiled. Rather than sadness I felt lucky, lucky that I was privileged enough to have this man in my life, and although our time was short, it felt like a lifetime and I was proud to have had a father like him. He was what made me who I was today, my sparkling diamond, and he was gone. I'd sent him to sleep and was happy with that thought. If I had my way, I would have stayed in that room with him forever, the silence of his death calmed my spirit, and it strangely felt nice, a moment of peace and purity I wanted to last forever.

I finally opened the curtain to see Preston and Gran standing outside. Of course Preston wanted to be right there for me, but Gran, I had no idea why she was standing there. I didn't want her anywhere near me and when I looked in her face, I couldn't hold myself.

'Why didn't you call anyone?' I shouted. 'My dad died alone, and you called no one?' I screamed.

'Nikki, come on let's just go,' Preston said as he put his arm around my waist to usher me away. 'This is a precious moment.'

He was right, so I bit my tongue and turned to leave. I just wanted to get home, but I couldn't calm myself down and kept thinking about that phone call.

'I need a cigarette,' I said as we got outside the hospital.

I stopped still to light a cigarette when Gran came rushing over.

'How dare you talk to me like that in front of everyone,' she shouted. 'You need to learn how to have respect.'

'Respect?' I shouted back. 'Respect for you, I'll never have respect for what you done. Why didn't you call anyone, Gran? Why, even if you didn't call me, why didn't you call someone else, anyone? We could have been with him,' I screamed even louder. 'You fucked it all up by making a fuss about who they call this morning. I would have called everyone like I always did, why would you take this away from everyone?' I shouted.

'You see how rude you are?' she shouted back. 'You're a wicked girl and I don't care if I never ever see or speak to you again.'

'Good, I don't care either,' I shouted back. 'My dad has just died, he hasn't been dead for five minutes and this is how you're acting, you disgust me.'

'He was dead when I got here,' she said.

'What's that got to do with anything? He still died alone because of you. I can't forgive you for this, do you understand?'

'Come on ladies,' Preston intervened. 'This really isn't what Mark would want is it? His mum and his daughter at each other's throats? Come on, it's not right, you're both going to have to communicate at some point. You've got planning to do, you need each other,' he said.

'I don't need her,' she viciously snapped.

I looked her up and down and thought to myself, yes you do, and one day you will, but there was no point in taking this argument any further. I chucked my cigarette on the floor.

'Come on let's go, I want to go home, it's over.'

'I guess so,' he said as he put his arm around me. 'But somehow I don't think this is the point where it really is over,' he said as he opened the passenger door for me.

I got in the car and stared out of the window while he drove us home. I flashed right back to when I was three years old in the back of the car, the day dad collected me from Claire's house. It was exactly

30 years ago, the very beginning of our journey. I stared at the lights of the cars as they drove by in the distance, remembering when dad told me they were Smurfs and smiled to myself as my tears fell. I would never hear his words again, his wise words that I once laughed about and said sounded like songs I'd never get out of my head. It was indeed the biggest chapter of life that certainly was over; it was over because whatever happened next would be different, and would always be different, because whatever was next, it would be just me.

Printed in Great Britain
by Amazon